THE NULL PROPHECY

THE NULL PROPHECY

MICHAEL GUILLEN

REGNERY
FICTION

The Author is represented by Ambassador Literary Agency, Nashville, TN.

Quote in chapter 34 from Carl Laemmle's *Frankenstein*, Universal Pictures Corp., 1932.

Regnery Fiction™ is a trademark of Salem Communications Holding Corporation; Regnery® is a registered trademark of Salem Communications Holding Corporation

Cataloging-in-Publication data on file with the Library of Congress

ISBN 978-1-62157-671-6

Published in the United States by
Regnery Fiction
An imprint of Regnery Publishing
A Division of Salem Media Group
300 New Jersey Ave NW
Washington, DC 20001
www.Regnery.com

Manufactured in the United States of America

10 9 8 7 6 5 4 3 2 1

Books are available in quantity for promotional or premium use. For information on discounts and terms, please visit our website: www.Regnery.com.

Distributed to the trade by
Perseus Distribution
www.perseusdistribution.com

ALSO BY THE AUTHOR

Bridges to Infinity: The Human Side of Mathematics

Five Equations That Changed the World: The Power and Poetry of Mathematics

Can a Smart Person Believe in God?

Amazing Truths: How Science and the Bible Agree

For Dr. John and Mrs. Jane Livermore,
Mr. John and Mrs. Norma Bowles,
and Dr. Hussein and Mrs. Karen Yilmaz,
who opened their hearts and homes to me
at critical times in my life.
With love and gratitude.

DISCLAIMER

This is a work of fiction, peopled by and involving foreign and domestic companies, institutions, organizations, and activities—private, public, and government—that are products of the author's imagination. Where actual names appear, they are used fictitiously and do not necessarily depict their actual conduct or purpose. For further reading on the very real science upon which this novel is based, the reader is referred to the bibliography at the end.

CHAPTER 1

CHILLY RECEPTION

Dallan O'Malley leaned into the squall, his face turned away from the howling, freezing madness. Small, hard snowflakes pelted the hood of his down parka—the pattering sound redolent of rainy days in the attic of his childhood home, where he often hid from his alcoholic father.

He squared himself and, squinting hard, searched the shrouded landscape. His escort, base commander Major John Brody, was no longer in sight. A shiver of fear halted him; a few heartbeats later he burst out laughing.

Flinging out his arms, he shouted, "This is freedom, baby!"

He lifted his head and sucked in the bracing air, snowflakes and all, then pushed ahead blindly. A dozen or so halting steps later he bumped

1

into the big man, who spun around and shouted, "There you are! You okay?"

"Top of the world!" Dallan cried out. "Top of the world!"

Brody waved him on. "Stay close!"

Dallan wondered what it would be like to live and work year-round up here, the northernmost human outpost on Earth. They called CFS Alert "Santa's Workshop." But in truth it collected military and environmental intelligence for the Canadian government, sharing whatever wasn't classified with clients worldwide, including Dallan's own U.S. Space Weather Prediction Center.

No way, he decided. *This place would wear thin really fast.*

Not enough women.

He thought of Lorena and immediately felt ashamed. Truth was he still loved her.

Eventually, a gaudy, mustard-colored shack with a fire-engine red entryway materialized out of the paleness—like a specter dressed for Mardi Gras.

A large animal, white and furry, dashed across his path. Startled, he looked to Brody.

"Arctic wolf!" the major shouted. "People here have never hurt 'em so they come right up to you. They're all over the station."

Once inside the building, Brody quickly led him to the magnetograph. The instrument didn't look like much—metal boxes connected by electrical cables to a computer monitor—but it was the reason he schlepped all the way up here on short notice from Boulder.

That, and to escape the mess with Lorena.

On Brody's orders, a technician cleared off a nearby table and then laid out a long sheet of graph paper.

"This is the pole strength for the past twenty-four hours," the base commander said, smoothing the paper with his hand. "Here's where it started wavering yesterday morning." He tapped his forefinger on the spot. "And we don't know why."

Dallan's mouth hung open. "Good god, it's like a jumpy stock market!"

"Yes."

He bent down for a closer look. "You sure this is for real?"

"Oh, yeah. We've checked and rechecked the system for glitches a gazillion times. It's as real as you and me."

It was instantly clear to Dallan why he'd been called. An instability this bad anywhere in the earth's magnetic field would be alarming. But up here at the pole, naturally a weak spot to begin with, it was extremely dangerous.

"What about the radiation levels?"

"So far, so good—no increases."

The magnetosphere was the main barrier protecting Earth from the sun's lethal radiation; it acted like sunscreen. Without it, the radiation would rain down on our heads like napalm, setting the atmosphere on fire and cooking everyone to death—literally.

He shot Major Brody an anxious look. "And the polynya?"

"I'll show you as soon as the weather clears."

★

SATURDAY, APRIL 22 (12:23 P.M. EASTERN DAYLIGHT TIME)

It took hours for the storm to play itself out, its legacy a thick layer of fresh snow and a heavy, pewter-colored sky.

The sun was a pale amber smudge just above the horizon. From now until fall it would circle round and round, low in the sky, bobbing up and down ever so slightly—the only clue for distinguishing morning, noon, and night.

A hulking, rattling, yellow Snowcat ferried Dallan, Brody, and a small military entourage out to the station's frozen runway, where they boarded a CC-130J Hercules cargo plane. Dallan knew from experience Hercs were the workhorses thereabout, shuttling heavy equipment, food, fuel, supplies, solid waste, and personnel between Alert and Thule, Greenland.

When they arrived in Thule, he looked up and gawked at the curtains of scarlet light fluttering overhead. "Northern Lights in broad daylight. My god!"

The Northern Lights were commonly seen in the night skies all over the Arctic. Like all aurorae, they were caused by charged particles from the sun blasting the upper atmosphere and making it glow. Because the spectacle happened tens of miles up, it was usually dim and could only be seen at night. Northern Lights bright enough to be seen during the day meant the bombardment was either unusually strong or infiltrating unusually low—or both.

"Wait till you see what's coming next," the major said. He tugged gently on Dallan's parka. "C'mon, let's go."

They hurried to a waiting skiplane, which flew them a short distance due west over Baffin Bay and set down on the snow. Before deplaning, Brody reminded the scouting party they'd be walking not on solid ground but on ice, springtime ice that was beginning to fracture.

"So everyone, please be careful, eh?"

Once under way, Dallan tried not to think too much about the pitch-black ocean lurking beneath his feet. His heavy, white rubber boots crushed the snow underfoot, making it cry out like rusty hinges.

The virgin-white terrain was mostly flat, but here and there were towering pile-ups of bluish-colored ice that looked to him like gigantic modern sculptures. Less than ten minutes into their hike, he came around one such icy heap and was arrested by the sight of a vast lagoon teeming with walruses, seals, polar bears, and scores of exotic-looking birds. Everyone stopped to stare at the unusual sight.

"Behold, the North Water Polynya!" Brody called out, sweeping a gloved hand in the direction of what he explained was the biggest warm-water oasis in the Arctic.

Dallan knew polynyas existed wherever there was frozen sea ice. But this polynya was huge, and it was the first time he'd actually seen one.

"Unreal!" he exclaimed.

"It's kept open by warm water welling up from below," the major said. "It attracts all kinds of whales: narwhals, belugas, bowheads, you name it. C'mon, keep walking, you ain't seen nothing yet."

On the polynya's southern shore they arrived at a campsite and met up with a small woman encased in black snow pants and a pink, furry-hooded parka. Brody introduced her as Dr. Rebecca Anawak, a marine biologist from the Isabela Oceanographic Institute.

Dallan took her all in—the aspects he could see, anyway.

Cute.

"Isabela," he said, fist-bumping her gloved hand. "That's in the Galapagos, isn't it? You're a long way from home."

"Yes and no. I grew up in these parts. I'm Inuit."

For the next few minutes Anawak filled him in on the bizarre animal behavior she and her assistants were observing since the previous morning. She finished by saying, "Come see for yourself—it's awful."

The biologist led them to an artificial blind at the water's edge. She handed Dallan a pair of binoculars, directing his gaze to a female walrus hauling herself out of the water with her tusks.

"Wow, I've never seen that before—the way they do that with their tusks."

"Keep watching," Anawak said. "She's being courted by the polynya's alpha male. He's over there." She pointed to a massive, pear-shaped walrus lolling in the water nearby.

Abruptly, he clacked his teeth and pealed like a bell—a guy thing, the biologist explained, caused by sacs in the neck filled with air. He then charged out of the water. But instead of displaying affection, as Dallan expected, the bull began goring the female with his saber-like tusks.

"Good god!" he cried out. "What the hell is he doing?"

"It's what we've been seeing," the biologist said. "It's insane."

The besieged cow howled in agony, causing the polynya's water fowl to leap into the air, their screeching and squawking a deafening cacophony. Dallan, still staring through binoculars, followed their frenzied flight.

What he saw next made him drop the glasses.

No! It's actually happening!

The tops of the scarlet clouds appeared to be hemorrhaging, their undersides a sickly shade of green.

"Jesus, Mary, and Joseph!" he bellowed. "The sky is catching fire!"

"Good god!" Brody's voice bristled with alarm. "We have to go, everybody!"

Dallan remained transfixed.

"Now!" Brody ordered. "*NOW!*"

CHAPTER 2

THRILL RIDE

SATURDAY, APRIL 22 (7:45 A.M. PACIFIC DAYLIGHT TIME)

DOWNTOWN SAN DIEGO, CALIFORNIA

The news van bearing Allie Armendariz and her crew zipped along Harbor Drive making good time. But she, seated alone in the rear, was too distracted by her phone conversation to notice.

Several blocks farther on, she clicked off her phone and shook her head. "Ay-yai-yai."

"What?" said Eva, not looking up from her laptop.

Eva Freiberg, her main producer and best friend, was only thirty-three, but already her unruly black hair was peppered with white, and the corners of her mouth and dark blue eyes were heavily creased.

"That was my brother Carlos. My sister's been taken to the hospital."

"Which one?"

7

"The Parker Center in—" She turned to Eva. "What does it matter?"

Eva looked up. "I meant, which sister?"

Allie shot her a look that said, *You need to ask?* "Lorena. Apparently she's had some kind of breakdown; the doctors are saying she's got delusional disorder, whatever that is. They're still doing tests."

Among her three brothers and two sisters, Lolo was the baby of the family—and the most rebellious. She had been born a preemie and always had a fragile, volatile personality.

Allie gazed out the window and began twisting a strand of her shoulder-length hair. "It doesn't sound good. And Dallan is MIA. Traipsing around the Arctic somewhere."

The previous week her brother-in-law had served Lolo with divorce papers and taken an apartment in Boulder, close to his work. Allie was praying they'd reconcile—but right now, as she stared blankly out the window, her cynicism concerning matters of love was winning out.

Believe, Miss so-called Christian, believe!

"It's a mess, an unholy mess."

"Which is why, my dear friend," Eva said—Allie could see a weak reflection in the glass of Eva brandishing a boney forefinger—"I intend to stay single."

Allie turned to her. "Yeah, right, like you're not already hitched."

Eva arched an eyebrow.

"To your work, *chica*, to your work."

Eva waved her off. "Yeah, yeah. Talk about the kettle calling the pot black."

She couldn't help grinning. "It's the pot call—"

The van braked suddenly.

"What?!" she crabbed.

"Traffic jam," Pitsy called out from the driver's seat.

Pitsy, her longtime chief cameraman, was a tall, thin, prematurely balding African-American man.

"You're kidding," she wailed. "On a Saturday morning?!"

Ten minutes later they came upon the reason for the jam: a long, rowdy parade of protestors in the bicycle lane, yelling and pumping large cardboard signs scrawled with various slogans: RED IS THE NEW GREEN...GREEN ENERGY IS A LIE...GREEN IS THE COLOR OF MONEY. At the head of the procession was a large banner announcing the group's identity: OCCUPY THE WORLD.

"And so it starts," she murmured, staring at the raucous spectacle. She was certain this had to do with the coming weekend's G-20 Summit in San Diego.

"You wanna pull over and get this on tape?" Eva said, peering out the window.

Occupy the World was a grassroots movement Allie was featuring in her upcoming primetime special. It was set to air in a month, smack in the middle of May sweeps, a special window of time when networks put on their flashiest programming in order to impress advertisers.

The thesis of her hour-long special dated back some six years. She'd been teaching physics at Harvard for a couple of years when she recognized a spectacular irony: science, widely expected to improve the human condition, was actually helping to bring about our destruction. She called the admittedly provocative hypothesis the "null prophecy"— after *null result*, a phrase scientists commonly used to describe an experiment that failed to produce a widely expected outcome.

"Well?" Eva pressed.

"I'm thinking."

Occupy the World was opposed to so-called green technology. It claimed (correctly) the sharp blades of wind farms were slicing and dicing innocent birds, including endangered species, even bald eagles. And the mirrored panels of huge solar farms heated the air immediately above them to 800 degrees, frying more birds than the Kentucky Colonel.

In Allie's estimation it was an illustration of the null prophecy in a nutshell.

"No," she said finally. "We're gonna be late as it is, and you know how I hate that."

★

SATURDAY, APRIL 22 (8:21 A.M. PACIFIC DAYLIGHT TIME)

They arrived at the north gate of Naval Base Point Loma and were cleared by security. The MP raised the wooden arm and waved them through.

A few minutes later Allie spotted a man built like a lifeguard and sporting red trunks and a white T-shirt standing with crossed arms in front of a hangar-like building. His attractive features were marred by a conspicuous frown.

"I think that's him over there and he doesn't look happy. Let me handle this."

Allie scrambled out of the van ahead of the crew.

"Dr. Sinclair?"

"Yes."

She was surprised at how handsome he was. She was expecting a geek.

"So sorry we're late," she said, extending her hand. "I'm Allie Armendariz."

He shook her hand. "Good to meet you."

"This is my producer, Eva Freiberg, and over there is our cameraman, Phil Pitman. We all call him Pitsy."

Eva shook Sinclair's hand. Pitsy, already unloading the equipment, gave him a quick nod.

"Everything's all set," Sinclair muttered. "Follow me."

Calder Sinclair claimed to have invented the perfect vehicle, a boat of some kind that supposedly ran on energy extracted from the quantum vacuum. Clean, limitless energy, he said, would change forever how people lived.

If true, she thought, he'd get the Nobel Prize in physics and become the most famous inventor since—well, since the creator of the wheel. But it was a very big *if*. She was always being solicited by quacks claiming to have invented a better mousetrap.

Eva walked alongside Sinclair just ahead of Allie. She overheard her producer saying, "She's still going to be able to ride with you, like we discussed, right?"

He nodded curtly and hastened them toward the water's edge.

A man of few words.

She gazed across San Diego Bay at the city skyline, her thoughts returning to Lolo.

I need to be there for her.

At moments like this Allie wished she had more free time and actually resented her job, her success, her whole way of life.

What have I become?

Who have I become?

As they neared the water she had a thought.

¿Por qué no?

After a moment's consideration, she decided—yes, she'd do it.

"Here she is," Sinclair said. He'd led them across the sand to a varnished wooden pier moored to which was a sleek, cherry-red vehicle. To her it looked like a cross between a ski boat and a rocket ship. It was roughly the size of a modern fighter jet.

Sinclair, grinning wryly, gestured to it extravagantly. "My *Hero*."

She looked at him askance and chuckled.

He stepped onto the pier, walked up to a metal footlocker, and proceeded to open it. "I named her after Hero of Alexandria."

"Ha, very cute," she said, recalling the first-century maverick who was considered the greatest inventor of the ancient world. Hero refused to believe in *horror vacui*, the then widespread conviction that a vacuum did not exist naturally and could not be produced in the lab either. "As I recall he never did manage to create a vacuum—though he died trying, poor devil."

Sinclair, having plucked a silvery garment from the footlocker, was pulling it on. "Yeah, but he sure was vindicated when Torricelli finally did."

When he finished dressing, he fetched out another suit and held it up to her.

"Here, this should fit you. It's Nomex."

Allie took the flight suit and looked around. "But where—?"

Smiling, he gestured to a large porta-potty a short distance away.

★

SATURDAY, APRIL 22 (8:25 A.M. PACIFIC DAYLIGHT TIME)

Everything about Allie impressed him—and helped to assuage his annoyance about their being late. For years he'd watched her reports on television and knew she had a first-rate mind. It was why he offered her the story.

But he was surprised by her genuine beauty. It wasn't just television smoke and mirrors. Her remarkable height—just short of his—long, wavy auburn hair, large emerald eyes, and creamed-coffee skin composed someone quite stunning.

It made him ache for his late wife, Nell—and his daughter, Sara, who'd recently left for Australia to study marine science.

"All set!" the producer called out. "Shake a leg everybody!"

Pushy, he thought. *But clearly efficient.*

A few moments later he and Allie eased into canvas sling chairs set up on the beach for the interview. The morning was warming up nicely; the sky was as blue as the water. It promised to be a picture-perfect spring day.

AA: "Dr. Sinclair, I'd like to—"
CS: "Please, everyone calls me Calder."

She smiled.

AA: "I'd like to start by asking you how *Hero* came to be."

Calder drew a long, deep breath.

CS: "All right. Well, as a kid growing up in Seville, Spain, near a river, I always dreamed of inventing a boat that'd go as fast as a rocket ship."

AA: "Why?"

CS: "I don't know. It just struck me the land and sky had already been conquered—and space, too. Oceans cover more than seventy percent of the earth's surface and to me they represent the final frontier. Still wide open and wild, you know? Ripe for the taking."

AA: "But there's more to *Hero* than just speed, right? Tell me about that."

CS: "Okay, well, when I was an undergrad at UCLA I started learning about the quantum vacuum, how scientists believe it's the foundation of all physical reality—the source of space, time, energy, and matter. I was so fascinated I started studying the work of guys like Hendrik Casimir, Dirk Polder, and Willis Lamb."

AA: "The pioneers."

He nodded, feeling thrilled to be talking to a kindred spirit.

CS: "What floored me was the idea a vacuum is not nothing. It actually houses invisible energy fields that are the source of *everything*. It's like science's answer to the idea of God."

Allie grinned and nodded.

CS: "I remember doing this one experiment. I put an inflated balloon and a pot of cold tap water under a glass dome and sucked the air out of it. The balloon grew bigger and bigger until it exploded. And the tap water boiled, even though it was still at room temperature. That's when a little bulb went off in my head and convinced me nothingness, or *seeming* nothingness, has amazing powers."

The surrounding stillness was rent by a loud air-raid siren.

"Cut!" the producer yelled.

"Sorry about that," he said. "It's only a munitions test. The siren always goes off to warn everybody on the base."

"What do you mean, munitions test?" Allie said.

"They're probably about to test insensitive explosives. Either that or the new sonar. This is one of the Navy's biggest installations in the world. There's always something going on here."

He caught sight of Allie giving her producer a knowing look.

"Is there a problem?"

"No, no," Allie shook her head. "Uh, I'm just wondering: is the test going to interfere with *Hero*'s run this morning?"

"Not at all. We're operating on different sides of the peninsula. Besides, *Hero*'s run this morning has been cleared by the Pentagon. They want to see it happen as much as I do."

"Roll camera!" the producer said in a rushed voice.

Allie appeared anxious about making sure the camera was rolling before pressing on.

> AA: "What you just said about the Pentagon's interest in today's test run—is it because *Hero* was created for military purposes?"

He raised himself in the chair to emphasize his response.

> CS: "No, I did *not* create *Hero* for military purposes. I created her to show the world that a clean, limitless energy source exists that has never been used before. It's a game changer."

Allie, hesitating, looked to her producer.

> CS: "Please, can we just move on? We were talking about how *Hero* works when the siren went off."
> AA: "Okay. Well, then, let's talk about how she's built. How strong is she? I mean her hull—how much punishment can it take? The ocean can be pretty brutal on ships. Just ask the engineers who designed the Titanic."
> CS: "She's virtually indestructible."
> AA: "No, really."

CS: "I mean it. It was a huge part of the challenge I faced. After figuring out how to extract energy from the vacuum, I needed to invent a casing for the Q-thruster hard enough—"

AA: "I'm sorry, Q-thruster?"

CS: "*Hero*'s main engine. I needed to make the hull strong enough to contain the pressures of matter-antimatter explosions. I finally created it: a laminate of boron carbide ceramic and stainless-steel-tungsten foam a thousand times tougher than what NASA uses for rocket engines."

Allie looked down at her notes before continuing.

AA: "So how do you see *Hero* being used? If not for military purposes, then—"

CS: "Who foresaw the future of air travel? Or cars? Or spaceships? One thing I can say for sure is my technology will relieve traffic congestion on the roads and in the skies by creating a viable transportation alternative. As I said, the oceans are wide open right now. With my technology we can build high-speed ships that'll ferry people from one country to another, faster, more safely, and more comfortably than airplanes. And with no pollution or fear of ever running out of fuel."

AA: "Faster than *flying*?"

CS: "You bet."

He paused for effect.

CS: "You'll see."

★

SATURDAY, APRIL 22 (10:03 A.M. PACIFIC DAYLIGHT TIME)

A small crowd of uniformed Navy bigshots gathered on the beach to witness the event. Inside *Hero*'s cabin, Allie was strapped snugly into the passenger seat, cocooned in suit, helmet, and gloves. Calder explained, like race car drivers, they needed to be protected against fiery collisions—an explanation that left her more than a little jittery.

Through the large, bubble-shaped windshield she watched Eva and Pitsy on the pier filming the prelaunch process. Two wide-angle lipstick cameras mounted inside *Hero*'s cockpit gave a clear view of the interior.

At Eva's request she went through one last sound check, after which all was ready. She gave them a half-hearted thumbs-up, suddenly second-guessing her decision to do this story. She swallowed hard and double-checked her harnessing.

Anything for ratings, right?

Calder, seemingly nerveless and seated in the forward compartment, ordered her people to evacuate the pier and reset on the beach. A moment later she heard him speaking on the radio.

"Point Loma, this is *Hero One*, over."

A flat male voice responded. "*Hero One*, this is Point Loma, we copy, over."

"*Hero One* requesting permission to launch, over."

A pregnant silence was finally broken by the words, "Permission granted. We've cleared the area of traffic. Good luck, Dr. Sinclair, over."

"Thanks, Scotty, over and out."

Scotty, Calder explained, was Point Loma's chief communications officer. Several moments later he began voicing the final countdown.

Her entire body resonated with the drumming sound of her accelerating heartbeat.

"Three...two...one. Ignition."

At first she was aware of only a high-pitched whirring sound. Then there was a loud explosion and abruptly she was slammed against the contoured seat with such violence she almost blacked out. She willed herself to focus, to speak coherently to the interior cameras.

"Hard to breathe...everything happening so fast...*Ay!* What was that?"

Later, when reviewing the video, she learned what she felt at that precise moment was *Hero* rising on her skis and hydroplaning across the surface of the ocean at four hundred knots.

"Calder!" she shouted into her helmet's mic. "Is everything okay?"

"Roger," he said phlegmatically.

A few moments hence the ride smoothed out dramatically. The sensation was like being in a glider plane—quiet, fast, enlivening.

"Wow!" she exclaimed. "This is amazing!"

It was going to be a challenge, for sure, to explain to her viewers how *Hero* worked. Perhaps she'd compare *Hero*'s source of power to an empty gas tank *that wasn't really empty.*

She realized people thought of a perfect vacuum as being the absence of anything and everything. But science, in its mind-bending way, believed a perfect vacuum still contained lots of invisible stuff—space, time, matter, and above all, *energy fields.* Sinclair was claiming to have found the Holy Grail of science: a way of tapping the enigmatic, ghostly fields for unlimited quantities of real, tangible, combustible power.

Her thoughts were interrupted by an ear-shattering buzzer. An instant later *Hero* seemed to slip out of control. The cabin shuddered with such vehemence she worried it'd break apart.

"Allie, listen to me—" Sinclair's voice broke off.

She felt *Hero* glancing off a wave and going airborne, felt her weight lift off the seat. A moment later the vehicle slammed onto the water with a heavy thud that rattled her insides. She then felt *Hero* swing around hard to port and saw through the expansive windshield a coastline pan into view.

They were heading straight for the Navy ships parked at Coronado Island!

Allie was about to cry out just as she felt *Hero* braking. Her helmeted head jerked forward while her captive upper body strained hard against the leather harnessing, causing the straps to creak. Several dizzying moments later the violent shaking quieted down and the vehicle sloshed roughly to a halt a mere few feet short of a Navy destroyer.

"Allie, are you okay?"

Hero bobbed gaily in the water.

"I'm so sorry. That was not part of the plan."

She let go of her breath, still trembling from the ordeal. "Yeah, I think so. But what in the world was that all about?"

Silence.

"The collision avoidance system," he said quietly. "Something went wrong."

They rode back to the pier without conversing. When they arrived, Calder shut down *Hero*'s engine. Navy ensigns scurried about the pier, roping the vehicle and lashing her to large metal cleats.

Allie quickly undid her harness, eager to get out.

Sinclair threw open the windshield, stood up, and removed his helmet. "Allie," he said, turning to face her, "I'm really sorry about the snafu. But *Hero*'s propulsion system worked perfectly. That's big news, right?"

She was still trying to regain her composure. "Yes—yes, it is."

"Are you open to giving *Hero* a second chance?" There was a silent pause. "I hope you are. You really need to, actually; it's important."

CHAPTER 3

FAMILIA

M oments after the closing hymn, *hermana* Diana burst into the Sunday school classroom to collect her two boys. "Allie, you missed a good sermon."

"*Sí, hermana*," she said, bundling up the boys' art projects—decorated crosses made of ice cream sticks—and putting them into a brown paper bag.

"It was about how the resurrection represents turning over a new leaf. Starting a new life. At one point, your brother asked if we knew what the first commandment in the Bible is."

Standing alongside the boys, her hands on their shoulders, Allie thought about it for a moment and immediately knew what was coming.

19

She was the only one in her family who wasn't married, divorced, or even engaged. By Old World Mexican standards, she was in danger of ending up a lonely *solterona*.

"*Sabes que es*, right?" Diana said.

Allie wouldn't be baited. "Of course. It's about worshiping only God and nothing else."

Diana didn't miss a beat. "Well, that, too, but no. It's in Genesis where God commands Adam and Eve to be fruitful and multiply."

La hermana Magaña entered the room. "Oh sister," she said, "you missed a really good one."

By the time the last children were returned to their parents, Allie was left questioning why in creation she was letting herself do this. Why during these past few months she'd been rising extra early on Sundays—contractually, her only day off—dressing up, and driving an hour out of her way, only to be—

Carlos appeared at the door. "C'mon, Allie, they need you!"

One look at her brother's brown, beaming face and any doubts about what she was doing vanished.

Estos son mis reices.

"Give me a hand," she said, instantly setting about to tidy the small room. "Unless it's beneath the senior pastor's pay scale." She chuckled.

"Yeah, right, my pay scale," he snorted, straightening the chairs. "Trust me, it's waaaay below yours, little sis. Besides, remember what the Bible says: 'If you want to be a leader, you have to be everyone's servant.'"

She paused and gave Carlos a wan smile.

He's the real deal.

And me?

Despite her religious upbringing, it wasn't until grad school that her eyes opened to the possible existence of God. At Cornell, enrolled in courses where she was learning about the deep-rooted order and beauty of the universe, she couldn't help but ask: *How did it all come to be?* The answer offered by science—that it was all a magnificent accident—was simply not intellectually satisfying. It required a gratuitous amount of faith in the scientific method—brilliant as it was—to believe such a shallow hypothesis.

By the time she arrived at Harvard, the possibility of a higher intelligence was very real to her. Seeking a credible elaboration on the nature of this posited deity, she dove into the sacred literature of the world's main belief systems: Hinduism, Buddhism, Islam, Judaism, even Transcendental Meditation. But she avoided the Bible because it wasn't exotic, not like the other religious literature she'd studied. It seemed unlikely to her the Bible contained anything earth-shattering she hadn't already heard a million times from her parents while growing up.

But she was mistaken.

After eventually reading the Bible from Genesis to Revelation, she learned Christianity's worldview was radically different than any other religion's. For example, God's favor was not limited to only a certain people; nor could it be earned by anyone, but was offered freely to one and all.

Most shocking of all, she learned, Christianity's worldview was identical to science's take on reality. Universal truths she'd learned as a physicist—for example, that absolute truth exists, time is linear, and significant parts of reality are hidden from us—jibed perfectly with fundamental truths espoused in the Bible.

The revelation was a game changer; it persuaded her to become a follower of Jesus. But to this day—five years after her conversion—she fretted that her Christian beliefs were still mostly intellectual. She didn't feel the kind of deep emotional and spiritual joy she saw in her brother.

It was why she'd returned to this church, founded by her parents and now pastored by Carlos and his wife, Alicia. Perhaps some of Carlos's bona fide spirituality would rub off on her. In the meantime, she told herself, she was at least reconnecting with the family, friends, and community from whom her ambitions and success had estranged her.

When they finished cleaning up, she grabbed her purse and followed Carlos out the door.

"I spoke to Lolo's doctor," she said in a quiet voice.

"Yeah, me too."

"It's serious. She's become convinced the world is coming to an end. What are we gonna do?"

"What can we do? Her world *is* coming to an end, as far as she's concerned. She was so hoping for a family. Our little rebel was finally growing up. It's awful." Carlos's husky voice broke; he hesitated.

"And Dallan—" Allie let out a small growl. "God forgive me, but I'm so angry at him right now I want to—"

"Allie, Allie. It's not his fault."

"Oh, really? No one knows what causes delusional disorder, but the research says stress is one of the main triggers. If Dallan hadn't filed for divorce—"

"C'mon, Allie, he doesn't even know what's happened. They can't reach him where he is—something about bad communications. But he's supposed to be back in Boulder tomorrow. Anyway, we can't change the past. Right now our baby sis is in trouble; that's all that matters. But she's in a really good hospital, okay? And I checked out the doctor—he's top drawer. So we've just gotta pray, Sis. We've gotta trust the Lord, surrender it to him."

"I know, I know..." She stopped. "But I have an idea."

After she'd explained it to him they resumed their walk to the church kitchen.

"What are they cooking this week?" she said, putting on a happy face. "I'm starving."

A tradition of the church was to offer the congregation a hearty meal following the service—a *comida*, it was called. She remembered it from childhood, when the ritual was started by her mom and dad.

"I'm not supposed to say," Carlos said with a knowing smile. "It's a surprise."

She groaned inwardly.

Oh, Lord, they've remembered.

When they stepped into the kitchen, Alicia and a group of church sisters cried out, "Happy birthday!"

Allie brought her hands to her mouth. "Oh, you guys! Thank you."

The giddy entourage led her by the hand to the parking lot. It was decorated all around with red, green, and white streamers and big, hand-lettered signs declaring Happy Birthday, Allie and Happy Easter and He Has Risen!

"When did you guys do all this?!"

"During the service, when you weren't looking," Alicia answered joyfully.

Mariachis strode out from the main building and began serenading her with "Las Mañanitas," the traditional Mexican birthday song. By the time they were done, the entire church—everyone colorfully dressed in their Easter finest—were gathered around her.

"Speech! Speech!" the crowd shouted.

She was used to doing live television, of having to vamp for hours if necessary. But this.

"Honestly, I was hoping you wouldn't know!"

Laughter.

"Don't worry, you're still young!"

The voice belonged to Albert Hernandez, the oldest son of her dad's best friend. He'd started chasing after her in kindergarten at Belvedere Elementary and now owned the largest Chevy dealership in East Los Angeles. He was still unattached.

She didn't feel young but chuckled anyway. "Yeah, right." Then she thanked everyone—*los queridos hermanos de la Iglesia Buen Samaritano*—who for the most part belonged to families she'd grown up with, who'd known her grandparents, her parents, and her brothers and sisters since they were born.

"You're like my family, you know?" Her voice was cracking. "You *are* my family and I love you. I love this church."

"We love you, Allie!" voices cried out.

She continued, "You know, just because I don't live in East LA anymore doesn't mean I've forgotten where I came from or who I am. I never want to forget. These are my roots and I'm proud of it. Thank you for loving me as much as I love you. God bless you."

She blew them all a kiss.

"Okay, enough already or I'm gonna start *chiando*!" Carlos yelled. "Let's eat!"

The church members cheered.

She saw them bringing out Mexican hot dogs, her favorite junk food. "What are you trying to do—make me fat?" she wailed, shaking her head.

Alicia, carrying a metal platter piled high with bacon-wrapped wieners, was quick to answer, "Actually, yeah!" and the others laughed.

Allie shook her head, smiling.

They never let up.

She spotted an apron on a nearby table and went to put it on.

"No way, girl," *hermana* Diana protested, "not on your birthday. Take a break."

But she insisted. She wanted to forget she was a year older and still single. She wanted it to be like any other day. She wanted to help serve. "You know what Jesus tells us," she said lightheartedly, tying on her apron. "He wants us to be a servant to all."

While dishing out food, she was repeatedly wished a happy birthday and asked how old she was. She gave them her stock reply: "Old enough to vote, okay? Reporters never give away their secrets."

When Albert's turn in line came he didn't need to ask her age. It was the same as his: thirty-four. "*Felíz cumple*, Alejandra. You're looking good."

"Thanks, Beto, you're not looking bad yourself."

He'd been Garfield High's star quarterback and still kept in shape. He had dreamy, caramel-colored bedroom eyes and she liked the way he combed back his straight black hair. But their worlds were very different now.

She held up a plain, bacon-wrapped wiener in a bun. "What do you want on it?"

"Like always, remember? The works."

She chuckled. "Still with the macho stomach."

"Hey, I hired two new employees this week. Business is booming."

She looked down and started heaping on the various toppings.

Here it comes.

"My offer still stands, you know. I found this great location on Cesar Chavez and Soto. We could start a chain."

Beto was after her to partner up in business—not to mention matrimony. No one had ever accused him of being a shrinking violet.

"I know," she said. "But right now I've got my hands full, brother. Maybe someone else."

"Never," he said, giving her a determined smile.

When she was done piling on the *pico de gallo*, pineapple, avocado, grilled jalapenos, and *crema*, she handed him the heavy *plato*. "Here you go, *patron:* one TJ dog with everything on it. Make sure you chew before swallowing."

At the end of the *comida* Allie went to her father, who was seated under the big sycamore at the edge of the parking lot. Her heart broke to see him without Mom.

Her parents had been an inseparable couple for forty-two years. For the first eight of them he was an atheist. But after witnessing what he believed to be the miraculous healing of her brother Carlos, he dropped to his knees and converted to Christianity. Afterward, the two love birds built this church from scratch using donated materials. Just like that, her father went from being Lupe the shoe repairman to the Reverend Guadalupe Armendariz—and her mother, from housewife to First Lady Betty.

Late the previous year her mom was diagnosed with early-onset Alzheimer's. Recently, because she was worsening, they needed to put her into a nursing home. It was a decision tearing away at her dad, who was sixty-one years old and still physically healthy.

She dragged over a nearby chair and sat next to him. "Hey, *Papá.* You need anything? Did you have enough to eat?"

He smiled and nodded. "How did you like our little birthday surprise? Everyone pitched in. We wanted it to be special."

"You really got me; I wasn't expecting it. Thank you."

She stared at his large, friendly face.

Don't say it.

"Now if you guys could only whip me up a husband..."

He gave her an indulgent smile, then reached over and placed his wrinkled hand on hers. "You're still young, *mija*, you'll get your chance. Be patient."

She shifted herself around in order to look straight at him. "Pa, I had my chance and blew it; you know that."

He pulled his hand away. "*Ay, Diosito, mija*, not Phillip again. Don't tell me you're still carrying that around."

Phil Gutierrez was someone she'd met in grad school at a seminar on the spatial correlation of galaxy clusters. They were first-years, she in physics, he in astronomy. Early on he came onto her with a fiery amorousness that spooked her. But after getting to know him, she came to believe their love was meant to be.

He was smart, sensitive, handsome, and wanted a family. Everything seemed perfect—until graduation. He was offered a job at Jodrell Bank Observatory in England, she, a teaching position at Harvard. In the end, she broke off their relationship and went to Cambridge. To this day that agonizing decision and its ghastly fallout still haunted her. In her weaker moments, despite Christianity's teachings and admonitions, she wondered how God could possibly ever forgive her.

No one must ever know the whole story.

Not even—

"*Papá*, you don't understand. He's married now and has two great kids. There are times when I think that could've been me. I have my career—which is great, I love what I do—but I want more." She paused. "I want to love a man like Phil, and be loved by him. But it's never going to happen, I just feel it. I had my chance and I blew it."

Her father sat up and sternly pointed a finger at her. "Don't talk that way; it's blasphemous. You're not God. You don't know what He has in store for you. I liked Phillip; he was a nice boy. But he's not the only man out there worth having. Dreams take sacrifice; yes, okay, you sacrificed. But look at you: you're beautiful, you're intelligent, you're successful. What man wouldn't want to marry you? Beto sure wants to."

She reared her head. "Dad, please!"

A silence fell between them.

Sacrifices.

If he only knew.

"I hear you're thinking about having Lorena move in with you," her father said quietly.

Einstein had been wrong about one thing: it *was* possible for information to travel faster than the speed of light. The Armendariz family grapevine was proof.

"Dad, she's all alone. I can't just let her fall apart without doing something."

"I know, I know, we all feel that way. The only question is, what's best for her?"

"What's best for her is to be with family. People who love her."

Her father shifted his gaze in the direction of the church. "I don't disagree. But she also needs professional help, *mija*." He paused and then looked at her. "And you are very busy."

Over the years her father made it abundantly clear to family and friends he was proud of her success. Even when she was a girl, a girl wanting to be a scientist, he'd always encouraged her to go after her God-given destiny. But his words now, although spoken gently and with evident love, felt like an indictment.

Who have I become?

"Your sister is telling everyone at the hospital 'the end' is about to happen and she wants to see Jesus coming back to Earth." His head fell, so all she could see was his thinning white hair. "*Pobresita.*"

A day earlier the doctor told Allie on the phone Lolo's delusional disorder appeared to be of the type called "grandiose." Furthermore, her delusions fell into the "bizarre" category, meaning they could not possibly happen in reality—at least, not as far as science was concerned.

The odd part, he further explained, was DD patients typically behaved normally until and unless the subject of their delusions came up or was challenged. So it was difficult to know how to treat them effectively; psychotherapy was a realistic option, but certainly not institutionalization.

She scooted her chair closer to her father and put an arm around him.

He lifted his face. "I know you mean well, *mijita*, but I want you to pray about it before acting, okay? There's no rush. She's in good hands at that hospital. Carlos checked it out."

Growing up, she had learned to trust her father's judgment, especially when it came to people and relationships. It was a gift she wished she'd inherited.

"*Sí, Apá*, I promise."

The two sat quietly together, watching and waving to the last of the people who were getting into their cars and leaving. She resisted looking at her watch.

"I hear you're not coming with us this afternoon to visit your mother."

This was the part of today she'd been dreading. "I've got to do an interview up north, in Mountain View."

He turned and trained his eyes on her. Those piercing brown eyes. As kids, they'd always marveled at their father's x-ray vision and quaked whenever it was turned on them. "He can see into a person's soul," *Mamá* would say. "It's what makes him such a good pastor."

"For your big special next month?"

"No, it's a live shot."

"Who are you interviewing?"

"Jared Kilroy. He's the new head of NeuroNet—a real whiz kid."

He continued looking at her.

"It's a big exclusive. No one's ever interviewed him before. No one's really ever seen him."

"That's good, *mija*, that's good," her father said, looking away and smiling weakly. "I'm proud of you."

There was an awkward pause in the conversation.

He turned to her. "But it's Easter, *mijita*," he said finally. "And your birthday. It's not right."

"I know, *apá*, I know. It's just that—"

What? That when push comes to shove, career trumps even family?

She stood up. "Dad, I'm so sorry but I better head out, otherwise I'm going to be late. Please tell *Mamá* I'll come see her this week, I promise. Give her a big *abrazo* for me, okay?"

She bent over to kiss him.

He took hold of her hand and looked up at her. "*Mija*, please be careful."

Tears blurred her eyesight, but she easily imagined the sadness in his kindly visage. "*Sí, Papá*, I promise; don't worry."

As she walked away, his last words echoed. "*Mija*, please be careful." She knew he'd meant it not just as a polite send-off but as a spoken prayer as well, a warning.

And not just about this afternoon's live shot.

CHAPTER 4

STORMY THOUGHTS

The monstrous Herc thumped safely onto the hard-packed, snowy runway. Dallan heaved a huge sigh of relief, joining in the eruption of applause from the plane's other grateful passengers. After the horrifying experience at the polynya and being grounded overnight in Thule, it felt good to be back at the station.

Deplaning, he cast a wary glance skyward. The sky looked more bloody, more garish than when they'd left the previous morning. The pole's magnetic shield was clearly deteriorating.

Heaven help us: it's gonna be like the polynya.

Brody came alongside him. "Be ready. We might need to evacuate, and pronto."

He answered with a curt nod.

As director of the U.S.' largest space weather forecasting facility, Dallan was used to reporting about solar storms, extra-bright aurorae, and disruptions to communications caused by radiation coming from the sun. But this…a possible complete collapse of the entire polar region's magnetic shield—a gaping magnetic hole! Without any protection whatsoever from the magnetic field, without anything to filter out the sun's lethal radiation—*good god!* People, property, the very air would be incinerated.

The bright yellow Snowcat rumbled up to the plane and stopped. Dallan watched the chief of staff jump down from the cab and rush up to the major. He overheard him say, "Sir, something's happening. You need to see this."

He, Brody, and the others piled into the Snowcat and were driven to the northern tip of the island.

"Oh, good lord!" Dallan exclaimed when he disembarked.

Stretching for as far as the eye could see was a frozen beachfront strewn with marooned narwhals. To him they looked like hapless, sluglike unicorns. Beyond the beach, the steel-colored Arctic Ocean teemed with still more whales making straight for shore.

"I expected this."

He and the others turned as one toward the voice; it was the Inuit biologist, Rebecca Anawak. Last night in Thule he'd convinced her to join them at the station until the polynya was safe again.

"What?" Brody said. "What'd you say?"

"It's the same as at the polynya—the same cause, I mean. The faltering magnetic field."

Everyone gathered around her.

"Go ahead," Brody prompted her.

"Many animals carry tiny magnetic particles inside their bodies. We believe they use them like built-in compasses, mostly for long-distance navigation. Homing pigeons carry them inside the muscles of their necks, rainbow trout inside their noses, whales inside their heads."

Dallan banged his gloved hands together and nodded. He knew where she was going with this.

"Joe Kirshvink at Cal Tech and others have done experiments and come up with a theory," she continued. "They believe there are troughs in the magnetic field—invisible highways—animals follow to get around."

"Like cars on freeways," Dallan interjected.

"Exactly."

He saw Brody light up like a third grader who suddenly understood fractions.

"So wait," the major said. "The problem we're seeing with the polar B-field is screwing up these invisible highways? That's why these animals are lost? Is that what you're saying?"

"Basically, yes," she replied. "And it's messing with their personalities too, as we saw at the polynya."

★

EASTER SUNDAY, APRIL 23 (9:35 P.M. EASTERN DAYLIGHT TIME)

That evening Dallan lay in bed staring restively at the ceiling. His dorm room was cozy enough and the black-out shades were fully drawn, but he was unable to fall asleep. His thoughts were in turmoil, surging from the events of the last twenty-four hours to Lorena and back again.

Every thought of Lorena ended with, *What have I done?*

The previous week he asked his lawyers to start divorce proceedings against her. It wasn't what he wanted, really, but he had no choice. She'd changed too much. The fun, high-spirited girl he first met and fell hard for had morphed into a conventional drudge.

He shut his eyes and rubbed his forehead brusquely, as if to erase all thoughts of the fiasco.

I never wanted children.

I told her that—over and over again.

Involuntarily, his mind was flooded again with images of bloody skies and beached whales. Moments later he found himself reliving the events of Friday afternoon that brought him to this nightmare.

He was at the Space Weather Prediction Center holding court with a gaggle of fifth graders.

★

"Every eleven years or so the sun goes bonkers," he explained. "Like you kids when you eat too much sugar."

The students laughed and nodded knowingly.

He pointed to the large screen on the wall of the SWPC's command and control room. "That's what you're seeing right now, live and in color: a sun that's pumped. We call it *solar max*."

The sun's surface, its chromosphere, was the very portrait of chaos. The tangled, twisting rivers of red-orange plasma suggested to his mind a nest of writhing red corn snakes.

A tall, lanky boy raised his hand. "Is that why there's gonna be a magnetic storm Sunday night?"

"You could say that. Geomagnetic storms happen a lot during a solar max."

He glanced furtively at the children's attractive young teacher, Ms. Bell, and noticed she wasn't wearing a ring.

"But you guys don't need to worry. The one we're predicting for Sunday is no biggie, okay? At most it might cause a little bit of radio and TV interference, that's all."

Ms. Bell raised her hand. "Dr. O'Malley, what about the Internet?"

"Yes, maybe that, too." He gave her a friendly wink. "Excellent question."

A ginger-haired, freckled-faced girl raised her hand. "What's a gee-o-mag-ne-tic storm, anyway?"

"Well, it's caused by a blizzard of invisible, electrically charged particles from the sun that slam into the earth. They're mostly electrons and protons—" he paused. "Uh, have you kids studied about them yet?"

There was a discordant chorus of yeses and nos. He looked to the teacher, who smiled and shook her head.

"Okay, then, let me put it this way. Electrons and protons are super-tiny particles that carry electricity. When they hit Earth's magnetic field way up there"—he pointed skyward—"they set off a chain reaction that creates big problems for us down here on earth."

"What kind of problems?" a kid called out.

He had an idea. "Let me show you. Follow me!"

He led the children to the visitors' auditorium, which was stocked with lots of fun demo equipment. Once on stage, he rolled out a Van de Graff generator, which looked like a giant metal globe. He invited the teacher to join him.

"If you don't mind," he said when she came alongside him, "I need you to stand on this wooden box." He took her hand and helped her mount it, in the process catching a whiff of her flowery perfume. "Lovely," he said *sotto voce*. "Thank you."

She tottered on her petite-sized green pumps, but quickly regained her balance.

"Okay, now, students, I want you to pretend this Van de Graff generator is the earth." He turned to the teacher. "Go ahead and place both hands on the globe."

She looked at him trepidatiously, but then did as requested.

Nothing happened.

"As you can see," he said, "nothing happens—everything's cool." He asked the teacher to remove her hands then flicked a switch; the machine roared to life with a loud, grinding sound.

"The globe is now being electrified. It's like the earth being bombarded by that hurricane of electrons and protons I told you about. It's creating a magnetic storm—and now watch what happens." He asked Ms. Bell to lay her hands on the globe once again.

She wavered.

He smiled. "Trust me, you'll be fine."

Reluctantly, the teacher placed her hands on the globe and instantly her long blonde hair rose straight up like stalks of dried wheat. The boys and girls pointed and laughed with unfettered glee.

Dallan quieted them down with his hands. "The magnetic storm is causing Ms. Bell's hair to rise like that—and if you were standing close enough, like I am, you'd hear her hair crackling from the electricity.

"In theory, if a magnetic storm were powerful enough, this would happen to your hair as well. Normally, though, magnetic storms—like the one we're predicting for Sunday—aren't strong enough to do that. Mostly they only mess up things like radio and cell phone reception. Nothing you'll probably even notice."

He switched off the machine and helped Ms. Bell off the wooden box.

"Okay, I think it's time—"

He was interrupted by the sight of his assistant rushing into the theater. A moment later the young man leaped onto the stage, rushed up to him, and spoke directly into his ear.

"We need you, sir. Right away."

CHAPTER 5

CASHING IN THE CHIPS

EASTER SUNDAY, APRIL 23 (4:00 P.M. PACIFIC DAYLIGHT TIME)

NEURONET CORPORATE HEADQUARTERS; MOUNTAIN VIEW, CALIFORNIA

For reasons nobody understood, but that Allie hoped to find out, Jared Kilroy was reared in complete secrecy. He'd never issued a public statement, except through his handlers, nor had he ever made a single public appearance. No one even knew his exact age, although prevailing wisdom placed him in his mid-twenties.

"I wonder what he looks like," she said to Eva. They were in the back seat of a limo that had just pulled into NeuroNet's vast parking lot. "Google Images has thousands of pictures that are supposed to be of him, but they're all different."

Two weeks earlier the young mystery man was named NeuroNet's new CEO, following the death of his ninety-year-old legendary father,

Jack. The old man founded the company decades ago and in 2000 received the Nobel Prize in Physics for co-inventing the computer chip.

Under Jack Kilroy's leadership NeuroNet grew to become the world's largest maker of integrated circuits. NeuroNet now employed more than 90,000 people and posted yearly sales north of forty-five billion dollars. The corporate giant comprised sixteen fabrication plants, or "fabs," and nine assembly and test facilities worldwide. NeuroNet microprocessors were in eighty percent of all existing PCs.

When the car stopped in front of the entrance she and Eva let themselves out and stood ogling the company's towering new office building. NeuroNet 2.0, they called it: Silicon Valley's newest hot property. Scores of uniformed musclemen were offloading chairs, desks, tables, and other furniture from a fleet of large vans.

"Wow," Allie said, "impressive." Her heart was racing. By network news standards this evening's exclusive interview was a huge "get."

Pitsy and the crew, who'd driven there ahead of time, were waiting for them at the entrance.

"How was the flight?" Pitsy asked.

Stu "tightwad" Siegel, their boss and president of Fast News, had given Eva and her permission to take a private jet.

"You know—same ol', same ol'," Allie deadpanned before laughing.

"Pretty awesome, actually," Eva said.

"What I wanna know is how you got Stu to go along with it," Pitsy said, pushing on the glass door and holding it open for them. "How'd he react when you asked him for it?"

"How do you think?" Eva said, rolling her eyes as she walked past him into the building. "The old skinflint."

Allie, following right behind, chuckled. She'd actually come to like Stu. Four years earlier, when she was still at Harvard, he had invited her to his office in New York City. There on the spot he offered her the position of chief science correspondent.

She quickly accepted on the condition she be allowed to live in Los Angeles, to be close to her family. Stu consented and later even helped get her manuscript about the null prophecy published, figuring a book tie-in would help boost ratings for the TV special. "I think you're onto something here, Allie," he'd said, "It'll be gold."

"Hey, it's the least he could do," Allie said about Stu's rare show of extravagance. "I'm giving up my Easter for this."

"Whoa, girlfriend!" Eva said. "Remember, you didn't need to be here. Stu knew I was willing to do the interview by myself."

Allie frowned. "And turn a major live spot into a taped piece? No way. Besides, I'm dying to meet this guy."

They walked through NeuroNet's lobby, gawking at the cavernous interior. At the reception desk they were checked in by a pretty, pale-faced young woman with spiked purple hair and lip rings. A few minutes later they were approached by a tow-headed, baby-faced teenager dressed in torn blue jeans and a black T-shirt emblazoned with the word BRAIN-STORM across the chest. A small, sorrel-colored horse was tattooed to the inside of his left forearm.

She guessed high-school intern.

Dang. The older I get, the younger they look.

"Allie Armendariz, right?" the boy said.

"Yes," she said, shaking his hand. She stared into his unusual, amber-colored eyes. "And this is my producer, Eva Freiberg, and our chief cameraman, Phil Pitman."

"Great, good to meet you all. Follow me. Everything's set."

This was her first time inside the new building and what she saw as they walked through the offices surprised her in a pleasant way. Google, Twitter, Facebook: the mainstream corporate environments of the digital age all had a certain Willy Wonka cuteness she liked at first. But she came to see them as childish attempts by the companies' geeky founders to be cool and worse, Orwellian. Playful, coddling environments, complete with free food and candy, ingeniously calculated to indoctrinate their mostly young, impressionable employees into cult-like corporate cultures while squeezing every ounce of productivity out of them. For her, there was far more Kool-Aid than cool in Silicon Valley.

But NeuroNet 2.0 was disarmingly understated. The chairs and couches being brought in were plump and inviting, the floor coverings warm and homey, the living-room-like lighting subdued. Had some management guru—Jared Kilroy himself, perhaps—discovered a new, unpretentious algorithm for enhancing worker productivity? Whatever the explanation, she liked what she saw.

The intern led them into a spacious, glass-walled conference room in which everything did indeed appear to be set up for the live interview.

"I'm sorry," Eva said, "I'm confused. We brought our own equipment."

"Is there a problem?" The question came from a slim woman with short hair, ramrod-straight posture, and stern demeanor. She was older than the intern, but not by much, and clad in a perfectly tailored charcoal-gray business suit.

Eva's face was reddening. "There is if you expect us to do the interview with your set-up."

"And why is that, may I ask? This equipment's all top-of-the-line."

Allie stepped in. "Sorry, but it's network policy. Unions and all that." She nodded at Pitsy to start setting up. "It won't take us long to set up."

"But we went—"

"It's okay, Maggie," the intern said, walking over to the young woman.

Allie thought it odd for an intern to be giving orders.

"I suppose I should introduce myself," he said, turning to her. "I'm Jared Kilroy. This is our public relations chief, Maggie Henderson."

EASTER SUNDAY, APRIL 23 (5:59 P.M. PACIFIC DAYLIGHT TIME)

"Stand by. One minute to air!"

It was Eva talking to her through the IFB, a custom-fitted earpiece. Allie was seated opposite Kilroy in front of an elegant, floor-to-ceiling bookcase. One camera was framed on her, another on him. A third camera was on both of them. Eva was out in the parking lot inside a capacious production truck, from which she could communicate directly with Stu in New York. The anchor there, Brett Halsey, was at that moment introducing the segment.

"Three...two...one. You're on, girlfriend."

AA: "Thank you, Brett."

She turned to Kilroy.

AA: "Mr. Kilroy, thank you for being with us this evening."

It felt weird calling him mister. He couldn't be older than eighteen or nineteen. Could pass for sixteen.

He nodded.

JK: "Sure, of course."
AA: "You've never appeared in public before. Why is that— why the secrecy?"

His face tightened.

JK: "If you don't mind, that's not what I'm here to discuss."

She squirmed, caught off guard by the terse stonewalling.

AA: "But you granted this interview. Why would you—?"
JK: "I agreed to the interview to talk about something very important to me."

This was live TV; she needed to roll with it or risk total disaster.

AA: "Okay, and what would that be?"
JK: "First off, let me say thanks. I've watched your science reports on TV. You're the best at what you do. Just like me. Just like NeuroNet 2.0. We don't plan to be my father's company anymore. That's why I'm doing this. Today, right here and right now, I'm announcing that

NeuroNet is going private and will be donating all of its profits to certain select charities."

She felt lightheaded. Was she being punked? She knew of reporters who'd been suckered in by fake news stories; their careers had tanked in the blink of an eye.

AA: "What do you mean? What charities are you talking about?"

JK: "My dad's generation was all about profits, right?—making the rich richer. My generation's all about the double bottom line: doing well by doing good; profiting for a cause, not just stockholders. We're going to be like Newman's Own, except a million times bigger. Our sales last year topped forty-seven point three billion dollars. That's a lot of influence."

AA: "You said, 'select charities.' What do you mean by that? What kind of charities?"

JK: "Charities like Hedge Clippers, Mind the Gap, Cornell's Center for the Study of Inequality—those kinds of non-profits."

She shifted in her chair, her mind desperately seeking its bearings.

JK: "See, we have a huge income inequality problem in our country and I want NeuroNet to be part of the solution. In the last thirty years the wealthiest one-percent increased their take by sixty-six percent, while for everybody else things got worse. The middle class in our country is disappearing. Minimum wage is worth twelve percent less now than in 1967. It's so bad that one in every four American workers has to rely on some kind of government handout. Bottom line: the U.S. is almost dead last in the civilized world when it comes to income equality: thirty-second out of thirty-four countries. That's obscene."

"Three minutes!" Eva said into her ear. "Enough with the politics, already. Ask him about the chip. *The chip!*"

A week earlier NeuroNet had released its latest microprocessor, the Quantum I; it was causing quite a sensation.

> **AA:** "Tell me about Quantum I. It's a real technological break-through, right?"
>
> **JK:** "Yes, well, as you know, it's the world's first one-mega-qubit microprocessor—the start of a new age."
>
> **AA:** "It's certainly taking the world by storm."
>
> **JK:** "Of course. With Quantum I's computing power your average PC can now run ultra-realistic simulations of everyday life that can forecast the future: the weather, stock market, climate—"
>
> **AA:** "But—"
>
> **JK:** "And that's just for starters. With Quantum I, theoretically you can digitize thoughts and memories and store them on a hard drive. One day you'll be able to download all that into the electronic brain of a robot that looks just like you. You'll be able to interact with others forever. It's the first step toward true immortality."

Dang, this guy is good.
But what a brat.

"Two minutes!" Eva said into her ear.

> **AA:** "The idea of a quantum processor isn't new. Scientists first started trying to build one more than ten years ago. How have you managed to do what others have failed at doing?"
>
> **JK:** "Because we're smarter than they are?"

She expected Kilroy to chuckle, or at least smile, but he kept a straight face.

AA: "How are you smarter? What was the key to your succeeding?"

JK: "Since anyone can and will reverse engineer Quantum I to find out, I might as well tell you. There were two huge problems we managed to solve. First, we found a way to cram one million qubits—one million quantum bits of processing power—into a tiny chip. No small feat. Second, everyone thought quantum chips needed to be kept super cold, at or near absolute zero. But we got around that by inventing a superconducting organic polymer that lets Quantum I operate at room temperature."

AA: "Jared, let me ask you about—"

Her IFB filled with static. She glanced at the TV monitor: the picture was breaking up. Moments later visual snow gave way to the cool, calm image of Brett Halsey in New York.

Allie turned to Kilroy. "Jared, I don't know what—"

But the Henderson woman, who'd been standing in the wings, barged in and hurriedly began removing Kilroy's mic. "Sorry, but this interview is over. Mr. Kilroy needs to leave—*now*."

Allie, opening her mouth to protest, watched helplessly as the hyperefficient sidekick spirited Kilroy out of the room.

★

EASTER SUNDAY, APRIL 23 (9:49 P.M. PACIFIC DAYLIGHT TIME)

FAST NEWS BUREAU; SANTA MONICA, CALIFORNIA

The executive jet landed at Santa Monica Airport and taxied to a waiting limo that whisked Allie to the network's LA bureau, a short distance away.

She strode into the newsroom. "Hey, *'mano*!"

She was hailing David Rodriquez, the young production manager on duty sitting at the rim—a circular arrangement of desks at the center of the newsroom. David was a devoted family man who, lacking seniority at Fast, had to work the swing shift, a sacrifice that endeared him to Allie.

"You guys figure out what the heck happened with my live shot?"

He stood up. "Yeah. The uplink people said it was a magnetic storm. Messed with the bird for a full hour. It's still not completely back to normal."

"Terrific! *Que mala suerte.*"

She stomped off to her office.

"Yo, Allie!" David called after her. "Is that guy really gonna give away all that money?"

Without looking back, she threw up a hand. "That's what he says. We'll see."

Inside her office she dropped heavily into a pink leather chair—a gift to herself the previous Christmas—and started fiddling nervously with her hair. Her stylist gave up long ago trying to break her of the habit.

A moment later Eva strode in and plopped into the King Louis XV chair facing Allie's antique painted desk. "Did you hear?"

Allie preferred to forget the entire miserable day. "About the magnetic storm?"

"No, China. It's a go."

"What? How do you know?"

"Have you checked your voicemail lately?"

She gave Eva a snarky look. "Sorry, no. I've been a little busy, in case you hadn't noticed. Any more brilliant questions?" She caught herself. "I'm sorry, *chica*. I just wanna go home and eat my way through a box of See's. Tell me what's going on."

"Just that the government's agreed to let you interview Dr. Tang about the unintended consequences of computer technology. The only thing is, you can't ask her any questions about accusations that China's military is developing secret plans for cyberwarfare."

Zhaohui Tang, one of the world's foremost experts on cyber security, rarely spoke to the press. Getting an interview with her was a major coup.

"*Ay!* But everyone knows the Chinese are up to no good."

"Yeah, but we'll have to live with it." Then Eva gave her a mischievous smile. "We'll figure out a way around it."

Allie stood, more than ready to call it a day. "Lord, this is frustrating."

"Let's sleep on it," Eva said, rising from the chair. "We've both had a tough day."

Putting on her coat, Allie shouted to her young AP, who sat in a cubicle just outside the door. "Amy! How's the G-20 story coming?"

Leaders and their entourages from twenty countries were flying to California to meet at the San Diego Convention Center over the forthcoming weekend. It was a huge news event in her own backyard; its timing would help promote her and the TV special, set to air in just three weeks.

Historically, G-20 summits were also a boon for protesters because of the enormous media attention they attracted. Usually, the demonstrations were desultory and disconnected; but not this time. According to special agent Mike Cannatella of the FBI, a person or persons unknown were secretly trying to organize the protests into one massive, violent rally against what anarchists called "The Machine," the totality of everything they considered wrong with today's mechanized, unfeeling, uncaring world.

Amy scampered in, notes in hand, and spoke rapidly: "We're getting the official agenda this week. Cannatella's flying in from DC tonight. I've confirmed your interview with him tomorrow morning. He can only give us a half hour because he's heading down to San Diego to set up shop. He's says there's definitely a secret agent provocateur."

"Great," Allie said. "I mean—you know what I mean. Great job. And stay on the Kilroy story. I want you to dig into this whole privatization scheme of his."

Eva agreed. "Get ahold of his peeps and tell them we want another bite of the apple, this time longer and taped, not live."

"One other thing," Allie said, watching Amy struggling to write everything down. "Get your hands on a PC with one of those chips in it. Give our IT guys a heads-up: I want them to check it out, put it through the mill. Let's see if it can do half of what Kilroy claims it can." She made a scoffing sound. *"Predict the future!* Yeah, right, we'll see about that."

She started twisting her hair again.

"What about Sinclair?" Eva said.

"What about him?"

"Are you gonna give him a second chance? My gut says walk away for now. You've got way bigger fish to fry and besides, he almost killed you yesterday."

CHAPTER 6

DESTINY

EASTER SUNDAY, APRIL 23 (10:30 P.M. PACIFIC DAYLIGHT TIME)

LA JOLLA, CALIFORNIA

Calder, still wide awake, was sitting up in bed, stewing over *Hero*'s near-disastrous voyage the previous morning. Despite his plea to Allie for a second chance he hadn't heard anything from her or her people.

He slapped the bed.

Call her! Pester her!

He turned to the bedroom window and stared at his reflection.

Forget it; just let it go.

Trust in fate.

His eyes fell.

No, he didn't dare do that.

★

THIRTY-THREE YEARS EARLIER

SEVILLE, SPAIN

Francis didn't realize how much noise he and the two dozen or so other kids were making until Sister Yolanda asked them to quiet down. She was the reverend mother's assistant and his favorite teacher.

"The bus driver can't hear himself think, children," she said. "We don't want to get into an accident, do we?"

"No!" they shouted.

A moment later the old bus squealed to a stop. Francis's best friend, Marin, twirled around in his seat and pointed toward the front. "*Mire el caballo!*"

Francis turned to look out the windshield. A bulky brown-and-white horse with hairy ankles was crossing the road, pulling what looked to Francis like a colorful circus wagon. Driving it was a sad-faced, dark-skinned man with shiny black hair. He was wearing an old suit without a tie. He glanced in the direction of the bus but didn't smile. Seated next to him was a dirty-faced boy about Francis's own age—seven or eight.

After crossing, the wagon turned onto a cart path paralleling the road and lumbered past the side window where Francis was seated. He pressed his nose to the glass and waved, but the boy looked away.

"*Gitanos*," he heard one of his foster siblings remark. "I wonder where they're going?"

"Maybe to get an ice cream cone, like us," Francis said.

"I don't think so, *niños*," Sister said. "Gypsies do not have money for such things. They're probably heading for their camp. It's not far from our convent, you know."

Francis turned to Sister. "Can we give them some money to buy an ice cream cone? For the little boy, at least. He looks sad."

"It's a very kind thought, Francis. You've made Jesus very happy."

He waited for Sister's further reply, but gave up when she turned away and began chatting with another boy.

He looked out the window again, but the wagon was nowhere to be seen.

You didn't answer my question.

During the rest of the trip into the city Francis wondered what his biological mother looked like. According to the sisters she was a *gitana* who died while giving birth to him. He tried picturing himself in place of the little boy on the wagon, but it was hard to do because his own hair and skin were so much paler than the boy's.

The summer sun was high in the sky, and hot, when they finally arrived in downtown *Sevilla*. Francis was mostly happy and certainly grateful to be living in the orphanage. The sisters were strict but kind. Yet sometimes it felt like a prison. He was looking forward to spending the afternoon walking around freely, the way normal kids always did.

And of course there was the *helado* to look forward to.

Before they exited, Sister told them to stay together or she'd have to cancel the field trip. They promised to obey.

Francis followed the others onto the crowded sidewalk of *Calle Sierpes*. They oohed and ahhed at everything they saw around them. His own eyes went straight to the pastries displayed in the large windows of *La Campana* right in front of him.

If only ...

They'd been walking for only a few minutes when Francis heard a child's loud voice say, "Mommy, look! Who are they?" He caught sight of a boy—again, about his age—strolling with his family and pointing in their direction. Francis watched the mother bend to speak to the boy, who immediately lowered his arm but didn't stop staring. Francis didn't like it and looked away.

A few moments later the family and his own group passed one another on the sidewalk. "*Huérfanos,*" the boy said with a sour face; the mother shushed him. Francis felt a warm flush and was tempted to say something back. But he bit his tongue because he really wanted that ice cream cone.

By the time they reached *Helados Rayas*, its line of customers extending out the door, Francis was suffering a king-sized hunger. But he'd learned to be patient. With so many kids at the orphanage, you usually weren't able to get what you wanted exactly when you wanted it.

"Now remember, children," Sister said, "each of you can have one scoop of your favorite flavor. But only one. *Entiéndenme?*"

"*Sí*, Sister," they answered in unison.

They began telling one another what flavors they were going to get, some changing their minds based on what others were planning to have.

"I'm getting a scoop of *Turrón*," Francis declared.

"Not me," Marin said. "I'm getting *nocciolossa*. It's got big globs of Nutella. Hmm."

Francis batted his hand at him. "Yeah, but *Turrón* has *two* kinds of nougat."

The back-and-forth continued while Francis and his siblings gradually worked their way forward. When his turn finally came, Francis announced his choice—he hadn't changed his mind one bit—and took hold of it with great care when the young woman in a white shirt and blue apron handed it to him.

Sister led them and their frozen treats to a nearby garden park. Some of them chose to sit on benches and others, like Francis, stayed on their feet. He laughed at a small, wiry dog doing tricks for his owner. He and everyone around him roared especially hard when the scruffy little *choo-choo* finished a backward somersault, then trotted over and shook his owner's hand.

Minutes later, when Francis was using his tongue to push the remaining ice cream into the cone, he felt a sharp pain in his left heel. It made him drop his cone.

"Sister! Sister!" he heard Marin cry out. "A dog has bitten Francis!"

Francis kicked at the mongrel, who was wolfing down the remains of his ice cream cone, scaring it away. Sister rushed over and squatted down to look at the wound. It was bleeding badly.

"We need to get you to a doctor!"

After a long, hurried, painful walk to a medical office, Francis sat nervously with Sister in a small, un-air-conditioned examination room as the doctor inspected the wound. His siblings remained outside in the waiting room, where the receptionist could watch over them.

"I was just eating my ice cream when he bit me," he whimpered to the doctor. "I wasn't doing anything wrong, I swear."

The doctor, a fat man with a small mustache, said, "Of course not. Nobody thinks you were. We have too many strays in the city. Don't worry; we'll fix you up."

The doctor turned to Sister and whispered something. Whatever it was, she seemed upset by it. They both asked him to stay in the room and went outside.

While he waited, his thoughts returned to the well-dressed boy on the sidewalk who'd pointed at him. In his mind's eye Francis studied the kid and his family with more than a twinge of envy. And resentment.

During the following weeks, the pain of that Sunday afternoon was multiplied manyfold on account of a series of shots he received in his upper leg. The doctor, Sister, everyone assured him the shots were for his own good and he wanted to believe it. But on those nights, when all the other kids were sound asleep, as he rubbed the swollen and sore needle marks and gritted his teeth against the burning pain, he gradually developed a theory about himself. He became convinced he was not only different from other kids but something about him—something beyond his control—caused God to be angry at him. It explained why he was born without parents. Why he had to live in an orphanage. Why he was bitten by a dog and dropped his cone.

He concluded he was being punished. Doomed to a life in which things, even when they started out happily, always went wrong.

★

EASTER SUNDAY, APRIL 23 (11:54 P.M. MOUNTAIN DAYLIGHT TIME)

PARKER CENTER FOR BEHAVIORAL HEALTH; DENVER, COLORADO

Inside the center's acute care unit Lorena was in bed having a nightmare about the end of the world. Her eyes flew open.

"Please!" she shouted into the darkness. "Help!"

The lights came on. It was her nurse. "Mrs. O'Malley, what's the matter? You're waking everyone up."

"It's coming to an end!" she said frantically. "I have to leave before it's too late."

The nurse, now at her bedside, tried taking her hand.

"Get away from me!"

"*Shhh*, please, Mrs. O'Malley, the world is not coming to an end. You were just having a bad dream. Now, pl—"

Lorena threw back her covers and pushed past the nurse. "I need to get out of here!"

"But it's the middle of the night."

"What's the matter with you?! The Bible says the end will come like a thief in the night. I need to get to Jerusalem!"

The nurse left the room in a huff and Lorena frantically began putting on her street clothes. Her stomach felt sick, but she ignored it.

Oh, how these people will regret their ignorance!

When she was finished dressing she grabbed her handbag and headed for the door. But just as she reached it, it flew open, knocking her backward onto the linoleum floor.

Nooo!

As the orderlies poured into the room and set about subduing her—when she felt the sting of the needle in her arm—she knew she was done for.

"Oh, sweet Jesus!" she screamed. "Wait for me! *Wait for me!*"

★

MONDAY, APRIL 24 (3:45 P.M. AUSTRALIAN CENTRAL STANDARD TIME)

CHARLES DARWIN UNIVERSITY; CASUARINA, AUSTRALIA

Sara, looking about desperately for help, spotted her intern partner. "Dirk! Get the vet! *Fast!*"

A few moments earlier the animal she and Dirk were assigned to rehabilitate—a juvenile short-finned pilot whale named Lulu—began thrashing around in her holding tank. Lulu was injured in a fishing net accident in Beagle Gulf and brought to the university's marine mammal rescue center for mending and subsequent rereleasing.

Sara raced around the tank trying to keep up with Lulu. She could see and hear similar crises flaring up in tanks throughout the vast outdoor facility.

"Please, Lulu! What's wrong, girl?"

When help finally arrived Sara and Dirk steadied Lulu while the doctor injected her with a sedative.

"She'll be fine now," the vet said before dashing off to the next frenzied patient.

Without thinking, drenched and sobbing, Sara turned and locked Dirk in a bear hug. An instant later, she pulled away.

"Oh my gosh, I'm so sorry!"

Dirk grinned amiably. "No worries, mate, I needed that."

CHAPTER 7

ANONYMOUS

MONDAY, APRIL 24 (7:30 A.M. PACIFIC DAYLIGHT TIME)

FEDERAL BUILDING; LOS ANGELES, CALIFORNIA

"Cut!" Eva called out. "Thanks, Mike, that was great."

Allie beamed at the mother lode she'd just received from Mike. There was enough here for a meaty segment on tonight's Special Report.

In only a half hour she'd gotten Mike to weigh in on many topics: increasing chatter in the blogosphere about China's secret plan to wage a cyberwar against the U.S. from outer space; massive protests expected at the coming weekend's G-20; and consequently heightened security for the summit, starting with its gala welcome reception on Saturday afternoon at San Diego's Mingei International Museum.

"The G-20 is what we designate a 'national special security event,' or NSSE," Mike explained to her, "which means my people are put in charge of intelligence and counterterrorism. The Secret Service on the other hand has lead responsibility for actually securing the two-day event."

She'd asked him how seriously Homeland Security was taking threats of violence.

"*Very* seriously. We're deploying four thousand state and local law enforcement officers," he said. "Some from as far away as Chicago. Also the National Guard, Coast Guard, and other armed services. Does that answer your question?"

She and Mike had worked together on numerous stories during the past four years, developing a close working relationship based on mutual trust and respect. He frequently remarked on how much he liked the thoughtfulness and fairness of her reports, as well as her reliability with off-the-record information. "You're not the average knucklehead reporter," he'd once said to her. "It's refreshing."

For her part, she liked Mike's no-nonsense approach to things and people. She was happy his star at the bureau was rising. Why shouldn't it be? His academic creds were through the roof: *summa cum laude* in computer science from MIT, law degree with honors from Harvard.

She also liked his physical features: hazel eyes, nicely trimmed, wavy chestnut-colored hair, and strong Mediterranean build. Altogether, he communicated potency—a strength on which one could rely.

"When are you guys planning to come down?" Mike asked her, referring to the summit's San Diego venue.

"Probably Friday, to get everything set up."

"Where are you guys staying?"

"Not sure. Hopefully, the Grand Hyatt."

Mike, being pressured by his hovering subordinates to get going, quickly buttoned his suit coat. "The protests are already starting—like Saturday's march and the tent cities popping up all over Balboa and Petco parks. The mayor's office tried denying them permits, but the ACLU took it to court and won. So we've got our hands full. Any help you guys can be…"

Mike didn't finish the sentence, nor did he need to. Allie understood completely. It was the unspoken tit-for-tat relationship common between reporters and sources, especially ones as battle tested as Mike's and hers.

"Of course," she said quickly. "But just one more thing before you go."

Mike's people stared daggers at her. She didn't care.

"What makes you so sure there's a secret instigator working to unify the protestors?"

Mike's flinty eyes locked on hers. "I'm willing to tell you, but not on camera. Strictly off the record. *Capisce?*"

She nodded. "Of course."

Mike made quick placating noises and gestures to his agents then led Eva and her into an office. Quickly seating himself at the computer, he beckoned them to his side.

"We have plants who've been covertly taping meetings of the various activist groups planning to disrupt the summit," he said, his fingers working the keyboard. "The video I'm about to show you was taken at a secret gathering of Planet First near UCSD last night. Mostly a bunch of college kids. I absolutely forbid either of you to speak about this to anyone, even your boss at the network. Got it?"

Allie agreed, feeling warm, the way she always did when she sensed a major scoop coming.

"Understood," echoed Eva.

The video on Mike's computer showed a crowd of about thirty people crammed into a small room. It was blurry and the sound was muffled, but Allie could understand most of what was being said.

"The resolution isn't great," Mike said, "but trust me, when the lab gets done with it we'll be able to see every freckle and hear every hiccup."

Abruptly, a person wearing a Guy Fawkes mask stepped into the frame. Allie and Eva looked at each other. "Who's that?" they asked simultaneously.

"Precisely," Mike replied. "That's what we're going to find out. But listen."

Mike cranked up the volume. The masked man—for clearly it was a male voice—was dissing the "military-industrial elites" and damning rampant technology for endangering Earth's plants and animals. By the end of the tape, the kids were on their feet pumping their fists.

"Wow!" said Allie, stunned by the artfulness with which the masked man had manipulated the idealistic crowd.

"For now we're calling him Anonymous," Mike said, "because that's the kind of mask that group tends to wear. They're known for—hold on."

Mike began typing away. A moment later large red lettering appeared on the computer screen. Allie and Eva leaned in for a better look:

News/Alerts from Occupy the World

To the community of users of the Burn server: The server is down until further notice. The data is still intact and there will be a forwarding address posted when and if the address is changed.

MicroSupport/UCSDComputingServices/burnisdown.html

"This is also off the record," Mike said. "It's a defunct website out of UCSD the university shut down last week. We're working with them to track down the author."

"Interesting that it's from UCSD," Allie said. "Just like Planet First."

Mike ignored her observation. "Take a look at the last thing they posted before the website was taken down."

On the screen appeared large red letters and yellow flames on a black background:

!!! We will obey on the first of May !!!
We are Anonymous. We are legion.
We do not forgive. We do not forget.
We will be heard. Expect us.

Allie and Eva gasped.

"But—I don't understand," Allie said, feeling positively hot now. "The first of May—that's the last day of the summit. What are they talking about?"

"Short answer, we're not sure," Mike replied, "we're working all the angles." He rose abruptly from the seat. "What we know is this: May 1 is an important day for anarchists and communists. It goes back to the last century, when the American Federation of Labor voted in favor of creating the eight-hour workday. But we're not sure whether this has anything to do with it—and if so, whether it's originating from someone at UCSD or somewhere else. Lots of foreign nationals in our colleges these days, you know."

He looked at his watch. "Look, I gotta scram. Remember what I said: not a word to anyone."

★

MONDAY, APRIL 24 (8:18 A.M. PACIFIC DAYLIGHT TIME)

"Can you believe our luck?!" Eva exclaimed.

After leaving the Cannatella interview and mounting the news van, they headed to a local, big-box electronics store. They were going to tape a report on the ongoing consumer hysteria over the Quantum I microprocessor, a natural follow-up to the abbreviated Kilroy interview. Not since the launch of the original iPhone or Pokémon Go had people gone so gaga over a piece of technology.

Allie shook her head. "You know I don't believe in luck anymore."

"Oh, please." Eva settled into her seat. "Don't get all religious on me. Call it whatever you want; we've hit pay dirt here." Pausing, she gave Allie a calculating look. "Now we just have to figure out a way around Mike's off-the-record thing."

Allie would've been floored by the remark if it weren't Eva making it. Her beloved producer was what the world called a good person; she'd give you the blouse off her back. But her professional aggressiveness sometimes caused her to say and do things that ventured into the unethical.

"I'm gonna pretend I didn't hear that, okay, *chica*? Let's just see what happens. Mike's been really good to us. The last thing we want to do is—"

Her cell phone rang.

"*Bueno?*"

Growing up, Allie always heard her father answer the phone that way. The small things helped keep her grounded, close to her roots.

It was Amy, her AP, on the phone; she sounded agitated. "The network wants you to beat it down to San Diego. There's a huge whale stranding down there and they want to go live ASAP."

"A whale stranding? But that happens all the time. Wait a sec."

She quickly briefed Eva.

"Absolutely not!" her producer exploded. "The Quantum story is way bigger. There's no way we're cutting out to cover a bunch of beached whales. *Oy gevalt!*"

Allie communicated the unanimous decision to Amy.

"But Allie," the young woman said, "you didn't let me explain. It's not just happening in San Diego. It's happening all over the world."

CHAPTER 8

DISTRESS CALL

The eighty-two-year-old Reverend Mother Abbess Yolanda Jimenez, OSC—a stooped figure in brown, black, and white—limped slowly across the dusty courtyard past the moss-covered cherubim fountain. Pausing, she looked up at the blue *Sevillano* sky in supplication to the One she was counting on to save the convent's orphanage.

Three months earlier *Sevilla* swore into office a young, new *alcalde* who was very enthusiastic about his progressive ideas. Professing to be concerned about the welfare of Spanish orphans, he quickly announced strict regulations about how orphanages throughout the city should be run.

His good intentions came with a very big price tag. The costs of updating the orphanage's 160-year-old facilities would shut them down unless she could find someone or some way to raise the needed funds. They had only until the end of May to comply.

While still looking skyward, beseeching the Heavenly Father, it came to her, *como una chispa de inspiración divina*. It was the sudden recollection of their humble operation's most memorable and illustrious alumnus: the orphaned boy whom they had placed with an American couple. They all moved to the United States when he was—what? Nine or ten, she recalled.

She'd heard somewhere he became a great inventor. If so, he would have the resources, the influence—above all, the motivation—to help. But how to find him after so many years?

Changing direction, she shuffled toward the storage building where the convent kept records of its residents and placements. After 160 years they were forced to pare down the paperwork to essential information only. Normally she would assign the task to one of the young sisters, but she decided to do it herself, in secret. She didn't wish to raise false hopes among the faithful in case her idea came to naught.

After several hours of digging she was not able to find much. But she hoped it would be enough to start things rolling.

The archival records, what was left of them, showed the person of interest came to them forty-two years earlier as an unnamed newborn. She remembered he was of mixed blood, but no details about his biological parents—except she was fairly certain the mother was from the local area and died giving birth.

The extant records further showed the sisters named the boy Francis, after the saint, and the adoptive parents were a Dr. and Mrs. Sinclair of the United States.

That night she was unable to sleep, so excited was she about the hopeful thought God had planted in her bosom. She watched the waxing moon drift across the small window of her stone-walled cell, then was struck by an idea.

¡Sí!

Moments later she was seated in front of her beloved, antique short-wave radio speaking in a quiet voice so as not to awaken the community: "*Saludos mis amigos en nombre de nuestro Señor Jesucristo. Este es Mateo 19:14. Necesito su ayuda. Busco a un hombre que de niño fue nombrado Francisco. Él fue adoptado por una pareja de los Estados Unidos llamado Dr. y Sra. Sinclair. Él es cuarenta y dos años de edad. Por favor, mis amigos, este es un encargo de la misericordia, más importante y más urgente. ¡Gracias! ¡Dios les bendiga!*"

Then she repeated it in English, praying that God would send angels to steer her plea to just the right pair of ears: "Greetings, my friends, in the name of our Lord Jesus Christ. This is Matthew 19:14. I need your help. I am looking for a man who as a boy was named Francis. He was adopted by a couple from the United States named Dr. and Mrs. Sinclair. He is forty-two years old. Please, my friends, this is an errand of mercy, most important and mo—"

Her broadcast was inundated by a tsunami of static. She smiled and nodded her head slightly. The enemy had been roused; she was on the right track.

"*Gracias, mi Señor,*" she whispered.

Then, ignoring the pain of rising from the seat and bending her arthritic joints, she knelt on the cold cement floor and began to pray.

And wait.

CHAPTER 9

WHALE OF A PROBLEM

A llie was standing on her mark in the sand, facing away from the ocean, ready for her live broadcast. They'd selected the Belmont Park stretch of Mission Beach for two reasons: it appeared to be the epicenter of the mass stranding; and its amusement park—famous for the Belmonty Burger and Giant Dipper wooden roller coaster—made an enormously telegenic backdrop. It reminded Allie of Coney Island, but upscale.

Next to her was Colin Berg, president of Planet First, who she was going to interview. Nearby, Eva was talking to somebody through her headset. Allie guessed she was getting last-minute instructions from Stu, who was at the main studio in Manhattan. The segment would be introduced by the anchor there, Ashley Folsom.

Pitsy came up to her. "This breeze is messing with the audio big-time. Try using your body to block it, like this." He helped to reposition her. "That should do it."

She surveyed the scores of whales and dolphins around them struggling for their lives. Volunteers were covering many of the animals with blankets and wetting them down. "I haven't been here in years," she said to Colin. "This is heartbreaking."

"Yeah, it is, for sure. Thanks for letting me be on this morning."

"Absolutely. You're perfect for this."

Since the start of the year, she and Eva had gotten to know Colin quite well. His group was being featured in her May TV special because of its vocal opposition to the unintended consequences of military technology. Planet First's YouTube video about whales and the Navy had thirty million hits and counting.

But the real reason they chose to interview Colin over other possible experts was the video Mike Cannatella had shown them earlier that morning. After the segment, she and Eva planned to take Colin aside and pump him about Planet First's protest plans for the G-20.

"We'll only have about four minutes," Allie said to him, "so keep your answers short, okay? If I think you're going long, I'll go like this." She nodded her head quickly. "When we're down to our last fifteen seconds, I'll kick your toe with my foot, like this."

Colin nodded nervously. "And you're gonna stick to the questions you told me, right?"

She reassured him there'd be no surprises.

At least not while we're on the air.

Eva rushed up to them. "They're giving you thirty more seconds, babe, so live it up." She studied Allie's hair with narrowed eyes and tightly pursed lips.

"What?" Allie said with faux irritation.

"I hate you. No one should have such beautiful hair." Eva reached out and relocated a strand. "Break a leg, girlfriend." Then she added: "Colin, babe, relax. You'll be great."

On a small TV monitor nestled in the sand at her feet, Allie was able to watch and listen to the pre-taped news package they had slapped together beforehand.

"According to officials at the National Marine Fisheries Service," her voice-over began, "the multiple strandings are unprecedented."

More than a minute later Eva yelled at her through the IFB. "Ten seconds! The out is 'hoping to find the cause.'"

"No theories yet," the voice-over continued, "but blame is being directed at everything from El Nino to solar max to off-shore military experiments. Marine biologists from around the world are flocking to the stranding sites hoping to find the cause."

Allie stood tall, took a deep, calming breath, and looked into the camera's glass eye.

AF: "And now Allie Armendariz joins us live from San Diego. Allie, what's the latest?"

AA: "Thanks, Ashley. I spoke to Adam Lucas just minutes ago. He's the communications director for the Marine Fisheries Service. According to him, the number of strandings worldwide is now up to five. Besides here in San Diego, strandings are being reported along the coasts of Japan, Australia, Spain, and Canada. It's got everyone stumped."

AF: "Tell us what's happening where you are now."

AA: "The stranding here started late this morning and, as you can see, there are dozens of whales and a few dolphins on the beach. Rescue workers are doing everything possible to keep the animals alive and comfortable. But as much as I hate to say it, strandings rarely end well."

AF: "Allie, I understand you have a special guest with you."

On cue, Pitsy's camera lens spun slightly—he was widening out to a two-shot of her and Berg.

AA: "Yes, I do. His name is Colin Berg and he's president of Planet First, an environmental group based at the University of California, San Diego. Colin, you and your group have a theory about what's causing these strandings. Tell me about it."

CB: "Yeah, thanks, Allie. The problem is San Diego has a huge Navy presence, one of the biggest in the world. In the waters between here and Hawaii, they're always testing bombs and sonar and it's hurting a lot of the sea life. Mostly whales and dolphins, which use sound to navigate."

AA: "But strandings have been going on forever, Colin. More than two thousand years ago *Aristotle* wrote about beached whales and dolphins."

CB: "Yes, but not to the degree we see nowadays. Old-style passive sonar doesn't work anymore. Our enemies have figured out a way around it. So the Navy is testing a new kind of sonar that's more powerful and more penetrating. They call it *active sonar*. To dolphins and whales, the difference is like going from soft rock to heavy metal.

"In its latest environmental impact statement the Navy admits its new active sonar exercises are harming up to six million whales and dolphins a year and permanently deafening more than three thousand a year. At Planet First we think that's outrageous."

She looked into the camera.

AA: "For the record, we asked the Navy for comment but they declined."

She turned back to Colin.

AA: "Colin, here's what I'm wondering: The strandings going on right now are not just confined to San Diego. Your theory doesn't explain that."

CB: "Yes, it does. The Navy has allies all over the world who are doing the same kinds of sonar and bomb testing. The problem is global. That's why we're seeing strandings everywhere. We're reaping the disaster the Navy has been sowing for years."

When the interview was over Eva came up to congratulate Colin. Then she subtly nodded to Allie.

"Colin," Allie said, "we're hearing you guys are planning something huge, something secret for the G-20."

The young man shrugged and shook his head. "Not true."

"C'mon, Colin," Eva said. "Be honest with us. We're not the enemy."

He looked down at his feet, kicking the sand nervously. "Look, you guys have been good to us but I have to watch what I say, okay? This has gotten way bigger than just Planet First. A bunch of others are jumping on the bandwagon."

"Like who?" Allie said.

"The Occupy people?" Eva ventured.

"No. Well, yes, they're involved I hear, but not with us. We don't see eye to eye on too many things. As far as we're concerned they're anti-environmentalists."

Allie wanted to sound sympathetic. "Because they're against green energy?"

"That's how it looks to us."

"But you were saying," Eva interjected, "others are jumping aboard."

"Hello there!"

The unexpected voice came from behind them. Spinning around, Allie saw Calder Sinclair rushing toward her. He looked upset.

"Calder? What a surprise."

"I'm sorry to barge in," he said, out of breath. "Do you guys have a moment?"

CHAPTER 10

THE CHOICE

MONDAY, APRIL 24 (4:45 P.M. PACIFIC DAYLIGHT TIME)

SAN DIEGO, CALIFORNIA

With the warm, yellow sunlight still reflecting brilliantly off the blue Pacific, Allie and the crew clambered back into the van and set out from Mission Beach to a nearby electronics store. They intended to pick up where they'd left off with the Kilroy story. The Quantum PC madness was sweeping San Diego as much as it was every major city in the world.

"I still say you've blown your lid," Eva said, scrutinizing her.

Allie laughed. "*Flipped* your lid—and no, I haven't."

Back at the beach Sinclair had pressed them to give *Hero* a second chance. At first she and Eva adamantly demurred. But then, surrounded by dying animals on the beach, a little bulb lit up in Allie's head. An idea to give Sinclair what he wanted *and* create a gonzo news story that'd bring huge attention to her and her TV special.

"Whatever you call it, you're crazy." Eva twirled a finger next to her ear. "*Messugah!*"

Allie raised her hands in self-defense. "Okay, *chica*, okay. So I admit it's either the most brilliant or the most hare-brained proposal I've ever come up with."

Her idea was to use *Hero*'s allegedly amazing speed and agility to try quashing the whale strandings around the world, to steer them away from the beaches. At first Sinclair had looked at her like she'd grown horns, but after some spirited back and forth he agreed.

"It's nothing but a stupid publicity stunt, Allie. And a dangerous one. He nearly killed you the first time out. It's looney tunes. I forbid it."

Allie shot her a glaring, questioning stare.

"As your friend, I mean," Eva said with a twisted smile. "As someone who loves you and is committed to protecting you—especially from yourself."

They rode in tense silence for nearly a mile.

"Look," Allie said finally, "I don't disagree with you about the danger, but you heard Sinclair: he's fixed the problem with the collision avoidance system."

Eva said nothing, sinking into her seat, arms folded, staring straight ahead.

"Look, *chica*, here's how I see it: if I do this and it doesn't save whales then I'll only have wasted a few days."

Eva unlocked her arms and stared at her. "A few days? *A few days?!* How about the rest of your friggin life?!"

"Language!"

Eva let out a long, low, guttural snarl.

"On the other hand," Allie continued, "if we pull it off, think about it: it'll be the most amazing story of my career and, yeah, you're right, amazing publicity for our special. What's wrong with that?"

Eva threw up her hands. "Do you have the hots for this guy? You do, don't you. I saw how you reacted when he showed up at the beach. You were all aflutter, like some stupid schoolgirl."

"Eva! *Stop!* I wasn't all aflutter—whatever that means."

But Allie knew exactly what Eva was saying. She fell silent for several moments and stared out the window.

Truth was, Calder Sinclair was the closest to a Phil Gutierrez she'd met yet. A scientist, smart, handsome, single; he'd mentioned to her he was a widower with a daughter off in college somewhere. And caring. He had to be, devoting his life to inventing something so intentionally noble—or *apparently* noble; it remained to be seen if he wasn't secretly working for the military.

"He's a nice guy," Allie said finally, "that's all. It doesn't mean I'd risk my life for him. Give me a break, for gosh sakes."

That's never going to happen.

Never. Trust me.

Despite her attraction to Calder—her wanting to get to know him better—she was not optimistic it'd ever lead to anything serious. Lightning rarely struck twice; it was a scientific fact. According to one study she'd never forget, seventy-three percent of singles on the hunt for "true love," after having let it slip through their fingers once before, never found it again.

Eva's eyes bored into her. "Listen to me, girlfriend, please don't do it. He's too—I don't know, strange. Too fanatical about that *Hero* of his."

Allie answered with a confused look.

"Don't pretend you don't understand. You need this gig like a hole in the arm. We've got the TV special; we don't need this—this weird little Lifshitz."

Allie leaned forward in her seat. "Eva! *Seriously?* Whatever you think about him, the guy's obviously some kind of brainiac."

"Yeah, like Dr. Strangelove. All testosterone and grey matter, no scruples."

Allie flung up her arms. "What are you talking about?! You spent exactly half a day with the man. How do you know he has no scruples?"

"Because I recognize the type. Remember, babe, I've been covering science a long time—longer even than you. While you were cloistered away at Haaahvard I was out here in the trenches getting to know these guys."

"These guys?"

"Yeah, the ones who do things just because they're into it, not because they've thought through the consequences." Eva sat up in her seat. "Look, why do you think I bought into your special? Put my heinie on the line for you when you were selling it to Stu?"

"For the ratings?"

Eva's eyes exploded. "No! I did it because I believe in the show's premise, your so-called null prophecy. Science has noble intentions—it's why I love this beat—but it's making life really scary, not just better. H-bombs, chemical weapons, killer robots. I just read a press release about these scientists who are using artificial intelligence to program a robot policeman who'll be fully autonomous. It'll be able to make life-and-death decisions completely on its own. God!—as if self-driving cars weren't terrifying enough. Is that creepy or what?

Allie looked at her for a moment. "Yeah, it is, actually. We should use it in the special." She fell back in her chair. "But what does all that have to do with Sinclair?"

"It's just a feeling I have about him. Like I said, I recognize his type. I don't doubt he means well with this *Hero* of his, but the whole idea of tapping into something we don't even understand…" Eva's voice trailed off. Then she said, "He reminds me of Teller, Edward Teller. Ever meet him?"

Allie nodded. Years before, as an undergrad at Stanford, she and a professor friend who knew Edward Teller dined at the famous scientist's house. He was a gracious host, at one point treating them to a piano recital. But it was clear Teller still felt misunderstood and unappreciated by his liberal colleagues, who vilified him for his leading role in the invention of the H-bomb.

"I'm sorry, *chica*," she said, "Sinclair is not Teller: he's not out to destroy. Yeah, *Hero* messed up and I was scared outta my mind. But we're talking about a guy who's quite possibly cracked the problem of finding a perfect energy source."

"That's what they said about nuclear energy." Eva paused. "Look, Allie, do what you want, but I'm against it. We have our hands full with the special and now with the whales and Kilroy—"

"Here we are," Pitsy called out.

The store was easy to spot because of the line of people trailing out the door and the rent-a-cops helping to keep order. Pitsy managed to find a parking spot and they all scrambled out.

Allie turned to Eva. "We've got to make a final decision by the end of today, okay? Sinclair says he wants to leave at first light tomorrow. So let's focus. I'm thinking I should do it."

Eva ignored her and set about helping Pitsy unload the equipment.

Allie stared at her. "*Hola!* Can I have some feedback here?"

Eva didn't stop what she was doing. "I've already told you how I feel. But if you decide to make the wrong choice"—she stopped and turned to give Allie a resigned look—"I'll be there to back you up."

"Even if it takes me away for several days?"

Eva went back to helping Pitsy offload the equipment. "I'll be there." And then, in a voice Allie was barely able to hear, she said, "Like I always am."

CHAPTER 11

TRUE LOVE

MONDAY, APRIL 24 (8:30 P.M. PACIFIC DAYLIGHT TIME)

SAN DIEGO, CALIFORNIA

I t was dark by the time Pitsy brought the van to a skidding halt opposite the entrance to the heliport. In the background was a high-pitched chorus of aircraft engines.

Allie jumped up from her seat and began gathering her stuff.

"So what do I tell Stu?" Eva called out from the rear of the van.

She did not stop moving. "That I'm doing it." Then she paused and looked over her shoulder at Eva. "Start thinking it out—how we can maximize coverage. I'll be back in—I don't know. Anyway, I'll be back. Meet me at the hotel tonight. Don't plan to sleep."

She sprinted into the terminal, cleared security, and climbed into the waiting chopper. This ride was on her own nickel. She didn't have the time or desire to wrestle with Stu over the expense.

An hour later the chopper set down gently on the rooftop landing pad of the hospital adjoining the Rio Hondo Nursing Center in Montebello, her mom's new home. She told the pilot she wouldn't be long and hopped out.

It was well past the nursing center's visiting hours but she'd called ahead and the supervisor had agreed to make an exception. It paid to be a well-known TV correspondent—and, more important in this case, a local girl who'd made good. Montebello was the next town over from East Los Angeles.

Inside the quiet, dimly lit building she approached the reception desk. "Allie Armendariz to see Betty Armendariz."

"Yes, we're expecting you," the young African-American woman chirped. "I watch you on TV all the time. I love your reports."

A moment later the head nurse appeared and escorted Allie through the wide, vacant hallways.

"Your father's here, as always," she said, approaching the door to the room. "We've all fallen in love with him." She held the door open for Allie—whispering loudly to her father, "Reverend, she's here"—then left.

Her father, slumped in a cushioned chair at the head of the bed, lit up at the sight of her. Her mom, tucked inside neat bedclothes, appeared to be sleeping. She'd always been an early bird: first one to bed and first one to rise. The disease hadn't changed that.

"*Apá*," she said, rushing to him, "I got here as fast as I could. You must be tired."

He rose and they hugged.

"Carlos'll be picking me up soon." He looked around. "I'll have the nurse bring another chair. I should've thought about it."

"*No, no te preocupes, Papá*. I'll just sit on the bed."

She settled onto the mattress and leaned in for a close look at her mother: the peaceful, slumbering face framed by wavy cascades of medium-length, pale auburn hair; the skin, gently lined yet remarkably smooth and still alive with color. It was impossible for Allie to imagine this lovely woman's mind was fading.

Her mother was and always would be her hero. As a young person, her *mamá* defied the wishes of her Cuban-Catholic family by marrying a Mexican who they considered beneath her station—and he was an atheist to boot. Later on, she defied her new husband's constant tirades against God by attending a nearby Pentecostal church. But despite all the defiance, following his conversion, she worked shoulder to shoulder with him to build a church that to this day faithfully served its mostly low-income congregation and Hispanic neighborhood.

Allie reached out and gently swept aside a lock of hair on the sleeping woman's forehead.

Oh, Mom, please come back to us.

Through the years *Mamá* had managed to be strong, yet tender. She fought convention, yet defended Latino culture's most precious old-world traditions. Supported her husband's sacred calling, yet achieved a high position of respect in her own right as the leader of *Buen Samaritano*'s vibrant women's ministry.

"How is she?" Allie whispered, still watching her mom's serene countenance.

"No change. The doctors are giving her some drugs to help her memory. But they say there's no cure."

She looked at him. "Science doesn't know everything, *Papá*."

"*Sí, mija*, whatever you say." He gave her a tired smile.

"Why are you smiling at me like that?"

"Nothing—I didn't even know I was smiling."

"You were. C'mon, what's up?"

Her father straightened up in the chair. "I was just thinking about how much I love you. That's all."

She half stood and bent way over to kiss his forehead. "Thank you, *Papá*, but sometimes I'm not so sure I'm all that lovable."

"*Mija*, of course you are. It's just that you're young; you're having to make some tough choices."

She settled back onto the bed. "Yeah, too tough."

He turned his world-weary eyes to her mom's reposing figure. "Believe me, I was the same way. But your mother saved me, you know."

"From what—starvation?" She chuckled, hoping to lighten the mood. "There was no better cook than Mom, that's for sure."

"No, from myself. When I was single, deep down I wasn't a happy person. I drank all the time and—well, you know the story." He stared blankly ahead. "Something was missing from my life and I sensed it; but I didn't know what it was or how I could find it. Then your mother came along." He grinned sadly. "Everyone needs someone like that, you know—to balance us out, to make us whole."

She shook her head. "People don't think like that anymore, Pops. Women especially. They don't like being told they need anyone to make them whole."

He looked at her. "How about you, Alejandra? Is that how you feel?"

"*Papá*, please. I came here to visit Ma, not to talk about me. I get enough of me at work. I just want to be quiet for a few minutes."

For the next short while she sat with her mother, stroking her hair, her cheek, her hand. This was the woman who'd given birth to six children and reared them grandly and gladly on a poor minister's income—meager not because of any stinginess from the churchgoers, but because of their own relative penury. In fact they'd been extravagantly generous with what little they had—and still were.

"I can't stop thinking about Lolo," she said softly.

"Oh?"

"I've prayed about it, like you told me. And I've decided that after I get back from my next assignment I'm going to visit her, see how she'd feel about moving in with me. I'll hire a full-time nurse; it'll be fine. At least she'd be closer to all of us."

"You're sure? It's a lot of responsibility."

"I'm sure."

"Okay, Alejandra, if you feel that strongly. We'll all help out, of course." He closed his eyes and after a few moments said, "That day I came home and saw all those men from your mother's church praying over your brother. Oh, man." He reopened his eyes. "I wanted to throw them all out! But something stopped me. Something bigger, stronger, more loving than myself made me just stand back and watch."

He teared up; he was recalling the moment he saw Carlos's crippling polio suddenly, inexplicably healed.

She edged nearer to him.

"I couldn't believe it," he continued. "His skinny, limp, little legs started filling out, right there in front of me. And when he stood up on them the next morning—*¡hijola!*—that's when I fell to my knees and committed my life to Jesus. How could I not? After what I witnessed with my own eyes, in my own living room." He swiped at his tears and met Allie's eyes. "If it hadn't been for your mother's faith, who knows what would've become of me. She gave me a second chance—God did, through her."

There was a brief silence.

Her mind wandered back to this afternoon's unexpected encounter at the beach with Calder Sinclair.

He seems lonely.

Needy.

I wonder if he believes in God.

"I wouldn't mind a second chance," Allie murmured. "I wish I could have what you and Mom—"

Her mother bolted up in bed and screamed at them. "*Qué pasa? Qué pasa?*"

Allie jumped off the bed.

"*Quién son? Por qué estan aquí? Por favor déjenme en paz! Déjenme en paz!*"

The nurse came rushing in with a syringe in hand. "She's scared is all. It's part of the disease—makes 'em overly nervous. This'll calm her down."

Allie hurried to the side of the bed opposite the nurse. "Ma, it's me, Alejandra. I came to see you."

Her mom stared at her wide-eyed, then with a terrified face turned away and thrashed around. "*Ay dios, no! Déjenme en paz!*"

Her father came alongside Allie and wrapped an arm around her shoulders. "She doesn't recognize you, *mija*. I sit here all day hoping she'll see me, know me. If I'm lucky, she comes out of her fog for a few minutes and it's like old times."

Allie watched helplessly as the utter bleakness and permanency of her mom's illness sank in. The guilt of not spending enough time with her mom in recent years made her stomach turn. She wanted to throw up.

Oh, Mamá! I'm so sorry!

Allie trembled violently; her eyes cascaded tears that quickly dampened the bed between her hands.

Oh, Mom, please come back!

Please recognize me!

Please, God, please!

Allie twisted about and embraced her elderly father hard, like a drowning child clutching a lifesaver.

"Oh, *Papá*," she sobbed, "Please forgive me. I'm so sorry. I'm so sorry."

CHAPTER 12

HIGH-SEAS COWBOY

TUESDAY, APRIL 25 (6:05 A.M. PACIFIC DAYLIGHT TIME)

NAVAL BASE POINT LOMA; SAN DIEGO, CALIFORNIA

Already in his Nomex flight suit, Calder stood on the pier gazing expectantly at the eastern horizon. Darkness was beginning its inevitable capitulation to dawn. It'd be light soon.

This time don't …

He slapped his cheek.

Stop it. This time we won't fail.

We can't fail.

He'd spent most of the previous three days overhauling the collision avoidance system. By a stroke of good fortune a recently released microprocessor, called Quantum I, was just what he needed. Its incredible

processing power and speed instantly enabled him to upgrade all of
Hero's ops, not just the collision avoidance system.

Still staring at the brightening horizon, he found its coloring a bit
strange. But before he could decide for sure, a black sedan quickly pulled
up and disgorged Allie and her producer, who looked pretty frazzled.

The camera crew already had been there for hours, setting up. These
two were bringing up the rear, cutting it close.

He called out to Allie, "Thought you might've changed your mind."

"Why?" she called back. "Didn't think I'd be crazy enough to give
you a second chance to kill me?"

He smiled broadly, shaking his head.

I like this woman! A breath of fresh air.

"I'll see if I can do better this time."

They both laughed.

He and Allie walked briskly toward the pier area, which in its present state of high activity gave the appearance of a street festival. It glowed
under the huge work lights mounted on small wheeled vehicles parked
all over the beach. Scores of people, mostly in uniform, scurried about
the central object of attention: *Hero*, floating majestically in the bay's
calm waters.

"She's beautiful," Allie remarked.

He swelled with pride at the sight of *Hero*'s sleek profile and polished
red skin, which gleamed under the spotlights. "Thanks for doing this,
Allie. You won't be disappointed. We won't let you down."

Allie gave him a stern look.

He stared back.

Lord, she's beautiful!

"You better not," she said. "I'm sticking my neck way out for this.
My people in New York think I've gone crazy. But I sold them on it and
they're expecting huge ratings."

"Chop-chop, everybody!" Allie's producer shouted. "We're live in
forty-five minutes! *Forty-five minutes!*"

At exactly seven a.m., he and Allie—ravishing in her flight suit—
stood at their assigned places on the pier alongside *Hero*. The main

engine was going through final prep. It was the part of the pre-launch process that never ceased to amaze him: creating the mysterious, all-important nothingness—the quantum vacuum—from which *Hero* derived her power.

"Go!"

Eva's voice bellowing at Allie through her earpiece was so loud he overheard it.

Immediately, Allie turned to him, her intelligent eyes radiating an inner excitement.

AA: "Dr. Sinclair, please tell us what's going on here."
CS: "Sure."

He raised a fist to his mouth and quickly cleared his throat.

CS: "Inside *Hero* is a stainless-steel vacuum chamber roughly the size of a tin can."
AA: "Her gas tank."

He bobbed his head and chuckled.

CS: "Okay, sure—her gas tank. It needs to be emptied completely."
AA: "Emptied of the air inside, right?"
CS: "Not just air—everything, every atom that's inside. We do that with a series of different vacuum pumps, each one more powerful than the last: roughing pumps, high-speed turbo-molecular pumps, ion pumps, titanium sublimation pumps. In the end, any atoms still bouncing around inside are nabbed by sticky chemicals coating the chamber's inside walls. They're special alloys we call 'getters.'"
AA: "Wow, that's a lot of work."
CS: "It is. Usually it takes days, although I'm working on speeding up the process. For this mission we've been prepping *Hero* since her last run this past weekend."
AA: "So is she ready?"

CS: "Let's see."

He leaned in to inspect the vacuum gauge.

CS: "Yupper. We're down to fewer than 0.001 atoms per cubic centimeter. Perfect."

AA: "Her tank's pretty empty, in other words."

He straightened back up and smiled.

CS: "Emptier than deep space."

AA: "So we're ready to go?"

CS: "Not necessarily. The chamber has to be absolutely cold as well. Otherwise you don't have a quantum vacuum."

AA: "And how do you do that?"

He realized Allie knew full well how to get something super-cold. She was just doing her job, playing the dummy, so he could explain it to people.

Must be hard for her.

CS: "We use what's called a dilution refrigerator. It involves bathing *Hero*'s vacuum chamber in liquid helium. That's what's causing the sputtering and hissing sounds you hear—and those bright white plumes of steam too."

AA: "The liquid helium—it's evaporating."

CS: "Yes, that's right. There are other steps to the process, but—here, let me see."

He leaned in to look at the digital thermometer.

CS: "Okay. The gauge reads 0.000000000001 degrees Kelvin. That's one-trillionth of one degree above absolute zero. Nearly 460 degrees below zero Fahrenheit."

He quickly straightened up.

CS: "So now that means we *are* go for launch!"

★

TUESDAY, APRIL 25 (7:39 A.M. PACIFIC DAYLIGHT TIME)

"Hold on," she said when the interview was over. "Can you please give me a minute? I forgot something."

He frowned. "Really? Allie, we've gotta go."

But she dashed off, saying, "It'll just be a minute, I promise."

"Please hurry!" he called after her. "And make sure you hit the bathroom. We won't be stopping until we get to Hawaii."

Moments later she found Eva outside the production truck, which was parked on the sand a short distance from the pier, fishing around for a piece of equipment.

Eva turned to look at her. "Allie!" What the—? You need to be—"

"I know, I know." She took her producer gently by the hands. They'd stayed up all night working out logistics: five locations (four of them foreign) in three days, with most of the travel happening on open water in the middle of nowhere. It was easily the most complicated assignment of their careers.

The good news, which they'd discovered by consulting with Calder, was *Hero* came equipped with a lightning-fast broadband communications system. It used ultrahigh-bandwidth dual Ku antennas linked constantly with civilian communications satellites. It meant they'd be able to broadcast live reports throughout the rescue mission—except perhaps in the extreme polar regions, where satellite coverage was unreliable and even nonexistent.

"Look, *chica*," Allie said, "I know we don't see eye to eye on this one. But I can't get into that tin can without our being totally okay."

Eva scoffed, "Oh please, babe. Don't get all smarmy on me now. We're cool. Pitsy and I'll do as much shooting on the special as we can— even the Tang interview—while you're out joyriding with this demented cowboy."

Allie swiped at her playfully. "Eva! *Ay, qué mala chica!*"

Eva pushed her away with a tight-lipped grin. "Go on, get outta here. Bag us a big one so I don't have to say, 'I told you so.'"

The two hugged and Allie rushed away wondering if she'd lost her marbles. But she had a premonition about Calder, that she could trust him. That their encounter, not just the *Hero* story, was meant to be.

Or is it just my imagination?

Or wishful thinking?

★

TUESDAY, APRIL 25 (8:05 A.M. PACIFIC DAYLIGHT TIME)

He and Allie were strapped into their seats. It was the final minutes of the countdown and once again the same small crowd of Navy brass from last weekend's test run was gathered on the beach.

"Calder, we're in a commercial break right now, but they're coming back to us very soon. Before they do, I have a question."

He was intent on finishing the pre-flight checklist. "Already?" he muttered.

"Get used to it. It's what we reporters do—ask questions. Your job, dear sir, is to answer them."

He was taken aback by her directness but let it slide because of her good humor. "Okay, fair enough. Shoot."

"You told me in our interview *Hero* is not intended to be a military vehicle."

He groaned inwardly.

Still harping on the military.

"Right, she isn't."

"Then why are all these military guys here? Why is your lab located on the Navy base?"

He paused, his shoulders dropping.

Good grief!

"It's a long story."

"We're going on a long journey."

"Once we're out of here, okay?"

Eva's voice played loudly over the cabin speaker, "You're back in ten, babycakes!"

He chortled. "I know she's not talking to *me*."

"Careful what you say from here on out, sailor. The world's about to hear your every word."

The thought of that gave him pause, but only briefly. He trusted Allie, believed she was the only person who could intelligently communicate to the public the importance of his achievement. Besides, he was keen on getting to know her better. She attracted him on many levels—certainly more than any woman he'd met since Nell died.

"We're back live from inside *Hero*'s cabin," Allie said in her reporter's voice, "minutes away from launch..."

His eyes were systematically scrutinizing the control panel. Moments later he saw what he was waiting for: an idiot light indicating the digitized itinerary was fully ingested by *Hero*'s navigation system.

Immediately, he thrust his arm up through the cockpit opening so people could see they were go for launch. The horde of spectators cheered as he lowered the large bubble-shaped windshield into place and locked it.

"Seat belts, kids."

Allie continued her reporting. "When we are near any coastline, like now, Dr. Sinclair will keep *Hero*'s main engine—her so-called Q-thruster—in low gear..."

After the mooring ropes were untied Calder pushed the round green button, initiating a rapid, automated sequence that ignited *Hero*'s engine.

Allie didn't miss a beat. "The whining sound you're now hearing comes from *Hero*'s fancy starting mechanism. Inside her vacuum chamber a super-high-intensity, titanium-sapphire laser beam—brighter than the sun—is colliding with an electron beam. The head-on collision of those two beams—"

There was an audible boom. *Hero* lurched forward.

"There it is!" Allie said.

Her enthusiasm made him smile.

"The collision of the two beams produces a tiny explosion so unbelievably powerful that right now it's literally ripping apart the quantum vacuum, unleashing a torrent of latent energy. That's what's propelling *Hero*. Unbelievable!"

Still smiling, he steered *Hero* slowly and carefully away from the pier.

He thought back to the origins of her ignition mechanism, inspired by theoretical work published in 2010 by Igor Sokolov and others at the University of Michigan. After doing some calculations, the researchers foresaw the possibility of using the head-on collision of a powerful laser and an electron beam to trigger a massive chain reaction inside a quantum vacuum. It was the quantum mechanical equivalent of the chain reactions used to ignite nuclear power plants.

Allie stayed on it. "It's like a spark in a roomful of dynamite. Except that *Hero*'s tank is empty, so it's like getting something from nothing. But nothing is not really nothing; it's really something."

He shook his head.

Man, she's good.

Really good.

"That's quantum mechanics for you, folks. For all of you hard-core geeks out there who want to know more, check out my Web s—"

"Rescue One, this is Point Loma. Please confirm your parrot is on. Over."

"Parrot?" Allie asked, interrupting her running commentary.

"*Hero*'s transponder. It lets the base keep track of our position."

He said to Scotty, "Confirmed. Over."

"Pinging you now," Scotty replied. "Stand by."

Several moments later Scotty came back on the radio. "Rescue One, this is Point Loma. We have you in our sights. Over."

"Excellent. Thanks for having my back, Scotty. Speak to you in two mikes. Over."

"Copy that. And everyone here sends their best. Make us proud. Over."

"Mikes?" Allie asked.

"Military slang for minutes."

"Ah, yes, the military," she tittered.

He rolled his eyes, concentrating on steering *Hero* southward away from Point Loma. To the left, a spring fog veiled Coronado Island and the city of San Diego, making their skylines appear ghostlike. He glanced up at the news copters circling overhead like vultures, noticing only one was marked Fast News. He'd given Allie exclusive rights to his story but it was impossible to stop others from horning in.

"Allie, I saw your report on the whales yesterday," he said, playing to her TV audience. "Good job."

"Thanks, I love being a reporter—even when a story isn't particularly lovable."

"What category does this assignment fall into?"

"Too early to tell. We'll see."

"Well, hang on. You're about to find out."

★

TUESDAY, APRIL 25 (8:15 A.M. PACIFIC DAYLIGHT TIME)

They left Mission Beach behind and were now reaching open water. Allie was still on the air.

"Here we go!" she heard Calder call out.

Abruptly, *Hero* sprang forward then turned sharply to the right. Allie's torso pressed hard against her six-point harness, leaving her breathless. She struggled to maintain her composure.

> AA: "Yikes! You can't feel it at home, folks, but we're off and running. Dr. Sinclair, what's the plan, exactly?"
> CS: "I'm going to use *Hero* to run interference between the shoreline and any large animal I see making toward it. With *Hero*'s speed and agility, we should be able to head them off."
> AA: "Can you explain to viewers: Why are you doing this? What does this mission mean to you personally?"

Calder didn't answer right away.

AA: "Dr. Sinclair? Can you hear me?"

CS: "Yes, Allie, yes. I was just concentrating on what I'm doing. This is tricky business. What was your question?"

AA: "Why are you doing this? What do you hope to accomplish?"

CS: "Wow. Well, first of all I want to show everybody what *Hero* can do. She's not just a scientific curiosity; she's the future of long-distance travel in my opinion—and much more. Hold on."

Hero skipped over a swell and came down with a thud.

CS: "Besides that, the technology I've invented to tap into the quantum vacuum has huge implications for our planet's future. We won't have to drill into the earth or tear her apart anymore looking for energy. Think of what that means to the environment, to every living creature on the planet."

Hero was executing a series of hairpin turns that made it hard for her to speak. "This is how I imagine a cow punch must feel who's trying to corral a bunch of wild mustangs," she managed to get out breathlessly.

She paused and sat back, picturing Eva safely ensconced inside the production truck.

You were right, chica: this guy's a cowboy.

Nearly a minute later Allie resumed.

AA: "What about these whales? What are your thoughts about them?"

CS: "I love the water and all the creatures that live in it. I always have. I've tried to pass that love on to my daughter, who feels the same way. Whales are among the most intelligent creatures on the planet, you know. It breaks my heart to see them doing this—beaching themselves. If I can use *Hero* to save even one of them—that's like the cherry on the sundae for me."

Hero continued racing up and down the coastline, speeding and slowing with equal abruptness, intercepting scores of animals. Remarkably, the craft was able to change direction on a dime, veering this way, then that way, seemingly without effort.

"Any speedboat might be able to keep some whales away," Allie explained to viewers. "But *Hero*'s incredible speed—let's see, right now we're averaging over 200 knots—her amazing speed and maneuverability make it possible to cover a much wider swath of ocean more quickly."

Just then, *Hero* turned extra sharply.

"*Whoa!*" she cried out.

"Sorry about that," Calder said.

"These animals are determined to beach themselves," she continued. "So heading them off once is not enough. *Hero* has to keep at it two, three, four times and be super quick about it."

The cabin suddenly filled with the clicks, cries, and songs of whales and dolphins.

"I've switched on *Hero*'s hydrophone so your viewers can hear the animals we're trying to save," Calder said.

She and Eva were prepared.

AA: "Thank you, that's awesome. Standing by inside our studio in Los Angeles is Dr. John Leland, a marine biologist who knows more about interspecies communication than anyone alive. In the United States alone his pioneering studies of whale and dolphin languages helped lead to the signing of the Marine Mammal Protection Act. Good morning, sir, can you hear me?"

JL: "Yes, I can. Good morning."

AA: "Dr. Leland, can you tell us something about the vocalizations we're hearing? In particular, are you able to tell if we're helping or hurting here?"

JL: "Well, I certainly can tell your presence is being felt. Word is spreading throughout the various pods that an intruder has invaded their territories. As to hurting or he—it's my impre—that the voi—hea—se—dicate..."

Eva's voice yelled through the IFB, "Hang in there, girlfriend! We're losing the uplink."

"You gotta be kidding! Here we go again," Allie protested. "What was Leland just saying? Are we helping or hurting?"

"I don't know," Eva answered, her voice sounding harried. "All we heard is what you did. I'll check with Los Angeles."

"What's going on?" Calder asked.

"Problems with the satellite."

Twenty minutes later the TV signal was still down.

"I don't know much about whale speak," Calder said, "but my LIDAR tells me we've cleared the water of all the animals that were threatening to beach. We'll hang around for a while longer, just to—"

"Allie, can you hear me?"

It was Eva.

"Yeah, go ahead."

"I'm sorry it's taken me so long. It's *mishegoss* here. Stu's having a cow over the satellite problems. It's like what happened with what's-his-face up in Silicon Valley—some kind of magnetic storm. Anyway, I got your answer: Leland says that from what he can tell you guys are doing a good thing. The animals seem to be changing course and singing a different tune. So keep going."

Allie immediately forwarded the good news to Calder.

"Okay, then, that's all I wanted to hear," he said brightly. "Next stop, Honolulu!"

CHAPTER 13

GUARDIAN ANGELS

Mother Abbess Yolanda had yet to hear from anyone regarding Francis, or whatever he was called now. A few of her many longtime radio interlocutors around the world offered advice but none of it paid off. That's why she was cheered by the possibility God had brought to the orphanage a *bona fide* guardian angel.

"Please come in, *Señor Paez*."

She led the tall, well-groomed man to the most comfortable accommodation in her unassuming office: an overstuffed chair upholstered in a repurposed eighteenth-century Andalusian tapestry. It was a Christmas gift from a local craftsman some ten years earlier.

She smiled at the children peeking through the open door, then surreptitiously waved them away. Everyone at Sacred Heart was excited by this visit because the parish priest told them *Sr. Paez* was interested in helping to rescue the orphanage.

"We're honored that you've made the trip to our humble home all the way from Madrid," she said, still standing. "May I offer you some refreshment? The boys and girls have made freshly squeezed lemonade from our own orchard. God bless them, they're selling it to help raise monies."

"Thank you, Reverend Mother. Yes, I think I will." He fanned himself. "I'm afraid I didn't dress properly for *Sevilla*'s heat."

She eyed his tailored suit and wondered how much it cost.

He must be quite rich.

After the lemonade was served and their friendly chitchat ran its course the man sat up straight. "Well, Reverend Mother, I trust the *padre* has explained to you our plan for saving the orphanage."

Her pulse quickened. "Only that you have taken an interest in our predicament and are prepared to help. God bless you, *señor*. We would not be in this situation if the government hadn't suddenly burdened us with many new rules and regulations. They're requiring us to update the electrical and plumbing systems for the entire campus. They're even demanding we have a resident physician, something we cannot possibly afford and that is not necessary anyway. In our 160 years the doctors of *Sevilla* have always taken very good care of the children."

He nodded empathetically. "Yes, that's wonderful, very commendable. Now as to our plan, I represent a group of investors who are interested in seeing *Sevilla* grow and prosper, to see it catch up with the times."

It was common knowledge *Sevilla* remained underdeveloped compared to Madrid and Spain's other big cities and she liked it that way. She cherished its small-city feel, family-friendly culture, and old traditions. But she could see things were changing: gated communities, giant chain stores, even the siesta—young people were no longer taking off the afternoon hours to eat and relax from their increasingly frantic lives.

"To that end we'd like to build you a brand-new facility."

Her hand flew to her mouth. "A new orphanage?"

"Yes, Reverend Mother. One that will more than satisfy the government."

She wanted to jump out of her chair and hug the man. "But that's wonderful!"

"Yes, Reverend Mother. And we've even found the perfect location; you and the children will love it."

For an awkward moment the two sat and looked at each other, she being thoroughly perplexed.

"But I don't understand..." she sputtered.

The man squirmed, as if sitting on something uncomfortable, then cleared his throat. "Your current location here by the Guadalquivir River will be the site of a beautiful new outdoor shopping arcade. And no ordinary one, either. It will be what they call a 'factory outlet,' *como los unos que los Americanos tienen.* And it will be solar powered. We'll use part of the land for a solar farm. The entire complex will be the first of its kind in all of Andalusia."

The man's enthusiasm did nothing to lessen her shock. "But *señor,* I don't understand. A shopping mall? Here? I thought you were going to save us."

"We are, Reverend Mother, we are! And it's not a shopping mall, it's a—"

"Yes, yes, but—"

"Look, Reverend Mother, I understand this is a lot for you to digest. But my investors and I believe that when you think and pray about it, you will see it's your best option. Your only option, really. What we are proposing is not a bad thing. The land we've chosen for the orphanage is beautiful, out in the country. And it will enable you to keep your doors open for another 160 years!"

"But the church, the history of this place..."

"We've thought of that too, of course. We will not be demolishing any of the main historic structures. We're hiring a very famous architect to renovate them in a respectful way. We've already heard from a major clothier interested in occupying the sanctuary—a very upscale brand name, very tasteful. And a sculpted monument to your ministry, which will include a permanent donation box, will be erected in a place of honor, at the very center of an elegant *al fresco* food court."

★

TUESDAY, APRIL 25 (9:32 A.M. PACIFIC DAYLIGHT TIME)

NEURONET FABRICATION PLANT; MOUNTAIN VIEW, CALIFORNIA

"Where is she?" Jared muttered to himself. He looked again at his cell phone: 9:32 a.m. Maggie was two minutes late.

He was standing just inside the entrance to NeuroNet's main fab, a one-million-square-foot facility located ten miles from corporate head-quarters. He breathed in deeply to calm himself, to remind himself of how good it felt to be free—to say *sayonara* to a lifetime of enforced confinement.

Idly looking around at the fab's cavernous space, he recalled his thirteenth birthday, when Maggie first spilled the beans about his incarcerated upbringing. She had learned the secret from her dad, his personal chauffeur.

His parents, she told him that day, lived in deathly fear for his safety. They worried he'd suffer the fate of his older brother, Jack Jr., who was kidnapped for ransom and ultimately murdered. After supposedly a whole lot of soul-searching, they decided it would be safest if Jared were randomly shuttled from one secluded property to another, accompanied only by a small troupe of very trusted servants, which included Maggie and her dad.

He scowled at the painful memory. It was like a perverted shell game! He glanced at his cell again: 9:34 a.m.

She has some nerve keeping me waiting.

He stared blankly at the fab and resumed his childhood recollections.

He surely would've gone bonkers back then—even committed suicide, which he'd thought about more than once—if not for computers. His old man made sure there was one in every room of every mansion Jared ever lived in. The Web became his best friend, the only way he was able to learn about and interact with the world—after quickly learning to defeat the severe restrictions his overbearing father had placed on its use.

He smiled at the memory then looked at his cell again: 9:35 a.m. "Damn!" he muttered.

Jared wanted Maggie to revere computers as much as he did—to value their supreme importance to people's lives. After all, his grand, altruistic vision for improving man's lot—for making amends for his father's insufferable greediness—depended on privatizing NeuroNet. And on the success of his first chip, Quantum I, which he had designed during those long, lonely years under virtual house arrest.

"Hey there," Maggie said, striding into the building. Her face looked tight, her eyes distracted.

He glared at her. "You're late."

"Sorry, lots going on we need to discuss."

"Not yet. You're my PR person now and you need to see how chips are made—it's awesome."

"Jared—"

But he wouldn't take no for an answer and told her so. Ultimately she gave in and, following his lead, put on a hair net and white bunny suit. The plant needed to be kept totally spotless—thousands of times cleaner even than a hospital operating room—because microprocessors were ultrasensitive to contamination.

He walked her into view of the vast assembly line, manned by both people and robots.

"*Ta-da!*" He swept a hand across the busy scene. "The chips that'll transform the world. That'll transform NeuroNet into the world's biggest philanthropist—bigger than Buffett or Gates. The chips that'll make up for my old man's sins." He gave Maggie a big, proud smile.

She answered him with an icy stare. "Jared, I'm not some TV camera so don't talk to me that way, okay? I really need you to stop and listen. We have important business to discuss."

He hired Maggie to head up NeuroNet's PR because there was no one on Earth he trusted more. But she could be a pain in the butt sometimes—like now.

"More important than these chips? Ha!" He took her hand and pulled her further into the fab's operation. "Did you know there are now more computer chips in the world than people? And they're talking to each other all the time, 24/7, running the world in ways large and small."

She scowled. "They don't run the world, Jared, people do. *People* tell your beloved chips what to do."

"True, true. But computer chips execute the orders—or not. And they chatter among themselves in a language all their own. When people are sleeping, chips are still awake, huddling, deciding, executing. And more and more we're totally trusting them, letting them do what they think is best. So, yeah, in the end they do run the world."

She shook her head and said nothing.

They came alongside the station where giant machines were spitting out small ingots of purified silicon, slicing them into ultrathin wafers. These were the foundations upon which miniature forty-story skyscrapers—Quantum I microprocessors—were built.

"My old man's first commercial chip, the thing that got him the Nobel Prize, went into the first-ever handheld calculator. Only geeks used them." He picked up a handful of wafers and waved them in front of Maggie's face. "But now *these*, these little slices of computer salami, control *everything*: military systems, Christmas ornaments, ATMs, cell phones, cars, spaceships—these guys have more clout than all the political leaders put together."

"*Jared!*" Maggie swiped at the wafers and missed. "Please, just listen to me for a moment."

He flung away the wafers and faced her. "What?!" he barked, swiveling his eyes skyward.

"Sometimes I just wanna quit, you know? You're like a baby. A willful, spoiled baby."

"You can't quit; I just hired you."

Maggie stomped her foot. "Your mother is after me to change your mind about what you're proposing to do, and I agree with her. It's nuts. Buying out the stockholders? Giving away NeuroNet's profits? Her lawyers are threatening to have you declared incompetent."

"Whatever!" He looked at her defiantly. "My mother is a control freak and now that my dad's gone she wants to dig her claws into me too. Forget it! *I'm* calling the shots now. What I say goes. End of story. Next."

Maggie shook her head and breathed hard. "An editorial in this morning's *Wall Street Journal* claims what you're proposing is illegal. That NeuroNet's bylaws—your dad's written intentions for the company—forbid it. The Security Exchange Commission is investigating."

"The SEC! Let 'em! Once we become a 501(c)(3) we won't be playing by Wall Street's greedy rules anymore." He trained his eyes on her as though they were flamethrowers. "*What else?*"

He softened his stare. Maggie was nearing the end of her rope—he could see that. He needed to be careful. He couldn't imagine life without her.

"That reporter woman, Allie Armendariz. Her assistant keeps bugging me about letting her interview you again. I've told her absolutely not. I don't know why you didn't hold a press conference in the first place, like I wanted. Now that you've singled her out it's gone to her head—and trust me, she's not going to leave us alone."

Jared hesitated and decided it was time to relent. "All right. No more interviews, unless you say so." Then quickly he took Maggie's hand. "Okay, Mommy? Can we get on with the tour?"

CHAPTER 14

GOING DEEP

At an average cruising speed of 500 knots, *Hero* took roughly five hours to annihilate the 2,275 nautical miles from San Diego to Oahu. Calder steered her into the slip reserved for them in the fashionable Waikiki Marina Resort. Choppers circled overhead while gawking, bathing-suit-clad spectators lined the famous white sand beach.

Allie, still on the air, made some hurried remarks about their arrival then quickly signed off. She had to pee badly.

"You holding up okay?" he said.

She was unstrapping herself as fast as possible. "Yeah, but I shouldn't have drunk so much water. I'll know better from now on."

The break lasted only long enough for them to freshen up and give interviews to local reporters. In the process they learned whales back in San Diego were still no longer beaching themselves, news that everyone hailed as encouraging.

Once at sea again, bound for Nagasaki, she reminded Calder about his promise to explain his military connection.

"We're not on, right?"

"No." Then she added, "I'll tell you whenever we are, trust me."

"I do, it's just that—anyway, I do."

A moment passed before he began. "It happened four years ago, when my wife died. Nell. She was a marine biologist working at a polynya in the Arctic, between Ellesmere Island and Greenland. Her specialty was whales."

"Polynya?"

"Yeah, I know, most people have never heard of one. It's a place on the ice where warm water currents create a lagoon that attracts all kinds of animals. I visited it many times. It's pretty amazing."

"So how did she die, your wife?"

Silence.

"They say it was a CME, a coronal mass ejection, or at least—"

"Wait a minute. I remember hearing about that. They said she was— oh, my gosh."

It all came back to Allie.

Coronal mass ejections—sudden cannon blasts of solar particles— usually weren't aimed at Earth. When they were, the particles bombarded the upper atmosphere, creating dazzling aurorae high in the sky. In some instances the radiation penetrated more deeply and disrupted communications.

In one horrific case, four years earlier, a CME was so powerful and the Arctic's magnetic defenses were so inexplicably weakened, radiation broke in and incinerated everything in its path, all the way down to the surface. The scientist—her name was Nell O'Reilly, as she recalled—was doing research outside on the ice when it happened.

"Oh, Calder, I'm so, so sorry. I had no idea she was your wife."

He didn't reply.

In the quietude she could hear and feel *Hero* hydroplaning across the choppy seas. She grew weightless whenever the vehicle became airborne, like a stone skipping across the surface of a pond. It was unnerving at first but she was getting used to it.

Still, as they hurtled across the open ocean at breakneck speed she was keenly aware of the danger. *Hero* was made of an impregnable ceramic-metal laminate, but she only of flesh and blood.

She wondered what Calder was made of.

"When Nell was alive," he said, breaking the long silence, "I set up my lab in Kangerlussuaq, on the west coast of Greenland—just to be close to her. It was great. During the week I worked on *Hero*; on weekends we came together and talked about the future.

"When Sara was born we homeschooled her. Like I told you before, she's in Australia now for an internship. You'll get to meet her—she's close to one of the stranding sites. She's nineteen, a great kid. I really miss her."

She waited for him to continue.

"When the commander of Naval Base Point Loma happened to hear the news of Nell's death and my research, he invited me to relocate to San Diego—offered to lease me an unused hangar on the base. It was in bad shape, he said, but he was willing to have it retrofitted according to my special needs. That meant making the building fireproof, bomb-proof, radiation-proof, you name it—to protect the outside world from the possibility of my quantum vacuum experiments accidentally exploding. In exchange for all that he asked me to grant the Navy certain rights to exploit my invention. It was an offer I couldn't refuse. At that point I'd used up all of my own money on *Hero*; I was close to being totally broke."

"What sort of rights? Do you worry about how the Navy might use your technology?"

"That's something I'm not free to discuss. But, anyway, their license is non-exclusive. It means I'm free, within reason, to take *Hero* into the marketplace, which is what I'm planning to do."

At length she said, "Well, this trip will help, that's for sure. You're getting millions of dollars' worth of free publicity."

She looked through the windshield at the white caps whizzing by. *As long as nothing goes wrong.*

★

TUESDAY, APRIL 25 (5:33 P.M. EASTERN DAYLIGHT TIME)

CANADIAN FORCES STATION ALERT; NUNAVUT, CANADA

Dallan spent an hour in the communications office trying unsuccessfully to phone his assistant in Boulder. The magnetic instability over the Arctic was allowing radiation to penetrate deeply into the upper atmosphere, making communications impossible.

Brody said he would've evacuated the base by now, but the magnetic disruptions were playing havoc with the aircraft's electronic navigation systems as well. It was unsafe for even one of his most experienced pilots to fly under these conditions.

Dallan walked into Brody's office for an update.

"There you are!" the major said from behind his computer. "Come have a look at this."

Becky Anawak, the Inuit biologist, was standing next to him. She looked at Dallan with large, doe-like eyes and smiled.

"Hey, Becky," he said, entering the room.

She looked positively beautiful without her bulky cold-weather gear on.

"Hey," she replied.

Dallan came alongside the two and bent forward to see the computer screen.

"It's the latest intel from our global net of magnetometers," Brody explained. "The information is sensitive but not classified, so I'm allowed to show you."

Dallan recoiled at what he saw. "What?! No way!"

The strength of the magnetic field directly above the North Pole was nearly gone. If the deterioration continued there would be a gaping hole in the field hundreds of miles across. When that happened solar radiation could penetrate freely into the atmosphere; bulldoze its way down through the layers of air until it ultimately reached Earth's surface. Everything within ground zero would be fried.

But that wasn't the worst of it. The map showed weak spots opening elsewhere around the globe, high above the cities of San Diego, Nagasaki, Humpty Doo in Australia, and Cádiz in Spain. If they continued growing, the same fate awaited those cities.

He looked to Brody. "For god's sake, when did this all start happening?!"

"After we got back from Thule. But until now we weren't sure how much of it was real. We're still not one hundred percent sure—the San Diego spot seems to be going away."

"But this is crazy," Dallan said, straightening up and running a hand through his greasy, unwashed hair. "What in the world's going on?!"

"That's what we were hoping you'd tell us," Becky said.

WEDNESDAY, APRIL 26 (12:17 A.M. MOUNTAIN DAYLIGHT TIME)

PARKER CENTER FOR BEHAVIORAL HEALTH; DENVER, COLORADO

Lorena decided it was time to make her move. Her plan to get away was simple: sneak out, take a cab home to get her passport, then continue on to the airport, where she'd fly to Israel.

She thought of Dallan and her spirits nosedived.

Forget it!

Nothing matters now but getting to Jerusalem.

Ever so stealthily, she eased herself out of bed and got dressed.

Fools.

For the past few days she'd pretended to go along with the doctors and nurses; to behave like a model patient so they'd relax their vigilance of her.

She recalled a verse in Matthew as she pulled on her sweater.

I am sending you out like sheep among wolves. Therefore be as shrewd as snakes and as innocent as doves.

They'll see.

Quiet as a church mouse, she cracked open her room's door and surveyed the dim hallway—first this way, then that.

The coast was clear. She rushed out on tiptoes.

A minute later, just as she was within sight of the front entrance, she noticed a man sauntering toward her.

No!

She quickly sized him up.

Janitor.

Looking around, she spied a women's bathroom and dashed into it.

Please, Lord, please. Protect me.

Locking herself inside a stall, she held her breath for what seemed like ages. But eventually she exhaled and soon thereafter worked up the courage to peek outside.

The man was gone.

She stared hard at the reception desk; it was unoccupied.

Now!

NOW!

Without hesitating, without thinking, she sprinted across the vestibule. Then she pushed through the revolving door and fled away into the cool night air.

"Thank you, Jesus," she whispered. "Thank you!"

CHAPTER 15

SEA OF QUESTIONS

WEDNESDAY, APRIL 26 (4:05 P.M. JAPAN STANDARD TIME)

EAST CHINA SEA

Allie was awakened by a bell-like alarm and Calder saying, "Okey-dokey, then, we're just about there."

"Nagasaki?" she croaked. Looking outside, she blinked at the sight of choppers overhead and a tall cityscape in the near distance. "So soon?"

"You nodded off and I let you sleep."

Between the extreme jet lag caused by zooming through multiple time zones, having to sit in one position without a break, and natural concerns about safety aboard an experimental vehicle, she had struggled to relax last evening. It surprised her she'd finally fallen asleep.

She stretched her arms.

The body knows what it needs.

The cabin alarm gave way to an intermittent, deep-throated horn.

"We've got traffic," Calder said—his voice, as nearly always, not betraying any emotion.

Abruptly, *Hero* slowed to an idle.

She looked outside and saw, dead ahead, a fleet of large boats with Japanese markings.

Whalers?!

"Harbor Police to Rescue One, can you read us? Over." The voice on the radio was heavily accented.

"Rescue One to Harbor Police. Yes, we read you. What's happening here?"

"Whaling ships. Please do not approach any farther. You are in violation of our territorial waters."

"Allie, can you hear me?" It was Eva's voice coming through her earpiece.

"Yes, *chica*, yes. I was just about to hail you. We've arrived in Naga-saki but they're telling us to stay away. I don't believe it."

"Well, believe it. Our chopper's streaming live video of it right now. Turn on your mic and start talking."

Fully awake now, Allie quickly cleared her throat and flipped on the audio switch. "This is Allie Armendariz inside Rescue One. We've just been given a warning by Japanese authorities to abort our mission. No explanation as to why, but it's not hard to guess what's going on."

Over the years she'd done many news segments on the Japanese whaling industry and its many controversies. That's why she was certain those ships out there right now were capturing wayward whales as they headed into shore—an atrocity akin to shooting fish in a barrel.

"Decades ago Japanese fishermen whaled their coastal waters to death. Since then, they—"

"Dr. Sinclair, please acknowledge our order. Over." The accented voice sounded stern now.

She stopped talking so viewers could see and hear for themselves what was happening.

"Yes, we copy, sir," Calder said. "Requesting innocent passage so—"

She spotted a trio of official-looking speedboats, all rapidly heading in their direction. "Calder, look!"

"Good lord!" he exclaimed. "These people are nuts!"

"Dr. Sinclair," said the radio voice, "this is your final warning. You are in violation—"

"Calder!" she cried out. "Please, let's just get out of here!"

In the blink of an eye *Hero*'s engine roared to life. For several anxious moments she watched over her shoulder through the windshield, then finally breathed easy—the boats giving chase were now well behind them. Still shaking, she reached up to worry her hair but her hand was blocked by the helmet.

WEDNESDAY, APRIL 26 (9:10 A.M. CENTRAL EUROPEAN SUMMER TIME)

POOR CLARES' SACRED HEART CONVENT; SEVILLE, SPAIN

Following this morning's Holy Sacrifice of the Mass, Mother Yolanda returned to her cell and donned her threadbare woolen robe. Shuffling across the room, she felt heavy knowing the Sacred Heart community—the priests, sisters, and kids—were all counting on her well-known, great faith to help save the 160-year-old orphanage.

She paused before the aged prayer bench, looked up and sighed, and then, bracing herself, slowly descended onto her knees. "Holy Mother, full of grace, come quickly to our rescue. For the sake of the orphans. For the sake of the Kingdom."

The plea went on for many minutes, after which she struggled to her feet.

"*Mateo 19:14*, this is Rising Son, can you hear me?"

It took a moment for her to recognize the handle of the incoming radio greeting. But then it came to her. It was her old friend the Reverend Mother Mary Pius from the Monastery of St. Clare in Nagasaki. Mother

Mary Pius helped found that community more than forty years earlier with a dozen sisters from the Poor Clares in Los Angeles.

"*Mateo 19:14*, this is Rising Son, can you hear me, please?"

Even though she was moving at top speed it took Mother Yolanda some time to reach the radio.

"*Mateo 19:14*, this is—"

"Yes, Rising Son, this is *Mateo 19:14*. How good to hear from you, Sister. It's been too many years. Over."

"Oh, thank heaven. For a while there I thought—yes, it's been far too long. How are you, my dear sister? Over."

After catching up on each other's life, Mother Mary Pius said, "I'm calling about the boy—the man—you are looking for. I believe I have found him for you, praise God."

Mother Yolanda, feeling a chill course through her frail body, wrapped the robe more tightly around herself.

"He was on television here in Japan. His name is Dr. Calder Sinclair. He has invented a special boat that can travel very fast."

Mother Yolanda began to weep and silently thank God for His faithfulness. She could not be certain this was indeed her man but knew she must try to make contact as quickly as possible.

"But how can I get ahold of him, Sister?" she said. "Do you have any ideas? Over."

"That's the best part, Sister. It's a miracle. The television showed a map of where he's headed. After Australia, which is his next stop, he's supposed to be in Spain. In Cádiz."

CHAPTER 16

HEART OF COLD

At Calder's request, the U.S. Navy hastily arranged an emergency pit stop at Keelung, a port city in northeastern Taiwan. It enabled Allie and him to hit the bathrooms before continuing to Australia.

Fifteen minutes out of port, *Hero* was once again flying across open water at (according to Calder) some 450 knots. Allie, nestled in her seat and feeling wooden with fatigue, listened with half an ear to Eva rave about the mission's success.

"The Nielson ratings for this morning's launch beat the Super Bowl. People are hooked. You guys are huge!"

"What's Stu saying?"

"Oh, my god, he's in hog heaven. In fact he's letting other networks carry a few of your reports a day. He's charging them a fortune."

Allie grinned and shook her head.

Note to self: ask ol' Stuey for a raise when I get back.

"So I made the right choice by coming, huh?" Allie winced. "Oh, man, I'm sorry, *chica*; I'm sorry. I'm just tired."

There was silence; then Eva said, "Hey, the San Diego stranding is totally gone. That's amazing, right?"

"No, *you're* amazing," Allie said, waggling her head in self-reproach. "What about Nagasaki? Why didn't they let us in? Is it what I'm thinking?"

"What are you thinking?"

"They didn't want us barging in on the stranding because they're fishing the poor whales, right?"

"Like shooting birds in a bucket."

Allie didn't have the energy to correct Eva's butchered saying. "It's disgusting."

"Yeah. And they're using the latest technology to do it: factory ships, diesel-powered whale catchers, everything. It's criminal. The whales don't stand a chance. Planet First and some other groups are threatening to take them to international court. We've got a camera crew at The Hague waiting to get it on tape for the special."

"Awesome. What about the Kilroy story?"

"Nothing new. The computers are still flying off the shelves; his family wants to commit him; and the little sh—the little punk's assistant isn't returning my calls for a second interview. But I'm not giving up."

Allie managed a tired smile.

The original pit bull.

"Anyway," Eva said, "that's it for now. Everything's fine; I'm on top of things. Get some rest; you sound tired."

"I had a long nap just before getting to Nagasaki. But it's hard sleeping in this chair and my mind's totally in a fog from all the time zones. But I'll be fine. Thanks for everything, *chica*. I mean it. *Dulce sueños*, okay? I know it's really late where you are."

"What's the latest?" Calder asked as soon as she signed off.

She filled him in on the mission's popularity and apparent success in San Diego.

"Great. Why don't you try grabbing some winks; it's a long way to Australia."

"I wish I could," she said, stifling a yawn. "I'll try."

Allie closed her eyes but after several futile minutes gave up.

She looked outside. Since leaving San Diego, *Hero* had been traveling in the same direction as the sun, which meant they had experienced only daylight. But as they sped southward to Australia, the reddening orb was falling into the Pacific Ocean like a stone. Several hours later the first star appeared in the darkening sky.

"Hey, Calder, make a wish."

"What?" His voice sounded tired.

"Star light, star bright…"

He chuckled weakly. "Wow, I haven't heard that since I was a kid."

She waited in vain for him to elaborate.

"So…you grew up in Seville? You don't look Spanish."

It took him a while to answer.

"I'm half Spanish—on my mom's side. My dad was British."

"Oh, really? My maternal great-grandfather was supposedly from Seville," she said. "One day I want to go there and find out. I hear it's a beautiful city." She added, "You speak the language?"

Again, silence.

"*Sí, muy bien,*" he said finally—with a surprisingly good accent.

"Wow, that's great," she laughed. "I like speaking Spanglish because it helps me stay grounded. I never want to forget where I came from, you know? I love my East LA roots. I love my family."

She fought away worrying thoughts of Lolo and her mom.

Moments later she realized Calder hadn't said anything to keep the conversation going.

Argh! It's like pulling teeth.

"What was it like growing up in Seville?"

"Good and bad."

He speaks!

"I was raised in an orphanage. I was told my biological mom died in childbirth and my dad was killed in a Jeep accident just before that. The sisters who ran the place were very nice—strict but loving. They were all like mothers to me."

Allie was listening with scrunched brows.

Dang, this guy's full of surprises.

Who is he, really?

"So how did you end up in the United States?"

"I was adopted when I was nine by a couple of American archaeologists. When I was seventeen they returned to the States. We lived in Westwood. My dad was a professor at UCLA, my mom was his lab director."

"Are they still alive?"

"No. They were in their fifties when they adopted me. They were never able to have biological children. Having me was like a miracle to them. They were great parents. I miss them a lot."

She had a million other questions but held her peace. Leaning back, she stared up into the night sky. The stars seemed close enough to touch. Closer than they ever did in the city.

The hum of *Hero*'s engine, the soft ride—punctuated occasionally by a gentle swerving this way or that, the result of *Hero*'s collision avoidance system steering them away from trouble—*Hero*'s skipping past swells, during which there were brief and exhilarating moments of weightlessness: it all combined to finally make Allie feel sleepy.

"Allie?"

Calder's voice seemed far away.

"Allie! Are you all right?"

She shook herself awake. "Yeah."

"Oh, good. You suddenly got quiet. I just wanted to make sure you were okay."

Allie sat up. "Yeah, yeah, I'm fine."

"Okay, good."

The cabin fell silent again, save for the natural sounds of the engine and ocean.

She closed her eyes once more, this time to picture Calder as a boy in Seville, immigrating to America in the grips of an impossible dream: to invent the ocean-going equivalent of a jetliner. She understood viscerally what he must be feeling right now, the enormity of what he needed to prove. To himself. To the world.

It was her story too.

An image formed of the white clapboard house on South Townsend Avenue near First Street, where she grew up. How far she'd come!—personally, professionally, spiritually.

Her eyes flew open and they bored deeply into the night sky.

She might as well have traveled to the stars.

"Calder," she heard herself saying, "tell me about Sara."

THURSDAY, APRIL 27 (1:54 A.M. AUSTRALIAN CENTRAL STANDARD TIME)

MINDIL BEACH, DARWIN; NORTHERN TERRITORIES, AUSTRALIA

Allie was brusquely awakened by the bell-like sound of *Hero*'s arrival alarm. She yawned, stretched, then looked outside with burning eyes. Helicopters were circling above an artificially lit stretch of rocky coastline strewn with beached whales.

Mindil Beach.

Standing beyond the rocky beach, behind a long length of yellow caution tape, scores of people and uniformed police gawked at *Hero*'s approach.

Dang, Eva wasn't kidding!

We're big news.

Calder was speaking on the radio. "No, we're heading straight in. Overnighting at the Skycity Darwin Hotel. Over."

Calder's plan was for them to herd whales in the morning.

"Awright then, mate, no worries." The radio voice had a strong, upbeat Aussie twang. "Welcome to Darwin."

She connected with Eva in preparation for her final report of the night.

"*Chica*, what time is it in San Diego, anyway? I've totally lost track."

"It's, let's see—9:25 in the morning. Wednesday. You're a day ahead."

"Oh, my gosh. I hope you're getting some sleep."

"Don't worry about me. Stu's feeling generous. He found us a great production facility here with little dorm rooms, like college. Knock this segment out and we can both hit the sack. Busy days ahead: things are getting worse in Cádiz and Canada."

"Oh, no, don't tell me," she said with a noisy sigh. "So what show are we breaking into this time? America's Newsroom, right?"

"Yeah, and they're pumped."

A few minutes later, as Calder steered *Hero* into shore, Ashley Folsom, the show's co-host, introduced the report.

"Thanks, Ashley. Even though it's the wee hours of the morning here in Darwin, we're being welcomed—as you can see from the aerial shot—by a huge crowd. What you can't see are the saltwater crocodiles and Portuguese man o' wars for which these tropical waters are infamous. Needless to say we're going to be extra careful when we disembark—we don't want to accidently become something's late-night snack."

Several minutes later, her report completed, Allie signed off.

"Perfect!" Eva said. "They loved it."

"What about the G-20? How's it going?"

"I told you, everything's cool. I've been talking constantly with Mike. One really interesting thing: he says the Anonymous guy was at a Planet First meeting yesterday—the day you launched—and pretty much gave away the whole show, how they plan to create one big demonstration. It's a huge break."

Allie felt herself getting warm. "Did Mike tell you what the plan is? Can we have the exclusive?"

"I'm working on it. I'm working on it. I'm only one person."

Allie detected stress in her voice.

"The plan is all laid out on a CD the Anonymous guy handed out. The FBI's mole got one. I'm trying to convince Mike to let us have a copy."

"Okay, okay, just please stay on it. And thank Mike for me."

"Of course. Also, I have some bad news about your sister. I'm sorry, I was going to call you when I first heard about it but didn't want to wake you. Your brother Carlos tracked me down a couple hours ago to say she's missing."

Allie was sure she was hearing things. "Say again?"

Eva repeated the news.

"Have they contacted the police?!"

"Yes, they've sent out an APB, but so far nothing."

"Oh, Eva, this is awful! I should come home. Right away."

"Your brother predicted you'd say that. He told me to tell you not to. There's nothing you can do that isn't already being done."

"That's what he thinks."

"Allie, really, think about it. What would you do if you came back now? Ride around in a police cruiser looking for her? Be reasonable. Everyone knows how much you love your family, but some things are out of our hands."

Silence.

"Allie, you still—?"

"Yeah, yeah. What about Dallan? Have they been able to contact him? Does he know about this?"

"Your brother keeps calling Dallan's office in Boulder. He still hasn't gotten back from the Arctic and his people say they can't get a message to him because of bad communications."

Still?!

Allie felt lightheaded. "Oh, *chica*. I should've listened to you and never done this story in the first place. What a huge mistake this was."

★

THURSDAY, APRIL 27 (7:25 A.M. AUSTRALIAN CENTRAL STANDARD TIME)

The two boarded the elevator wordlessly.

Calder pushed the first-floor button then looked at her with concern. "How'd you sleep?"

Allie's face was ashen; her eyes lacked their usual sparkle.

"Not so good; I was thinking of Lolo all night. Thinking I should get back."

His stomach did a somersault.

The story of my life.

Every time things are going well …

"Well, just let me know what you want to do." Hoping to lighten the mood, he added with a jocular Aussie accent, "I'll do this mornin's wrangling m'self, if I hav' to—no worries, mate."

She grinned weakly. "Thanks, Calder."

A moment later the elevator stopped and its doors parted.

"Daddy!"

Sara, standing in the lobby with the hotel manager and several others, rushed forward and embraced him.

"Sara, baby!"

"Oh, I'm so sorry I wasn't here last night," she cried, squeezing him tightly. "I'll tell you all about it later."

"Never mind. Let me look at you!" He held her at arm's length and was thrown by how grown-up she looked. She had Nell's sandy blond hair, cut short, and pale blue eyes. "Wow, are you a sight for sore eyes." Calder turned around. "Allie, this is my daughter, Sara."

Allie stepped forward and the two hugged. "I've heard so much about you from your dad. It's so great to finally meet you in person."

Sara, disengaging, said, "Dad has told me all about you too. Thanks for what you're doing. Isn't it awful what's happening? Dirk and—oh, my gosh." She whirled around. "Dirk!"

A moment later she was joined by a young man about her age. He reminded Calder of a scruffy young Prince Harry.

"Daddy, this is Dirk Cannon. He's from Sydney. He's interning with me."

Calder looked him over while pumping his hand. "Good to meet you, Dirk. Why don't—"

The hotel manager appeared and announced breakfast was set up for them inside a private banquet room.

They entered the room, which was decorated nautically, and sat at a round table by a large picture window overlooking the ocean. From this vantage point no beached whales could be seen.

Calder sat down between Sara and Dirk; Allie settled into the chair directly across from him. The waiters served eggs benedict with tomatoes and beans.

"I love your name, Allie," Sara said. "Is that what your parents named you or is it short for something?"

Allie smiled. "It's short for Alejandra, which supposedly means defender of mankind. My dad now kids they should've named me Ignacia—Iggy for short—because it means fiery one, which is how I turned out."

"You?" Calder said, hoping to keep the conversation light. "I'd say you're more cool than fiery." He realized instantly it had not come out right. "I mean, cool under pressure. I couldn't do what you do. You're very good at it."

"Well, thank you, *señor*," Allie said with a quick wave of the hand. "Anyway, it's a great TV name. Easy to remember."

"Thank you for letting me join you for breakfast, sir," Dirk said. "I told Sara I didn't want to butt in on your time together, but she insisted."

"Yeah, well, she's hard to resist," Calder said. "I mean—anyway, yes, by all means, it's good to have you with us."

During the meal Calder watched Sara with disbelieving eyes. She was no longer the little girl he used to tuck into bed and read to sleep.

Or the one who, following Nell's death, woke up frightened in the dead of night and asked to sleep in his room.

"How's Lulu doing?" he asked.

"Oh, Daddy, that's why we weren't here for your arrival last night."

The *we* made him feel left out somehow.

"Lulu was acting crazy all day and night yesterday. But after midnight—right around the time I was thinking you were arriving—everything suddenly started changing."

"Yeah," Dirk said. "It was way strange."

Calder saw Allie perk up.

"In a good way, strange?" she said. "Or a bad way?"

He smiled.

The old Allie.

Always on the job.

Sara and Dirk answered at once. "A good way!"

"Lulu's like her old self," Sara said, then turned to Calder. "Oh, how I wish you had time to see her."

His insides churned at the thought of having to leave Sara so quickly. He knew from here on their lives would continue diverging. His aloneness would become more and more complete.

They were nearly finished with their meal when Sara said, looking from him to Allie, "So how'd you guys first meet?"

"*Hero*'s big public debut last Saturday at Point Loma," he said. "Allie was the only reporter I could trust."

"Thanks, Calder," she said, dipping her head. She arched a brow. "It was quite a debut."

Sara laid down her fork. "My dad's always watched your segments on TV and made me watch them, too."

Allie laughed, dabbing her mouth with a napkin. "You make it sound like it was a chore."

"Oh, no," Sara said, looking mortified. "I didn't mean it that way. It's just that whenever your segments came on he'd ask me to watch with him. Your segments are legit. I still can't believe you're here and I'm having breakfast with you."

When they all finished eating and began rising from the table, Calder said quietly to his daughter, "Sweetie, can I see you for a moment?"

The others made a quick exit, leaving them alone in the dining room.

He gently took his daughter's hands. "Sara, honey, I want you to know how happy I am for you. Seeing you today..." He couldn't finish the sentence. It was as if he were saying good-bye to Nell all over again.

"I know, Daddy."

He took a moment to collect himself. "I'm worried about you—about your safety, I mean, way out here by yourself."

"I'm not alone, Daddy, and besides, I need to grow up. You and Mom always took good care of me. I need to prove I can take care of myself now."

He gave her a crooked smile. "You don't need to prove anything to me, sweetie."

"Not to you, to me. I need to prove it to myself."

He studied her face with pressed lips.

"Look, Dad, stop worrying. You worry too much, you always have. You need to believe in me."

He wanted to explain to Sara it wasn't her—it was *life* he didn't trust. But this was not the right time or place.

"You're right, sweetie," he said with a tight smile. "I need to let go."

The two hugged long and hard.

Afterward, he said, "You know, I'm really proud of what you're doing out here and I can't wait to meet Lulu." He pecked her on the cheek. "After this is over, okay? I'll make a special trip and you can show me all around your new digs."

"Deal. And Daddy? I really like Allie. You deserve to be happy again."

His eyes widened and mouth slackened.

She gave him a toothy smile. "Just saying." Then, taking him by the hand, she walked him out.

★

THURSDAY, APRIL 27 (8:35 A.M. AUSTRALIAN CENTRAL STANDARD TIME)

A police detail walked Allie and Calder out to the hotel parking lot, where they were greeted by a lively swarm of well-wishers and reporters. The Lord Mayor of Darwin formally welcomed them and then surprised everyone by announcing the whales had stopped beaching themselves.

"It happened overnight, while we were all sleeping," she said. "It's like a miracle!"

Allie and Calder exchanged puzzled looks while the crowd cheered loudly.

For the next half hour, she and Calder gave interviews and signed autographs. Then they said their good-byes to the well-wishers.

A security detail escorted them, Sara, and the Lord Mayor to the water's edge, where *Hero* was moored. There, Allie paused to drink in the beautiful scenery. Scores of colorful sailing vessels bobbed in the bay's sparkling, azure waters like so many butterflies. Her chest reverberated with the heavy thumping caused by helicopters circling overhead, the cobalt sky unmarred by even a single cloud.

What in the world am I doing here?

She paused to utter a silent prayer for Lolo's safety.

Please, God.

She was tempted to end it here. To fly back to the States and start cracking the whip on everyone and everything, the way she always did.

But Eva was right. Truly, there would be nothing for her to do back home but wait, just like everyone else. It would drive her crazy and she, in turn, would drive everyone else crazy.

She looked over at Calder, who was saying farewell to Sara.

Besides, she was needed here.

Reluctantly, she climbed aboard the sleek, red rocket-boat and strapped herself into the seat. She took in a lungful of the warm, moist air and held it for a moment before anxiously letting it out. The next leg of the journey would be the lengthiest of all: twenty-eight hours, requiring four pit stops.

CHAPTER 17

SIGNS AND WONDERS

THURSDAY, APRIL 27 (9:24 A.M. ISRAEL DAYLIGHT TIME)

KING DAVID HOTEL; JERUSALEM, ISRAEL

After enduring overnight connecting flights to Tel Aviv and a car ride this morning to Jerusalem through rush hour traffic, Lorena was now stuck in a slow-moving line at the King David Hotel waiting to be checked in.

"Lord, give me patience," she said loudly enough for the employees at the front desk to hear.

A fair-skinned, aristocratic-looking lady immediately in front of her wheeled around and shot her a sour look.

Lorena looked past her and said even more loudly, "The world is about to end, people. Let's speed it up here!"

A hotel staffer materialized at her side. A uniformed soldier with a rifle slung over his shoulder advanced toward her as well.

"Ma'am," the staffer said, "is there a problem?"

Fearing eviction, she calmed herself and sighed plaintively. "You don't have enough people on duty here. I am very tired and just want to check in."

"Yes, ma'am, we're doing our best. Please, I ask for your patience."

She watched irritably as the staffer and soldier jabbered in Hebrew, or whatever it was. Afterward they both looked at her queerly before finally withdrawing.

The soldier did not go far. He parked himself close by and kept his eye on her, which made her feel uncomfortable. Dirty somehow.

"He's probably a fornicator," she muttered. "Like Dallan."

The aristocrat spun and scowled.

Five minutes later, when Lorena's turn finally came, she stepped up to the counter and was addressed by a stylishly uniformed hotel clerk.

"Good morning ma'am, I'm very sorry for the wait. Welcome to the King David. Name, please?"

"Lorena Armen— uh, O'Malley, Lorena O'Malley. I have a reservation. I'd like a room on a high floor with a view of the Eastern Gate, the one Jesus walked through."

"Yes, ma'am, I'll do my best." The clerk looked down at her computer screen and worked the keyboard. A moment later she said, "We have you staying for a week, is that right?"

Lorena snorted. "It's not up to you or me."

"Excuse me?"

"Never mind, I'm sure you wouldn't understand. That's fine. Just check me in, please. I'm very tired; I've been travelling all night."

"Yes, ma'am, of course. Let me see what we have available." The clerk looked down and studied the screen for what seemed like an eternity. Then she looked up. "I'm sorry, Ms. O'Malley, all our rooms with a view of the Eastern Gate are occupied. But you know, there is some debate about which gate Jesus actually went through. I hear some scholars believe—"

Lorena, feeling something deep within her snap, held up her hand. "Please stop! I don't want to hear it."

"What is the trouble here?"

She wheeled. It was the military man.

"Fornicator! Fornicator!" she yelled. "Get away from me!"

A long, blurry moment later, as she was being dragged away, she told herself the prophets of old had been similarly mistreated. Emboldened by that fact, she recited Paul's prophetic words all the way out of the hotel:

> I will show wonders in heaven above
> And signs in the earth beneath:
> Blood and fire and vapor of smoke.
> The sun shall be turned into darkness,
> And the moon into blood,
> Before the coming of the great and awesome day of the Lord.

THURSDAY, APRIL 27 (5:35 P.M. ISRAEL DAYLIGHT TIME)

HADASSAH UNIVERSITY MEDICAL CENTER ER; JERUSALEM, ISRAEL

Lorena woke up in a daze, her head full of cotton. She gave the room a quick once-over.

Where am I?

It certainly wasn't the hotel. It looked like a—

Frantically, she turned to her left and then to her right and found the buzzer. A few moments later a nurse arrived, all smiles and officiousness.

"Where am I?" Lorena shouted. "What are you doing to me? I'm an American citizen, you can't do this to me!"

"Please, Mrs. O'Malley, we're only here to help."

"I said, where am I? You can't keep me prisoner."

"Please, Mrs. O'Malley, no one's keeping you prisoner. An ambulance brought you here from the King David Hotel. You passed out; we just want to make sure you're okay."

"But where am I? What is this place?"

"It's an emergency room, one of the finest in all of Jerusalem. We're affiliated with the Hadassah University Medical Center."

"I don't need a hospital. I need people to leave me alone. I need to rest, that's all."

"Yes. Well, you can speak with the doctor; I know he wants to order some tests. We've just been waiting for you to wake up."

"I don't need any tests! I know my rights. I want to get out of here. You can't stop me!"

"No, we can't. But it wouldn't be wise to check out before being evaluated. Passing out can be a symptom of something serious. Don't you want to find out?"

Lorena would have none of it.

"Well at least stay for dinner then," the nurse said. "The food here is excellent and they're just about to serve it. Then you can talk with the doctor. How does that sound?"

She stopped.

She *was* tired.

And hungry.

Lorena leaned back on the pillows. "Okay. But I'm not staying. So get the paperwork ready for me to sign out. I don't need to talk to any doctor."

The nurse, visibly frustrated, turned on her heel and stormed out. A short while later an orderly carried in her dinner and set it down on the bed table: steak and latkes.

She inhaled the meal then left the bed and walked to the window. The hospital was situated atop a large hill; the view from her room was spectacular.

She gazed out at the lighted monuments, her eyes roaming the scenery. She caught sight of the so-called Garden Tomb of Joseph of Arimathea, located in the near distance below. Some claimed Jesus was buried there but she considered it a blasphemy.

Tourist trap.

She closed her eyes. She imagined Dallan entering the room right then, exploding with joy at the sight of her—like when they first…

"Oh, my love!" she'd say, drinking in his strong, handsome face and smiling eyes. "You came! I knew you would! Come here, look!" She imagined pointing out the window. "You see those two gray domes way in the distance? The ones all lit up? Past the big gold dome. Do you see?"

He'd take her hand ever so gently, ever so tenderly. "Yes, baby, I do. I see them."

"Good, because that's where we're going."

"When?"

"Soon, *mi amor*, soon."

Staring out at the city lights below, mesmerized by their beauty, she began quietly reciting the prophetic scripture she'd committed to memory:

> And then shall appear the sign of the Son of man in heaven: and then shall all the tribes of the earth mourn, and they shall see the Son of man coming in the clouds of heaven with power and great glory.
>
> And His feet shall stand in that day upon the Mount of Olives, which is before Jerusalem on the east, and the Mount of Olives shall cleave in the midst thereof toward the east and toward the west, and there shall be a very great valley; and half of the mountain shall remove toward the north, and half of it toward the south.

"Ahem."

The small noise made her jump. Her gaze jerked toward the door and landed on a slender, fair-skinned man in a white coat. He was smiling.

"Mrs. O'Malley? I'm sorry, I didn't mean to startle you. I'm Dr. Silverstein. I understand you want to check out before letting us run some tests?"

She squared herself in his direction. "Yes, that's right. I'm just tired, that's all. It was a long trip from America and they were taking forever at the hotel—that's why I fainted. I'm feeling much better now that I've slept some and eaten."

He frowned. "Well, we can't detain you against your will. But if you insist, you'll need to sign a paper that says you're checking out against medical advice. The hospital can't be held responsible in case something happens to you."

She remained stone-faced. "Fine, I understand."

"And I will need to ask you some questions as well, before we can let you go. It's standard protocol."

CHAPTER 18

UNMASKED

From the back of the black stretch SUV Jared nervously chewed his lower lip, watching the sleek white and blue HondaJet touch down with a squeal of rubber and puff of smoke.

Can't wait to see her reaction.

After the plane rolled to a stop opposite the SUV, its front cabin door pivoted downward, becoming a staircase. A moment later Maggie appeared at the opening. As she walked down the steps, he scrutinized her face.

She's not happy.

He scrambled out of the car. "Maggie, baby!"

"Jared, this better be good or so help me..."

133

She hurried past him and dove into the back seat. Jared climbed in after her and the driver shut the door. "Maggie, c'mon. This is important." He leaned in to kiss her but was rebuffed.

The limo began moving.

"Where are we going? Why'd you bring me all the way down here?"

He hesitated before answering. He was already in San Diego on important business and decided it would be the perfect place for the very private conversation he needed to have with her.

But there was also another reason.

"I thought a change of scenery would help relax you, that's all." He spoke as tenderly as he could. "I know the past three weeks since I became CEO have been pretty intense for you."

Maggie stared daggers at him. "Jared, you have no idea what a can of worms your charity scheme has opened with your family and shareholders. Tomorrow you've been ordered to appear in court to—"

He sat back. "*Psh!* To what? Explain myself to some puppet judge? Forget it. It ain't gonna happen."

"What are you talking about, forget it? They'll arrest you for contempt of court. They'll—"

Jared reached out to calm her, but she drew back and scowled.

He sat back again. "Okay, I get that you're upset. But when you hear what I have to tell you, it'll change everything. You'll see."

The two rode in edgy silence as the limo travelled south on Cabrillo Memorial Drive toward Point Loma. Eventually, they reached the VA's vast and picturesque Fort Rosecrans Cemetery. For as far as he could see, on both sides of the road, white marble gravestones stood shoulder to shoulder in neat ranks and files like soldiers permanently at attention. It crossed his mind that many innocent people would probably have to die in order for there to be a new world order.

Phase transitions.

There's no other way.

Years ago on the Web he learned meaningful change rarely happened gradually. It first required complete destruction of the old order—like with ice. To change it into a liquid, you needed to blast the ice with heat, to destroy its rigid crystal structure.

He decided back then that in order to replace the current rigged economy—where the grasping one percent lorded over the ninety-nine percent—he needed to destroy it. Utterly destroy it.

In his mind it was also like Stanford's marching band. After arranging themselves in an orderly formation on the football field, they always broke ranks and went completely bonkers—ran around like maniacs—before settling into a different orderly formation.

The limo pulled up to the quaint-looking Old Point Loma Lighthouse.

Maggie growled. "What in the world?"

"Please, Maggie. Trust me."

Grudgingly, she followed him to a nearby dirt trail. Along the way they had an elevated view of Coronado across the inlet to the east.

"Look at that view!" he said, hoping to break the ice.

"Yeah, great," she said, hardly looking. "Let's just get this over with."

The trail led them toward the Pacific Ocean side of the point, to the apron of a large tidal pool. The surf pounding the coastline's massive, sharp-edged rocks was deafening. To the north were towering sandstone cliffs that plunged straight down to a giant boulder field and the churning sea.

Nervously, he searched around for signs of other people and saw none, just as he'd expected. He looked up. The sapphire sky was flawless—like the complexion of a child. The air was warm and still.

He gestured for Maggie to sit down on a large rock but she refused, though her body language had softened noticeably.

She looked around. "I have to say, this is really beautiful."

He cleared his throat. "Maggie, you know how much I love you, right?" His mouth was suddenly dry. "And one day..."

The quick, amorous look on her face hit him like a wet-handed slap.

Oh hell—she's expecting me to propose!

Maggie smiled and made a gentle move in his direction. She took hold of him and guided him onto the ground, all the while eyeing him lovingly. "Yes, go ahead. One day..."

"Okay," he said anxiously, "well let's start with the obvious, which is that my old man was a greedy bastard."

Maggie's face fell. "What?!"

"Hold on, hold on, please listen."

She let go of him and sat back.

"I remember my mother always saying, 'Your father is counting on you to take over one day, Jared.'" He mimicked his mother by wagging his finger in a theatrical way. "'You're the future of NeuroNet.'"

"Jared, why are you dredging this up ag—"

He stilled her with his hand. "Please, Maggie, hear me out. It's important you understand what I'm about to tell you."

She gave him a wary look. "Go ahead."

"Fat cats like my parents care more about profits than people, even more than their own families. Their greed has ruined the world. A long time ago most people made a living off the land or with their hands and had relatively equal chances of making an honest living. But now, forget it. Some hard-working farmer in Cambodia earns about a thousand dollars a year and dies when he's fifty-seven years old; while some self-absorbed wonk in Silicon Valley earns more than one hundred times that and lives nearly eighty years. How's that fair?"

"Jared—"

"You promised you'd let me finish."

Maggie shook her head and pursed her lips.

"Today, nearly half of the world's wealth belongs to the top ten percent of the population." He paused for emphasis. "But I have a plan to change that."

She folded her arms. "Yes, oh yes, how I know it well—the charities."

"No, not just that. There's more. That's why I asked you to come here, so I could tell you."

She stared at him suspiciously.

"My plan will create a level playing field again, equalize things between the haves and have-nots." He studied her for a reaction. "What do you think of that?"

"You really want to know?" She unfolded her arms. "I think you're a spoiled rich megalomaniac with too much time on his hands. Really, Jared, what you're talking about is impossible." Her voice was rising. "Communists have tried it for years and they've only made things worse. No one can—"

"Oh, yeah? Well hear me out. I've been working with a bunch of activists who plan to protest at the G-20 summit this weekend here in San Diego. I've been giving them money and coaching them. They're my secret army."

"They're your what?! What are you—?"

"Listen. I've convinced them to band together to create one monster demonstration, the biggest in history. The cops have no clue what's about to hit them."

"Jared, that's—"

"No, wait, that's not all. I—"

She sprang to her feet. "No, Jared, that *is* all—I've heard enough. You're now the CEO of one of the most powerful companies on the planet and all you want to do is throw it all away. Throw *us* away—and for what? For some twisted revenge plot against your father?! Well, I'm done. I'm outta here."

Jared leaped to his feet. "No, hold on, you can't go!" He could hardly find his voice he was so angry. "You think this is just about sticking it to my father? No, Maggie, it's not! It's what I've been waiting for my whole life. All those years in exile together—I thought you'd be proud of me. You, of all people. You know how deeply I feel about injustice and greed."

"God, Jared, yeah! But this! *I'm* against injustice but what you're doing and how you're doing it—who died and made *you* God?" She paused, as if searching for the right words, then roared, "Jared, you can't do this! It'll ruin everything!"

She rushed back to the trail.

Jared ran after her and easily caught up. He grabbed her arm and whirled her around. The horrified look on her face made him cringe.

"LET GO OF ME!" she demanded. Then she screamed, tore herself loose, and sprinted up the trail once again.

He renewed his chase—determined to make her understand, to explain the rest of his plan—and easily outran her. He grabbed her arm, pulled her close, and slapped her cheek.

"Listen, just listen!" he insisted.

She spit in his face. "You monster! I'm gonna have you locked up!" With inhuman strength, she pushed him down and doubled back toward the ocean, dashing up the rocky coast toward the sandstone cliffs. "LEAVE ME ALONE!" she screamed without looking back. "GO AWAY!"

Picking himself up, he resumed the chase. Moments later he caught up with her again and held on with a tight grip. She wrestled with him fiercely.

"LET GO OF ME, JARED! YOU'RE CRAZY! I'M CALLING THE POLICE ON—"

She tore herself loose, but just as she turned to flee, her foot slipped on a smooth rock and she fell backward. He heard the dull thud of her head slamming against a large, wet, rounded boulder. The nearby surf reared up and flung itself against the coastline, drenching them both.

Dripping wet, Jared stared wide-eyed at the glistening, prone body of his lifelong friend. A pool of blood formed beneath her head. He bent down but was afraid to touch her.

"Maggie? Are you all right? Please be all right. Talk to me, please."

But there was no answer, and a split second later he was bowled over by yet another savage breaker.

CHAPTER 19

FREEDOM REVISITED

Dallan paced the radio room floor in his felt boot liners like a caged animal. It had been days since he'd spoken with his people in Boulder.

I need to warn them.

They need to know what's happening up here.

"It's still a no-go, Dr. O'Malley. I'm sorry," the communications officer said, sad faced. "I'll keep trying."

His shoulders fell. During the previous forty-eight hours the magnetic disruption over the Arctic worsened to the point Alert was now completely cut off from the rest of the world. Airplane navigation systems, radio communications, even the Internet—all of it was being addled by the intensifying magnetic storm.

He left the radio room and headed for the dorm. He entertained thoughts of drinking himself to sleep, hoping when he awoke things would be back to normal.

"Hey there."

The voice snapped him back to reality. It was Becky.

"Oh, hey, Becky."

Over the past few days he and she had become well acquainted. He'd even told her about his filing for divorce, about wanting to put married life behind him and move on—to feel free again. She was empathetic, but so far hadn't noticeably warmed up to him.

Dallan looked at her with a gnawing hunger.

Give her time.

He felt a wave of shame.

I'm sorry, Lolo, I'm sorry—it's how I'm wired.

He swiped his hand across his eyes.

Oh, stop already.

Becky was smiling curiously at him. "You okay?"

"Yeah, yeah. Just frustrated is all. I've been trying to get through to my people with no luck."

She nodded. "I hear you. I was just heading out for some fresh air— I'm going stir-crazy in here. Want to join me?"

He quickly agreed and minutes later, after throwing on his cold-weather gear, met her outside. He glanced at the thermometer hanging next to the entrance: minus seven degrees Celsius.

Twenty-one degrees Fahrenheit.

"Wow, a heat wave," he said.

"Yeah. We should be wearing shorts."

He followed her to the snowmobiles, both of them armed with FNC1 rifles. It was regulation protection against feral animals, mainly polar bears.

Flurries were trickling down from an overcast, Dalí-esque sky.

"Where are we going?" he said, staring up nervously at the aurora glowering down at them. During the past two days, like everything else being affected by the magnetic storm, the aurora had worsened; it was vaster and more colorful than before.

"You'll see."

They mounted their snowmobiles and drove away. But before going very far they paused alongside the solitary gravesites of Canadian crew members whose Avro Lancaster crash-landed in 1950. Nine upright crosses were silhouetted by the low-lying sun.

"What a lonely way to go," he said in a small, faraway voice.

What have I done?

They pulled away and for many minutes Becky led them southward toward Crystal Mountain. Gradually, the low buildings of the ice station grew smaller and smaller along the northern horizon until they vanished completely.

The snow-splotched slate and shale terrain gave him the impression of a grayscale moonscape. The region, he learned from Brody, was drier than the Sahara Desert, which meant the air was usually as stark and clear as the lunar sky. But not today. Today it was like being inside a shaken snow globe.

When they had traveled so far across the monotone tundra nothing and no one could be seen anywhere, Becky brought her snowmobile to a stop, cut the engine, and climbed off. He did likewise.

Slowly, he turned in place, taking in the desolation, straining to hear a sound other than his own breathing. The silence was so profound, the visual field so blank, he felt both dead and alive.

Perfect freedom—is this it?

Becky's voice made him jump.

"I wanted you to see why my people call this place *Nunangata Ungata*—'Beyond the Inuit Land.' I was born in *Grise Fjord*, 725 kilometers south of here. It's as far north as the Inuit have ever settled."

He found the information interesting but didn't have the energy or desire to respond.

"Dallan, I can tell something is bothering you."

Staring into the cold, gray nothingness, he nodded. "Yah."

"It's none of my business but you're not alone. It might feel that way, I know, but even out here in the middle of nowhere, I believe God is with us."

He turned to her. "You believe in God? I didn't think your people, the Inuit—"

"Yeah, well it's complicated. Like most Inuit I grew up believing everything has a soul and everything is connected. Animism. Nature worship."

"Right. Worship the creation, not the creator."

She looked skyward then toward the distant mountain. "The first time I met a Christian I was a freshman in college. A history professor from Greenland. We became good friends and eventually I came around to his way of thinking."

He followed her gaze toward Crystal Mountain. "Why?"

"Lots of reasons. But mostly I was attracted to the idea of a single god. Inuit believe in lots of gods. Lots of everything actually. To them even a single body has lots of souls."

He looked over at her. "You're kidding."

"No. Your arm, your leg, your ear. If you get hurt, it means part of your body has lost its soul. The idea of a single god is simpler. More scientific."

"How so?"

"Occam's Razor—you know." She flung her arms out for emphasis. "Given all imaginable explanations for something, science always favors the simplest one."

"Hmm. I never thought of Christianity that way. I just grew up going to church. Took it for granted."

"So you believe in God too?"

He needed to think about how to answer. "I guess I do. I mean, I go to church, or at least used to. After I filed for divorce..."

"Yeah, I understand."

"My biggest problem with God is all the bad stuff that happens all the time—that's happened to me and the people I love."

"Tell me."

"Oh, it's a long, sad story. It doesn't matter—I'm over it now."

"We have time. I'd like to hear it."

He invited her to sit on the ground with him. The sky was getting darker, the snowfall and aurora more intense.

"I grew up in Columbus, Ohio. My dad was an electrician who drank away most of his weekly paycheck. My mom was too afraid to stand up to him when he beat me. One day he up and left us—my mom, two brothers, two sisters, and me. Just like that. I was the oldest, so I became the man of the house. I dropped out of high school to make us some money."

"But you have a PhD."

"That came later. After Mom died and my brothers and sisters were old enough to fend for themselves, I went to night school. Studied my as—studied day and night on weekends. That's how I became a scientist."

"Dallan, that's an amazing story."

"That's not all. My mom was very religious, a dyed-in-the-wool Irish Catholic. Went to mass like clockwork. Made all of us kids go with her. By the time I got my PhD, though, I had stopped going to church. Stopped believing in God. I didn't have time for either of them."

He held up a finger for emphasis. "Then I met this amazing woman: Lorena Armendariz. She blew me away, she was so beautiful. And smart. She had an economics degree from Yale. She was a preacher's kid—Pentecostal—but didn't want anything to do with God either. She grew up with all these rules—no dancing, no drinking, no short skirts, blah, blah, blah—so when she left home all she wanted to do was have fun. Make up for lost time, just like me, you know?" Dallan looked out at the mountain. "I'm telling you, we were a perfect match."

His eyes dropped. "But then, about two years ago, her older brother got to her. A real Holy Roller. Started filling her head about going back to her roots. About having a family before it was too late." He paused and looked around at the barren landscape. "At first she didn't listen. But then one day I caught her reading a Bible. We started fighting. Next thing I know she wanted to go to church and started talking about having kids. 'It's time to grow up,' she said."

"So what happened?" Becky said in a quiet voice.

"What else? I loved the woman. I started going to church with her. But I put my foot down when it came to having kids. I'd already been a father once, as a boy. I wasn't going to get saddled with that load ever again. But then she said it was either having unprotected sex or no sex at all."

Becky shook her head. "Wow."

"Yeah. And she meant it. So I gave in to her. But only once. Right afterward I could see the rest of my life being spent as a slave. I could kiss my freedom good-bye. Forever." He remained silent for a moment. "That's when I decided the marriage was over. Lorena was not the woman I married. Everything about our relationship became one-way. She was unwilling to compromise, to see things my way. That's why last week I asked my lawyer to serve her with divorce papers."

"How did she react?"

He gave Becky a defeated look. "How do you think? She freaked out. Threatened to fight me all the way. Accused me of being a womanizer and worse. It was pretty ugly."

He scrambled to his feet, his stiff muscles nearly upsetting his balance. "I told you it was a long, sad story."

Becky stayed seated.

He lifted his arms and let them fall. "And now here I am with no wife, no life, and a gutful of guilt."

He began pacing.

"Guilt?" she said.

Without stopping, he looked over at her. "Lorena was—is—a great girl. One in a million. Deep down I still know that. She doesn't deserve what I'm doing to our marriage—blowing it up because I don't want kids."

Becky stood up and came alongside him, keeping pace. She laid a gloved hand on his padded forearm. "First off, you're not a bad person for wanting to be free." She spoke in a voice so gentle he could barely hear it. "Who doesn't want to be free from people and things that make demands on us? Who doesn't want to be free from a conscience that rubs our weaknesses in our face? From a God who seems to let bad things happen?"

He spat into the air. "You've got that right."

"But what does freedom look like without all of those burdens, Dallan? It's not very pretty either. If we only do *what* we want, *when* we want, we become slaves to our own selfishness. It's not attractive and it sure isn't freedom."

Becky stopped and stomped her feet. "Oh, wow. There was a time when I could stand out in the cold for hours and not feel it. Getting old stinks."

He stopped too. "You're not old."

"Older, then. It still stinks."

Abruptly, she closed her eyes, held out her arms, and began chanting—in her native tongue, he guessed.

When she finished she looked at him. "I just said a prayer for you."

"Yeah? What did you say?"

"I'd rather show you." Her hand swept over the scenery. "Look around, Dallan. Right now everything looks bleak, right? But at this very moment, hiding here and there beneath the ice, life is starting to assert itself. By next month you won't recognize this place. There'll be wildflowers and birds and butterflies everywhere. It'll be beautiful!"

She turned her face upward and sucked in the cold air. "Our lives go through seasons too. You're in a season of desolation, I can see that—thumbing your nose at commitment, shaking your fist at God. You told me a moment ago you had a long, sad story to tell, but you were over it." She looked squarely at him now. "No, you're not, Dallan. You're still being controlled by what your father did to you and your family. You're still his slave, and will be until you can release him and truly move on. That's what it means to grow up and be free."

Becky's words struck him like a bolt of lightning. Time stopped. He felt hollow, his ears rang with the indictment.

She's right!

My old man follows me everywhere.

Even out here I'm not free.

He stroked his temples. He felt dizzy and his head hurt.

Suddenly, he was ten again, ducking as his old man threw a left hook at him. After hearing his mom scream, he sprinted up the stairs, hiding in the attic behind a fortress made of boxes filled with junk. His father was shouting, "You can't hide from me, you little sneak! C'mere and take it like a man." Dallan saw himself covering his head, his ears, his eyes. "No! Leave me alone! Leave me alone!"

"Dallan!"

He stiffened. He didn't recognize the voice.

"Dallan! Are you all right?"

Who??

He shook himself back to consciousness.

Becky had a hold of his shoulders. "Dallan! Please, are you all right? Speak to me."

"Yeah, yeah, I'm fine," he murmured, collapsing. He took a few moments to collect himself. "You should've been a preacher."

She plopped down next to him. "What?"

He didn't answer right away.

"Nothing," he said finally. "It's just that you made me realize something I never saw before."

"What is that?"

"That I'm my father's son."

Becky looked on without saying anything.

He stared at the mountain. "That's why he hated me; that's why he left us. He wanted to be free. He wanted freedom, not a family." His body shuddered; he could not contain the tears or the anger. "Oh, Becky, what a fool I've been. What a mess I've made. Me—not my father— *ME!*"

Baby, please forgive me!

Dad…forgive me.

I see now.

Becky waited for him to quiet down then said, "Dallan, life isn't a Happy Meal, that's for sure. And wanting to be free of all its problems doesn't make you a bad person. It's normal. But what I've learned is that true freedom, true joy, comes only when we make peace with our past and rise above our selfishness; when we spend our lives on others, not just on ourselves. I pray God will help you understand that even in the midst of bleakness and despair, there's always the awaiting discovery of something beautiful."

He had been listening to Becky while staring up at the heavily clouded sky. Now he lowered his gaze and saw with crystal clarity what he needed to do—even though it terrified him.

"Thanks, Becky, more than you know." He scrambled to his feet. "But we better get back now, okay?—I don't like the looks of those clouds."

★

THURSDAY, APRIL 27 (3:47 P.M. EASTERN DAYLIGHT TIME)

By the time they were halfway back to the ice station the snow flurries had evolved into a full-fledged snowstorm. Dallan, blinking constantly to keep from being blinded by the wind-driven flakes, widened his eyes when the aurora's red and green flames suddenly took on an ominous-looking, pinkish-purple hue.

"Becky!" he roared over the noise of the engines, gesturing skyward.

She glanced up, nodded, and opened the throttle all the way.

He followed suit.

Moments later—heavy snow peppering his face, wind howling in his ears—he sensed the temperature spiking. Then he gasped in disbelief at what he saw happening: the aurora appeared to be falling from the sky!

Frantically, he scanned the open terrain. But there was absolutely nowhere for them to hide.

"Dallan, look!"

He turned to see Becky pointing up at a large bird being whipped about by the blustering crosswinds. Its body was glowing with a powder-blue light!

"Keep going!" he shouted, struggling not to panic.

The ice station broke into view on the horizon. At this rate, he figured, they'd reach it inside ten minutes.

The surging air temperature was now transforming the snowy blizzard into the semblance of a howling, swirling tropical hurricane. Dallan felt as though he were suffocating; the powerful gusts were ramming his face, making it hard to breathe. The melting snowflakes pelted his exposed flesh with the stinging ferocity of a sandstorm. He could barely keep his eyes open.

He willed his snowmobile to go faster.

"*HELP!*" Becky screamed. "*Aieeee....*"

Squinting in her direction, he saw her and the snowmobile somersaulting through the multicolored air. Both landed hard on the wet ice and slid in different directions. He hit the brakes and was thrown from his seat. He landed on his stomach, which knocked the wind out of him. The heat was stifling.

"DALLAN!" she cried. "HELP!"

He made a move to go after her but just as he righted himself, he heard the air hissing. He looked up: the aurora's violet-stained hemline was coming down on his head. From his reflection in the wet, icy ground, he saw his hair begin to rise and glow blue. Saw the same thing happening to Becky across the way.

He struggled toward her on hands and knees. "Becky! Hold on! I'm coming!"

But the vicious, irresistible wind bucked his every effort to reach her.

Then he froze at the sight of what looked like a large, multihued candle flame in the near distance—speeding in their direction. In a moment he realized it was actually a towering vortex, a whirlwind of fiery air, bristling with lightning.

Jesus, Mary, and Joseph!

He stared, spellbound, as the frenzied twister zigzagged capriciously across the glistening, fantastically colored landscape, ripping open the ice like a giant zipper and roaring like a freight train. He was well aware eddies were able to form within aurorae high in the sky; he'd observed them on many occasions in space weather satellite photos. But to see one at ground level.

Oh, god! It's heading for Becky!

He screamed and clawed against the overbearing wind like a spooked horse straining at tied reins. But the hellish-looking, deafening tornado would not stop. In an instant it bore down on Becky's squirming, prone body then skipped away like a child's top, leaving no trace of her behind.

Laying prostrate in the slush, encircled by the crackling, multicolored aurora, his face thrashed by the driving rain—he wanted to rip out his insides.

"Why?!" he howled. "Why?! Why?! WHY?!"

CHAPTER 20

RUDE AWAKENING

The bell-like cabin alarm startled Allie out of a fitful sleep.

"Cádiz," Calder said in a perfect Spanish accent through her headset.

She rubbed her sore eyes.

Does he ever sleep?!

She stretched her arms and glanced outside. High in the night sky she thought she saw an odd coloration. After staring hard at it, however, she chalked it up to starlight playing tricks on her weary eyes.

"Rise and shine, girlfriend."

It was Eva hailing her on the IFB.

Allie flipped the communications switch. "What's the latest on Lorena?"

151

"Okay, here it is. I tracked down the Denver detective myself and he said they still haven't found her—"

"*Ay!*"

"No, let me finish, there's more. They have a solid lead. The detective told me, and this is an exact quote, I took it down word for word: 'We did an expedited search of the area right after the initial call and came up empty. But then we discovered she boarded a plane. Her final destination is Tel Aviv. We've—'"

"Tel Aviv?!"

"Hold on, hold on, I'm not finished. He said, 'We've alerted Interpol and the Israeli authorities and they told us Mrs. O'Malley had reservations at the King David Hotel in Jerusalem.'"

"Oh, thank God. But why Israel?"

But even as she said it, she knew. Like herself, when Lolo went off to college she turned her back on everything she'd grown up with: family, friends, faith—but more egregiously than Allie. She became a real hell-raiser; and when Dallan came along, it didn't help. They were birds of a feather.

About a year back, though, Lolo started changing—growing up, everyone said, *finally*. She wanted to settle down and have kids. She even started reading a Bible Carlos gave her. She called Allie with all kinds of questions about the End Times, especially the Second Coming. She was fascinated by the prediction that when the end came, Jesus would descend upon the Mount of Olives—which was in Israel.

"Never mind," Allie said. "What else did he say? Are they going to the hotel?"

"They were planning to, but he said the hotel reported some sort of incident involving your sister. She was taken to an ER; they're trying to find out where."

What?!

"Is she okay?! What happened?"

"That's just it, we don't know. Israeli authorities literally just found this out and the Denver detective is waiting for an update."

Allie took a deep breath to calm herself. "What will the police do when they find her?"

"The detective said they'll order her to return to Colorado."

"*Ay, yai, yai!* Call me the moment they make contact. I wanna talk to her before they do anything; she'll listen to me. And look into flights from Cádiz to Jerusalem, just in case. Under no circumstances is she to get on a plane before talking with me, understand?"

"Sure, no problem. I'll get on it. There's other news too. Not about Lorena—other stuff."

She wasn't interested; her mind was entirely on Lolo.

"You there?"

"Yeah, yeah, go ahead, what?"

"First of all, the bad news."

Allie shut her eyes and shook her head.

Like everything so far hasn't been bad news!

"The stranding in San Diego has started up again, worse than before. And it looks like the same thing's happening in Australia. You already know about Spain and Canada—both strandings are getting worse. The same in Japan."

Allie's heart sank but she said nothing.

"And our wunderkind friend, Jared Kilroy, has gone missing. The police are looking for him."

"He's been kidnapped?!"

"No, I mean they're *after him*."

"Why? What do you mean?"

"That woman we met at NeuroNet who I didn't like? Kilroy's PR person, Maggie Henderson? She was found dead near the old lighthouse on Point Loma. Fatal head injury, they're saying."

Allie inhaled sharply and her hand flew to her mouth. "Oh, my g—!" Then something clicked. "Oh, no. Don't tell me they think Jared did it!"

"They're not sure, but right now he's suspect *numero uno*. Cannatella tells me the problem with Kilroy is he's one big fat unknown. Nobody knows anything about him, not even his own mother—who, by the way, has been on TV defending him, even though she's still furious about his nonprofit idea." Eva paused. "Speaking of which, because of all the publicity about the murder and Kilroy's disappearance, the Quantum PCs are flying off the shelves faster than ever. The whole thing is totally weird."

Allie felt *Hero* slowing down. She gazed out the windshield. City lights were coming into view.

Something is missing …

A moment later it hit her.

No helicopters.

"Hello, Allie, you still there?"

"Yeah, yeah. Look, stay on top of the Kilroy story and check on those flights to Jerusalem. I need to get going here, we're pulling into port."

"No, wait, one more thing. The Spanish government's not going to let you wangle any whales."

"Wrangle," Allie said wearily. "Calder's *wrangling* whales."

"Whatever. But it's not what you think. They've had a problem with speedboats trying to do what you're doing and people have been injured. One teenager was killed today. So they're clamping down: no more herding whales. But they're thrilled to have you. They've got a whole welcoming thing planned for you tomorrow morning. Nothing tonight, so you can go right to the hotel. A driver is waiting for you at the dock."

THURSDAY, APRIL 27 (8:37 P.M. PACIFIC DAYLIGHT TIME)

POINT LOMA PENINSULA; SAN DIEGO, CALIFORNIA

Jared continued his escape up the four-mile-long Point Loma peninsula, but darkness was slowing him down. Since morning he'd been alternately laying low and stealthily picking his way through the rocky, brushy, hilly terrain of the U.S. Park Service's Cabrillo National Monument and the Point Loma Ecological Reserve.

He paused under a clear, starlit night and cursed himself for losing his cool. For inadvertently destroying the one person in the universe whose company he'd always sought and treasured.

He hung his head, his arms falling limply at his sides.

She's gone.

Forever.

In his mind's eye he saw Maggie's terrible, unexpected reaction to his plan, which she hadn't even let him fully explain. Her hysterics. Her threatening to expose him, to have him committed. If only she hadn't wrestled with him. If only she hadn't lost her footing on the wet rocks and smashed her head against them.

She would still be alive.

Oh, Maggie, Maggie.

Please don't be mad at me.

He froze and listened.

A dog.

No—dogs.

He broke into a run, pushing recklessly through the thick underbrush. A branch slapped him in the face.

Right after Maggie's fatal fall his first instinct was to book it to his La Jolla beach house. Now he wasn't so sure. It was likely the police would be watching it. Would be staking out all his houses, in fact. And NeuroNet too.

An idea flashed into his head. Stopping, he whipped out his smartphone.

A few minutes later, the task accomplished, he angled to the right and redoubled his speed.

★

FRIDAY, APRIL 28 (7:05 A.M. CENTRAL EUROPEAN SUMMER TIME)

PORT OF CÁDIZ, SPAIN

"Mother Yolanda!" Calder cried out when she was presented to him by the city's *alcalde*. "Oh, my goodness! What a surprise!" He embraced the diminutive, ancient-looking nun with care, fearful of breaking her.

He held her for a long while, barely conscious of being surrounded by city officials, reporters, and TV cameras.

"*Mijo*," the old woman said, following the hug.

Calder felt himself choke up. No one had called him "my son" in ages.

She said, a song in her voice, "*Que bueno a verlo, mijito, hasta tantos años. Es un milagro. Gracias a Dios!*"

Calder's Spanish was still plenty good enough for him to know exactly what she'd just said: "How very good to see you, my little son, after so many years. It's a miracle. Thanks be to God!"

His spirits flagged when he listened to the Reverend Mother explain her reason for tracking him down.

"Oh, Little Mother..." His voice failed him. He could not—would not—tell her the truth: despite his remarkable invention, despite the effusive publicity he was receiving, he was hardly more than a pauper. He had no money in the bank and in fact was deeply in debt, having mortgaged everything he owned to subsidize his expensive dream. He expected to reap financial benefits from the success of this trip, but right now he dared not offer this saint any false hopes.

Staring into her still bright eyes, he sought desperately to find the right words. But before he could speak, the light in her happy expression dimmed noticeably. At first he read it as disappointment but quickly decided it was something else.

It's something—beatific.

With a weathered hand the nun gently stroked his cheek, as a mother would when soothing a distraught child. Her touch was electric and left his senses reeling; made it difficult for him to pay attention to her words.

"Do you remember what we always told you, my son?"

He shook his head.

"We said: 'God has singled you out for a very special purpose in life.' The sisters and I sensed it, prophesied it the moment you were delivered into our care on Christmas morning, swaddled in a purple woolen blanket."

As he listened, painful, happy recollections long since shelved and forgotten tumbled forth, nearly knocking him off his feet.

"You had a quick mind and an easy smile," she continued. "We all loved you and were heartsick when you left us, although we were happy for you."

He remembered the day he said good-bye to the sisters—to God as well, as it turned out. His forever parents were not religious and soon he found himself adopting their secular worldview. Science quickly became his chief preoccupation, his reason for living, replacing the Christian faith Mother Yolanda and the sisters brought him up to love.

The stooped nun continued, her eyes glistening with evident joy, "And now I am happy, my son, because I see you are indeed doing God's will. It's the best gift you could've given to us." She patted his arm lovingly. "Do not worry about us. We are in very good hands."

He loathed departing from this precious woman without saying something positive. Something meaningful, profound even. But what?

"Little Mother, please pray for me." He froze. He had no idea why he'd said that. It just spilled from his mouth.

"Of course, my son." Her tanned, leathery face was beaming, rosy with the morning rays of the warm Andalusian sun. "I will consider it a privilege to pray for you."

She walked with him toward *Hero*. "Thank you for seeing me today. I know you are a very busy man."

Just before climbing into the ship he gave the angelic little woman one last hug.

A moment later, when they disengaged, she was beaming. Leveling her wizened eyes at him, she said quietly, tenderly, "And remember, *mijo*, whenever any of us fails to get what we want or expect, it does not mean God is indifferent. Almost always He allows us to experience loss and failure so ultimately we can succeed in fulfilling His great purpose for our lives. Something bigger than ourselves and our own human desires."

FRIDAY, APRIL 28 (8:15 A.M. CENTRAL EUROPEAN SUMMER TIME)

Allie watched the old nun waving at them as *Hero* slowly backed away from the port of Cádiz. Her mind was still brooding over the newsflash Eva gave her earlier that morning about Lolo. The police found the ER, but her baby sis had checked out. No one knew where she was.

Allie's impulse was to abandon the rescue mission and fly immediately to Jerusalem. But once again Eva talked her out of it. "Carlos is ready to fly to Jerusalem, if need be," she argued. "But right now, he says, there's no point—not until the police find her. And anyway, think about it: if she checked herself out of the hospital, that's some kind of good news, right? It means she's not hurt or anything."

Eva was probably right.

Still …

But then there's Calder.

I can't just abandon him.

She rousted herself back to the moment. She felt *Hero* gaining speed; they were heading out to open water once more.

"You looked really surprised when you saw Mother Yolanda," she said.

"That's because I was. Jeez, I haven't seen her in forever."

"Were you happy to see her? You seemed a bit upset at the end."

"Oh, no. I was happy to see her all right. It's just that—it's okay, never mind. I was definitely happy to see her. Just sad I had to say goodbye. She's so old. Who knows…"

He's hiding something.

A moment later he said, "Good news about the whale stranding, huh?"

At the morning's event Cádiz officials informed them the animals had stopped beaching themselves overnight, all on their own.

"Just like in Darwin," he said.

She swallowed hard. "Calder, there's something I haven't told you."

"Yeah?"

"Last night Eva told me the San Diego and Australia strandings have started up again. No one knows why. I was going to tell you right away. But we were both so tired and I didn't want you to be discouraged."

Silence.

At last he said in a sullen voice, "Great, thanks for being so considerate."

She sensed something was gnawing at him and not just the bad news about the whales. She'd seen it in his face back at the port. The old nun unnerved him somehow.

"Calder, if I'm not being too personal, may I ask you a question?"

"Allie..." There was an edge to his voice.

"Never mind."

She settled into her seat but couldn't relax. She tried distracting herself with the passing scenery; but she had long since grown tired of seeing only water. Finally, she broke open the book she packed for the journey: *Can A Smart Person Believe in God?*

After what seemed like a long while Calder's voice broke the strained hush.

"Allie, I'm sorry."

She set down the book and glanced at the chronometer. It had been a full two hours since they last spoke to one another. A record.

"No, Calder, really, I'm the one who's sorry. I talk too much. It comes from being alone so much of the time."

"You? Alone?"

"Yeah. Everyone assumes that because I'm on TV I have this glamorous life. That when I'm not trotting all over the world doing my reports I'm at parties hanging out with Brad Pitt and the gang. Truth is, when I'm on the road—which is a lot—my workdays always lead to an empty hotel room. That's the reality of my life. So I guess being here with you in this tiny cabin...Well, I can't help but talk." She stopped herself. "Like I'm doing right now. *Ay, caramba*, I'm so sorry."

She heard Calder chuckle.

"Calder, may I—?"

"Go ahead, ask."

"Well, it's just that I'm wondering. I overheard you ask the old nun to pray for you. Why? Was it a specific request? Or a generic request?—which is how it sounded to me."

Calder didn't answer right away.

"You don't need to tell me if it's too personal. Like I said—"

"Allie! Stop, *por favor*, give me a chance."

She forced herself to be quiet.

What's going on with you, girl?

But she knew.

For the first time since Phil, since committing the biggest blunder of her life, she was actually feeling a glimmer of hope.

Oh, stop.

Stop deluding yourself with wishful thinking.

That scientific study she once read—about the long odds of finding true love a second time. She called it to mind once more.

Face it, mija, lightning doesn't strike twice.

★

Her question was so completely out of line that Calder's impulse was to shut her down. But he didn't and knew why: he was falling in love with this bright, beautiful, nosey reporter.

"Truth is, Allie, I have no idea why I asked Mother Yolanda to pray for me. The words just came out of my mouth. The craziest thing is that I don't even believe in prayer. Or God."

"You don't?"

"No. And you?"

"Yes—although I didn't always."

He thought back to his adoptive parents. They eschewed religion, ridiculed it, actually, and called it a superstition. At first he wasn't so sure, given his earnest belief that God existed and was punishing him for some reason. But then it occurred to him that maybe he was, in fact, being superstitious; perhaps his misfortune was just bad luck. It didn't improve his outlook on life any. But it did remove the guilt he'd felt for so many years.

"When I was in grad school," Allie continued, "I learned about black holes, multiple universes, dark energy, singularities, the big bang—you know the drill. My professors believed in them, asked us to believe in them too, even though none of them is directly observable and probably never will be. Their supposed existence is based entirely on a certain way science connects the dots, on particular interpretations it gives to circumstantial evidence."

She stopped.

"Yeah, and?" he said.

"Well, after a while it hit me. For a lot of my colleagues science is a religion. Their entire reality is logical-materialism. Their Bible is the laws of nature. Their god is the human mind, which is only too happy to deify itself."

He was tempted to debate with her but his reunion with Mother Yolanda made him realize he'd never really given serious thought to religion—not as a grown-up anyway. "So, you believe in God but not in science, is that what it boils down to?"

"What?! Of course I believe in science. It makes life easier in some ways and increases our understanding of the universe—*and* its Creator. That's natural theology."

"What is?"

"The belief that God reveals Himself not just in the Bible but in the study of nature as well."

"And you believe that?"

"Yes. It's one of the main reasons I love science."

"But Allie, help me out here. You claim to love science, yet in your TV special you're gonna say it's doing us in. I—"

"Yes, but you need to remember that for Christians the end of this life isn't the end of the story—it's only the beginning. For us, science isn't just a worthwhile discipline. It doesn't just give us the ability to explore God's creation or His nature. It also gives us the ability to destroy the world as we know it. In all those ways science is a key part of God's plan. That's the ultimate message of my TV special."

"Whoa!" he said, his thoughts in utter turmoil. "Allie, I can handle quantum mechanics and even life's craziness, like being orphaned or my wife being killed in some random way. But not the idea of a God who has some special, far-out purpose for the world or my life. From my experience that purpose can only spell trouble for me."

"So you prefer to think of it all as bad luck? Calder, that isn't very—"

"Allie, enough, please. Thanks for answering my questions and being so honest. To be continued, okay?"

As they turned northward toward the Arctic Circle for their final task Calder marveled at how well *Hero* was performing. After her disastrous public debut last weekend it was a wonder she hadn't malfunctioned, not even a little bit.

Maybe my luck is changing.

Or maybe there is a God after all.

He ruminated on the spiritual disinheritance he'd suffered since saying good-bye to Mother Yolanda and the sisters so many years ago. His thoughts led to a disturbing image of the yawning chasm clearly separating him from this woman he was beginning to love.

Little Mother, please pray for me.

There it was again, that inexplicable impulse!

He couldn't stop himself.

Little Mother, please pray for m—for us.

★

FRIDAY, APRIL 28 (12:30 A.M. PACIFIC DAYLIGHT TIME)

POINT LOMA PENINSULA; SAN DIEGO, CALIFORNIA

He paused to catch his breath. "Atta boy!" he said to himself.

Jared was standing on the outskirts of the Navy's sprawling Point Loma military complex. He took out his cell phone. According to its GPS and the map of the base from the Navy's website, he'd broken through the southern boundary and was within eyeshot of the Submarine Learning Center.

Fighting off gory images of Maggie's bloodied body lying twisted on the rocks, he looked back over his shoulder at the brooding darkness that was the nature reserve he'd just traversed.

Get a grip!

It's all about the revolution now.

It's gotta happen.

Turning to face the base again, he peered hard in the direction of the learning center. At this late hour it looked deserted.

Perfect!

CHAPTER 21

SHEER MADNESS

*H*ero was fast approaching the southern tip of Greenland, the halfway point of their journey to the Arctic. The cabin resounded with Eva's staticky voice hailing them.

"*Sí, chica*," Allie replied instantly, "you're on speaker. What's up? What've you got for me?"

"Nothing new about your sister, sorry. I'm calling because we've been trying to get through to the ice station in Alert. It's the only inhabited place close to the stranding site; but no one's answering our calls. The Space Weather Prediction Center is reporting a major magnetic storm all over the Arctic. Stu's worried—we all are—about what you guys might be getting into."

"Are you saying we should turn back?"

A hissing, crackling silence followed. Then Eva's voice resumed. "Calder, what do you think? Is *Hero* equipped to handle a magnetic storm?"

"Well—it's a good question."

Allie wasn't reassured by Calder's equivocation.

She was certain he knew magnetic storms produced aurorae in the thermosphere, sixty miles above the surface and higher, which posed no physical threat to *Hero*. But the ship's delicate electronics systems were another thing entirely.

"Calder," she said, "what about *Hero*'s collision avoidance system?"

She didn't want to face another situation like what happened in San Diego last weekend, when a failure of the collision avoidance system almost got them killed.

"If I hadn't installed the new chip," Calder answered, "I'd say there would be something to worry about. But now she's got backups to her backups—I'd say we're good to go."

★

FRIDAY, APRIL 28 (7:46 A.M. EASTERN DAYLIGHT TIME)

DAVIS STRAIT; NORTHWEST TERRITORIES, CANADA

Allie, listening to Eva on the IFB, kept looking up. Multiple aurorae were painting the heavily overcast sky in an unnatural, menacing way.

"Ten seconds!" Eva said. "I just hope he knows what he's doing."

Allie was thinking the same thing but chose not to admit it. "Of course he does. Have a little faith, *chica*."

"Yeah, right. Three...two...one. You're on, girlfriend."

Allie greeted viewers with far more brightness than she was feeling. "Dr. Sinclair tells me we're less than thirty minutes from our destination—the northernmost beachhead of Ellesmere Island. Right now we're cruising through Davis Strait toward Baffin Bay at roughly 500 knots.

Greenland is on our right while the Northwest Territories are on our left. What you probably can't see—hold on."

She yanked a lipstick camera from the bulkhead and aimed it skyward. "The Arctic is being hit by a magnetic storm and as you can see it's creating all kinds of aurorae. Usually you see these only at night. Seeing them in broad daylight is a rare treat."

She halted, realizing she'd almost said, "rare *threat*."

★

FRIDAY, APRIL 28 (8:09 A.M. EASTERN DAYLIGHT TIME)

BAFFIN BAY; ELLESMERE ISLAND, CANADA

Hero's deep-throated horn yanked Calder's attention away from the ugly-looking sky.

"Isn't that the collision alarm?" Allie cried out.

"Hold on, Allie!"

For the next few moments he wrestled with a situation he didn't entirely understand. Then he spotted the problem and instantly activated the emergency brake.

"Allie!" His heart was banging against his rib cage. "Hang on!"

She screamed.

Hero shuddered to a halt.

He blinked hard at the phantasmagoric sight. All around them the surface of Baffin Bay was being ripped to shreds by the manic struggles of hundreds upon hundreds of whales, climbing over one another to gain the nearby beach.

Good god!

An instant later his eyes swept skyward. Something about the hideous-looking colored lights was changing. Seconds later he realized what it was: the aurorae were dissipating.

He swiped at his eyes to make certain he wasn't hallucinating.

This just keeps getting weirder and weirder.

"Are you seeing this?" Allie said.

He dipped his head apprehensively. "Oh, yeah." Then his gaze lowered.

The churning tangle of whales was unraveling, the surface of the water settling down. Moments later, with the complete departure of the aurorae, the maniacal behavior stopped altogether and the animals began to disperse, like football fans after a game.

At length the coastal waters were calm and clear enough for him to reignite *Hero*'s Q-thruster. He decided it was time for a pit stop. Time to figure out what the devil was going on and what their next move should be.

"I'm going in for a surf landing," he said. "You up for some fresh air?"

★

FRIDAY, APRIL 28 (3:11 P.M. ISRAEL DAYLIGHT TIME)

JERUSALEM, ISRAEL

Lorena, sporting a contented smile, crossed the street onto Mordehai A'liash. The weather was skin-temperature warm with a slight breeze—*yet another perfect blessing from God*, she exulted.

The previous evening, when the ER doctor peppered her with questions—designed, she knew, to figure out if she posed a danger to herself or others—she felt the Holy Spirit's help in answering them perfectly. Then after her departure from the hospital, the Lord guided her to a small, clean hotel well away from the King David, where she was able to get a delicious, undisturbed night's sleep.

Now, her pulse quickened. After hours of walking across town she was within eyeshot of her first destination: a warehouse on the outskirts of northern Jerusalem. As she neared the main entrance, she read with great excitement the large, hand-lettered sign: **Temple Mount and Land of Israel Faithful Movement.**

For the past year she'd been sending in donations to support the movement's goal of taking back the Temple Mount from the Arabs and building on it the long-prophesied Third Temple. According to the conventional interpretation of Scripture, reconstructing the Temple was a prerequisite for Jesus's second coming. She herself believed Jesus's return would *precede* the new Temple, but either way she was all for what the movement was doing.

Stepping through the entrance, she saw several brawny men with ropes and wenches struggling to load a massive marble block draped with an Israeli flag onto a flatbed truck. No doubt it was what she'd read about on the movement's website: one of the five-ton cornerstones hewn from a local quarry and destined for the rebuilding of the Temple.

During the week to come, on *Yom Yerushalayim*—the annual national holiday commemorating Israel's capture of Old Jerusalem during the Six Day War—the movement's supporters would march from Ammunition Hill to the sacred Mount, where they'd attempt to lay the cornerstones. Each year since 1989 they were prevented from doing so because Jerusalem police feared violence from Muslims, whose own religious shrines currently occupied the Mount. But Lorena was praying this year would be different.

A bespectacled, elderly man supervising the effort looked in her direction. "Mrs. O'Malley, is that you? Oh, my goodness, *shalom! Shalom!*"

Asher Hershkovitz, head of the Temple Movement, looked exactly as he did in online photos: a rangy Alan Dershowitz whose curly, grey hair was topped with a black embroidered kippah. She'd phoned him earlier, telling him of her visit and describing her appearance.

He rushed to her with widespread arms. "Welcome! *Welcome!*"

"Asher, my brother. How wonderful to finally meet you!" She embraced his tough, slender body and kissed both sides of his taut, grizzled face.

"My feelings exactly. You've been so generous to our cause and now I get to thank you in person." He looked around. "And Dr. O'Malley? Is he here too?"

She brushed back some stray hairs. "No, I'm afraid he's too busy. Always working, you know. But he sends his greetings."

"Come, let me show you the cornerstones! We have three of them now, thanks be to God—and to loyal friends like yourself."

A moment later they came alongside two massive stones sitting on the ground—the third stone already on the truck. Each marble block, she knew, was anointed by orthodox rabbis.

"May I touch?"

"Of course, of course."

Feeling great reverence, she ran her fingers gently across the rough-hewn surface.

"As you know, we're getting ready for next week's march," Asher said. "This year, I just feel it. *This year,* nearly two thousand years after the destruction of the Second Temple, the prophecies of Isaiah and Micah finally will be realized and the way cleared for the Messiah." He took her hand and kissed it. "You being here is a good sign."

She did not challenge Asher's belief in the conventional order of events—Temple, then Messiah. It was not the right time, nor would it be appropriate. She believed deeply in Asher's cause, admired him as a man. He was a war hero who witnessed Israeli soldiers reclaiming the Holy Land in 1967; who felt betrayed, like many others, when then Defense Minister Moshe Dayan immediately returned religious control of the thirty-five-acre Temple Mount to Jordan and endorsed Muslim laws preventing Jews from even praying there.

"Where are you staying?" Asher asked. But before she could answer he waved his hands. "Never mind, never mind, it doesn't matter. You must stay with Myra and me. She would be devastated if you didn't."

CHAPTER 22

MAGNETIC THERAPY

FRIDAY, APRIL 28 (8:15 A.M. EASTERN DAYLIGHT TIME)

NUNAVUT, CANADA

As she and Calder climbed out of *Hero*, Allie looked up and down the deserted beach. "It's so strange."

"What?"

"The whales. One minute they're careening for the beach, next minute—poof!—they're all gone. It's weird."

Calder was hammering a metal stake into the gravelly beach, to which he would tie *Hero*'s mooring rope. "That's what I wanted to talk about before planning our next move. The whole thing's got me stumped."

She stared out at the steel-colored water. "And it's not the first time, if you think about it."

"What do you mean? I've never seen anything like this before."

"It's the first time we've seen it with our own eyes, yes. But think back to what happened in Darwin and Cádiz. The strandings stopped spontaneously *while we were there*—we didn't have to do any wrangling. In fact the only time we've had to was in San Diego, when we started out." She looked at him. "Don't you think that's odd?"

Both remained silent—Calder securing *Hero*, she staring out at the gray horizon.

The air was calm but frigid. She hugged herself and stomped her feet; they weren't properly dressed for arctic temperatures. She scanned the shoreline once again for the slightest clue. Her mind began to wander.

Dallan's up here in the Arctic somewhere. Or was.

Does he know about Lolo?

Does he care?

How do people stand living in this kind of isolation?

It's beautiful, but …

"After rats, humans are the most adaptable creatures on the planet," she said finally. "Did you know that?"

Calder chuckled. "That's so totally random." Then he added, "How do you know all this stuff?"

"It's my job."

"Speaking of adaptability, I remember hearing about the rats in Chernobyl. They're supposedly bigger and fatter now than before the reactor accident. They love the radiation. It's incredible."

"It's true—I've reported on it." She kicked at some loose, gray rocks. "So what do you wanna do?"

Part of her wanted to beat it back to San Diego; the G-20 leaders would be arriving tomorrow. But during the past several days her body had taken a major beating from the long hours of confinement, fitful rest, and severe jet lag—not to mention the unending updates she needed to broadcast. She bridled at the thought of climbing back into *Hero* right away and toughing it out another thirteen hours with maybe only one pit stop.

Besides, this bizarre mission, which was getting stranger by the minute, had become an even bigger story than the G-20. According to Eva the ratings worldwide were through the roof and still climbing.

"The ice station Eva told us about is not far from here," she said, making up her mind. "About a half-hour walk. I wouldn't mind stretching my legs and getting to someplace warm."

Calder readily agreed and they set off.

The stony ground was covered with snowy patches. Twenty minutes into the hike it began turning icy, which made for treacherous footing.

"What the—?!" she said, stopping and pointing. "Calder, look at that!"

Just ahead of them was an icy field strewn with what appeared to be singed corpses of some sort.

"They look like foxes—wolves—birds too—what's left of them. *Ugh!*"

Calder had kept walking and was closer to the ghastly scene. "Good god, what could've caused this?" he called out. "It's like the place was torched."

She caught up with him. "Look there!" She was gesturing to the tops of buildings in the far distance. "I don't know about you, but I'm running the rest of the way. This place gives me the creeps."

Less than ten minutes later they arrived, short of breath, at a boxy gold and red structure; it might've been an oversized outhouse. Stepping inside, they were greeted with looks of astonishment from the three people inside.

"Hello!" exclaimed a young man in military uniform, dropping what he was doing. "Who are you? Where in the world did you come from?"

After they explained things, trying to catch their breaths in the process, the man visibly relaxed, although not entirely. She wondered what his first impression of them must have been. Spies? Terrorists? After all, per Eva, this place was a military watchdog installation.

The young officer offered them a hot beverage—a polite way, she thought, of making certain they stayed put. "I need to get Major Brody," he said anxiously, making a quick exit.

When the major arrived and was fully briefed he shook his head in wonderment. "We've been out of touch with the world for the better part of the week, so you can understand how surprised we are to see you. It's surreal, actually."

"We totally understand," she said. "We didn't mean to scare you."

"No, no, please." The major's countenance turned serious. "But tell me: you must've seen what just happened, eh?"

She jumped on the question. "Yes, we were going to ask about that. What happened to all those animals out there? It's like they were incinerated."

"That isn't what I meant. I was talking about the sudden disappearance of the magnetic storm."

"The aurora?" Calder said. "Oh, yeah, we saw it all right. We were out on the water and all of a sudden the skies cleared."

"And the whales, too," she said. "One minute they're all over each other trying to beach themselves and then the next moment"—she snapped her fingers—"they're heading back out to sea. It's like someone flipped a switch or blew a whistle or something."

"That's how it was here as well—with the magnetic field, I mean," Brody said. "It started last Friday. The magnetic field above the Arctic began fluttering then actually disappearing, bit by bit. We have no idea why. Yesterday it vanished completely, left a magnetic hole a thousand miles across. But now, suddenly, the polar field is back to normal. It's the most amazing thing I've ever seen."

Allie was feeling positively warm. "You had a *hole* in the magnetic field?"

The major nodded. "A huge one and now, nothing."

Her mind was busy connecting the dots. "So that explains the daytime aurorae. The amount of radiation flooding through the hole must've been *huge* to create that much light. But the stranding." Then it struck her. "Wait a minute. Was it caused...?"

"Yes," Brody said. "We think the magnetic disruption is behind the stranding. A visiting biologist here was the first to explain it to us. Whales depend on the magnetic field to navigate; they use it like we use a magnetic compass."

Her mind was in overdrive. "But then, what about all the other strandings? Does it mean—?"

"Hold on." Major Brody held up a hand. "What other strandings?"

★

FRIDAY, APRIL 28 (8:57 A.M. EASTERN DAYLIGHT TIME)

CANADIAN FORCES STATION ALERT; NUNAVUT, CANADA

The major was surprised to hear strandings were happening in four other places throughout the world. "As I said," he explained, "we've been cut off for the past several days." Immediately, he led Calder and her to a large room at the back of the red and gold building.

"This is our magnetograph," he said, pointing to a piece of equipment, the likes of which Allie recognized. "We use it to monitor the magnetic field above the Arctic, twenty-four-seven." He walked them over to a metal table atop which was a long strip of paper. "Here's the first thing I want to show you: this is the printout of what just happened to the field, right when you guys arrived. Look here." He traced the jagged line graph with his finger. "Here, as you can see, the field has virtually disappeared—then suddenly—right here—it comes back to life. Like Lazarus in the Bible."

Her thoughts were racing, stumbling over one another.

Could it be?

But it's impossible!

"Let me show you something else, just as puzzling." He led them to a nearby computer monitor and hit some keys. "Our Internet just came back, so I can show you this. It's a false-color image of Earth's entire magnetosphere, not just the polar region." He zoomed in on the image. "You see those red smudges?"

To her they looked like a face full of red sores. "What are they?" But then she took note of their locations.

Sweet lord!

"They're magnetic holes in the making," the major said. "And they coincide perfectly with the coordinates of the strandings you just told me about. They're small now, only a few miles across, but—"

"Wait. What are you saying?" Calder said.

"That the world is in trouble," she interjected, "serious trouble."

Calder turned from her to the officer. "Major?"

"She's right. If the field keeps thinning out over those locations, they'll experience the same things we have."

She locked eyes with Brody. "And not just beached whales, right? You never answered my question, major. What happened to those animals out there?"

★

FRIDAY, APRIL 28 (9:21 A.M. EASTERN DAYLIGHT TIME)

"Please, have a seat," Brody said, gesturing to the room's well-worn furniture. "We can talk more comfortably in here."

Before answering her question about the singed animal corpses, he'd hustled them out of the red and gold structure, across the station grounds, to the main building, and into his cluttered office.

"Yesterday a terrible thing happened here," he began, settling into a rickety wooden swivel chair behind his desk. "We're still trying to figure it out; but we lost one person—the biologist I mentioned to you earlier, Dr. Becky. Another scientist was hurt, a visitor from the States."

A wave of chills coursed through her body. "What's his name?"

"Dr. O'Malley—Dallan O'Malley."

She leapt from her armchair. "Oh, my gosh! I know him! He's my brother-in-law."

The major looked dumbly at her.

"He's married to my sister. Where is he? Is he all right?"

She was surprised by how genuinely she cared to know, given her current resentment of him.

"Well he went through a lot, I can tell you that," Brody said, still looking dumbstruck. "But he'll survive. I can arrange for you to see him."

"Yes, that'd be great, thank you."

Brody hesitated. "Do you want to do that now? Or do you want to hear what happened to him first? And the animals, too?"

She resumed her seat. "No, please go ahead."

"Yes, please," Calder agreed, looking every bit as astonished by the coincidence as the major.

"Well, as I said, we're still debriefing Dr. O'Malley, still trying to piece together exactly what happened. But from what he tells us, yesterday in the late afternoon, at the nadir of the magnetic crisis—right when the field totally disappeared—we believe unfiltered solar radiation poured through the hole with so much power it made it all the way down to the ground. I imagine it must've been something like a bomb, a dirty bomb, maybe."

She noticed Calder shift uncomfortably in his seat and began twisting her hair.

It's awful.

He's thinking of Nell.

"And that's what happened to the animals out on the ice?" she said, still eying Calder.

"Yes, we think so, poor creatures. The only mercy is it probably happened in the wink of an eye."

She turned to the major. "What about Dallan? Was he burned too?"

"That's the miraculous part. He said it looked like a giant, fiery twister and acted like a tornado. When a tornado barrels through a town, its destruction can be selective—one house could be blown to smithereens while the one next to it could be left untouched. When the twister made landfall it got Dr. Becky but not him."

The room fell silent for a long moment.

Allie, still worrying her hair, finally said, "Can I see him now?"

"Of course." Brody stood up. "Oh, my gosh, he's going to be surprised."

★

FRIDAY, APRIL 28 (9:41 A.M. EASTERN DAYLIGHT TIME)

"Here it is." Brody gestured to Dallan's room.

She turned to Calder. "You sure you don't want to meet him?"

"No, you go ahead."

The major cracked open the door and poked his head inside. "Someone here to see you." Then he backed away and let her go in alone.

"Allie?!"

Dallan, lying in bed under khaki-colored sheets looked as shocked as if he'd seen a ghost. His forehead and right hand were swathed in white bandages.

She swallowed hard.

Be nice.

"Hey, Bro. Surprise!"

"Yeah, but how—where—??"

She walked to his bedside and quickly filled him in on how they got there. She refrained from mentioning anything about Lorena.

He whistled. "That's unbelievable. This has to be the craziest thing you've ever done—and you've done some pretty crazy things."

"Yeah, well—can I sit down?"

"Of course, please. I still can't believe you're real."

She took the only seat in the room. "I've got some other stuff to tell you, but first, tell me about *you*. I hear you survived a killer tornado of some sort? Are you okay? You look pale, but honestly I was expecting way worse, given what the major told us."

"Just bruises and some minor burns is all; nothing serious." His expression turned dark. "My friend wasn't so lucky. It was horrible. That's the worst part; I can't get the images out of my head." He shook his head quickly as if to rid himself of the memories. "Anyway, I'll be fine. I just heard about the storm—that it's gone. I'm arranging to fly back to Boulder. I've been away for a week. They probably think I'm dead."

Allie, straightening in the chair, cleared her throat. "Dallan, I'm afraid I've got some bad news."

Minutes later, after bringing him up to speed on Lorena, she stood. "I hate to lay it all on you like this, but since you've been cut off for—"

He waved his hands. "No, no, you had to. But, please—just give me a few moments to digest everything, okay? Wow." He made an effort to prop himself up on the pillows.

She watched, wavered—

Be Christian.

She helped him sit up.

"Thanks."

"Of course."

She sauntered to the window. Her impulse to vent on Dallan was gone. He looked so miserable. So defeated.

Besides, if her sudden suspicions about the mission, about …

But it can't be true.

It's ridiculous.

It's just a coincidence.

She stared out at the bleak landscape.

The middle of nowhere.

We need to get back to San Diego.

I need to think this through; do some calculations.

Oh, Lord, help me.

Help us all.

"Allie, I don't know what to say."

She held her gaze out the window.

"First off, I'm really ashamed of myself." His voice faltered. "I don't know why my life was spared—Becky's the one who deserved to live, not me. But yesterday I made the decision that when I got back home I was going to meet with Lolo and see if we couldn't work things out."

She wheeled. "What? Why the change of heart?"

He looked away. "It's—it's something Becky said to me yesterday. Out on the ice. I'd never thought about it that way."

"Thought about *what*, what way?"

He turned to her, but she could see it in his eyes: his mind was a thousand miles away. "Allie, it's just that—you're a Christian, right?"

She raised an eyebrow. "Trying to be."

"So you know all about the importance of forgiveness, right?"

What is he babbling about?!

"Go ahead."

"Well, I can't say *I'm* a Christian—I don't know what I am, really. But for most of my grown-up life I've been carrying this guilt because of my childhood, you know?"

Oh, Lord, here we go again, the sob story.

"Allie, I felt really guilty about filing for divorce, okay? But I wanted to escape. Your sister was talking about having a family. It scared the bejeezus out of me. I didn't know what to do, so I ran away—just like my old man."

"Dallan, you don't need to tell—"

"No, please, just listen. I don't think it's a coincidence you're here. It's spooky, really, because it's just what I needed."

She wanted to leave. "Dallan—"

"Allie, what I'm trying to say is yesterday out there on that ice"—he jabbed his bandaged right hand toward the window—"I was brought to my knees, *literally*, and I forgave my dad. *For the first time in my life*, I forgave my dad. I let him go. Set myself free. And now—right here, right now—I want to say I'm so sorry to you for the hurt I've caused Lolo and the entire family." He locked eyes with hers. "I love Lolo, Allie. Can you please forgive me?"

She hesitated. "Dallan, I'm not the one who—"

There was knocking at the door. A voice from behind it said, "Dr. O'Malley. Your plane is ready whenever you are."

Dallan didn't take his eyes off Allie. "Okay, thank you."

She walked up to his bed and rested her hands on the sheets. "Dallan, I love my sister—and if anything happens to her..."

Be Christian!

"...but I'm trying to be a good Christian. So, yes, Dallan, I'm going to try hard to forgive you." She folded her arms and stood up straight.

"At the same time, Brother, you say you've changed? You say you love Lolo? I'm going to need to see some evidence of that before I can believe you."

★

FRIDAY, APRIL 28 (10:27 A.M. EASTERN DAYLIGHT TIME)

The lumbering Snowcat came to a stop alongside *Hero*. The craft was still right where they'd left her: tied to a stake driven into the rocky beach.

She, Calder, and Brody hopped off.

"Thanks for the lift," she said, eager to head home.

"Yeah, thanks," Calder said.

"She's a beauty, all right," the major remarked, walking up to *Hero* and giving her the once over. "How did you say she works?"

Allie rushed to unlock the windshield.

"It's actually pretty simple," Calder said, pulling the stake out of the ground. "I've come up with a way to tap into the vacuum's virtual energy fields."

"Whoa! Whoa!" Brody said, his hand shooting up. "In English, please. I'm a military guy, not a scientist."

Heaving open the windshield, Allie decided to help speed up the conversation. "According to quantum mechanics, a true vacuum is not really nothing. It's filled with invisible energy fields. Science calls them 'virtual' fields. Dr. Sinclair here has figured out a way to tap into that energy."

Brody laughed. "No kidding. Sounds like science fiction to me."

"Except it's real," Calder said, stowing away the metal stake and mooring rope in *Hero*'s rear compartment. "We've traveled around the world literally on an empty gas tank."

"That's right," she said, donning her helmet. "According to physics, it *is* possible to get something from nothing. In fact, cosmologists think it's how the universe began."

Brody was rubbing his chin, looking skeptical. "No way."

Eager to bring this elementary back-and-forth to a close and shove off, she said, "Think of it this way: in the beginning was the vacuum and the vacuum was with God and the vacuum *was* God." She stepped into the rear passenger compartment and, addressing Brody as she might an undergrad back at Harvard, delivered the punch line of her deliberately theatrical soliloquy. "Then the vacuum swelled like a pregnant woman and *whoosh!* The universe was born."

Calder smiled at Brody. "It's called the big bang."

CHAPTER 23

UNWELCOME VISITORS

Jared sat up and stretched. He ached all over.

He spent a quiet night sleeping amongst cleaning equipment inside a huge, unoccupied building he found shortly after arriving on the base. With luck, he discovered a small back door that was unlocked.

Slowly, groggily, he surveyed the building's dusky interior, squinting for a better look. It was a hangar of some sort, converted into what appeared to be a fancy research lab.

He took out his cell phone and glanced at the screen: Friday, April 28, 7:27 a.m.

Then it hit him.

Maggie.

Oh, Maggie!

He crumpled back into his hidey-hole, all the grisly images and details of the previous day's nightmare inundating him. For a long while he stayed there, rocking back and forth.

At last he forced himself to sit up.

C'mon, deal with it.

Focus!

May 1 was only, what? Two days away. He needed to lay low until then.

He contemplated his scheme's big finale after the G-20 protest. His mind flashed to his thirteenth birthday.

Oh, Maggie.

Focus!

It was immediately following Maggie's horrifying revelation on his thirteenth birthday that he set his mind on liberating himself and anyone else oppressed by extreme wealth. He vowed to make things right in the world, to help the ninety-nine percent suffering at the hands of the arrogant one percent.

Very quickly his online research taught him about a worldwide army of hacker-activists, or hacktivists, called Anonymous, the "final boss of the Internet." They called themselves defenders of freedom—above all, free knowledge and free speech.

With swelling amazement he read about the group's 2008 assault on Scientology's main computer system using, among other cyber-weapons, software called Low Orbit Ion Cannon; their 2010 denial-of-service attacks that disabled computer systems belonging to PayPal, Visa, and MasterCard; their 2011 subversive, online protests that helped stoke the Arab Spring unrest in Egypt, leading to the resignation of President Mubarak; and on and on.

Equally impressive to him was the hacktivism of an Australian lone wolf named Julian Assange, who'd begun his work using the handle Mendax. As a young man Assange was widely credited with hacking a NASA computer system and using it to reposition one of its orbiting satellites.

In 2006 Assange founded a nonprofit organization called WikiLeaks, which published hacked information on the Web—sometimes with powerful consequences. During the 2016 U.S. presidential election Assange released hacked emails from the Democratic National Committee ultimately causing the resignation of its chairwoman, Debbie Wasserman Schultz.

Jared also read about a super-brash black hat hacking group called LulzSec, which beginning in 2011 successfully attacked computer systems belonging to Fast, PBS, a bunch of UK banks, the U.S. Senate, the CIA, police stations, and many others.

Learning about all this hacktivism, he quickly became convinced the most awesome instrument of liberation at his disposal was right in front of him: computers.

That's when he began to conceive Quantum I.

He grinned to himself, picturing the scene on May 1, a split-second after midnight. He imagined himself being interviewed by an awestruck reporter. Maybe that same woman, Allie Armendariz.

"So how did you pull it off, Jared?"

He would smirk. "By realizing that in today's computerized world the most powerful weapon on the planet is the keyboard. From a living room, anyone with the right smarts can wreak havoc on the status quo—instantaneously, through the Web.

"Think of history's wickedest viruses—Storm, Melissa, ILOVEYOU, Sasser & Netsky, MyDoom—on steroids. Then think of a Trojan horse so monstrous, so indestructible no computer security system, no antivirus program on the market could possibly defeat it.

"At the appointed moment, my Quantum I chip released a Trojan horse exactly like that into cyberspace, where it began cloning itself. The clones spread like a plague, riding the Internet at the speed of light, attaching themselves to websites, e-mails, documents, infecting every computer, TV, printer, smartphone, and server on the planet. Then quietly, qubit by qubit, they began unraveling the global oligarchy.

"First, the clones produced a denial-of-service worm, which caused government and corporate websites to crash. Then the clones seized control of the computer systems of Fortune 500 companies and their equivalents worldwide, turning them into zombies. Now, under my control, those computers are coughing up their innermost industrial and financial secrets—all of which we're posting on NeuroNet's website."

The reporter would stare at him with wide eyes. "But why? Why are you doing this? You told the world you wanted to do good, not destroy civilization as we know it."

"But that's exactly *why* I've done this. Today's electronic civilization, today's economy, is stacked against the little guys. They don't stand a chance against corporate greed and government corruption. The only way to fix the problem, the only way to bring about meaningful change is to wipe the slate clean and start from scratch—send the world back to the Stone Age.

"You see, the key is realizing that in this day and age you don't, and can't, destroy the rigged system with bombs or politics. You destroy it *electronically* by revealing its dirty little secrets—the billions of secrets propping up the wealthy and enslaving the poor. Bank account numbers, social security numbers, passwords, classified information, e-mails, phone numbers, addresses—Quantum I is pulling back the curtain on all of it, so no one will have power over anyone else. Destroying secrets, destroying privacy—it's the great leveler. More effective than a bazillion A-bombs."

"But what about *you*? Where do you fit in all this chaos?"

"Even as we speak, the Quantum I virus is utterly sabotaging the old, crooked system and putting me and my army in control of all information. You'll see, in the weeks ahead, under my rule, everyone will get a bank account with the same amount of money in it. Since I will effectively become the world's central bank, after erasing all existing account records, I'll make sure the reallocation of wealth is fair to everyone, not just fat cats like my old man."

An unexpected sound snapped Jared out of his make-believe world. He hunkered, his muscles taut and ready to send him flying out the door. Looking around him, he seized the handle of a hefty broom. Then he waited, straining to make sense of the sounds he was hearing.

People.

One voice stood out from the others. A woman. Clear, bossy.

"Pitsy, right here," it ordered. "It's the perfect spot."

Pitsy.

Pitsy.

He knew the name. Then it came to him.

It's the people from Fast News!

"They're setting up the podium over there and the sun's going to be setting over there, so it's perfect. Right here."

★

FRIDAY, APRIL 28 (7:23 P.M. MOUNTAIN DAYLIGHT TIME)

BOULDER, COLORADO

On the flight to Boulder, Dallan kept hearing Allie's voice.

I need evidence.

Evidence.

Evidence.

She'd see it soon enough. In spades.

The sun was lowering by the time his plane touched down. His intention was to head straight for the office and arrange for a leave of absence; they could manage without him for another few weeks. Tomorrow he'd fly to Jerusalem to help look for Lolo.

Striding through the airport, he kept glancing out the oversized windows. It was the first time in a week he was seeing the sun set. He smiled. The gathering darkness came as a relief—like exhaling after holding your breath for a long time.

He booted up his cell, expecting to find messages from the Denver detective he contacted before leaving Alert. Instead, there were six missed calls from the SWPC.

He dialed his assistant, who answered after the first ring.

"Dallan! Oh, thank goodness!"

"What's up?"

"Well, first of all, we're all really upset to hear about Lorena. The police called here looking for you."

"Yeah, I know. Thanks." He added, "Is that it? Is that why you left me all the messages?"

"Oh, man, no. It's the sun. Where are you? When can you get here?"

★

SATURDAY, APRIL 29 (9:32 A.M. CHINA STANDARD TIME)

SHANGHAI JIAO TONG UNIVERSITY; SHANGHAI, CHINA

Dr. Zhaohui Tang—sitting in her office, as always—did not feel kindly toward her nation's close neighbors, the Japanese. She never had and this was one more reason.

For the past seventy-two hours she'd been following with mounting anger the news of Nagasaki's reprehensible whalers just across the East China Sea, less than five hundred miles away. Now she was truly furious. A China Central TV reporter was saying the whalers' rapaciousness had apparently triggered some kind of ripple effect suddenly afflicting China's very own shores.

"The mass stranding off the coast of Shanghai began about an hour ago..."

★

SATURDAY, APRIL 29 (11:04 A.M. AUSTRALIAN CENTRAL STANDARD TIME)

CHARLES DARWIN UNIVERSITY; CASUARINA, AUSTRALIA

Sara rushed to the edge of Lulu's tank. The juvenile pilot whale was re-exhibiting signs of madness after being normal for the past few days— ever since Sara's dad was there.

"Dirk!" she yelled, reaching out to Lulu in an attempt to quiet her down. "Over here. *Quick!*"

CHAPTER 24

HOME AGAIN

FRIDAY, APRIL 28 (7:35 P.M. PACIFIC DAYLIGHT TIME)

SAN DIEGO, CALIFORNIA

During the long return trip to San Diego, Allie aired reports about the deadly Arctic tornado and the magnetic holes growing and shrinking in various parts of the world. "It's as if they have minds of their own," she explained, "which makes it hard to predict what will happen next." She also broke the news about the hypothesized connection between the magnetic anomalies and whale strandings; the strandings appeared to come and go in step with the holes.

Eva told her the news reports were causing a sensation, with other reporters frantically trying to play catch-up. "This is gonna make your arrival a bigger story than ever, so get ready for an onslaught. But don't worry; I'll be there to manage things."

In actuality Allie was distracted by a multiplicity of other concerns. For one, the seeming coincidence between their rescue mission's own movements and the comings and goings of whale strandings and magnetic anomalies—as just happened in the Arctic. And for others: Lorena's disappearance, Dallan's odd behavior, and her growing amorous feelings for Calder and her befuddlement about what to do about it.

As the San Diego Bay came into view—awash in a darkening, golden light—her mind pushed aside all the worries and was seized by a single, euphoric thought.

Unbelievable! He's done it! He's made history!

He'll probably even get the Nobel Prize!

Hero's loud arrival bell shattered the silence inside the cabin.

"Calder, congratulations!" she said. "It's amazing, really. This is going to change everything!"

"Thanks, Allie."

On this final leg of the mission Calder had opened *Hero*'s throttle nearly all the way, just to prove how fast she could go. According to him she averaged 551 knots.

Hero glided slowly across the water toward Point Loma for their grand entrance. The sun was setting; lights were coming on.

Earlier, they were told civilian watercraft would be banned from the area for security reasons. But a gaggle of helicopters and blimps circled noisily overhead. They were joined by earsplitting, deep-throated air horns blasting from Navy ships anchored all around them.

It reminded her of the Fourth of July.

"Calder, before we both get swallowed up by the media circus, I just want to say thanks for letting me tell the story."

"Allie, thank *you*. I would've gone bonkers out there by myself. Really."

She giggled. "So I didn't drive you crazy with all my questions?"

"Are you kidding? They helped keep me going." Then he said, "Anyway, now it's *my* turn to ask a question."

"Sure, go ahead."

"Would you consider going out to dinner with me? To celebrate?"

She froze for a moment and then said, "Of course. When? Uh, let me check with—"

"Welcome home, girlfriend!" Eva's voice over the IFB was extra loud. "Can you see what's happening? Stu's cut a deal with just about everybody in the world to let them cover the arrival up close. It's a zoo out here. I've never seen anything like it."

"Hey, *chica*. Yeah, I see it."

But her mind was on Calder's surprise invitation.

Dinner!

"You're on in three," Eva said. "Are you ready?"

"What?"

"You're on in three minutes—so get ready. Brett's doing the intro. This is your big close-up, babycakes!"

Several minutes later Allie took a long, relaxing breath, flipped the switch, and on cue began broadcasting: "Yes, hello, everyone—as Brett just said, we're only minutes away from pulling into the naval station. The big headline this afternoon is *Hero* has performed flawlessly throughout the entire three-day mission. It appears Dr. Sinclair has done it. He's discovered a whole new energy source that will change the course of human history—and that's no exaggeration."

FRIDAY, APRIL 28 (7:47 P.M. PACIFIC DAYLIGHT TIME)

When the lighted landing area came into clear view he was shocked by the size and color of the spectacle awaiting them. He'd never seen so many TV cameras. Even the Navy band was out in full force, performing "When Johnny Comes Marching Home Again."

Be careful what you ask for.

"I warned you," Allie said. "Get ready."

"Yeah, right."

After Navy personnel lashed *Hero* to the pier he shut down her systems, one by one. "Thanks, ol' girl," he whispered, patting the console.

Allie was on the air when he said to her in a loud voice, "Ready to go ashore?"

"Ay, ay, sir." Then she said, "That was Dr. Sinclair. He's about to open the hatch, so I need to sign off now. Brett, it's good to be home! Back to you."

He pushed open the windshield and heard an ovation that rivaled ones he'd witnessed at USC-UCLA football games. The applause and cheers continued—the band played "The Stars and Stripes Forever"— while he and Allie wriggled out of the cabin. They stood on the pier for a few moments to regain their land legs.

He waved both hands at the delirious throng, which appeared to be equal parts military and civilian. Then he turned to Allie, clasped her hand, and lifted it in a gesture of victory. "Allie, you deserve this."

The crowd went wild.

"Thank you, Calder," she said. "Thank you, everybody!"

Halfway to the podium he and Allie were met by the governor. "Welcome home, Doctor, welcome home! Bravo! Bravo!" He gave Calder a hearty, telegenic handshake, all the while smiling into the cameras. Then facing Calder, he whispered, "I'm going to say a few words then turn it over to you, okay?"

Calder nodded.

"Allie, well done," the governor said, leaning forward and giving her a quick handshake.

He then marched up to the podium with its large bouquet of microphones and waited for the attendees to quiet down. When finally they did, he said, "The Nobel laureate Pearl S. Buck once remarked, 'The young do not know enough to be prudent and therefore they attempt the impossible—and achieve it, generation after generation.' This evening we're here to bear witness to the completion of an expedition every bit as audacious and significant as man's first landing on the moon. More so, really, when you consider the implications of what Dr. Sinclair has achieved. Not since the invention of the wheel or the automobile or the airplane, not since humans first dreamed of finding a perfect energy source—limitless, clean energy—has there been a moment such as this.

You all know him. You've been following his daring journey into the history books. Ladies and gentlemen all over the world, it's my honor to welcome home to California—Dr. Calder Sinclair!"

Calder, feeling faint, rocked on his heels.

Is this real?

Has the curse finally lifted?

But he knew from long, painful experience he wouldn't know for a while yet.

Bellying up to the microphones, he stood silently while the crowd whooped it up. He scanned the happy faces, indicating his gratitude with quick nods, but paused when he spotted Allie's producer. She was at the back wearing a headset. He gave her a wink and she replied with two upraised thumbs.

The wiry-haired wizard behind the curtain.

When the applause finally played out he opened his mouth, not knowing what he wanted to say. He wished Allie were standing alongside him.

"Thank you," he said hoarsely. He cleared his throat. "Before anything else, I'd like to acknowledge and thank my cockpit companion: TV's number-one science reporter, Allie Armendariz." The throng erupted anew.

He turned to her and shouted over the deafening noise, "Thank you, partner! Thank you!" Smiling broadly, she bowed slightly and gave him a snappy salute.

He faced the multitude again and began speaking. "For me, this day represents the culmination of a lifetime of work. It began with a simple dream to build a speed boat as fast as a jet plane. As I grew older, the dream became more ambitious, more mature until finally I became convinced the quantum vacuum held the answer to all our modern problems. That instead of tearing into the earth looking for coal or oil or gas—instead of blanketing the landscape with acres of ugly solar panels and deadly wind-powered generators—everything we ever wanted, ever needed, existed within what most people assumed contained absolutely nothing: a perfect vacuum.

"Along the way lots of people told me it couldn't be done. That I was tilting at windmills. Well, it so happens I grew up in a part of the world, Spain, where tilting at windmills is considered a high calling, and committing to not give up until succeeding, a sacred duty.

"I didn't do this alone. I've been helped all along, in ways large and small, by many people. Some of them, like my parents, are dead—may they rest in peace. But some are still alive. And among them is a very special woman I'd like to single out right now.

"She was like a mother to me when I was very young and still is. I had the privilege of seeing her when we were in Cádiz. It was a great surprise. She is the Reverend Mother Abbess Yolanda Jimenez, a Franciscan nun who runs the orphanage where I grew up. She needs our help."

He explained the orphanage's plight and asked people to help save it from certain death. "If it hadn't been for Mother Yolanda and the orphanage I wouldn't be standing here before you now. And *Hero* would not exist. For that, and for your warm welcome today, I will be eternally grateful. Thank you!"

FRIDAY, APRIL 28 (10:34 P.M. PACIFIC DAYLIGHT TIME)

Three hours following the start of *Hero*'s welcoming ceremonies, the only ones left were TV people breaking down equipment, cleaning crews picking up trash, and a local radio reporter wrapping up an interview with Calder at the pier.

Standing close by, Allie spotted a bulky figure rapidly approaching.

"There you are!" the figure called out.

She narrowed her eyes for a better look.

Carlos!

"*Shhh!*" she said to him, quickly gesturing him to follow her. When they were a respectable distance away from Calder's interview she hugged him. "Wow! How great to see you, Bro. Thank you for coming!"

"I would've been here sooner but the security people didn't believe I was your brother. I told them to tell you, but they refused because you were mobbed. They finally let me in just now, after your producer vouched for me."

"Oh, Carlos, I'm so sorry. But it's really awesome you came. It's the best homecoming I could have. Thank you!" She hugged him again. "How's Lolo? Anything new?"

He shook his head. "No, they're still looking. The detective in Denver told me the Israeli police are doing everything possible to get the word out—even asking the media for help. They don't want anything to happen to her that would cause an international incident. Our little sis is big news."

Her face fell. "But not good news."

"We need to have faith, Allie; she's in God's hands."

She nodded bleakly. "Yeah, I know." She looked away and back. "How's Mom?"

"No change. But no worse either."

"And Dad?"

"Fine, fine, you know him: your biggest cheerleader. When I left, he was at the church with all the *hermano*s watching your reports on the big-screen TV we set up. It was like a huge fiesta, food and everything. You shoulda been there."

He laughed at himself. "*Que tonto*! Duh. You know what I mean."

She laughed. "I know. I wish I'd been there too."

"Hey, since I'm here I was wondering: Can I see inside the hangar? I've been following your trip and I find it really interesting even though I'm not smart like you."

She took a swipe at his arm. "Oh, c'mon—you're not dumb. But hold on, okay?"

She waited for Calder's interview to finish and then went over to him with Carlos in tow.

"Calder, this is my big brother, Carlos."

"Oh, hey, good to meet you." The two shook hands. "I heard a lot of great things about you on the journey."

"She lies," Carlos laughed.

"Nah, I bet not." Calder looked to her. "She loves her family, that's for sure. She's lucky to have you guys."

"Calder, Carlos wants to know if he could take a peek inside your hangar. I know you're tired and probably—"

"No, no. I'm so full of adrenaline right now it's gonna take me days before I can sleep. Let's do it!"

It took just a few minutes to walk across the sand from pier to hangar.

"Let's go through the back door," Calder said, leading them to a small, inconspicuous entrance. "I always leave it unlocked in case I forget my keys—which is way too often."

"Absent-minded professor, huh?" Allie joked.

"Uh, guilty as charged."

CHAPTER 25

NO REST FOR THE WEARY

FRIDAY, APRIL 28 (10:53 P.M. PACIFIC DAYLIGHT TIME)

NAVAL BASE POINT LOMA; SAN DIEGO, CALIFORNIA

Jared was starving. Since morning, when he first began hearing people outside the building, he decided to stay hidden. As the commotion outdoors steadily increased, he readied himself to bolt at any moment, but no one ever entered the place.

It didn't take him long to figure out the babble of voices belonged to people preparing for the arrival of that spaceship boat he'd heard about in the news. For the past several hours, from the security of his nook, he heard all the speeches over the public address system.

With the party outside apparently over, he dared to stand up to stretch his legs. A few moments later he heard voices and quickly ducked.

"Let's go through the back door," a man said. "I always leave it unlocked in case I forget my keys—which is way too often."

"Absent-minded professor, huh?"

A woman.

"Uh, guilty as charged."

When the door opened Jared made himself as small as possible.

Someone turned on the lights. He shrouded his eyes against the sudden brightness.

"Can you hold on? I need to go to the bathroom," the female said. "I haven't gone since Panama City."

He readied himself as the voices moved quickly away from him, heading further into the hangar.

Now!

Go!

In one swift, quiet motion, he leapt up, pushed through the door, and sprinted away into the darkness.

★

FRIDAY, APRIL 28 (10:59 P.M. PACIFIC DAYLIGHT TIME)

When she returned from the restroom, Carlos and Calder were chit-chatting.

"Not talking about me, I hope," she said in jest.

"No," her brother said. "I was just telling Calder how everyone at our church followed your guys' whole mission."

"I'd like to meet your family one day," Calder said. "They sound like really cool people."

"They are," she said. "But we better get on with the tour. I gotta powwow with Eva before heading to the hotel. Lots happening."

Calder led them to the center of the hangar and explained the purpose of the tall stage-like structure there. A ramping scaffold wound around its perimeter, like the threads of a screw.

"This is where *Hero* sits when I have to work on her."

"Her throne," Carlos said.

"Yeah, you could say that. I can raise and lower her using this hydraulic lift and access any part of her by walking along the scaffolding."

"And it's just the one vehicle, right?" Allie said. "There's no backup?"

"Right, no backup; *Hero*'s a very expensive machine."

She smiled. "Well, after this, I predict you're gonna be able to afford building her a sister or two."

Carlos was sweeping his eyes around the place. "It's so clean. Like a hospital."

"*Hero*'s insides contain some very precise, delicate technology," Calder said. "One speck of dust in the wrong place could be disastrous. That's why the building is under positive pressure."

"What does that mean?"

"Special ventilation fans constantly keep the inside pressure higher than the outside, which helps keep dirt and air pollution from coming in."

Allie looked up at the very tall ceiling. "This place reminds me of the VAB at Cape Kennedy—you know, the vehicular assembly building, where they put together the huge rockets."

Calder nodded. "Actually, it does. I've seen it."

He swept his hand across the massive facility. "The layout's pretty straightforward—divided into quadrants." He started pointing. "Over there, to the north, is propulsion. Over on the west side is navigation. On the east is life support. And over there, by the door we just came through, is payload. In each—"

Her phone sounded.

"Oh, dang, I'm sorry. It's probably Eva wondering where I am." She glanced at the caller ID then answered. "*Bueno?*"

"Allie?" The voice sounded winded. "It's Dallan."

★

SATURDAY, APRIL 29 (8:15 A.M. CENTRAL EUROPEAN SUMMER TIME)

POOR CLARES' SACRED HEART CONVENT; SEVILLE, SPAIN

When her cab arrived at the convent, Mother Yolanda smiled at the colorful, handmade paper decorations hanging on the outside of the main office building. She was used to receiving a warm welcome whenever she returned from a long absence, but this ...

The rising sun was heralding a bright new day, but her body and spirits were feeling the wearying effects of the long, disappointing journey. She paused a moment to steel herself.

God will provide, He always has.

The driver helped her out of the car and immediately the kids ran to meet and swarm about her. *"Ay, mis niños!"* she said, bringing her hands to her cheeks. *"Que bellísimos son!"*

She stooped, taking the children into her arms one by one and kissing them, allowing herself to be swept up by the joyous homecoming reception.

"Mother Abbess! Mother Abbess!"

Her assistant, Sister Theresa, was hurrying toward her, holding the front of her habit off the ground to avoid tripping over it.

"Yes, Sister," she said, alert to the look of extreme joy on Theresa's young, smooth face. "It is good to be home, thank God."

"Indeed, Mother Abbess, indeed! Welcome home! I have such news to report. We've all been waiting to tell you together."

Yolanda always had a guarded reaction to being told there was unexpected news. The prowling enemy never rested. But in this case she thought Theresa's evident jubilation boded well.

"What is it, my child?"

"Donations!" Theresa's hands plunged into her habit's hidden pockets and drew out fistfuls of paper money, telegrams, and checks. "People saw you on television with the American inventor, heard about our need, and are sending us money! Praise God, it's a miracle! Our prayers have been answered!"

★

SATURDAY, APRIL 29 (12:23 A.M. PACIFIC DAYLIGHT TIME)

Allie, aboard an executive jet bound for Boulder, had her eyes closed but wasn't sleeping. Her restless thoughts vied between Lorena, who was still missing, and the truly scary news story she was about to break to the world.

When it rains it pours.

According to what Dallan told her on the phone, the sun was about to detonate a killer CME, a coronal mass ejection. Under normal circumstances, he explained, CMEs hitting the earth weren't big news; they happened regularly and at their worst caused severe magnetic storms. But given the growing holes in the magnetosphere, a CME happening now constituted a very real and present danger to the planet. It could lead to the kind of catastrophe the Arctic just experienced or that allegedly killed Calder's wife—or worse.

Dallan explained the president was planning to address the nation about the potential disaster, but that if she hurried over, she could be the one to break the news before anyone. She guessed he was trying to ingratiate himself with her, to show he was serious about turning over a new leaf. But she didn't care about his motives, only the story.

Shifting in her seat for a more comfortable position, she yearned for the hotel room she gave up for this emergency. She loved the Manchester Grand Hyatt in San Diego and was counting on getting a good night's sleep in preparation for the next day's G-20.

"You awake?"

Her eyes flew open. "Eva," she whispered. "What? I'm trying to sleep here. I'm gonna look like *caca* in the morning."

Eva glanced around the darkened cabin. Pitsy and the crew were also on board. "Sorry, sorry. I just got a call from Stu."

"Terrific, good to know," she said irritably.

"He said the White House just contacted him. The president wants to tour the whale stranding site in San Diego tomorrow afternoon the minute he lands in the city. It's a huge photo op."

Allie looked at her blankly, still not understanding why all of this couldn't have waited until the morning.

Eva gave her a big, self-satisfied grin. "Allie, he's been following your reports of the rescue mission and today's big arrival. He wants to meet you guys. The prez wants *you* and Calder to brief him on the whale strandings!"

CHAPTER 26

AMBUSH

SATURDAY, APRIL 29 (3:45 A.M. PACIFIC DAYLIGHT TIME)

SAN DIEGO, CALIFORNIA

Calder, in the back seat of the limo with Burton Sager, was questioning the location of this morning's live TV show. At Allie's behest, the veteran PR agent was helping him out with the tsunami of interview requests.

"I just don't understand why Mission Beach with a bunch of dying whales," he griped. "Why not at my hangar? Why not next to *Hero*?"

The car was exiting the 5 Freeway, headed for Sea World Drive. They were running late.

"Networks like their anchors to be where the action is. They were going to do it at your hangar but changed their minds when news broke about the magnetic holes. It'll be fine; this is important. They're the number-one morning show in the country."

When the car arrived at the beach he and Sager were met by the police chief and a dozen officers.

A police escort?

"The mayor wants to make sure you're well taken care of," the chief said, shaking his hand.

Calder looked about in the dark and spotted two large gatherings of demonstrators across the street. They were holding lowered picket signs and arguing loudly with one another.

At this ungodly hour?

Why are they here?

The police escorted him past the demonstrators, who hooted at them, and then past a barricade of white sawhorses and yellow caution tape.

"Good morning!" said a woman dressed in white Capri pants and a burgundy blouse. Her hair was pulled back tightly in a ponytail.

Calder easily recognized the popular anchor of the morning show, Dusty Robins. He shook her hand, forcing a smile. "Sorry for being late."

"It's okay. It's an honor to meet you, Dr. Sinclair, thank you for coming." She also greeted Sager and then jerked a thumb in the direction of the protestors. "I hope they didn't hassle you too much."

"No big deal," Calder replied. "But who are they?"

"They're mostly kids from Occupy the World and Planet First. We're hoping they don't go for each other's throats this morning. One group blames the beached whales on Navy experiments and the magnetic holes on climate change. The other blames it all on the environmentalists. Go figure." She added casually, "Some even blame *you* for making things worse."

Calder reared his head. "What? How do they figure that?"

"Yes, thank you, I agree. Anyway, I wouldn't worry about it. All they want is publicity. You're just a convenient target."

"Great," he muttered.

"Did you manage to get any sleep?" she said, leading them across the sand.

He wagged his head. "Not really. It's been nonstop interviews since I arrived, with reporters from every imaginable time zone. I'm just hoping I can make it through this interview. I don't know how you people do it, getting up so early and being all smiles."

"It takes practice: I've been doing this show for nine years now. Let's get you some coffee real quick. Follow me." She glanced at her smartphone. "We go live in twelve minutes."

She led them into a large trailer parked in the sand. "How do you like your coffee?"

"Straight up."

"And you, Mr. Sager?"

"Milk and two sugars."

After her assistant served them coffee, Robins said. "C'mon back outside. I want to introduce you to our other guest."

Calder looked to Sager then to Robins. "Other guest?"

"Yes, for a reaction to what you've just done. It's someone who knows you: Dr. Terry Bradstreet."

"Oh lord, not him."

"What? He's president of the California Academy of Sci—"

"Yes, I know. He's my worst critic. Has been for years."

Sager pulled Calder aside and asked him for an explanation.

"Never mind, I can handle him. Actually, it'll give me a chance to say, 'I told you so.'"

"You wanna pull out?" Sager pressed. "You can, you know. You don't have to take any cra—"

"No, let's just do this and get out of here."

He and Sager followed Robins out of the trailer. They walked a short distance across the sand to a tall, thin man in tan slacks, button-down powder-blue shirt, and navy blazer.

Robins spoke first. "I understand the two of you know each other."

"Yes, we do," Bradstreet said with a feeble smile. "Morning, Calder."

Calder stared arrows at him. "Morning, Terry. Good to see you." He looked away and said under his breath, "Not."

A frazzled-looking bald man wearing a headset rushed up to them. "Five minutes, Dusty! New York needs you all out there—now!"

The three quickly positioned themselves on the sand in front of the main camera—he on Robins's right, Bradstreet on her left. The beach all around them was lit up; massive black, white, and gray shapes lay everywhere. Scores of volunteers were speaking softly to the distraught animals, dousing their bodies with buckets of seawater.

Calder winced at the ghastly sound of the whales clearing their blowholes and sighing, of the juveniles crying pitifully. Many in the final stages of dying were on their backs, their gigantic, fluked tails curled skyward.

"One minute!" the bald man shouted.

Moments later, on a small monitor nestled in the sand, Calder watched the show's opening graphics.

Some fifty feet away, the demonstrators came alive.

He smirked.

Like trained seals.

Calder glanced over his shoulder at the slogans on the now dancing signs: SOLAR FARMS KILL…HOLY SMOKE—STOP THE SLAUGHTER…GO GREEN, NOT SOLAR…BAN ALL RADAR…MAKE PEACE, NOT WAR…CLIMATE CHANGE: WHALE OF A PROBLEM! The two groups took turns shouting, like warring football fans: "Stop the Navy!" "Stop the greenies!"

He turned back to the small monitor. The introductory graphics gave way to a shot of the cheery-faced anchor. At the bottom of the frame were the words: FRINGE OR FRONTIER?

What the—?

The bald man cued her.

"Good morning!" Robins said. "I'm here at Mission Beach, where the strandings continue to worsen beneath a hole in the earth's magnetic field scientists say is growing. We'll have the latest updates on that for you in just a minute.

"But first we begin our live coverage with a man who knows all about what's happening with the strandings. Last evening, after three days of trying to stop whales from beaching themselves, he came home to San Diego to a hero's welcome as the world watched and cheered."

They played snippets from yesterday's ceremonies: *Hero*'s arrival, the governor's introduction, Calder's own speech.

Suddenly he felt a nudge from behind, his cue to enter the frame.

DR: "Dr. Sinclair, thank you so much for joining us this early in the morning. Here in California it's only four o'clock and I know you haven't had much sleep."

Calder nodded unenthusiastically.

CS: "Thank you. I'm grateful to be here."
DR: "How does it feel to be home?"
CS: "Terrific. It's always good to be home."

For the next few minutes Robins had him quickly walk viewers through the three-day trip, querying him about the Japanese whalers, the Reverend Mother, and how he and Allie handled going to the bathroom and getting sleep.

DR: "Looking back on it all, what would you say was the highlight of your trip?"

Calder shifted his feet in the sand, numbed by a chilly, predawn breeze and the litany of mostly inane questions.

CS: "The highlight? I'd say proving *Hero* actually works as advertised. I couldn't have hoped for a better performance from her. She was a real trouper."
DR: "You claim she runs on nothing but air, is that right?"

Calder stifled an urge to scream.

CS: "No, not air. And not nothing. That's the point. She runs on the quantum vacuum. People often think a vacuum is

nothing. They remember learning that way back in science class, but it's wrong."

DR: "So, when you say 'quantum vacuum,' what exactly do
you mean? Is there some simple way you can explain it to
us?"

Calder, taking in a lungful of air, nearly gagged on the stench of the
beached animals.

CS: "When you suck everything out of an enclosed space—a
jar, let's say—there's always something left behind. Science calls it 'vacuum energy.' It's invisible and exists in a
kind of twilight zone state, but I've figured out a way to
extract it and put it to work."

DR: "Oh, wow, that sounds complicated."

CS: "Well, yes—but—well, think of fracking, where you
extract leftover natural gas trapped inside the ground.
That's kind of what I do. I've invented a way to liberate
leftover energy trapped inside the vacuum."

DR: "Oh, I get it. Kind of like squeezing blood out of a turnip,
huh?"

Robins chuckled at her own cleverness, thanked him, and then
looked directly into the camera.

DR: "Now, for an outside opinion on all this we're joined this
morning by another respected scientist, Dr. Terry Bradstreet. He's president of the California Academy of Sciences."

Bradstreet stepped into the frame and smiled—somewhat smugly,
Calder thought.

At the same time, Calder felt someone taking hold of the back of his
shirt and tugging it gently, his cue to step back from the limelight. His
stomach muscles tightened. His mouth felt dry.

DR: "Dr. Bradstreet, thank you so much for being here. You heard what Dr. Sinclair just explained. Tell us—what do you think?"

Bradstreet, clearing his throat, shot a glance at Calder, then turned to the camera. He seemed confused about where exactly he should be looking.

TB: "I want to be careful how I express myself. I've known about Dr. Sinclair's work for some time, although only anecdotally, through secondhand claims and reports. And that's my main concern here. I have enormous respect for Dr. Sinclair personally—he has one of the finest minds I know—but everything we've heard him tell us this morning is highly speculative. Most serious scientists don't agree with his ideas and claims, and it doesn't help that he's never published a single paper on the subject."

DR: "I'm not a scientist. But isn't history full of mavericks who turned out to be right? Like Christopher Columbus or the Wright brothers? And didn't Dr. Sinclair just prove himself with *Hero*'s mission around the world?"

TB: "*Hero*'s performance does seem like proof, on the surface. But he's not allowed any of us to inspect her. We have no way of knowing, really, what powers her. Publishing your results in a peer-reviewed journal is the only legitimate way science can judge the veracity of any new claim, especially one that flies in the face of conventional wisdom, as this does. Dr. Sinclair's claims about *Hero*'s power source challenges the laws of physics, the laws of thermodynamics. It smacks too much of a perpetual motion machine, which we all know is impossible. If published properly, his claim could be independently tested by others elsewhere. The problem here is there's no paper trail, just allegations."

Bradstreet took a breath and then continued, clearly warming to his critique.

TB: "I don't mean any disrespect—"

Calder hit his limit. He stepped back into the frame.

CS: "No, Terry, that's exactly what you mean. You complain
about my not publishing, but what you don't say is that
all the papers I've submitted to the journals over the years
have been rejected. The truth is, peer review sounds great
in theory, but in practice it's little more than a pretentious
euphemism for an old boys' network."

Bradstreet held up a hand.

TB: "Dr. Sinclair, please, this is neither the time nor place—"
CS: "Oh, but it is. I realize you prefer doing things behind the
scenes—like axing submitted papers that challenge the
status quo. But what makes you and your so-called peers
think you have a corner on the truth? Who made peer-
reviewed journals the judge and jury of all science? I bet
you'd be the first one to criticize the early church for
excommunicating people whose opinions it considered
heresy. But science today does it all the time, using the
peer-review process as an excuse."

Calder noticed the protestors had stopped their chanting. Like everyone
else on the beach, they appeared to be mesmerized by this clash of titans.
Bradstreet hiked himself up and sniffed.

TB: "I think you're being a bit melodramatic, Dr. Sinclair. No
one's excommunicating you. I'm merely pointing out that
if you wish to be taken seriously you've chosen the wrong
platform for announcing your claims. It suggests grand-
standing. Worse, it smacks of opportunism. Of riding the

coattails of a truly urgent and frightening worldwide crisis."

DR: "Dr. Bradstreet, I'm not sure you're being entirely fair to—"

Calder felt himself swaying on his feet. Automatically, one of his hands flew to his forehead, the other to his chest. He heard Robins asking, "Dr. Sinclair, are you okay?"

The voice of his PR agent, standing behind him, asked, "Calder, what's wrong?"

"What's going on with him?" the bald man exclaimed. "Oh, my god—catch him!"

CHAPTER 27

HERE COMES THE SUN

When her plane arrived in Boulder Allie was whisked directly to the SWPC, where Dallan—bandaged but fired up—quickly briefed her. Afterward, she retreated to a vacant office, where she did stand-up yoga exercises while going over the questions in her head.

"Five minutes, everyone!" she heard Eva shout. "Five minutes!"

Allie made her way out to the SWPC's cavernous command and control room. Two SWPC employees were standing in for Dallan and her so Pitsy could adjust the position of a klieg light. A short distance away Eva was hunched over a bank of monitors.

"That's it!" she cried out. "The shadow's gone. Leave it!"

213

This was to be a three-camera shoot, a sign of the story's importance. The main camera would frame Dallan and her, with the giant, wall-mounted LED screen appearing behind them. The second camera would be used for the wide shot. The third camera—a steady cam controlled by a roving operator—would handle close-ups.

"Pitsy," Eva sang out, "swing camera one a little to the left."

Allie half-watched while she pumped herself up mentally.

"No, the other left," Eva said. "Whoa, that's it! Lock it down."

Dallan appeared alongside her. "Allie, something was just handed to me I want you to see." He held out a sheet of paper. "It's from one of our theorists."

She looked at the document: a world map with six red markings on it—centered over the north pole, south pole, San Diego, Nagasaki, Humpty Doo (between Darwin and Kakadu), and Cádiz. "Yeah, so? It's like the map Brody showed me up at Alert."

"Yes, but do you see? They form a pattern. Like on a Chladni plate, except three-dimensional."

She was familiar with Chladni plates. She used them at Harvard to teach students about resonance. They consisted of a metal plate dusted with sand. When the plate was made to vibrate—for example, by stroking one of its edges with a violin bow—the sand particles danced around and settled into fabulous patterns. Like sand art.

She scrunched her brows. "A resonance pattern?" She paused. "But that would mean—"

"Exactly."

"Okay, everybody. Places!" Eva shouted. "Time to make the donuts!"

Moments later she and Dallan were standing on their marks, listening to Eva's countdown. At zero Allie heard through her IFB the New York anchor—Ashley Folsom—introducing her.

"For our top story this morning, a Fast News exclusive: we go live to the Space Weather Prediction Center in Boulder, Colorado, and our very own Allie Armendariz. Allie?"

Stretching to her full height, Allie looked into the main camera lens and assumed her best broadcaster's voice.

AA: "Thanks, Ashley, good morning. With me is Dr. Dallan O'Malley, director of the SWPC. He's just returned from the Arctic where, as you can see, he sustained some injuries."

She turned to Dallan.

AA: "Good morning, sir. I know we're not here to talk about your health but I thought to mention it because viewers are sure to be wondering about your bandages."

DO: "Good morning, Allie. Yes, well, I'm fine, really. It looks worse than it is. But thank you."

AA: "Good to hear. Now, you have something very important to report about the sun, right? Something that could affect us all. Tell us about it."

DO: "Yes, that's right. Yesterday at eleven a.m. Rocky mountain time our technicians noticed a blister growing on the face of the sun. Take a look."

On the screen behind them was a video of the sun's brightly lit, red-orange-yellow chromosphere. Its sinuous texture reminded her of bloody muscle fibers. Dallan used a handheld laser pointer to highlight the trouble spot, which was located in the northwest quadrant. It looked like an open sore.

DO: "Here you see it in the early stages of an eruption we call a CME, or coronal mass ejection. Think of a CME as a solar flare on steroids; it's the most powerful explosion known in the solar system."

Abruptly, the small blister swelled into a gargantuan bubble.

DO: "Here now is where it started bubbling up into a huge blob of very hot, glowing gases."

A moment later the blob exploded into a flash of blinding, white light.

DO: "The eruption occurred early this morning, less than two hours ago, and blasted a *hundred billion tons* of electrically charged particles into space. It's like a huge, radioactive sneeze."

She was eager for Dallan to get to the point.

AA: "And why should we be concerned?"

DO: "Well, most CMEs explode away from Earth, so they never matter to us. But this one is coming right toward us, at about 360 miles per second."

AA: "Per *second*?"

DO: "Right. That's more than a million miles per hour. At that rate it'll hit us head-on in about three days—on Tuesday."

AA: "What exactly—?"

DO: "By the way, when I say hit, I do mean *hit*. The CME has an energy equivalent of *360 million one-megaton H-bombs*."

She flinched at the statistic.

AA: "Can you explain what all this means. What should people be worried about—or *should* they be worried?"

DO: "The short answer is that it depends on how well our magnetic field holds up."

AA: "Please explain."

DO: "As you know the earth is cocooned inside a giant magnetic field—like a protective bubble or force field. Its outer boundary is about 40,000 miles away on the side facing the sun; farther on the side facing away. So if the field holds up when the CME slams into it, the damage will happen far away from us."

AA: "Forty thousand miles away or more."

DO: "Ideally, yes."

AA: "But what if the field doesn't hold up? I mean, you just said the CME is equal to 360 million megatons of TNT. What if it breaks through? What happens then?"

She knew the answer, of course: people and property would be incinerated. Like the nuclear bombing victims of Hiroshima and Nagasaki. Like Nell. Like Dallan's biologist friend and all those animals on the ice at Alert.

DO: "Honestly? We don't know, because there's never been a recorded CME this big."

She didn't challenge his prevarication; she understood Dallan didn't dare speak too bluntly about the worst case scenario for fear of triggering a panic.

DO: "Let me put it in perspective. Right now the sun is going through a very active period—we call it solar max, okay? On average it's spitting out three to four CMEs a day. Most of them go off in directions away from the earth. But of those aimed at our planet, the typical CME contains about one billion tons of electrically charged particles. The one heading at us right now is a *hundred times* bigger. We have no way of knowing how well the magnetic field will hold up to something of that size and power."

AA: "Which raises the question of the holes developing in the magnetic field at six locations around the world. I reported about that yesterday. Aren't people beneath those holes in special danger?"

Dallan, pressing his lips hard, hesitated. On the TV screen appeared an enhanced, updated version of Brody's map, showing six red sores.

DO: "I don't want to overly scare anyone—and remember we're still three days away from anything happening. But, yes, the magnetic holes are like wide-open doors that will let the CME pour in. So in those six regions where the magnetic field is weakening, residents living beneath them should definitely think about protecting themselves."

She knew she needed to press him on this, but tactfully.

AA: "Against what? What sort of danger are those people in, potentially?

She turned to camera.

AA: "And I want to stress the word *potentially*. As Dr. O'Malley is saying, this is still very early in a rapidly developing situation; the last thing anyone should do at this point is freak out."

She faced him once again.

AA: "Right?"
DO: "Yes, absolutely. During the next seventy-two hours we'll be working closely with the White House, Congress, the National Academy of Sciences, FEMA—we'll all be huddling to come up with the most intelligent way of protecting lives and property."
AA: "In the meantime can you give our viewers an idea of what dangers are possible, realistically speaking?"
DO: "Right. So when the CME first collides with the magnetic field it'll be like a Mack truck slamming into a Volkswagen Beetle. On the day side, facing the sun, the CME will squash the field. On the night side, it'll blow it away. These sudden distortions will induce spikes of electricity that'll wreak havoc on any kind of electrical equipment—both on the earth and in space."
AA: "You mean like satellites?"
DO: "Exactly. So people can expect their cell phones, radios, and satellite TV reception to be disrupted, even cut off completely. Again, we can't know for sure. But anything electrical will surely be affected to some degree."

AA: "What about aurorae? In the Arctic yesterday, when the magnetic field was weak, I saw some in the daytime. Can we expect the same to happen here?"

DO: "Yes, take a look."

On the TV screen were stills of colorful, oval-shaped aurorae centered over the north and south poles—images produced, Dallan said, using data from the Polar Operational Environmental Satellite system.

DO: "As you know aurorae happen when charged particles hit the upper atmosphere—about sixty miles up and higher. The impact makes the different air molecules glow different colors. We usually see aurorae only in the polar regions because the magnetic fields there are naturally weaker than elsewhere on Earth. But when this CME hits I expect we here in the United States might see aurorae as far south as Texas or Cuba. Nothing to worry about because they're so high up; but it will be something very unusual and people who don't know better might be alarmed at the sight."

She was impressed with Dallan's ability to explain complicated things without sounding too condescending or too esoteric.

AA: "Any other dangers we need to wor—be prepared for?"

DO: "Yes, there's one other important danger. All those charged particles I told you about? A hundred billion tons? They're like the biggest sandstorm you can imagine, multiplied a billion times. And, worse, the particles are so tiny they can go right through your skin and damage your DNA. That's a big danger if the magnetic field doesn't hold up."

AA: "A sandstorm of radiation."

DO: "Yes. If the field gives way, we need to brace ourselves for physical damage—not just electrical interference. Physical damage to property; but also possible *genetic* injury to our bodies, to animals, plants—anything that has DNA."

AA: "But how in the world do we protect ourselves from that?"

DO: "Mainly by staying indoors. But Allie, we have many more details about how people can protective themselves, their pets, and their property on our website."

AA: "And viewers can see the address on the lower part of the screen there."

A lower-third graphic appeared on the TV monitor showing the address: http://www.swpc.noaa.gov/index.html.

DO: "Yes, and I suggest people keep checking in on it because we'll be updating it constantly from now until the moment of impact—and then afterward as well."

AA: "Assuming our computers are still working at that time, right? Dr. O'Malley, thank you so much. We'll be staying in close contact with you during the next three days. Please stay safe."

CHAPTER 28

GOING IT ALONE

SATURDAY, APRIL 29 (8:30 A.M. PACIFIC DAYLIGHT TIME)

NAVAL BASE POINT LOMA; SAN DIEGO, CALIFORNIA

ESTIMATED TIME TO IMPACT: 66 HOURS 18 MINUTES

After fleeing the hangar, Jared made it to a small, deserted storage building not far away. There, tucked in a corner behind some crates, he slept soundly all night.

He awoke with a start, froze, and listened.

Nothing.

Chill, man, chill.

He dug out his smartphone and, heart racing, fired it up. He mostly kept it turned off now to conserve battery power, but also because he knew police could track his location whenever it was switched on.

Not that they could do it easily; the phone was registered under a phony name. Only one person had the number—the man handling the little G-20 surprise not even the protestors knew anything about—and even he didn't know Jared's true identity.

He stared at the awakening phone and after a few moments saw it.

GOOD TO GO

The text message he'd been hoping to receive from his confederate.

He pumped a fist.

Yes!

The fun would begin this evening, in a matter of hours.

He rose to his feet, stretched, and cautiously exited the shed, pausing just outside to scrutinize his surroundings. His eyes were drawn to the brightening morning sun—there was something odd about it. Using his hand for shade, he saw what appeared to be a pale, tangerine-colored halo around it.

Weird.

His stomach growled; he desperately needed to eat. His phone, his only lifeline, needed charging as well.

His plan, hatched overnight, was to attend the morning's Woof Walk at the Admiral Baker picnic area. According to the ad he'd read in the base's online newsletter, *Navy Life: This Week*, the event was a one-mile walk for military families and their dogs benefiting some kind of Navy charity. He didn't have a dog but if challenged had an idea that was sure to work.

All the way to the park he was careful to stay in the shadows. When finally he got within view of the event he was relieved to see most people were dressed casually, not in uniform. He'd easily blend in. A band was performing and there were all kinds of booths, including—thank goodness—vendors selling food. A show arena at the edge of the park was alive with handlers and gaily costumed dogs practicing acrobatic tricks. The largest part of the crowd was gathered around the starting line.

"Hey!"

The high-pitched voice came from behind him. Fighting the urge to run, Jared took a deep breath and wheeled. He saw a girl roughly his own age approaching him. She was being pulled by a toy poodle on a leash.

"Where's your dog?" she asked.

Jared nonchalantly stuffed his hands into his pockets. "Aw, I'm just visiting. My dad's a defense contractor. Makes pumps for nuclear attack subs."

"Lucky you." She came up to him and the little, curly haired pooch began giving him the olfactory once-over. "You get to skip school."

Jared feigned a frown. "Not really. I'm homeschooled." Then he said, "Hey, after this thing's over can you show me around?"

"Sure," she said, smiling coquettishly. "Are you living on base?"

"Yeah. How about you?"

"Yeah. Ballast Point Village."

"No way! Me too. Small world, huh?"

They set off together toward the festivities, the poodle leading the way.

"Yeah, small world," she echoed cheerily.

SATURDAY, APRIL 29 (9:16 A.M. PACIFIC DAYLIGHT TIME)

LINDBERGH FIELD; SAN DIEGO, CALIFORNIA

ESTIMATED TIME TO IMPACT: 65 HOURS 32 MINUTES

Allie was met at the airport by three Secret Service agents—two men, one woman. One of the men—presumably the leader—informed her the president was already at the beach.

"We need to pat you down," said the female agent.

"Go for it," Allie said, lifting her arms.

Her gaze drifted eastward toward the morning sun. Sure enough, it was ringed by a gauzy, orangish fringe—proof positive the CME was heading right for Earth.

"It's already a huge cloud," Dallan told her just before she departed. "But as it travels across space, it balloons. By the time it reaches us, it'll be monstrous—probably about fifty million miles across."

"All set, thanks" the agent said to her, turning then to Eva.

More than anything else right now, Allie wanted to be near her family, to make sure they were all protected against the CME. She wanted to be in Jerusalem looking for Lolo. She wanted to be with Calder, with whom she'd talked a few minutes earlier on the plane after hearing about his collapse on the air that morning.

Sacrifices—always sacrifices.

But what choice did she have? She needed to be here.

Help me, sweet Jesus, my life is out of control.

"Okay," the lead agent said. "We can go now."

Allie and the crew followed the dark-suited men and woman to the news van and waited for them to inspect it as well. Once on the road, their motorcade passed through numerous fortified checkpoints. The lead agent explained Mission Beach was closed to the public and so were streets for at least a mile around.

When they arrived, Allie—wired for sound; trailed by Eva and the crew, camera rolling; and flanked by Secret Service Agents—tramped across the sand and waded into the crowd surrounding the chief executive. She approached him with a smile and an extended hand. "Good morning, Mr. President. It's an honor to meet you."

She had not voted for him but respected the office.

"Allie, good to meet you. Martha and I watch you all the time. Saw your report this morning." He gestured to a nearby gray whale struggling for its life and shook his head. "This is just awful. I expect to learn a lot from you today."

"Yes, sir, whatever I can do. Dr. Sinclair's very sorry he couldn't make it. He's in the hospital and wanted me to give you his warmest regards."

"Thank you, Allie. I'll be calling him later today to see how he is. He's impressed us all with that vehicle of his. Made his country—the world—proud of what he tried to do for the whales."

As the president's sprawling entourage walked haltingly along the whale-strewn beach, reporters and TV cameras shadowed the procession like seagulls dogging a fishing boat.

"Allie, tell me, how does this stranding compare to the ones you saw at the other sites?"

The president, though ostensibly addressing her personally, was clearly playing to the cameras and reporters leaning in to record the conversation.

Politicians.

Not that most scientists she interviewed were any different. They too did more than their fair share of spinning and outright dissembling to protect their turf, reputations, and grant monies.

"The only real differences are the species," she said. "Here in San Diego we're seeing mostly Eastern North Pacific gray whales. From February till about July these grays migrate from breeding grounds off the coast of Mexico to summering grounds in the Arctic. If everything were normal they'd simply be passing through these waters. This is an atrocity."

She went on to itemize the other species being affected at the other locations.

"Marty Glauber tells me it's all being caused by the magnetic holes," the president said. "You agree?"

Allie knew the president's science advisor, Martin Glauber, from Harvard. He was a good guy.

"Well," she said, "it's the best explanation so far. Whale strandings generally are a mystery to science. We think it has something to do with their built-in compasses getting jammed or sabotaged somehow. Disturbances in the magnetosphere could definitely do that."

She was tempted to bring up what Dallan had shown her—the image of the resonance pattern. But he'd asked her to wait until it was double-checked.

"And the Japanese," the president said. "Did they really challenge your presence in Nagasaki? Were you threatened with violence?"

It was all over the news the president was planning to rake the Japanese prime minister over the coals during the G-20 for his country's ravenous appetite for whale meat.

"Well, I was scared, that's for sure. They radioed us beforehand, warned us we were approaching their territorial waters. Then they sent the harbor police to chase us away."

"Would you say your lives were endangered by their actions?"

"I'm not sure I'd go that far." Allie was mindful that everything she was saying could—almost certainly would—land on the evening news. "I'm just glad Dr. Sinclair was able to get us out of there fast enough to avoid a real confrontation. If he hadn't I'm not sure—well, let's leave it at that."

Ten minutes later, when the president was ready to depart, he asked her to follow him back to his limo. There he said, "I'd like you and Dr. Sinclair to head up a special emergency task force. I've cleared it with Marty. He respects you a lot."

She was barely able to find her voice. "Yes, sir. But a task force on what?"

"All this," the president said, motioning widely toward the beach and sky. "Marty tells me it's all getting worse, the strandings, the magnetic holes—and now the solar threat. The leaders coming to this summit are pressuring me for a solution, for a way to reassure the public. It's why we didn't cancel or relocate the summit. We want to show the world we aren't afraid—and that there's hope."

"But what about your safety, sir? And the safety of the other leaders? Aren't you risking too much just to make sure people don't overreact?"

"Worldwide hysteria is no small thing, Allie. We need to do everything possible to avert it. Besides, there are contingency plans to insure our safety—but that's off the record."

"But why me, Mr. President? There are Nobel Prize winners, even Marty, who are more qualified."

"Yes and no, Allie. Yes, I could put some pinhead in charge who knows more about one particular subject than you do. But I need someone who has the big picture. You know all the major players; you're up to speed on everything. You and Dr. Sinclair have just seen firsthand what's happening all over the world—no one else has."

"But—"

The president held up his hand. "Allie, I know your plate's already full; I can understand why you wouldn't want this kind of responsibility on top of everything else. But the public knows and trusts you. They relate to you, and you know how to talk to them. That's extremely important in this case. And you're a scientist of no small reputation. As I said, Marty was the first to suggest the idea." He added, "Plus, you know about tight deadlines."

She smiled weakly. "Well, that much is true."

"Allie, I'm giving you and Dr. Sinclair the full resources of the White House. Use everything you learned on your mission. Consult with whomever you want anywhere in the world. Form a blue-ribbon panel, whatever, but come up with a plan. And fast. I need to announce a solution by tomorrow evening—at the latest."

★

SATURDAY, APRIL 29 (9:18 A.M. PACIFIC DAYLIGHT TIME)

SHARP MEMORIAL HOSPITAL; SAN DIEGO, CALIFORNIA

ESTIMATED TIME TO IMPACT: 65 HOURS 30 MINUTES

Calder threw back the covers and sat on the edge of the bed, ready to walk. "I'm fine I tell you!" He'd had enough doting from Sager and the doctors. "I just want to get back to *Hero* and be left in peace."

He looked away from Sager and chewed on his lower lip.

Oh, c'mon…stop acting like a prima donna.

He knew the hospitalization wasn't to blame for his crabbiness. Nor was it the over-the-top publicity he was getting. Nor even the morning's abortive TV show—Bradstreet, the loose accusations, the lack of respect.

No, it was Allie and—

His head dropped. He slapped the bed.

I'm just tired.

He reminded himself of what *Hero* had just accomplished.

You should be dancing in the streets, man!

Sager exploded out of his chair. "Look, Calder, please, just wait till the test results, that's all." He brandished an index finger. "And you better get used to all of this. I know it's a pain. But your life's never going to be the same, whether you like it or not."

Calder slowly wagged his lowered head. Lots Sanger knew.

Nothing ever changes for me.

Not for the better.

He breathed hard.

Oh, get off it already!

He lifted his chin, gripping the edge of the mattress. "All right, all right. But only until the test results."

CHAPTER 29

URGENT BUSINESS

SATURDAY, APRIL 29 (7:25 P.M. ISRAEL DAYLIGHT TIME)

JERUSALEM, ISRAEL

ESTIMATED TIME TO IMPACT: 65 HOURS 23 MINUTES

Lorena pushed back from the dinner table. "Myra, if only we had shawarma this good in the United States. You ought to start a chain."

"Oh, please," Myra Hershkovitz demurred. She was collecting the dirty dishes. "It was nothing. If I'd known you were coming I would've prepared something special."

"It was perfect," Lorena said, feeling genuinely grateful.

Asher jumped out of his seat at the head of the table. "I must turn on the TV. Yonit Levi is doing a news segment on us tonight."

"Yonit Levi?" Lorena said.

"She's the anchor of the prime-time news show on Channel 2," he said from the living room. "Very popular. She interviewed me the other day. I hope they don't do a hatchet job on us, like the others have."

After helping Myra clean and put away the dishes, Lorena joined Asher who was glued to the TV set.

"It should be coming on soon," he said, staring at the screen. "It looks like they're keeping us for last."

She gave Asher a gentle pat on the back before taking a seat on the couch next to him. "In the United States we always save the best for last."

Asher looked away from the set and gave her a warm smile. "It's good to have you with us."

"Thank you, Asher, it's good to be here." Then she said, "I have a question."

"Yes?" His eyes remained on the TV set.

"Why did Dayan give religious control of the Temple Mount back to the Muslims right after capturing it? It's not just because the Mount is considered too sacred for Jews to walk on, right?"

Asher made a face. "Aach! He was afraid of how a billion Muslims and the Jew-hating world would react if Israel were to begin rebuilding the Holy Temple. He was afraid of human beings, you see, not the God of Israel. He did not trust the promises of God, that He would always stand with the forces of Israel, especially when we set out to rebuild His Temple."

"Do you think—?"

Her attention was snatched away by an image on the TV screen. An image of her.

"Oh, look!" Asher said.

But they both fell silent when they heard the anchor say, "Local police and the U.S. Consulate are asking for the public's help in locating this missing American woman who disappeared from a hospital in Colorado four days ago. She is now believed to be in the Jerusalem area. The woman's name is Lorena Armendariz O'Malley...."

★

SATURDAY, APRIL 29 (10:47 A.M. PACIFIC DAYLIGHT TIME)

MISSION BEACH; SAN DIEGO, CALIFORNIA

ESTIMATED TIME TO IMPACT: 64 HOURS 1 MINUTE

Allie, having just said good-bye to the president's science advisor, was about to go looking for Eva when an unmistakable male voice boomed out from behind her.

"Look who's here," it said.

She whipped around. Mike Cannatella and Eva were rushing toward her.

"Welcome back, stranger," he said, offering his hand.

"Mike!" she exclaimed, accepting his hand and pumping it vigorously. "Good to see you, good to see you."

"Look, I've gotta leave with the motorcade but I've told Eva some stuff I thought you guys ought to know." Then he said, "What did you and the president talk about? Anything you can tell me?"

She decided not to be coy with the man who'd always been so forthcoming with her. But she also couldn't resist turning the tables. She said in a put-on voice, "I'll tell you, but it's strictly off the record. *Capisce?*"

★

SATURDAY, APRIL 29 (10:53 A.M. PACIFIC DAYLIGHT TIME)

ESTIMATED TIME TO IMPACT: 63 HOURS 55 MINUTES

They rushed back to the van, Eva demonstrably unhappy about the president's request of Allie.

"You have no time!" she said, flinging her hands into the air.

Allie ignored Eva's rant and reached for her cell phone. "I have to tell Calder."

"But my god, Allie, the G-20 starts *tonight*. And wait till you hear what Mike just told me."

Allie stopped mid-dial. "What? What did he say?"

Eva, speaking so rapidly Allie had a hard time following everything, said the FBI lab finished analyzing the CDs the masked man handed out. "The CD contains computer script like they've never seen before."

Allie suddenly felt warm all over. "What do you mean?"

"Mike said it's like some kind of security code. An antivirus program designed to protect against viruses no one's ever heard about. It's got them stumped."

Allie began twisting a strand of her hair into a corkscrew. "An antivirus program?"

"Miss Armendariz?"

Startled, she looked behind her and saw a youngish, well-groomed Hispanic man dressed in a dark suit. She recognized him as one of the agents who'd been with the president on the beach.

He held out his hand. "I'm Agent David Aragon with the Secret Service. I've been asked to stay with you in case you need anything. President's orders."

"Really?" She cast a look at Eva who shrugged and smiled ironically. Looking back at the agent, she said, "Well, thank you. That's, uh, terrific."

She started walking away, beckoning him to follow. "We were just heading back to the van. We need to get to the ho—"She spun around to look at him. "Actually, you know what? There *is* something you can do to help me."

★

SATURDAY, APRIL 29 (11:52 A.M. PACIFIC DAYLIGHT TIME)

SHARP MEMORIAL HOSPITAL; SAN DIEGO, CALIFORNIA

ESTIMATED TIME TO IMPACT: 62 HOURS 56 MINUTES

Calder, in bed propped up on pillows, was listening impatiently to the doctor discussing test results.

"The good news is you appear to be healthy as an ox. But you were severely dehydrated when they brought you in. And your body is suffering from extreme exhaustion. I'd prefer it if you stayed here for at least another day; but if you insist, I'll let you leave, on the condition you go straight home and rest." He wagged a finger at him. "No work whatsoever, you hear?" He turned to Sager. "And absolutely no more interviews for now. I'm serious."

Calder thanked the physician and said he wanted to leave immediately.

"Sorry to have been such a bear, doc," he said, scrambling out of bed. "I just want to get back to *Hero*; she's been sitting outside since we arrived." He added, removing his hospital johnny, "Man, I'll tell you this much: I wouldn't be Brad Pitt for a million dollars. Having to deal with all that publicity all the time. It gets old, real fast."

"Yeah, well, you *are* him now, like it or not," Sager said. "I told you—get used to it."

A few minutes later, when he was dressed and about to sign discharge papers a nurse had just handed him, his cell phone jangled. It was lying on the bed table.

Calder lunged for it. "Hello?"

"Calder, it's Allie. Are you sitting down?"

★

SATURDAY, APRIL 29 (12:52 P.M. MOUNTAIN DAYLIGHT TIME)

SPACE WEATHER PREDICTION CENTER; BOULDER, COLORADO

ESTIMATED TIME TO IMPACT: 62 HOURS 56 MINUTES

Dallan, at his desk nervously twiddling a pencil, was on the phone with Detective William Brady of the Denver Police Department. "I wish I could find a way out but I just can't."

He squeezed the bridge of his nose.

Oh, Lolo, please be okay.

Please forgive me.

"I understand completely, Dr. O'Malley, I'll notify the Israeli authorities right away."

"Thank you, detective. Tell them I plan to fly over there right after all of this blows over."

If it does.

"Sure. And don't beat yourself up over it. You have your hands full, everybody knows that. The missus and I saw you on TV this morning. She wants me to buy one of those underground shelters. Is it really going to be that bad? You made it sound like the end of the world was coming."

Dallan's thoughts froze.

The end of the world—my god, could Lolo be right?

Don't be stupid.

"It's serious, all right," he said. "But the end of the world? No."

"Oh, good."

"Problem is, though, we've become so damned modern. Back when we lived in caves or rode horses and read by candlelight we didn't need to worry about stuff like this. But nowadays—Anyways, we just need to be prepared for the worst and hope for the best, that's all."

CHAPTER 30

OUT OF CONTROL

Calder stared blankly out the backseat window of the speeding limo. The two Secret Service agents escorting him were explaining that protecting the president and foreign leaders at events such as the G-20 depended on concentric rings of perimeter security.

He shook his head slowly.

This is ridiculous.

"Everything's out of control," he muttered.

He wanted to be heading home or to the lab—not to some stupid hotel. He should've insisted Allie tell him on the phone what the supposedly big news was. "I'd rather tell you in person, if you're up to it," she said. "It's something really big and it involves you."

It better be good.

He needed to focus all his energies on figuring out how to mass produce *Hero* at a reasonable cost.

Assuming the world survives.

And he needed to find a private investor to fund the manufacturing, *pronto*. He wasn't comfortable depending solely on the Navy anymore.

Time to move on.

He thought of Allie.

Yeah, time to move on there too.

He'd fallen hard for her, but their differences were just too great. It was no use pursuing a dead end.

They drove past checkpoint after checkpoint, the nested layers of protection the agents described to him. When at last they pulled up to the Manchester Grand Hyatt he was hustled through the lobby. The place was abuzz with people he pegged as mostly reporters and government apparatchiks.

He was led down a long hallway to the door of a conference room. When he was shown inside, Allie and Eva were sitting at a small round table. A dozen people—most of them young—were scurrying about or huddled in deep conversation near a banquet table covered with food along the right-hand wall.

"Calder!" Allie sang out, waving gaily at him.

"We'll be right outside the door in case you need us, sir," one agent said to him.

He crossed the room and sat down heavily next to the two women. "Allie, what's this all about? What's going on?"

Her smile faded quickly. "Calder, are you all right? You don't look well."

"I'm fine," he lied. "Why am I here? What's so important you couldn't tell me on the phone?"

She looked at him guardedly. "Calder, I can see—"

"Allie, please! Just spit it out. Why did you bring me here?"

"The president wants us—you and me—to head up an emergency committee to figure out how to protect Earth from the CME heading our way."

He slapped the table hard. "Allie, that's insane!" He shot to his feet and began stomping about the room. "And why didn't he tell me himself?"

She stared back at him, her green eyes the size of dinner plates. "Calder, he was expecting *both* of us at the beach, remember? He told me he was going to call you at the hospital but obviously he didn't. The man's got a lot on his shoulders. He told me he's getting huge pressure from the other leaders on this."

Furious, he glanced around the room. Everyone was staring at them now. "Can we please take this outside?"

SATURDAY, APRIL 29 (1:02 P.M. PACIFIC DAYLIGHT TIME)

ESTIMATED TIME TO IMPACT: 61 HOURS 47 MINUTES

Calder, his stomach churning, didn't speak while Allie led them through several doors to the outside, to a metal bench in a small, elevated garden overlooking San Diego Bay. Seaside Village, alive with people, lay immediately beneath them. Coronado Island loomed in the near distance. They were tailed by the Secret Service agents.

He plopped down on the bench and stared out at the water. He felt nourished by the warm sunshine and gentle sea breeze.

Allie sat next to him. He heard her say, "Do you mind, fellas? A little privacy?"

He turned and saw the agents dip their heads and retreat to a respectable distance—still within eyeshot.

He turned again to the bay.

"Calder, what's going on? Something's bothering you and it isn't about the task force."

He felt his body stiffening. There were so many things he wanted to say to her, he couldn't make up his mind where to start.

"Look, Calder, I watched a recording of what happened to you on TV this morning with Bradstreet. Them ambushing you like that, I'm really sorry it happened. Actually, I'm more than sorry. I'm angry about it.

"Unfortunately, it's an old tactic used by reporters who've been scooped on a major story. They cast around for a different angle and are willing to say or do just about anything that takes the headline in another direction. It's usually sensational in a negative way."

"If it's such an old trick," he said, rounding on her, "then why didn't Sager see it coming? I was made to look like a fool in front of the entire world. This is my life's work we're talking about here, Allie."

Painful images sprang from the deep shadows of his mind and ambushed him: the condescending look on the Seville boy's well-scrubbed face; his pampered-looking lips spitting out the word, *huérfano*; the special afternoon in the park spoiled by a dog bite and dropped cone; the excruciating shots that followed; Bradstreet's insufferable haughtiness.

He shook his head. "I just want to get back to my work."

"But Calder this is part of it. You can't expect to change the world without taking it on. And not just on your terms—*its* terms. It's never pretty."

She stood up and looked down at him. "Einstein—remember? The academic world brutalized him when he first came out with relativity. Said it was nothing but Jewish physics. Same with Wegener. And Galileo."

She resumed her seat and said quietly, "And now it's Calder Sinclair's turn." She paused. "You said this was your life's work. I know that. The question is do you think it's worth fighting for?"

Calder looked away at the magnificent vista before him. His eyes picked out a large sailboat, which appeared to be tacking toward the marina. It reminded him of the sailboats crisscrossing the sparkling turquoise waters off Mindil Beach.

You deserve to be happy again.

That's what Sara said to him after breakfast on that happy day in Darwin.

Tell it to God.

If he exists.

He looked askance at Allie who was staring out at the water also.

But I love this woman.

He curled his lips.

Forget it.

He spoke without taking his eyes off the sailboat, which was nearing the slips. "Allie—look, I'm sorry about my sour attitude. It's just that after four-plus days of nonstop television—" He turned his head toward her and made an all-encompassing gesture with his hand. "All this commotion—this is *your* world, you love this stuff, I can see that. I went looking for it, I admit it. But I've had more than enough now. I'm beat and I'm pissed and all I want to do is go home and get a decent night's rest."

She met his eyes. "Calder, I know, believe me." She hesitated, bunching her hands in her lap. "I don't see the *locura* anymore, the craziness, because—well, as you say, it's my world. And yeah, I love it. It's like a drug, the news business. When I go on vacation, which is not often, I get antsy after just a few days—even after just one day—and I start monitoring the news. If something breaks I can't stop myself: I call the network to see if they need me." She shook her head. "Just hearing myself talk about it right now—it's nuts, really, sick in some ways."

He felt a wave of empathy. "I know what you mean. I've always been a workaholic too. It got worse after Nell died and Sara went away. I'm basically a hermit now. *Hero* is my closest friend. I love her the way I would a person, which is pretty twisted, right? Having you on the trip was like, I don't know—like a spring day." He rearranged himself on the bench so his whole body was facing her. "You made me feel my luck was changing, especially after *Hero* completed the mission with flying colors. But then it all started unraveling. Like always. That's why I reacted the way I did."

"What do you mean, 'unravelling, like always'?" she said, tucking her feet beneath herself.

He hesitated, looking away, then back again at her. "This is probably gonna sound weird to you."

"Try me."

"Well—it's just that I think I really like you—and I'd like to get to know you better. But part of me—and maybe I'm just tired—but part of me is thinking, why bother? We're very different people—me and my obsession with *Hero* and having no time or patience for the idea of a god—and you with your crazy, jet-setting schedule, glaring lights, non-stop demands, and posturing blowhards." He looked away. "And your Christianity." He paused, expecting her to blow up. But she didn't. "Besides, every time something good happens to me it gets ruined some-how. Look at what I have to deal with, even now—even though *Hero* has succeeded. The naysayers never quit, never stop trying to make me out to be a quack." He turned to her and threw up his hands. "It's the story of my life."

She undid her legs, squared herself in the bench, and stared out at the water.

"Wow, so that's it. Pretty heavy."

"Yeah."

She turned to him. "Now let me tell *you* something, Dr. Sinclair. I really like you too. Last night, when you asked me out to dinner it was like…"

She hesitated.

"What?" he said. "Like what?"

"Like lightning had struck twice."

He bunched his brows and inclined his head.

She gave him a sad grin and wagged her head. "Long story. It's just that you made me really happy—the happiest I've been in a long time. But then my mind—my vaunted, brainiac mind—started kicking in. I began doubting the possibility of anything coming of it, of us, because of your atheism."

He leaned back and rolled his eyes. "Ah, yes, my atheism. It's exactly why—"

"No, it's not what you think. It's not that you don't bel—"

"Oh, thank god—there you are!" Eva came running up to them. "Allie—"

Allie shot up a hand. "Not now, Eva."

"But—"

"Not now! Give me a few minutes."

After Eva retreated, she said to him, "Look, Calder, we can finish this later. Right now you and I have serious work to do."

He started up from his seat. "*You've* got serious work to do—count me out."

She reached out and kept him from standing. "Think of Bradstreet, for goodness sake—how stupid it'll make him look when it's announced the president of the United States has picked *you*—not some establishment wonk—to help save the world."

He hesitated.

"Please, Calder, we don't have much time. People's lives are at stake."

His eyes went out to the water again and noticed the sailboat. It was being moored.

Sara.

"All right, he said finally. "Where do we start?"

Allie slapped her thigh. "Now we're talking. I've already started. We don't have time to bring people together physically so I've been on the phone with some of my top sources from all over the world, including Dallan's people at the SWPC and the president of the National Academy of Sciences. And here's what I'm getting from them." She paused and said warily, "And please, Calder, I'm just the messenger here, okay?"

He stood. "What? What are they saying?"

"Well—that you and *Hero* might be our best hope."

"What?!"

"No, wait. Hear me out. And remember, they're looking at the situation from a distance. Objectively, through fresh eyes."

He plunged his hands into his pockets and, head down, started pacing. "Go ahead."

"Well, let's start with what we already know. In Darwin, Cádiz, and Alert, the whale strandings stopped and the magnetic holes went away all by themselves—at least for a while. And it happened right when we arrived, or a few hours after."

He stopped and looked at her. "Yeah, but—"

"I know, I know. You think it's a coincidence. But c'mon, Calder, you don't really believe that."

Calder resumed pacing, his insides tingling.

Could it possibly be?

Rubbish!

"Calder?"

"What?"

"You *know* what." Allie eyed him mercilessly. "Somehow, *Hero* is having an effect on the earth's magnetic field. I've been thinking a lot about it ever since Alert and have my own ideas. But I'd rather hear from you first."

Eva stormed up to them yet again.

"Allie, *please*! You've got to listen. There's a major situation developing. We need to go *now!*"

Allie looked from Eva to him and was about to speak, but he cut her off.

"Like I said—your world, Allie, not mine." He flung his hands into the air and waved her away. "Go. Go!" Then he added, "You know where I live."

CHAPTER 31

LUNACY

SATURDAY, APRIL 29 (1:38 P.M. PACIFIC DAYLIGHT TIME)

SAN DIEGO, CALIFORNIA

ESTIMATED TIME TO IMPACT: 61 HOURS 11 MINUTES

The news van—and KU satellite truck used for live shots—followed Agent Aragon's black sedan through deserted streets cordoned off from the public. The bright afternoon sun made everything sparkle.

Allie was in the van's back seat next to Eva, concerned simultaneously about Calder's acerbic behavior and why neither Carlos nor her dad had returned her repeated calls.

"Hello. Are you with me?" Eva was waving a hand before Allie's eyes. "Have you heard a word I said?"

"What? Oh, I'm sorry, *chica*—go ahead."

"From the start?"

"Yeah, I'm sorry."

"I was saying Mike told me the protesters started showing up separately about forty-five minutes ago: Planet First, Occupy the World, and a bunch of others. At first they avoided each other. But gradually the groups started drifting toward each other, hooking up, blending, behaving like one."

"So Mike was right about Anonymous."

"Looks like it. But he says the numbers are already way higher than expected. He's on the scene now—that's where we're heading. Stu wants us to hit the grass rolling."

Allie looked at her quizzically. "Do you do that on purpose?"

"What?"

"Never mind."

Eva shouted toward the front of the van. "You hear that, Pitsy? As soon as we get there, off-load the camera. Wireless mic and sun gun, that's it. We have to be nimble."

Sun guns were handheld, battery-operated lights used for complete freedom of movement.

"Roger that," he answered.

Allie reached for her cell, intending to retry Carlos, when it jangled. "*Bueno?*"

"Allie!" It was Carlos' voice. "I'm so sorry. I just saw your message."

"Oh, thank God. Is everyone okay? Mom, Dad?"

"Yeah, everybody's fine. It's just that after we saw you on TV this morning we've been getting the church basement ready for the solar flare."

"Oh, great idea, great idea. What about Mom?"

"We're talking with her doctor. He's trying to see what the home's gonna do with all the patients. Worst case—"

"Bring her to the church basement."

"That's what I was going to say. The doctor is cool with the idea, if it comes to that. The *hermanos* are bringing food, blankets, everything we'll need to hole up. How long do you think we'll need to stay there?"

"I'm not sure. But to be safe, plan on at least a couple days. Good thing you guys have bathrooms down there and a kitchen. It's perfect. Just make sure everyone goes down there well before the CME hits, okay?—you never know with this thing. And make sure you have plenty of first-aid supplies. You need to be prepared for anything and everything. How about Lolo? Any news?"

"No, nothing. It's as if she's disappeared. It's really scary. The police over there say they're doing everything possible. We need to surrender her to the Lord. There's nothing else we can do."

Eva was frantically motioning to her now, mouthing the words: "We…almost…there."

"What about you, Sis?" Carlos said. "Everyone's asking. They're worried about you being out there."

"Listen, Carlos. I'm gonna be fine. I gotta go, okay? But I'll be fine. Tell Mom and Dad—tell everybody I love them—and to please, *please* be careful. I gotta go."

"Okay, Sis, okay. But you be careful too. We're all praying for you. I love you."

"I love you too, Bro. Bye."

The van pulled up to a large, squat, tan-and-orange structure with a red roof. Across its façade were the words: HARRY WEST GYMNASIUM. There was no parking lot, so Pitsy jumped the curb and parked on the patio area in front of the main entrance.

"Everybody out!" Eva commanded. "*Pronto!*"

Allie glanced at her watch. Ten minutes was all it had taken to travel from the hotel, through the Gas Lamp Quarter and East Village, to this gym belonging to San Diego City College.

"This is where Mike is headquartered," Eva said, leading the way. "They're using it for command and control."

They rushed inside, but the liaison officer immediately intercepted them, saying Agent Cannatella was way too busy to speak to the press.

"But he knows we're coming," Allie insisted. "He spoke to my producer here just a few minutes ago."

"Yeah, well, that was then, this is now. We've got a major situation blowing up and everyone's on the job, sorry."

"Where exactly are the protests happening?" Eva said.

"They started on the soccer and baseball fields. But now they're spilling over into Balboa. That's why it's a red alert."

Allie immediately grasped the gravity of the matter. At this very moment, inside the Mingei International Museum in Balboa Park, less than a mile north, the luncheon reception marking the official start of the G-20 Summit was under way. The police dared not allow the protesters to get any closer.

"Let's go!" Eva said.

Just as they turned to leave, a loud voice echoed from deep within the gymnasium. "Hold up!"

A moment later Mike emerged from the horde and strode toward them, looking grave.

The liaison, abruptly straightening, said, "I told them you were too busy, sir."

"Not for these guys, I'm not," Mike said, brushing past the man and shaking Allie's hand.

"Thanks, Mike, but if you're—"

"Look, I don't have lots of time but here's the scoop." He smiled at her. "And you can quote me: it's for the record."

She felt a rush of warmth for this man. In many ways they were members of opposing camps; but at heart they were undeniably birds of a feather.

She whipped out her narrow, dog-eared reporter's notebook. "Shoot."

"We're having to call in the National Guard and military reservists from the Army and Navy. We estimate the crowd of protesters at a hundred and twenty thousand—at least. And it's growing by the minute."

"A hundred and twenty thousand?!" Allie scribbled the figure into her notebook and underlined it.

"Exactly our reaction."

"So this is what the masked man was up to—just like you said."

"Well, we're not sure. It's also the solar thing. Your report this morning and all the reports afterward have really put a nickel into these people—the environmentalists especially. They're blaming the corona-mass-whatever on human carelessness, on what we've done to the earth."

"But that's ridiculous!" Allie exclaimed. "We don't control the sun. It's ninety-three million miles away, for Pete's sake."

"Yeah, well, tell it to the protestors. And most of them are college kids. Makes you wonder what they're teaching them nowadays, doesn't it?"

She flashed to her days at Harvard, caught a glimpse of how far she'd come from its ivy-covered walls. "Yeah, well, they're not learning basic astronomy, that's for sure."

"What about the Anonymous guy?" Eva said. "You haven't caught him yet, I take it."

"No," he said curtly.

"You think he's here today?"

"Most probably. But we have no idea what he looks like."

"And the antiviral thing," Allie said. "Any more on that? What does it mean?"

"The lab guys are still playing with it. We have no idea." Mike looked at his watch. "Look, I have to go back in there before they start yelling for me. I'll have one of my men escort you out to the protests. They're not letting the press get too close but I'll make sure you get a front-row seat."

"Thanks, Mike, but we're all set. The president assigned me a Secret Service agent." She gestured to Agent Aragon who was standing a short distance away.

Mike nodded to him, then looked to her. "Great, so you're in good hands."

Responding to an impulse, she stepped forward and gave him a warm hug. "Be careful, Mike, okay?" She quickly disengaged and stepped back.

"You, too." He wheeled to head back into the crowd and then stopped. Turning, he said, "Hey! Let's have lunch when this is all over, all right? Trade war stories."

"Absolutely!" Then she added. "But it's gotta be my treat."

He laughed. "Whatever you say. Anyway, you make a whole lot more moolah than me." And with that he disappeared into the gymnasium's chaos.

★

SATURDAY, APRIL 29 (2:03 P.M. PACIFIC DAYLIGHT TIME)

ESTIMATED TIME TO IMPACT: 61 HOURS 11 MINUTES

In the soundless, starlit darkness of space, 22,233 miles above Earth's surface, above the *Sturm und Drang* of human existence, the solar X-ray imager of the GOES-15 satellite caught sight of something noteworthy in the atmosphere of the sun. Exactly as it was programmed to do, the orbiting sentry immediately sent the digitized color image to the U.S. Space Weather Prediction Center.

A short while later its robot eye spotted another noteworthy disruption in the sun's atmosphere.

And another.

And another.

★

SATURDAY, APRIL 29 (3:03 P.M. MOUNTAIN DAYLIGHT TIME)

SPACE WEATHER PREDICTION CENTER; BOULDER, COLORADO

ESTIMATED TIME TO IMPACT: 61 HOURS 11 MINUTES

Dallan was at his desk when the computer began to chime. At that same instant, his assistant rushed in to explain the GOES-15 satellite had just detected the eruption of a Class X solar flare.

"Damn!" This had been his worst fear since announcing the CME. "Just what we don't need!"

A few minutes later the computer chimed again.

"No, *NO!*" He pounded the desk and then, leaning forward, peered at his computer monitor through narrowed, intensely focused eyes. He wanted to make certain he wasn't just seeing things.

★

SATURDAY, APRIL 29 (2:13 P.M. PACIFIC DAYLIGHT TIME)

SAN DIEGO CITY COLLEGE; SAN DIEGO, CALIFORNIA

ESTIMATED TIME TO IMPACT: 61 HOURS 1 MINUTE

When they reached the scene of the protests, Allie and the crew hurried out of the van.

"*Ay, caramba!*" she said. "This is crazy!"

She'd covered protests before, including some on the Washington DC Mall that were enormous. But the one before her was denser and noisier than anything she'd ever seen. In a single, unified chorus they were shouting:

"OMG! CME! OMG! CME!"

"Pollution no! Justice yes!"

"Technology no! Justice yes!"

"Fat cats no! Justice yes!"

Adding to the racket were police choppers circling overhead. News copters too—including, she noticed, one from her own network.

Flanking the melee on the right and left, trying to keep the protesters in check, were rows of law enforcement officers wearing black riot gear and carrying large Plexiglas shields. She could see they were vastly outnumbered and sooner or later would be forced to retreat to accommodate the mushrooming crowd.

While Eva helped get the KU truck ready for the live shot, Allie remained standing on the sidelines, taking in the bedlam, hoping to spot someone who could be Anonymous. But it was no use. There were too many protesters wearing masked costumes, most of them homemade and garish. A giant papier-mâché bird covered in fake blood. A large-headed, sinister-looking businessman chomping on an outsized cigar. A walking globe of the Earth with a surface that looked scorched. And to make matters worse—sprinkled throughout were hundreds of protesters wearing Guy Fawkes masks.

Eva rushed up and gave her a wireless, handheld microphone flagged with the Fast News logo. "Here you go, girlfriend. The bird'll be up in less than a minute. Stu says be careful."

Minutes later, with the protesters framed behind her, she went on the air. "I'm here at the San Diego City College soccer field, where record crowds are gathering to protest everything from big business to green energy. Official estimates place their number at more than one hundred and twenty thousand and growing fast. You can't see it from here, but we're told the crowd is spilling over into the adjacent baseball field and is attempting to advance to the southern border of Balboa Park. That's less than a mile from where the G-20 reception is being held. According to the FBI, the city is calling in the National Guard and reservists from the Army and Navy. Already on the scene are hundreds of police, some from as far away as—"

Loud, piercing, chirping sounds rent the bright, clear air. Instantly, the protesters stopped marching and chanting, dropped their placards, and covered their ears.

She quickly covered her left ear with her free hand and buried the mic in her bosom. She knew what this was: an LRAD, or long range acoustic device. Its high-pitched squeals were capable of inflicting a bad headache or worse—permanent hearing loss.

As she recalled, riot police first used LRADs against protesters at the 2009 G-20 Summit in Pittsburgh. Based on how that confrontation played out, she knew the police would follow up, if necessary, with tear gas and rubber bullets.

Accompanying the LRAD's deafening squeal, a painfully amplified, stern voice filled the air. "BY ORDER OF THE CITY OF SAN DIEGO

CHIEF OF POLICE I HEREBY DECLARE THIS TO BE AN UNLAW-
FUL ASSEMBLY. YOU ARE ORDERED IMMEDIATELY TO DIS-
PERSE. IF YOU DO NOT, YOU MAY BE ARRESTED AND/OR
SUBJECT TO OTHER POLICE ACTION."

Eva yelled at Allie through the IFB, "Keep talking! Keep talk—no,
wait! The network's breaking away. Toss to the space center."

The space center??

SATURDAY, APRIL 29 (3:28 P.M. MOUNTAIN DAYLIGHT TIME)

SPACE WEATHER PREDICTION CENTER; BOULDER, COLORADO

ESTIMATED TIME TO IMPACT: 60 HOURS 21 MINUTES

Dallan, facing the TV camera in the SWPC's main room, waited
nervously for his cue.

"Go!" said his assistant, standing just off-camera.

"Good afternoon. Five minutes ago, at 3:23 p.m. Mountain Daylight
Time, one of our satellites detected a series of eruptions in the atmosphere
of the sun. We've identified them as x-ray storms. Because they travel at
the speed of light, they will begin slamming into our atmosphere in fewer
than three minutes. The strength of the impacts is hard to predict because
each flare is different, but the eruptions did saturate—overwhelm—our
detector.

"The main effects will be felt on the dayside of the planet, the side
facing the sun. This includes disruptions to radio communications, cell
phones, and the GPS satellite system. If you live there, we also recommend you stay indoors as much as possible and not travel by air—as
precautions against any x-rays that might make it through the atmosphere.

"You might be wondering if this has anything to do with the CME
heading our way. The simple answer is, *yes*. These x-ray storms are like

the flashes of lightning that sometimes precede a major thunderstorm. The brunt of the storm, the giant swarm of radioactive particles that makes up the CME proper, is currently seventy-eight million miles away and still traveling at more than a million miles an hour. According to our best forecasting models, it's on track to hit us in less than sixty-one hours.

"If anything changes we'll immediately send out an alert. In the meantime we urge you to stay tuned to your local news media for instructions affecting your city or town. For the latest satellite information and images, please go to our website."

★

SATURDAY, APRIL 29 (2:33 P.M. PACIFIC DAYLIGHT TIME)

SAN DIEGO CITY COLLEGE; SAN DIEGO, CALIFORNIA

ESTIMATED TIME TO IMPACT: 60 HOURS 17 MINUTES

Allie wasn't able to catch what Dallan was saying because of the LRADs' relentless, ear-shattering chirps and broadcasts. The armored vehicles were now slowly rolling through the vast crowd, scattering screaming protesters in all directions.

"…OTHER POLICE ACTION MAY INCLUDE ACTUAL PHYSICAL REMOVAL AND/OR THE USE OF NONLETHAL MUNITIONS, WHICH COULD CAUSE INJURY TO THOSE WHO DISOBEY…"

She gaped at the madness while awaiting her cue to resume reporting.
This is what the Apocalypse will be like.
Please, Jesus …
Eva screamed into her ear: "Allie! We gotta—"
"Ms. Armendariz!" Agent Aragon was at her side, looking anxious. "I need to get you out of here right away—orders."
She wasn't used to being bossed around by anyone—other than Eva. "What are you talking about? I'm about to go back on the air."

"Please, ma'am, I'll explain later."

"Sorry, no!"

Freedom of the press, baby!

At that moment there was a palpable change in the crowd's behavior. Many of the police began banging their riot sticks against their shields. Then she saw a sudden break in their ranks, both on the right and the left. Quick as a flash, scores of them began laying siege on the protesters. There was gunfire. Then, unbelievably, officers began battling among themselves!

She couldn't make any sense of it.

She heard Aragon apologizing and felt herself being physically hoisted off her feet.

"Wait!" she cried.

"You'll thank me later," he said, whisking her away from the explosive scene.

★

SATURDAY, APRIL 29 (8:36 P.M. PACIFIC DAYLIGHT TIME)

NAVAL BASE POINT LOMA; SAN DIEGO, CALIFORNIA

ESTIMATED TIME TO IMPACT: 54 HOURS 14 MINUTES

Under a star-studded night sky, Jared stepped merrily and stealthily back to the storage shed. He'd had a chill day with Haley, the girl at the Woof Walk, and even managed to stuff his empty belly with food. The two agreed to meet after church tomorrow, at which time he planned to further a scheme he'd hatched last evening.

As he pranced along in the balmy darkness, constantly looking this way and that for any threats, he hooted to himself. People thought military bases were impenetrable.

Ha!

No place was impermeable.

He chortled at the recollection of the homeless woman who snuck onto MacDill Air Force Base in Florida on four separate occasions, each time living there for weeks before being discovered. It made the news some years back because MacDill—supposedly protected by huge security—was headquarters for Central Command, the place where the United States directed military ops all over the friggin world.

Once inside his hideaway, he booted up his smartphone and saw it immediately—the message from his G-20 confederate:

MISSION ACCOMPLISHED ☺

Turning off the phone, he curled up and snuggled into his bunched up jacket. A few minutes later he drifted into a sound sleep.

CHAPTER 32

CROSSROADS

She pulled up to the security kiosk at Naval Base Point Loma. Her eyes burned and her body felt like lead; she'd been up all night.

The MP stepped out of the hut. "Yes, ma'am, good morning."

"Morning. Allie Armendariz, Fast News—here to see Dr. Sinclair." She handed him her press credential.

He took it and said, "Yes, Ms. Armendariz, I know who you are. Is he expecting you?"

"It's complicated. We're working together on an urgent matter for the President of the United States, but I haven't been able to get through to him. So I think it's probably best if you contact Alvaro Martinez, the chief press officer. He'll vouch for me."

"Yes, ma'am, give me a minute, please." He retreated into the guard shack.

Yesterday, her afternoon and evening had been monopolized by reporting on the x-ray storms. So far, thankfully, they were not making it all the way down to the surface. The lower and middle layers of the ionosphere—the so-called D and E layers more than fifty miles up that normally filtered out solar x-rays—were doing their jobs well, absorbing most of the brutal onslaught. Nevertheless, the resulting disruption to the ionosphere, as well as some leaked x-rays at lower altitudes, were messing with electronic communications.

She'd also been kept busy by the horrifying turn of events at the G-20 protest rally. According to Mike, some of the out-of-town police officers imported by the Secret Service turned out to be imposters. Without provocation they opened fire on the protesters, killing fifteen and wounding dozens. That was when he ordered Aragon to remove her *post-haste* from the frontlines.

"But why?" she asked Mike. "Why would those fake policemen do that?"

"Good question. As best we can tell, to create anarchy. They knew with all the confusion it would be next to impossible for us to finger any one person for the crime. And they used unregistered guns. Absolutely no accountability."

"But I mean, *why* would they want to create anarchy? Who's behind it? Not the masked guy, right?—that wouldn't make any sense."

"No idea," Mike said. "But we're gonna find out, if it's the last thing we do."

The guard re-emerged from the hut. "Okay, Ms. Armendariz…" The wooden arm swung upward. "…you're cleared to go in. Do you need directions?"

She shook her head. "I know my way, thanks."

Calder lived in Ballast Point Village, one of the nicer residences on the base, reserved for military families and defense contractors. Pulling up to his condo and seeing no driveway, she parked her vintage Jag on the street.

Her cell phone jangled. She glanced at the screen. Eva again.

"*Bueno?*"

"A—ie, it's—e."

Whether it was a consequence of the x-ray storms still hammering the upper atmosphere like Nazi buzz bombers or the worsening magnetic holes, she couldn't be sure. But the fact was conversing by cell phone had become impractical.

It's why she was showing up at Calder's place unannounced. After brief phone conversations with him last night between news reports, she'd been unable to connect with him at all. Not by cell phone, not even on his house or lab phones—which was odd because most land lines were still operating fairly normally.

In fact, this morning she spoke with Carlos on a land line to make sure everyone was still okay. They were, but Lolo was still missing.

"Eva, can you hear me?" she shouted, getting out of the car.

Static.

"If you can, I just got to Calder's. What's up?"

Yet more static.

"Eva, I can't hear you. Try again later. Good-bye."

She walked up to the front door, knocked, and waited, her nerves clanging like a fire alarm. A moment later the door opened. Calder looked rested but not entirely happy to see her.

★

He looked through the peephole, hesitated, then reluctantly opened the door.

"Morning!" Allie said. "Hope I didn't wake you."

She looked beautiful, as always.

"No, no. I was just on my way to the lab, actually."

"Oh."

He opened the door wider. "But come in, come in."

She stepped inside. "I tried calling ahead but I got a fast busy signal on both your home and lab phones."

He led her into the house. "That's because I took the receivers off the hook. People just won't leave me alone. I'm even getting calls from Hollywood producers who wanna make a movie about me."

"I warned you, remember?"

"Yeah, yeah, you did. I was naïve. I just wanted *Hero* to get the credit she deserves, not become.... Never mind. How 'bout a cup of joe?"

"Yes, *please*. Make mine a double; I'm about to collapse."

He went to the kitchen, poured Allie and himself some coffee, then came out and handed her one of the cups. "Let's go to the living room."

They sat at opposite ends of the overstuffed, fawn-colored couch. "So—"

They'd spoken simultaneously and now laughed nervously.

"Go ahead," he said. "Ladies first."

She grinned from behind her steaming coffee. "Oh, that's good. So you still think I'm a lady."

He chuckled. "Yeah, I do."

★

SUNDAY, APRIL 30 (4:46 P.M. CENTRAL EUROPEAN SUMMER TIME)

POOR CLARES' SACRED HEART CONVENT; SEVILLE, SPAIN

ESTIMATED TIME TO IMPACT: 43 HOURS 2 MINUTES

Mother Yolanda was saying good-bye to the well-dressed man who proposed to swap their venerable property for a place well away from *Sevilla*. She had just finished describing the miraculous windfall the convent was receiving from generous donors all over the world.

"Please, if anything changes, Reverend Mother," he said, "you know how to get in touch with me. You know our offer would have benefited many people, not just the orphanage."

"Yes, my son." She plunged her hands into the habit's oversized pockets, feeling for the rosary beads. "Please go with God and our sincere thanks."

"Take care of yourselves," he said, walking out. Then he stopped and looked up at the sky. "They're saying one of the holes is right above this region."

She had no idea what nonsense he was saying and was eager for him to leave.

"Yes, my son, yes. But we're all in God's hands, always."

When at last the man left, she looked up. The sun was encircled by a soft, gilded crown and the sky had a festive red tinting. Could it be a sign of their sudden good fortune?

She lowered her head and briefly closed her eyes.

Thank you.

Earlier in the morning she notified the parish priest that they already had enough money for a full-time, resident doctor and all the upgrades the new government was requiring of them: better electrical wiring, smoke alarms, lead-free plumbing, proper handrails on the staircases—the list went on and on.

Entering her cell, she made straight for the shortwave radio, eager to inform the world about God's surprising provision. But on the radio there was nothing but white noise. No matter how much she tried finding a clear channel, the static was unrelenting.

At last she gave up.

"Yes," she said to herself, smiling. "I might've known."

Sliding off the seat, she spoke quietly but firmly to someone or something invisible whose presence she felt.

"Well," she said in conclusion, "I can be just as stubborn. *Do you hear me?* Just as stubborn."

Tomorrow she would try again.

★

SUNDAY, APRIL 30 (5:46 P.M. ISRAEL DAYLIGHT TIME)

JERUSALEM, ISRAEL

ESTIMATED TIME TO IMPACT: 43 HOURS 2 MINUTES

Lorena rambled furtively through the narrow passageways of Old Jerusalem. She paused to gawp at the lowering sun and darkening sky, both of which were unusually colorful.

"Crosses, very good price."

She turned and saw an old vendor, his brown face wrinkled and weathered, his vacant, cheerless eyes dark. He was holding up a small, colorful wooden crucifix.

"For you, Miss, ten percent discount."

She stared blankly at the old man, her thoughts casting back to the previous evening. After her photo appeared on the evening news, Asher—God bless him—offered to shelter her from the authorities; he was completely sympathetic to her plight. At first she accepted. But by late afternoon today she decided to leave—and not just to avoid risking trouble for Asher's household or righteous cause.

It was because the time was quickly nearing for her to be in place for Jesus's return. The scary news about the giant solar flare and magnetic holes confirmed her conviction: the Second Coming was happening *before* the rebuilding of the Temple. The End was less than two days away!

"Don't worry, old friend," she said to Asher upon her leave-taking. "I'll be fine."

Myra gave Lorena a shawarma to go and a headscarf to help conceal her identity. Lorena left the house with the black, flower-patterned headscarf securely wrapped around her head and so far it was working beautifully.

She looked around guardedly and then stepped forward for a closer look at the seemingly ancient crucifix.

"Ten percent, ten percent," the weathered vendor said eagerly, handing it to her.

Taking hold of the relic, she went weak in the knees imagining the extraordinary event that was about to happen right here in Jerusalem. The event Christians had been anticipating for more than two thousand years.

She spoke in a faint voice to no one in particular. "He's coming back."

"What? What you say, Miss?"

She shook herself. "Huh? What?"

"You say something, Miss. You want cross? Fifteen percent."

"Yes, yes, I'll take it."

After paying, she clutched the holy artifact to her bosom and wandered away. "I'm coming, sweet Lord," she whispered ecstatically. "I'm coming."

CHAPTER 33

SHIFTING SAND

A llie reached down into the leather bag at her feet. "Okay, so let me show you something."

She handed Calder a map of the magnetic holes.

He looked at it and then her. "Yeah, so what? It's what Brody showed us up in Alert."

"Yes, but there's more. You know about Chladni plates, right?"

"Of course."

"Yesterday morning when I was at the Space Weather Center my brother-in-law Dallan—you met him up in—"

"Yeah, what about him?"

Just before we went on the air he told me one of his analysts noticed a pattern in the locations of the magnetic holes. It fit a 3-D Chladni plate pattern. At the time it seemed like just a curiosity. But last night it came to me—a way to protect us from the CME."

"Go ahead."

She got down on the floor, extracted more papers from her giant purse, and laid them out on the coffee table. They were carpeted with handwritten calculations.

She motioned to him. "C'mon, sit down with me."

He placed his mug on the end table and joined her on the floor.

"Now, before I tell you, I want to warn you: it's a bit out there. But it fits both with the Chladni pattern and what we talked about yesterday—that *Hero* seems to have an effect on the magnetic field."

He made a face. "Oh, lord, not that again."

"Yes, that again. You can't deny it, Calder—unless you're willing to believe it was a giant coincidence that on three separate occasions the whale strandings—which are caused by the magnetic holes—stopped happening exactly when we arrived."

He looked away into space. In fact he *had* been thinking about it, and she was right—the plain evidence was too suggestive of a connection to be dismissed as coincidence. But that would mean ...

He shook his head.

Just like always.

Just when things are going well.

"C'mon, Calder, we've been through this. Work with me. When I'm finished, if you think I'm all wet, then *you* come up with another plan that makes sense."

His hand brushed away the idea. "Go ahead, go ahead."

"*Hero* gets energy from the quantum vacuum, right?"

"Yes." His voice was hard.

"So I'm presuming that means you've figured out a way to cause the vacuum to resonate, right? At just the right frequency to create matter-antimatter pairs."

He felt himself tensing up.

"Yeah, the head-on collision of the laser and electron beams inside the chamber is what does it. The collision rattles the vacuum just right, so it spits out electrons and positrons. The pairs then collide with each other and explode. The energy from all the explosions is what propels *Hero*. It's that straightforward."

He was reminded of the many years it took him to figure it all out. He'd always been impressed with how a wine glass shattered when hit with sound waves of just the right frequency. In creating *Hero*'s engine, he'd used the same principle. Vibrations of just the right frequency jostled the vacuum's invisible electromagnetic energy field so violently that, in a manner of speaking, it shattered it into countless electron-positron pairs, like so many shards of glass. Since matter and antimatter exploded on contact, he realized the creation of those pairs could be harnessed as a mighty propellant.

"Okay, good," she said. "So here's what I think is going on." She sat up straight. "I think the violence inside *Hero*'s vacuum chamber is generating collateral harmonic vibrations that are radiating out into the greater quantum vacuum"—she made a widening gesture with her hands—"like ripples in a cosmic-sized pond."

His shoulders slumped. "Oh, please."

"No—no—remember, you yourself said it: the quantum vacuum is the foundation underneath *everything*. It's everywhere. And it quivers, like Jell-O. Thwack it hard—like you're doing inside *Hero*'s chamber— and who knows how far afield the harmonics of the disturbance will reverberate—theoretically, to the ends of the universe."

He shook his head vehemently. He'd contemplated that possibility a long time ago—and discounted it. According to his computations, the amplitude of any stray ripples quickly diminished with distance and therefore couldn't possibly have any palpable effect on the environment at large.

He explained it to Allie, but she wasn't satisfied.

"Did you ever consider the possibility of constructive interference?" she said. "The possibility that all those small ripples could add up to something big, especially if *Hero* were in continuous operation for long periods of time?" She leveled her gaze at him. "You've been running *Hero* for some weeks now, yes? Even before our journey."

He was stopped by her allegation. What she was saying—it was like when Sara was a kid and he pushed her on the swing. If he timed his little pushes just right, very quickly they added up to something so powerful Sara would be flying high, squealing with joy.

"Yes, but—"

"No buts, Calder. Have you ever done any calculations on the scenario I just mentioned? Yes or no."

"No, but—"

She slapped the tabletop. "Well, I have. I did some calculations last night when I couldn't sleep."

He stared at her with incredulity.

This woman is inhuman!

"Let me tell you what I found."

★

MONDAY, MAY 1 (12:35 A.M. AUSTRALIAN CENTRAL STANDARD TIME)

CASUARINA COASTAL RESERVE; NORTHERN TERRITORIES, AUSTRALIA

ESTIMATED TIME TO IMPACT: 42 HOURS 43 MINUTES

Sara was walking the beach alone, navigating by the light of the vivid colors swirling high in the night sky; they were brighter than a full moon. She stopped and stared up at the mesmerizing sight. It was as if some demonic entity were stirring a cauldron of green and red poison.

Shivering, she pulled her light jacket more tightly around her.

She made the trek to the isolated coastal reserve to think. Living beneath a magnetic hole, watching the sky turn colors, dealing with Lulu's worsening bouts of craziness—all of it was creeping her out. But it was the internship that unsettled her the most. It wasn't working out as she'd hoped.

She resumed walking. The sand, still warm beneath her naked feet, felt good.

A few minutes later she stopped again and sat down cross-legged, facing the ocean. The auroral lights played on the waves like thousands of tiny, dancing fairies.

She remained in that position for some time, absently watching the sparkling waves and the dark horizon beyond them.

Somewhere out there—

Oh, Dad.

She missed him so much it ached—and knew deep down it was the root cause of her despair.

She was dating Dirk and enjoyed his company, but he wasn't her dad—not by a long shot. From their talks it seemed Dirk was interested in eventually landing a cushy academic position at a university or wildlife center close to Sydney. His biggest aim in life was to earn tenure so he could hang out with animals and not worry about anything else.

It was a decent enough ambition, but she yearned for something more thrilling, more adventurous. She hoped for a life like her dad's. Difficulties and all, it was exciting. She was incredibly proud of his historic accomplishments with *Hero*.

Suddenly feeling the urge to speak with him, she scrambled to her feet and looked around for the quickest way back to her dorm. But in the sickly light, a sudden movement caught her eye—a large bird alighting on a nearby rock.

She squinted for a better look.

It can't be!

A bright flash of whitish light high up in the sky stole her attention—a meteor?—but only for a moment. She returned her gaze to the odd-looking bird and moved slowly toward it. The conviction of what she was seeing grew stronger with every step. A few moments later, when she was close enough to erase any doubt, she gasped.

"*Leucophaeus atricilla!*" she whispered. "But that's impossible."

The Laughing Gull in front of her was not a rare bird. But it was in the wrong hemisphere, thousands of miles away from where it ought to be.

"You should be laughing your way north to Cape Cod right now, buddy," she cooed to it. "What in the world are you doing here?"

★

SUNDAY, APRIL 30 (12:01 P.M. PACIFIC DAYLIGHT TIME)

NAVAL BASE POINT LOMA; SAN DIEGO, CALIFORNIA

ESTIMATED TIME TO IMPACT: 38 HOURS 47 MINUTES

Jared met Haley at the Ballast Point Village Rec Center at noon, as planned.

"How was church?" he said.

She made a face. "Boring. All I could think about was meeting you here."

The girl reminded him a little of Maggie, but he put it out of his mind. There were important things to accomplish before tonight's detonation of the Quantum virus.

"So whatta you wanna do?" she said flirtatiously. "I know this spot over by—"

"Maybe later, okay?" He spoke gently; he didn't want to put her off. "Right now I need to use a computer."

Seeing her pretty little face fall made him soften his approach even more.

"Just for a few hours, I mean." He took her hand. "Then we can go anywhere you want, okay?" He added, "I'm sure you have homework. Do it while I'm on the computer. Then we can have the whole rest of the day free."

Her pout became a smile. Leaning in, she gave him a quick peck on the cheek before leading him to the rec center.

The facility housed the usual games—foosball, ping-pong, billards—as well as a widescreen TV and a bank of computers. Haley dragged him over to the help desk and introduced him to the resident tutor, a short-haired guy who Jared guessed was in his twenties.

"New here?" the tutor said.

"Yeah, my dad makes water pumps for the Navy. We're here for just a few days."

"Yeah? Where you from?"

"Connecticut."

"Really? I'm from Connecticut too. What city?"

He hesitated. "Stamford. But hey! I have a whole lot of homework to do. Can I use one of the computers?"

The tutor looked at him quizzically. "Yeah, sure, that's what they're here for."

Jared took Haley's hand and started walking away.

"Say!" It was the tutor guy. "What did you say your name was?"

Jared took a deep, exasperated breath and said, "Sinclair—Billy Sinclair."

SUNDAY, APRIL 30 (12:05 P.M. PACIFIC DAYLIGHT TIME)

NAVAL BASE POINT LOMA; SAN DIEGO, CALIFORNIA

ESTIMATED TIME TO IMPACT: 38 HOURS 43 MINUTES

She and Calder were still sitting on the floor of his living room, drinking their umpteenth cup of coffee and rehashing for the umpteenth time the very same argument. He was clearly in denial—she could see no other explanation for his obstinacy.

"One more time," she said, struggling to maintain a patient voice. "Ripples in the quantum vacuum can interfere constructively with each other, exactly the way *all* waves can. Sound waves, water waves—it doesn't matter. You know what I'm saying."

She thought back to when she taught this stuff to Harvard undergrads. Showed them what happened when, in a shallow pan of water, waves advancing from opposite sides clashed head-on like ranks of enemy soldiers. Wherever the waves interfered destructively—a peak coincided with a valley—they cancelled out. Wherever they interfered constructively—a peak coincided with a peak—they built upon one another. The totality of those constructive highs and destructive lows—the overall image they produced—was called an interference pattern.

The very same physics explained a Chladni plate. If applied properly, vibrations of just the correct frequency made the surface warp resonantly into a distinctive pattern of high spots and low spots, which was easily made visible with sand. The grains hopped up and down on the resonating plate, sliding off the peaks and settling into the valleys—the end result looking like a work of art.

A similar resonance phenomenon was being instigated by *Hero*. She was sure of it. Tiny, rogue quantum perturbations from innumerable point sources within the Q-thruster's vacuum chamber interfered with one another, as they radiated outward—ultimately inducing a resonance pattern in the magnetosphere. In her opinion, the physics was inescapable.

Calder remained stone-faced. "Of course. But—"

"No, hold on. Given certain reasonable assumptions—about the size and shape of *Hero*'s vacuum chamber; about the frequency and amplitude of the quantum ripples; about the size and shape of the earth's magnetosphere—given those reasonable assumptions, my calculations show an interference pattern with six valleys."

She paused, twisting her hair.

Dios, I hope I have this right. I'm so tired.

"Yeah," he said, "go on."

"And their locations match exactly the latitude and longitude of the six magnetic holes."

He began to protest.

"Oh, c'mon, Calder!" She grabbed the Brody map and waved it in front of him. "This is no coincidence and you know it."

"No, I don't. No, I don't."

"Yes, you do! The calculations don't lie: *Hero*'s operation is distorting the quantum vacuum for hundreds of thousands of miles all around her. She's turning an entire spherical region, including the magneto-sphere, into a three-dimensional Chladni plate."

"Oh, please—listen to yourself!"

"No, you listen to *yourself*, Calder. My calculations clearly show unintended quantum vibrations from *Hero*'s chamber are radiating outward, interfering, and causing the magnetic field lines in space to dance around like sand grains on a Chladni plate. The vibrations are creating a gigantic, 3-D interference pattern that has six bowl-shaped valleys, six low spots, six *holes*."

"Rubbish! I told you, the ancillary ripples from *Hero*'s vacuum chamber can't possibly be significant that far away. You don't know what you're talking about. Besides, the whale strandings began *before* the rescue mission. They and the magnetic holes have nothing to do with *Hero*!"

"Calder!" Her insides were a nauseous miasma. "We've been through this a million times already. You've been testing *Hero* for how long now? Weeks, right? Well before our mission. You know that's right."

He jumped up from the floor and began stomping around, saying nothing.

Her eyes followed him. "Look, I know this is far-out. But it fits the data." She lowered her voice. "And it doesn't take away from what you've accomplished."

He stopped dead and snorted. "Oh, really? OH, REALLY?! Imagine what Bradstreet will say if this turns out to be true. It'll be the end of my work, my whole life's work. So please, stop with the patronizing."

"Calder, you've spent your life devoted to science, to the truth. I know this is a hard pill to swallow. But you have to have faith that—"

"Oh, please, don't start that again!" He was shouting now. "I told you, I don't have faith in anything but my bad luck. It's the one thing that's never failed me."

She gaped at him wide-eyed.

She could never live with this man.

Oh, stop.

You're just tired.

She took a deep breath. "Calder, my proposal has nothing to do with my belief in God or your belief in luck. Show me where my calculations are wrong and I'll take back everything I've said. I'll leave you alone and you won't have to deal with me or my beliefs ever again."

Roughly, irritably, he ran a hand across his face. After some hesitation he held out that same hand to her. "Let me see them again."

She sprang to her feet and handed him the pages scrawled with her computations. Then she fell down heavily onto the couch.

What if I've made a mistake?

What then, Miss Brainiac?

There was knocking at the door.

"You get it," Calder mumbled, pacing, his face buried in the pages.

She went to the door and opened it.

"Finally!" Eva exclaimed, pushing her way inside. "My god, Allie. The world's falling apart and you're nowhere to be found."

"What? What's the matter?"

"What's *not* the matter? Let's start with the fact that at this very minute the G-20 is being relocated here to the base."

CHAPTER 34

ON BOARD

She had no choice but to follow Eva out the door, leaving Calder and their unsettled business behind. Her attention was immediately drawn to the sun's orangish halo. It was larger and brighter than before—as expected.

God help us, we're running out of time.

She lowered her gaze and saw Agent Aragon standing next to his black sedan.

"I see you brought the troops with you," she said, waving to Aragon. They hurried into Eva's car, which was parked behind the sedan.

"Just to warn you," Eva said, "Stu's having a cow."

Allie buckled herself in with an irate flourish. "Yeah, well, let him. I'm only one person and none of this'll matter if we all get fried to death."

Eva pulled away from the curb and sped off, following the agent's car. "Hush! Just listen. You're about to go on the air and there are things you need to know."

"Go ahead."

"The x-ray storms are intensifying. They've grounded air travel, even Air Force One. The radiation above thirty-three thousand feet is now way too dangerous; satellite communications are going south—including TV satellites. Stu says they're taking a beating and lots of them are biting the dust. The network's having to go back to the old days: UHF and VHF broadcast towers."

Allie touched her forehead and shook her head. "Lord! I remember Dad telling us how they used to use rabbit ears to get good reception."

Her thoughts froze.

Apá…the church basement.

It might not be strong en—

Then an idea came to her.

She'd get Aragon on it right away.

"…that bad yet," Eva was saying, "but Stu says to keep broadcasting anyway and not worry about it. The other thing is people here are starting to lose it. The strandings, the holes, now the x-ray storms and the CME—they want out. They're jamming the streets to escape."

"But where do they think they're going?"

"Arizona, New Mexico, Nevada—anywhere to get out from under the magnetic hole. Some people are actually leaving on foot, the traffic is so bad. It's total *mishegoss*."

Allie stared at her in disbelief. "But the streets were fine this morning. Why all of a sudden?"

"It's the morning shows. They got people all hyped up with horror stories about past CMEs and how the magnetic holes are getting worse. The last straw was the G-20 deciding to evacuate here to the base. That's why Stu made me come after you. I've been trying to get you on the—"

"Yeah, yeah, I know."

"Anyway, we'll be there in just a few minutes. You'd better start…"

As Eva yacked on, their car quickly passing one military building after another, Allie's thoughts returned to Calder. She wondered what he was making of her calculations.

More than ever now, everything was on the line.

★

SUNDAY, APRIL 30 (12:47 P.M. PACIFIC DAYLIGHT TIME)

ESTIMATED TIME TO IMPACT: 38 HOURS 1 MINUTE

Calder, alone in the living room, let Allie's papers flutter to the floor. He could no longer deny the truth. He felt dizzy and nearly lost his balance. He quickly made for the couch and spilled across it like a drunken sailor.

I knew it was too good to be true.

He flashed to one of his all-time favorite black-and-white movies: Carl Laemmle's *Frankenstein*, starring Boris Karloff and Colin Clive. He loved the scene where Clive stands up to the small-minded, naysaying scientist Dr. Waldman right after achieving the supposedly impossible and dangerous aim of bringing the dead back to life.

He'd long ago memorized the soliloquy's exact words.

Dangerous! Poor old Waldman. Have you never wanted to do anything that was dangerous? Where should we be if nobody tried to find out what lies beyond? Have you never wanted to look beyond the clouds and the stars or to know what causes the trees to bud and what changes the darkness into light? But if you talk like that, people call you crazy.

But if I could discover just one of these things, what eternity is, for example, I wouldn't care if they did think I was crazy!

He squeezed his eyes tightly. It turned his stomach to think of *Hero* in the role of the infamous monster.

Yet math didn't lie; Allie's computations were irrefutable.

My destiny, my great purpose. Right.

Just more bad luck.

He recalled a quote he'd once read or heard. Something like: "Whom the gods would destroy, they first drive crazy."

Not gods, God.

Allie's *supposed God.*

What a crock.

For a long while he didn't move. Deep down he'd known something was amiss ever since Cádiz, the second time he and Allie were told the whale stranding had disappeared spontaneously—on the very night they—

Hold on!

He sat bolt upright.

Yes, it just might work!

Rolling off the couch, he grabbed his car keys and raced out the door.

SUNDAY, APRIL 30 (1:03 P.M. PACIFIC DAYLIGHT TIME)

ESTIMATED TIME TO IMPACT: 37 HOURS 45 MINUTES

Pitsy set up the live shot just outside the base's northernmost entrance, through which the dignitaries were expected to be passing shortly. Allie, standing on her mark, gazed up at the sky. The air high up was blushing red and green. Out of habit her hand went straight for her hair.

"Don't even think about it, girlfriend!" Eva shouted through the IFB.

Allie's hand instantly retreated.

"They're less than a minute away. Stand by."

Seconds later she was on the air: "I'm standing at the north entrance to Naval Base Point Loma—and as you can see behind me, the motorcades are beginning to arrive. The president's press secretary announced late this morning that, out of an abundance of caution, the G-20 leaders are being brought here to complete their meetings."

A video clip showed the press secretary urging the public to stay calm and to follow the instructions of local officials. He said the president would be making an important announcement later in the day.

"Just minutes ago," Allie continued, "at one o'clock Pacific Time, the governor declared Southern California to be in a state of emergency. He vowed to impose martial law if necessary."

She tossed to a video clip of the governor looking glum. Sternly, he warned that the extra police and military backups already here for the G-20 would be used whenever and wherever it became necessary to maintain civil order. He singled out San Diego and Los Angeles, where the first and worst signs of mass hysteria were breaking out. He said people were free to evacuate, but curfews would be strictly enforced and lawless behavior would not be tolerated.

Allie continued, "Streets leading out of San Diego and Los Angeles are backed up for tens of miles. Reports of rioting and looting have been minimal but we're told a run is beginning on emergency supplies. For the latest, we go now to our reporter in downtown San Diego, Heidi Shore."

The cutaway showed a female reporter standing at a street corner surrounded by bumper-to-bumper traffic and sidewalks crowded with people pushing and shoving their way forward. On their backs, in their arms, in hand-powered carriages of one sort or another, they were hauling personal belongings and goods of every description.

"Heidi, tell us what's going on."

"Allie, it's pandemonium here as people are trying either to get out of the city or to hoard essentials. I've covered lots of disasters but never anything like this." She paused to button-hole a young man passing in front of her. "Excuse me, sir. Can I ask you what you're doing down here?"

The teenager mugged for the camera. "This is like totally cray, dude! My buddies and I are getting some camping gear and heading out to a cave in the desert."

A middle-aged, well-dressed woman said, "I came down here this morning to do some regular shopping, but now I'm not sure what to do. This is very scary."

An excited UPS delivery man said, "It's like the end of the world or something. I'm calling it a day and beating it home. I've been trying to reach my wife and kids but I can't get through. All the phone lines are either jammed or not working."

Heidi turned to camera. "Allie, it all started just about an hour ago. The streets went from being normal to this." She gestured to the stalled traffic. "It began right after the Space Weather Prediction Center announced the magnetic holes are getting worse and the White House press secretary reported the G-20 Summit was moving out of downtown to the Navy base. We'll certainly keep an eye on the situation. But for now, reporting live from downtown San Diego, I'm Heidi Shore. Back to you."

CHAPTER 35

LOST SOULS

SUNDAY, APRIL 30 (2:16 P.M. PACIFIC DAYLIGHT TIME)

NAVAL BASE POINT LOMA; SAN DIEGO, CALIFORNIA

ESTIMATED TIME TO IMPACT: 36 HOURS 32 MINUTES

For an uninterrupted hour Allie reported live from outside the Command Administration building, where the G-20 leaders were gathered. Finally, the network cut away to a brief commercial break.

"*Chica*, I need to get back to Calder," she said to Eva via the IFB. "Someone else can do this."

"I know, I know. Hold on."

Allie waited—and waited.

"*Chica*, what's going on. Hello?"

Eva came back into her ear. "Okay, okay, I just spoke to Stu. He says just one more report and you can go."

"No! That's what he keeps saying. I really need to—"

"Stand by. In ten.… "

Allie growled.

"Go!" Eva said.

On the TV screen was a woman standing in a tidal marsh located fifty miles north of the Golden Gate Bridge.

> AA: "As if the mass strandings aren't enough, now this: birders from all over the world are spotting species where they aren't supposed to be. With me now is Gillian Woods. She's chief science officer at Point Blue, a conservation group based in Petaluma, California. Gillian, tell us what's happening."
>
> GW: "Well, as you said, bird watchers are seeing vagrant species everywhere. We expected something like this, but not so widespread. Migrating birds are like whales—they use Earth's magnetic field to navigate. It's clear they're having to fly blind because of what's going on. Let me show you what I mean."

On the screen appeared video of a warbler. Its small blue body was set off by black and white highlights and a bright yellow chest.

> GW: "This is a Northern Parula. Normally these little guys migrate along the Mississippi and Atlantic flyways. But now we're seeing them here on the Pacific coast. One hundred sightings so far in the Bay Area alone."

Allie instinctively looked around her, half expecting to see some strange bird flying by. Moments later, after finishing the interview with Gillian, she quickly segued to the second part of the report.

> AA: "Joining us now is Kyle Post, winner of this year's World Series of Birding. It's a competition held annually at the

start of every spring in New Jersey. Hello, Mr. Post, can you hear me okay?"

On the screen appeared the image of a balding, middle-aged man wearing combat fatigues, a pair of expensive-looking binoculars hanging from his neck. He was standing in a vast meadow beneath a gray, overcast sky.

KP: "Yes, Allie, I can hear you fine. I watch you all the time. It's great to be talking with you."

The man spoke with a thick New Jersey accent.

AA: "Great, thanks. First of all, tell us quickly: what exactly is the World Series of Birding?"

KP: "Sure. It's a bunch of teams that compete all over the state to see who spots the most bird species in a twenty-four-hour period. My daughters and I—the Marshketeers— that's what we call ourselves—we've been competing for more than ten years and what happened today is something totally new, totally far-out."

AA: "Tell us about it."

KP: "Well, early this morning we were tromping into this meadow here, Cape May Meadows."

The man jerked his hand to indicate the grasslands surrounding him.

KP: "The girls and me were pretty sleepy because we'd been up all night. But then I hear this call and I perk up. I can't believe it. I tell myself I'm more sleepy than I thought. You know, I'm hearing things."

AA: "Yes, go ahead."

KP: "Well, I stand there and I hear it again, clear as a bell: *Fee-reet! Fee-reet!* I tell the girls and they go, 'We didn't hear anything.' And when I insist, they say, 'C'mon, Dad, stop pulling our legs.' Except now I know I'm not hearing things. It's for real."

AA: "And what was it, sir? What kind of bird did you hear?"

KP: "It was a Western Wood-Peewee, which is impossible because it's a western bird and this is New Jersey. All we see out here are Eastern Wood-Peewees. And they go *pee-a-wee? Pee-a-wee?* This one was going *Fee-reet! Fee-reet!* Big difference, right?"

AA: "Absolutely. So you ended up being right—it was a Western Peewee?"

KP: "Big as life."

AA: "And you took a picture of it, I understand."

On the screen appeared the photo of a medium-sized bird with a grey-olive upper body and a pale yellow underbelly, perched in a small birch tree.

KP: "Yes, and it wasn't just me. When we got to the finish line, everybody was trading stories about birds they'd seen that didn't belong here. Like I said, in all my years of doing this competition, this is a first. Very weird."

★

SUNDAY, APRIL 30 (2:38 P.M. PACIFIC DAYLIGHT TIME)

ESTIMATED TIME TO IMPACT: 36 HOURS 10 MINUTES

Allie stepped inside Calder's lab and yoo-hooed loudly. When no one answered, she began searching the facility.

She was struck anew by its spaciousness, orderliness, and hospital-like cleanliness. Against spotless white walls stood massive tables cluttered with expensive-looking mechanical and electrical equipment. At the very center was the hydraulic lift, encircled by a winding platform—vacant at the moment because *Hero* was still moored to the pier.

When Allie reached the lab's far, northeast corner, she found Calder standing before a control panel covered with buttons, switches, and multicolored lights. It was attached to a large, box-like structure with small windows that looked like a walk-in freezer.

She rushed to his side. "I was hoping I'd find you here. I was just at your condo and you weren't there."

"Worried I might've flown the coop?" He spoke to her without taking his eyes off his work.

"Not at all."

"Anyway, perfect timing—*stranger*."

"I know, I know. Stu just wouldn't let me go." She snarled through closed teeth. "But I'm here now and we don't have a whole lot of time. Did you look at my calculations?"

"Oh, yeah." He said it nonchalantly and still didn't look at her. "That's why I'm here."

"Which means?"

He continued minding the console and didn't answer.

"Calder! Stop! Look at me and tell me what's going on."

At last he faced her. He was smiling.

She placed her hands akimbo. "I'm serious. Tell me. *Now*."

"Okay, okay. When I started going over your figures I was sure I'd find something wrong. But I didn't. And that's when I knew you were right. Actually, I knew it all along. I just didn't want to admit it."

There's a newsflash.

"And..." Impatiently, she spun her hand in circles to prompt him.

"Well, I was ready to throw in the towel, to be honest. But then I thought of something."

"What?!"

"That if *Hero* really does have an effect on the magnetic field, it's not a complete negative—the way you made it out to be. We can turn it into a positive. You said *Hero* caused the holes. I'm saying she can fix the holes."

She threw up her hands. "Calder, hallelujah! That's exactly what I was going to tell you before Eva showed up."

He blinked at her. "Oh?"

"Yes! Look, it's like fighting fire with fire. The ripple effect started everything, created the magnetic holes. But I think if we're clever enough, we can use the same vibrational mechanism to quell them. I'm not exactly sure how yet, but that was my plan."

Calder, turning back to the control panel, said, "Well, that's my plan too. Let me show you something."

She watched him push buttons and flip switches, as he spoke.

"Like you said, it's all about resonance. But resonances can be destroyed as easily as they're created, right? Actually, *more* easily, because a resonance by its very nature is fragile. It arises only under very precise conditions and at a particular frequency."

She smiled.

Yay! This is the Calder I know and love.

"Yes," she said. "And unless the required conditions are maintained, the resonance eventually dies on the vine."

"Right! But we don't have time to wait around for that to happen naturally, do we?"

According to her calculations, it would take weeks for the resonance pattern driving the magnetic holes to dissipate on its own—way too late to protect Earth from the CME. The pattern had to be destroyed by some well-directed, intervening force—like a hand coming in and wiping the sand pattern clean off a Chladni plate.

"Absolutely not," she said. "So what's your idea?"

"A picture's worth a thousand words." He pointed to the walk-in freezer. "This is a reverb chamber. I made it several years ago, to test out an invention—a modification of *Hero*'s propulsion system that would make her supersonic."

"Supersonic?! You mean—?"

"Yes. It would allow *Hero* to travel faster than sound. I was going to tell you about it at the right time."

"How much faster?"

"Way faster. Theoretically, she...hold on. Do you know about Haisch's theory of inertia?"

She nodded. "Sure—the one he published with Puthoff and Rueda, right? Back in the 90s?"

"Yeah."

Bernhard Haisch, Alfonso Rueda, and Hal Puthoff believed inertia was caused by an invisible energy field in the quantum vacuum. Any accelerating object was slowed by the field, their calculations appeared to indicate, the way a swimmer was slowed by water. That inescapable resistance to movement—caused by the vacuum's omnipresent, ghostlike energy field—was what science called *inertia*.

"Why do you ask?" she said.

"Because *Hero*'s supersonic booster is based on their hypothesis— that inertia is an extrinsic trait caused by the quantum vacuum."

She frowned. "Really? A lot of physicists don't take the Haisch theory seriously, you know. Glashow has argued against it. It's really way out there."

"Just like *Hero*, right?"

"Calder, I'm just saying—"

"Never mind, just watch" he said, looking disgusted. "Seeing is believing." He gestured in the direction of the window in front of them, just above the panel. "See that tank of water in there?"

She peeked in and saw something that looked like a round, above-ground swimming pool. "Yeah."

"The water in the tank represents the virtual fields in the quantum vacuum, okay?" He pointed at a TV monitor that showed the underwater image of a toy sub. "That toy sub there represents *Hero* traveling through the vacuum fields."

He switched off the chamber's interior lights. The water in the tank glowed with a steady neon green.

"I put phosphorescent dye into the water to make things easier to see." He flipped another switch and bright white lights inside the dark chamber began to strobe, like in a vintage disco bar.

Allie frowned.

What in the world?

"Ready?" he said.

"Totally."

"No, I mean *you*. Are *you* ready?"

She questioned him with her eyes.

Let's go, already!

We're wasting time!

"You get the honors. Just press the yellow button here when I tell you. Okay?"

"But—"

"No buts."

She pressed the button at his prompt.

"Keep your eyes on the sub."

The tiny sub, immersed in glowing green water, drifted slowly forward.

"Is that it?"

"No, keep watching."

She kept one eye on the little sub and the other on Calder working the control panel. Abruptly, she heard a chest-thumping bass hum coming from within the chamber. Tiny ripples appeared around the edges of the sub, like those surrounding a fluttering goldfish fin. The hum grew louder and louder—then a split-second later the toy sub shot across the water and smashed into the opposite side of the tank.

She gave a shout and Calder's hand hit a large red button. The hum immediately stopped and so did the ripples.

"What was that?" she said.

Calder's bright face broke into a smart-alecky grin. "*That*, my dear Allie, was the solution to our problem."

★

SUNDAY, APRIL 30 (4:07 P.M. PACIFIC DAYLIGHT TIME)

ESTIMATED TIME TO IMPACT: 34 HOURS 41 MINUTES

Jared, ducking behind a large bush, scanned the area in front of him before making a run for it.

He'd intended to spend the whole day with Haley. But with the G-20 suddenly on base and the nosey tutor asking so many questions, he chose to ditch the girl and execute his plan of escape.

Certain the coast was clear, he dashed to the next convenient hiding spot, a dumpster. For the next fifteen minutes he darted from cover to cover, getting closer and closer to the water.

The G-20 commotion was actually working in his favor. With security concentrated around the main admin building, this part of the base was unusually deserted.

Finally, he got as far as the back of the building he'd first slept in. From there he could see the boat; it was still in the water, unattended.

Yes!

It crossed his mind that Maggie would disapprove of what he was doing, yell at him to grow up and behave.

But she's dead.

When at last he arrived at the sleek, red vehicle, he quickly set about putting to use all the intelligence he acquired by hacking into Sinclair's lab computer at the rec center today. If all went according to script, this crazy-fast ship would take him not just away from the base, but out from under the magnetic hole that loomed like the Grim Reaper over Southern California.

CHAPTER 36

STOLEN VEHICLE

SUNDAY, APRIL 30 (4:26 P.M. PACIFIC DAYLIGHT TIME)

NAVAL BASE POINT LOMA; SAN DIEGO, CALIFORNIA

ESTIMATED TIME TO IMPACT: 34 HOURS 22 MINUTES

With the two of them in total agreement over the plan, Calder and Allie quickly went their separate ways: she to inform the president, he to bring *Hero* into the lab to make the necessary modifications.

Jumping into the tow truck, he started up the engine and steered for the pier.

★

Jared pounded the ship's dashboard and then tried again to get it started.

Nothing.

He pushed the green ignition button again and again, but without success.

Then ...

It was just a small noise, a high-pitched whirring sound, but promising nonetheless. He quieted himself and held his breath. A moment later the rocket boat was purring like a well-tuned Maserati.

Quickly, Jared doubled-checked the body harness. But just as he went to throttle up, his ears picked up another sound. This one coming from the outside.

★

Calder approached the pier and caught sight of *Hero* moving away from her moorings.

Am I seeing things?

Drifting?

He stared hard.

Oh, god, no—someone is stealing her!

Instantly, he stopped the truck, jumped out, and dashed toward the water. "Hey!" he yelled. "Hey!"

★

After passing through layers of security, Allie finally made it into the main admin building. MPs directed her to a large conference room, where she found a milling crowd of high-level government bureaucrats waiting to be called on for this or that task by their respective leaders.

They also serve, who sit and wait.

She spotted Marty Glauber in the middle of the room and waved at him. He responded like a child laying eyes on Santa Claus.

"Allie, Allie—oh, my god," he said rushing to her side. "I've been trying every which way to reach you by phone. The president's waiting. What do you have for him? I hope it's good. They're eating him alive in there. Blaming your *Hero* guy—Sinclair, the United States—for what's happening."

"What?"

"I know, it's lunacy. But that's politics. What do you have?"

Allie smiled. "Let's go somewhere quiet. Bring your laptop."

★

At first Calder was paralyzed with indecision. To whom do you report a stolen vacuum-powered speedboat? But soon enough he settled on driving to the base police department.

The chief was a beefy MP who wore a blue camouflage-patterned uniform and cap, ankle-length black boots, and a black leather utility belt supporting a holstered weapon and various storage pouches.

"And you didn't authorize anyone to take her out for any exercises?"

"No! Absolutely not."

"Did you actually see anyone inside?"

"No. But chief, she was going way too fast to be on her own. Besides, I could hear the roar of her engine. And she made a one-eighty before heading out to sea. There *had* to be someone inside steering her."

The chief looked at him as if to ask another question, but then relented. "Okay, look, we've never had a situation like this before, understand? We'll have the Coast Guard dispatch all their patrol boats right away." He added, "But if you're right and someone's deliberately stolen her, I remember reading in the newspaper—she goes about what? Four, five hundred knots?"

"About that, yes."

"Sir, at that rate—well, let's just put it this way. At that rate, I don't know of any boat on the planet that could chase her down. But we'll try."

CHAPTER 37

FALSE START

Eva was kibitzing with her on the IFB.

"You've hit the big time, girlfriend. *The president of the United States!* Just don't forget me when you're First Lady."

"*Chica!* He's married." Allie glanced at her watch.

What's taking Aragon so long?

"Yeah, yeah," Eva said, "but I've seen how you and Mr. *Hero* act around each other. You can't fool Mama Freiberg." She bellowed, "Ten seconds!"

Allie felt clammy. She'd never introduced the leader of the free world before.

"Go!" Eva said.

Allie welcomed viewers, told them where she was—in front of the main administration building at Naval Base Point Loma—and explained that in a short while the president would be addressing the nation.

She'd been told the president's message was being broadcast via the Emergency Alert System. The EAS, she knew, was a select network of broadcast, cable, and hard-wired pathways that included, when necessary, military communications satellites. The satellites had outer shells and computer chips (called rad-chips; she'd done a report about them once) specially hardened to protect against high-level radiation.

But she also knew the EAS was relatively new. Its most recent nationwide trial resulted in technical malfunctions, including test messages that were muted, duplicated, and reverberant.

"Vamp!" Eva said in her ear. "He's running late."

"We're told the G-20 meetings originally scheduled were mostly scrapped today because of the mounting crises threatening the world. In just a few minutes the president is expected to announce a plan for sparing us from the worst of the threats. Of course I'm speaking of—"

"He's ready! Toss to him in five...four..."

"Excuse me. I'm being told—ladies and gentlemen, the president of the United States."

Allie could see on the monitor the president was dressed in a dark suit and red tie, sitting at a desk surrounded by the other G-20 leaders. Their somber expressions said it all.

"Good evening," the president began. "Tonight the world faces two natural enemies threatening our planet at the same time. All day today these leaders and I have been exploring every imaginable option for protecting ourselves. We discussed and debated them, all the while bearing in mind the very limited time we have to deploy any kind of meaningful defense. Along the way we looked to our best scientific minds for guidance, for their best ideas about what we can do. About what we *should* do.

"And now, as a result of those careful deliberations, I'm pleased to announce we have reached a consensus. Tomorrow morning Dr. Calder

Sinclair of the United States Navy will launch an initiative we hope will quickly repair the magnetic holes hovering over major portions of the planet. We are calling this brave initiative Project Joshua because Dr. Sinclair's plan is to destroy the magnetic holes with nothing more than vibrations.

"I'm not a scientist so I won't attempt to explain it to you. I've instructed my press secretary to prepare and distribute to the media a document that will explain the essential parameters of Project Joshua in terms we laypersons can understand. We will attempt to post it on the White House and United Nations websites, but for now the World Wide Web is not functioning reliably. Furthermore, my science advisor, Dr. Martin Glauber, will be holding a press briefing right after this.

"My fellow Americans, my fellow humans around the world, I call on each of you to remain calm. Right now, after the CME, fear and hysteria are our worst enemies. Keep listening to your local authorities. They will be issuing instructions on the best ways for you and your loved ones to stay safe.

"If you're a person of faith, I ask you to initiate prayer vigils. Ask your church, synagogue, temple, or mosque to pray for Dr. Sinclair's mission. For our country. For the earth. For everyone and anyone, wherever they might be this night, who stand in harm's way.

"Thank you. May God bless America. And may God bless our planet."

★

Allie decided to skip Marty's press briefing in favor of getting in her car and rejoining Calder. She was satisfied with how the president had communicated the plan, except for the part about Calder being affiliated with the Navy. She knew that wouldn't make Calder happy.

As she approached the lab she glanced toward the water; *Hero* was no longer moored to the pier.

Good.

Stepping into the building, she called out to Calder.

No answer.

Argh, always too busy to listen.

Walking in farther, she saw the empty hydraulic lift and was instantly gripped with foreboding.

"Calder!"

She raced to the far-left corner of the lab, where she found him the last time. He wasn't there. The reverberation chamber was quiet and dark.

She stood still for a moment, wondering what was going on and where Calder might be. She started rushing back to the car. She'd tell Eva. Recruit her help.

"Allie!"

She froze. "Calder! Where are you?"

"Over here by the lift."

Running up to him, she immediately noticed his long face. "Where have you been?" she said, out of breath. "Where's *Hero*?"

He seized her by the forearms. "I've been looking for you. You're not going to believe it."

★

She found Eva inside the production trailer, parked outside the main admin building, and quickly told her what happened.

Eva stared deep into her eyes. "You're kidding me, right? Tell me you're joking."

Allie shook her head miserably.

"You're not joking. *Oy!* How did it happen? Who could've done it? And why?"

"Look, *chica*, right now my main worry is telling the president. *Dios!* How am I going to break it to him?"

A short while later she was standing face-to-face with Martin Glauber.

"Allie, you're kidding, right? It isn't funny."

"Marty, I've never been more serious in my life. You've got to tell the president."

"Me? He's in there right now being congratulated by everyone, getting pats on the back. He just finished telling the world not to worry, that help is on the way. And you want *me* to tell him it's all off? That the world is screwed? Oh, no, this is on you, Allie. *You're* the one who's going to tell him."

★

MONDAY, MAY 1 (11:02 A.M. CHINA STANDARD TIME)

SHANGHAI JIAO TONG UNIVERSITY; SHANGHAI, CHINA

ESTIMATED TIME TO IMPACT: 30 HOURS 46 MINUTES

Zhaohui Tang, fighting hard to stay alert, nodded off. Instantly, her chin snapped back up and her eyes flew open. For the past eleven-plus hours a small army of her brightest grad students—along with an even bigger, worldwide throng of her most successful alumnae—had been diligently trying to defeat her newest brainchild: software to make Web browsers absolutely hack-proof.

The revolutionary add-on took her three years to design and debug. This was its final test, and so far it was withstanding everything being thrown at it.

She slowly rose from her chair. "How is everyone holding up?" she said hoarsely.

The students assured her they were fine. They were seated at computers lining the walls of the spacious computer lab. The alumnae, hearing her on the open mic, reported the same.

"I'm having lunch brought in for everyone," she said to the students. "If the add-on keeps holding up, we will make an announcement tomorrow. It will bring great honor to our university and country."

★

SUNDAY, APRIL 30 (8:32 P.M. PACIFIC DAYLIGHT TIME)

NAVAL BASE POINT LOMA; SAN DIEGO, CALIFORNIA

ESTIMATED TIME TO IMPACT: 30 HOURS 16 MINUTES

Allie emerged from her meeting with the president feeling heavy. She lumbered through security, conferred briefly with Glauber, and then stepped outside. She hesitated before making a beeline to the production truck.

Eva looked like a nervous wreck. "What did he say? Stu wants you to do an exclusive cut-in right away."

Allie shook her head despondently. "The president's not happy. Wants me to stay mum about what's happened."

"What? No way!"

Allie plopped heavily into the nearest chair. "Eva, cut the man some slack. He's putting no less than the chairman of the joint chiefs—the highest-ranking military guy in the country—on the case right away. He says wherever *Hero* is, they'll find her. I'm willing to give him some time before blowing the whistle."

She began twisting her hair.

Is this really me talking? Willing to sit on a huge scoop?

"But—"

"*Eva!* It's not always about the story. I'm learning that now. You should too."

CHAPTER 38

PLAYING WITH FIRE

SUNDAY, APRIL 30 (8:45 P.M. PACIFIC DAYLIGHT TIME)

PACIFIC OCEAN; VICINITY OF NORTHERN CALIFORNIA

ESTIMATED TIME TO IMPACT: 30 HOURS 3 MINUTES

Jared slowed *Hero* to a stop in the deep waters opposite Northern California but kept the engine idling; he didn't want to risk her not firing up again.

He glanced at the onboard chronometer: 8:45 p.m. Pacific daylight time.

11:45 p.m. eastern.

He wanted to get as far away from the United States as possible, but was pausing briefly—just fifteen minutes—to ring in the Quantum virus.

Afterward, he'd zip off to one of the mansions he had called home as a child.

Maybe I'll even go back to mansion-hopping.

He banished the thought as too depressing.

Narrowing his eyes, he peered through the windshield, but it was too dark outside to see much. A whale spouted close by. In the near distance to his left, a brightly lit, off-shore oil rig held its tangled head high above the surface of the sea, like a boxy, four-legged giant on stilts. Miles away to his right, tiny points of light sparkled along the coast.

His eyes looked past them. Somewhere inland lay Mountain View and NeuroNet.

Oh, Maggie—you don't know what you're missing.

He stared blankly into the night and tightened his lips.

It could've been awesome, you and me.

Still strapped securely in the seat, Jared leaned back, closed his eyes, and focused on what was about to happen. It was the realization of a lifelong dream to rid the world of injustice. To abruptly reverse the disastrous, tyrannical progress of big science and big business and big government. To yank the world back to a primitive time when people were more equal than they were now.

He smiled. Starting in just a few minutes life would become simple again. Small again. Human-sized and human-friendly again.

He surveyed the innumerable glittering lights of the coastal cities and imagined them being summarily snuffed out when the computer-controlled power grids of the world crashed—one of the first casualties of his virus.

He wondered how his hacktivist allies would react when he announced to the world—which he would, just as soon as he had the chance—that he was the masked man. That they were now members of a hand-selected army entrusted to enforce a new world order.

If they followed his instructions, they would've already downloaded the CDs he gave them—protection against the virus. After the virus exploded, he'd assign lieutenants to each region of the world. Their job: hack key sites debilitated by the virus—major banks, ATMs, Fortune

500 and other multinational corporations, government agencies, the media. Bleach existing financial records and create new ones, so wealth could be redistributed fairly. Every adult in the world would receive an equitable amount of money in a personal bank account created for them.

His lieutenants would hack the virus-weakened computer systems of law enforcement agencies and judicial systems, obliterating forensic evidence, fingerprints, criminal records, verdicts, the names and jail sentences of inmates. The justice systems of the world would be so screwed up, he wouldn't need to worry about the law.

Jared kept staring at the chronometer.

C'mon, already!

He thought of the big-chested cook from his childhood saying to him, "A watched pot never boils." Maybe he'd track the kindly woman down, hire her to cook for him, and even give her a mansion of her own.

A strange, sharp sound from the dashboard snapped him out of his reverie. *Hero* began to shudder. Alarms were going off.

Before he could get a grip on what was happening, *Hero* lunged forward like a wildcat pouncing on prey. His head was thrown back, his body smashed against the seat.

★

MONDAY, MAY 1 (12:00 P.M. CHINA STANDARD TIME)

SHANGHAI JIAO TONG UNIVERSITY; SHANGHAI, CHINA

ESTIMATED TIME TO IMPACT: 29 HOURS 48 MINUTES

Zhaohui Tang, slumped in her chair, was awakened by shouting.

"Something is happening! Something is happening!"

It took her a moment to realize that, despite herself, she had nodded off. Her grad students were in an uproar.

"Dr. Tang, wake up, wake up!" one student cried out. "Our computers—they've detected something awful!"

★

SUNDAY, APRIL 30 (9:00 P.M. PACIFIC DAYLIGHT TIME)

PACIFIC OCEAN; NORTHERN CALIFORNIA

ESTIMATED TIME TO IMPACT: 29 HOURS 48 MINUTES

Pinned to the seat, Jared looked frantically all around, straining to figure out what was happening. From the haphazard forces on his body, he could tell *Hero* was moving hectically, first in one direction then another, like a tight end juking his way to the end zone.

The panel's digital readouts were vacillating uncontrollably. The images on the main video monitor looked fractured.

What the hell is happening?!

With all his might, he managed to get his right hand to move. To stretch in the direction of the red, all-stop button. But when he pushed it, nothing happened.

Damn!

With superhuman effort, he willed both hands to punch fiercely and randomly at *Hero*'s controls. But the demented vehicle would not obey. Her maniacal movements were now jerking him about so violently he felt like prey in a hyena's jaws.

He shut his eyes hard and tried to think of what else he could do. Opening them again, he hoped it was all a dream.

Then it came to him. Something he remembered from hacking *Hero*'s operations manual. Instantly, he groped for the lever that controlled the ejection seat. But before he was able to find it, he saw it—the giant oil rig. It was coming at him so fast there was no time even to scream. Only to experience the twin sensations of an explosive impact and a towering wall of brilliant yellow flames.

Followed by utter darkness.

CHAPTER 39

HOPE OR DESPAIR

Allie and Calder were working together in bleak silence at a corner table inside the lab. She was helping him get the supersonic booster flight-ready, on the chance *Hero* would be found soon.

Her thoughts were on family. It'd been nearly nine hours since she—

"Can you hand me those needle-nosed pliers over there?" Calder said, without looking up.

"What happens if they don't find her?" she said, handing him the tool. "We need to come up with a Plan B."

He turned to her. "You don't think I've been racking my brain about that for the past two hours?"

She was drawing a total blank too.

If only he had a backup vehicle.

Or even a backup vacuum chamber. They could put it aboard a supersonic jet and fly it from hole to hole before the CME struck.

But he didn't. And even if he did, it was no use; all planes were grounded because of the x-ray storms.

Sweet Jesus, I surrender.

Help us.

"That TV special of yours." He continued working, with his head down. "You don't really believe in that stuff, do you?"

She was tightening a screw. "What stuff?"

"The idea the world's gonna end and all that."

She set down the screwdriver and looked at him. "Actually, I do. And I believe we're steadily making it happen. With our science."

"With our science?! You're blaming science?"

"I'm blaming us. A gun by itself is benign. It's the person squeezing the trigger that's bad."

"So we *want* to bring about the end of the world—is that what you're saying?"

She continued looking at him, even though his own attention was still on his work. "No, not necessarily—although there are people bent on using science and technology to create fear and anarchy: suicide bombers, hackers—"

"But Allie—"

"But mostly it's all the unintended consequences of science that'll end up doing us in. I really believe that."

His eyes remained focused on his work. "But Allie, c'mon. That's pure speculation. You're a scientist. You should be dealing in facts."

"I am." She leaned in. "Calder, look at me."

He stopped working and obeyed; their eyes met.

"Look," she said, "did you know medical science is now the number-three killer in the U.S.—just behind heart disease and cancer? Number three! And in five years it'll probably become number one."

He curled his lips, shook his head skeptically, and turned back to his work.

"Shake your head all you want, it's true," she said. "Our doctors use more technology than doctors anywhere else, except Japan—MRIs, CAT scans, PET scans, the whole nine yards. Yet our treatments kill more people than those in countries using less technology. It's called iatrogenesis—death by high-tech medicine, literally."

She resumed her work and they both remained silent.

"I don't know," he said at last. "Maybe we *will* end up killing ourselves—or maybe science will find a way to save us, I don't know. It's just I hope you're not insinuating this has anything to do with some superstitious prediction in the Bible about the world coming to an end. That would be totally ridiculous."

She stayed on task, resisting the urge to lash out.

A few moments later he said, "You have nothing to say?"

She shook her head. "Calder, you're entitled to your opinion—I respect that."

"And?"

"And nothing. Let's just keep working. And hoping."

"No, I really want to understand how you can believe in God and the Bible and all the rest of it. Someone of your intelligence and sophistication. I just can't wrap my head around it."

She stared at him. "Calder, you believe in luck, right?" She hesitated, wanting to express herself in a non-combative way. "How is *that* scientific?"

★

Calder stiffened. "Luck is about probabilities, numbers you can calculate. It's not some hocus-pocus about a god controlling everything.

I used to believe in that stuff when I was an orphan—that God existed. It made my life a living hell because the only way I could make sense of all the bad things happening to me was that God hated me. Not anymore, thank you very much. It's a whole lot saner to chalk up all the bad stuff to happenstance."

"Calder," she said, looking at him, "I'm really sorry to hear that. I had no idea."

"I'm over it now."

They both resumed their work and did not talk.

She was the one to break the uneasy stillness. Minutes later he heard her say in a gentle voice, "So, Calder, tell me—you believe in odds, right? Then why do you believe the odds are stacked against you? If life is truly controlled by the throw of dice, you should have as much good luck as bad, no?"

He scanned the workbench. "Let's not talk about it, okay? On your left, a piece of red wire, please."

She reached over and handed him the entire spool. "I'm sorry, but you're the one who wanted to understand my beliefs. You see, I believe in odds too, just like you. In particular, the impossible odds of anyone ever being able to understand everything with complete confidence. Descartes discovered the only thing he could be absolutely sure about was that he was alive. Everything else required some degree of faith."

He clipped off several short lengths of wire.

Please stop.

"Atheists have faith in the power of nothingness. They believe the universe was created by natural laws acting for a long time on nothing, on randomness. But where did the laws themselves come from?"

He was concentrating on soldering three wires together. "Science doesn't have all the answers, okay? Nor does it pretend to, the way religion does."

"But atheists believe they *do* have all the answers. Including the answer to the biggest question of all: does God exist?"

Calder tried tuning her out. He touched the hot iron to the solder wire, watched the shiny, liquid metal enrobe the twisted bare wires—but she wouldn't stop talking.

"No matter how clever anyone thinks they are, Calder, they can't account for the universe we see today by believing in nothing."

"How 'bout the vacuum?" Calder knew he was just being cute.

"Exactly. The vacuum is not nothing. How many times have you said that yourself? It only masquerades as nothing. In fact, it's filled with all kinds of goodies, like a cosmic-sized *piñata*. But where did all those goodies, the virtual energy fields, come from, huh? So you see, to explain the universe, you always need to start with *something*. And whatever that something is—that's your god."

He slammed the soldering iron back onto its stand.

"Allie, for god sakes, please—I'm sorry I asked. Can we give it a rest now?" His voice sounded harsher than intended. "Allie, I'm sorry. It's just that—"

"No, Calder, it's okay." She stopped working, turned, and headed toward the exit. "I'll be right back."

He hesitated, and then ran after her.

"Allie, wait!"

He caught up with her at the main door, gently took hold of her, and turned her around.

"What?" she said.

For an eternal moment he stood looking deep into her eyes.

Something about this woman ...

"Calder, I—"

Abruptly, he pulled her to himself and pressed his lips to hers, long and hard.

★

The lights in the lab flickered.

She was still in Calder's arms, her mind reeling from their long, dizzying kiss.

He abruptly let go. "Oh, lord, what now?"

The lights went out altogether.

"Don't move," he said, "Let me go check the fuse box."

He fetched his smartphone from his shirt pocket, activated its flashlight, and dashed off.

A minute later she could hear banging sounds coming from the back of the lab. "Calder? Are you all right?"

The distant reply came quickly. "Yeah. The breaker wasn't tripped—there's just no power coming in. It's weird. I'm switching to the emergency generators."

She scanned the darkness. The only things visible were the bright screens of computers sitting on benches all over the lab.

Must be running on batteries.

But there was something odd about them—their displays were breaking up.

The overhead lights came back on. But the computer displays continued behaving strangely.

It struck her like a hammer.

The CME!

"Calder! I've gotta go! I'll be at the live truck!"

She rushed outside, but immediately was stopped cold by the sight of headlights moving fast in her direction.

CHAPTER 40

TRUST

SUNDAY, APRIL 30 (9:58 P.M. PACIFIC DAYLIGHT TIME)

NAVAL BASE POINT LOMA; SAN DIEGO, CALIFORNIA

ESTIMATED TIME TO IMPACT: 28 HOURS 50 MINUTES

Her eyes went from the headlights, which she now could tell belonged to several military Jeeps, to the night sky. It was mottled with swirling colors, as before, but gave no evidence the CME had struck early. *Then what—?*

The motorcade halted in front of her. Agent Aragon jumped out of the lead vehicle.

"Finally!" she said under her breath.

Earlier today, given the severity of the X-ray storms, she decided the lab would be a far safer refuge for her family than the church basement.

With Calder's blessing, she asked for Aragon's help. "Anything you wish," he said. "President's orders."

He rushed up to her. "Ms. Armendariz, I'm so sorry it took so long. The streets are jammed like you can't believe. And—"

"It's okay, it's okay," she said, peering anxiously in the direction of the idling convoy. "Thanks for making this happen; I can't tell you what it means to me."

As she spoke, her brother hurried toward her, followed closely by Albert Hernandez.

Beto?

"*Dios*, it's good to see you, big brother," she said, giving Carlos a bear hug, adding as sincerely as she could, "Good to see you, too, Beto."

When they finished embracing, she said to Carlos, "Go ahead and tell 'em to get out."

"Who?"

"The family, *tonto*." She took a step in the direction of the vehicles. "I wanna show you guys where—"

Carlos reached out and detained her. "Wait a minute, Sis. They didn't come. Only me and Beto—and we're not staying."

"What? Why?"

"Not here. Somewhere pri—"

Calder rushed out of the lab. "Allie, what in the world's going on?"

"It's my family. You remember Carlos, my brother. And this is Albert Hernandez, a family friend."

After a flurry of hellos she led Carlos into the lab. "So what's going on?"

He took her hands. "First of all, everybody's really grateful you thought of them. But they didn't come on account of they didn't want to be in your way."

She pulled away. "But that's ridiculous, they wouldn't be in my way. It's a big lab, for Pete's sake."

"It's not only that, Allie, it's..."

"What? Tell me."

He shrugged his shoulders. "It's just that Alicia and I don't feel comfortable abandoning the congregation. She and the *hermanas* have fixed up the church basement with cots and everything. They've even made all kinds of food. Everyone's coming to wait out the storm together. We'll be fine."

She was suddenly nauseous. "I know Carlos, I know. You told me and I thought it was a good idea—at first. But now I'm worried it might not be safe enough! This thing is—"

"Allie, you know the people of the church. They're not just *believers*." He made a fist and tapped it against his heart. "They *trust*. There's a big difference, you know. Even Satan believes. But *los hermanos* are surrendering this thing to the Lord because they truly trust him. *Con todo sus corazones*, with all their hearts."

She gaped at him. "And Mom and Dad, are they still—?"

"Yes—just like I told you before. Beto's having a limo pick them both up and bring them to the church—along with a nurse. You know Beto, *primera clase* all the way."

She had to admit it, Beto was a good man—despite his annoying relentlessness.

"And Lolo? What's gonna happen to her?" She flung herself at Carlos and held him hard. "Oh, Carlos, what's going to happen to our baby sister?"

She began to weep.

"I know, Sis, I know." His voice faltered. "I spoke with the Denver detective just before coming here. It wasn't easy getting through because of the bad phone lines. He said they hadn't heard anything new from Interpol." He paused. "He also told me that truthfully, with everything going on, it's not—"

"Don't say it, don't say it," she said, letting go of him. "Let's just pray."

Carlos uttered a brief prayer and then said in a quiet voice, "Well, Beto and I better be getting back. We'll be fine, Sis. Don't worry."

She took a deep breath. "I'll walk you out."

Arm in arm, they stepped out of the brightly lit lab and into the night.

"Hold on, I have a surprise for you," Carlos said.

As he ran to the parked vehicles, she caught sight of more headlights heading their way.

Dang, it's like Grand Central Station all of a sudden!

Carlos returned quickly, clutching a bulging paper bag, Beto at his side. "A care package from the *hermanas.*"

"A dozen of their best tamales," Beto chimed in, beaming. "*Son de rez y* Texas style, just the way you like 'em."

Before she could thank them, the new cluster of headlights pulled up, accompanied by the sound of screeching tires.

A large MP jumped out of the lead Jeep. "Excuse me, ma'am. We're looking for Dr. Sinclair. It's urgent."

She ran inside and found him still working on the supersonic module. "Calder, someone needs you right away!"

They both sprinted outside.

"Yes, here I am," Calder said.

"Dr. Sinclair, sir," the MP said, "they've found her."

"Hero?"

"Yes, sir. They're flying her back this very minute." Then the large man's face dropped. "There's only one thing."

CHAPTER 41

A NEW DAY

Mother Yolanda was waiting at the door of the bank when the security guard unlocked it and welcomed her in. She was carrying an old cloth bag filled with the cash, checks, and money orders the convent received from people all over the world. The total was far more than they'd prayed for: $451,345.22—enough even for an endowment, she hoped.

"*Buenos dias*, Reverend Mother," the bank president said, coming quickly toward her.

She smiled. He seemed so young to be in charge of *Banco Sevillano*. "*Buenos dias*, my son."

"Is this the deposit? Let me help you with it."

Back at the convent, the sisters had vied for the privilege of delivering the heavy bundle to the bank. But she felt called to carry it herself, despite its heaviness.

The young man took the bag and led her to his private office. "Okay, now." He settled into a high-back, brown leather chair behind his massive desk. "You have many options for what to do with the money. I will do my best to explain them and to advise you. But in the end it will be your choice. You understand, *sí*?"

She nodded and grinned, amused at how young people often spoke to her—as though she were senile.

"Give me just a moment while I start up my computer," he said. "You are my first appointment today and the most important one of all."

She sat back and surveyed the office.

So fancy.

The orphanage had been doing business with *Banco Sevillano* for many decades.

"I remember your father, may he rest in peace, when he was running the bank. He was a good…" Something appeared to be wrong. She could see it in the young man's furrowed brow. "Is there a problem?"

"One moment, please, Reverend Mother." He stood up and left the room.

It immediately crossed her mind that the enemy might be at it again. He had not relented since the beginning of their good fortune.

On her way to the bank this morning even the traffic lights stopped working. One after another, they either went out or blinked constantly. The sisters warned her the sun was threatening to do such things. But she knew better.

The lights in the bank faltered.

She fumbled for her rosary beads.

Yes, the enemy is on the prowl.

She would need to be especially alert today in handling the money. The sooner it was deposited the better.

The banker returned, still wearing a vexed look. "Mother Yolanda, I'm sorry for the delay."

"What is it, my son?"

"Well, I really don't know how to explain it."

"Try, my son." Then she added, asking God to forgive her mischievous jab, "But please use plain words because I am a simple old woman."

The young banker laughed self-consciously. "Well, to put it simply, Reverend Mother, when I accessed your account just now, it showed a balance of $7,777,777. And no one can explain why. There's no record of a deposit, it just appeared that way moments ago. Like magic."

★

MONDAY, MAY 1 (1:04 P.M. CHINA STANDARD TIME)

SHANGHAI JIAO TONG UNIVERSITY; SHANGHAI, CHINA

ESTIMATED TIME TO IMPACT: 28 HOURS 44 MINUTES

Zhaohui Tang, sitting with her grad students before a wall of outsized computer screens, stared in utter amazement at the telemetry and fluttering imagery on display.

Her proprietary diagnostic program was tracking the lightning-fast proliferation of the unfamiliar virus that erupted an hour earlier. The Trojan horse, ferocious beyond anything she'd ever seen, was hitching rides on search engines, browsers, e-mail servers—doing everything possible to replicate itself and infect the entire World Wide Web.

At the moment it was targeting computer-controlled public systems—local, regional, and national—appearing to give priority to power grids, telephonic networks, and the media. She watched helplessly as it attacked China Radio's broadcast system and the People's government websites—including military ones—with fiendish alacrity.

For now, the lab's computer system—independently powered by natural gas generators and protected by her new add-on—was holding up to the brutal onslaught. But she knew it was only a matter of minutes, if that long, before the malware-fighting add-on succumbed and the entire system crashed.

A female student burst into the room looking distraught. "Professor!"

"Jia, what is wrong?"

"Everybody in the university is fleeing! Power is down all over the city. People are screaming that we're being attacked."

"It's a computer virus," Zhaohui said calmly, remaining in her chair in front of the giant screens. "And it's not just Shanghai. We've been tracking it. Electricity is out everywhere, all over China, all over the world. It's a massive cyberattack. But we must remain calm."

★

MONDAY, MAY 1 (2:36 P.M. AUSTRALIAN CENTRAL STANDARD TIME)

CHARLES DARWIN UNIVERSITY; CASUARINA, AUSTRALIA

ESTIMATED TIME TO IMPACT: 28 HOURS 42 MINUTES

Sara was sitting on her bed trying without luck to reach her dad by e-mail. For some reason her computer, like her cell, was no longer working.

"Arghhh, c'mon!" she said, banging on the keyboard.

The dorm room lights went out.

Moments later Dirk burst through the door. "Sara, you in there?!"

"Yeah, right here."

"Oh, thank god. Electricity's down all over the university! It's like totally spooky-crazy."

★

MONDAY, MAY 1 (8:10 A.M. ISRAEL DAYLIGHT TIME)

MOUNT OF OLIVES; JERUSALEM, ISRAEL

ESTIMATED TIME TO IMPACT: 28 HOURS 38 MINUTES

The noise of a padlock being unlocked made Lorena sit up.

Jamil!

She'd spent the night sleeping in a niche in the subterranean cemetery called the Tombs of the Prophets, on the western slope of the Mount of Olives. Jewish and Christian tradition held—and she believed—these tombs once housed the remains of the Bible's last three prophets—Haggai, Zachariah, and Malachi—plus dozens of their disciples. In the fifth and sixth centuries BC Zachariah and Malachi prophesied about the End Times and the coming of the Messiah.

Lorena knew Zachariah 14:4 by heart and began whispering it to herself: "On that day his feet will stand on the Mount of Olives, east of Jerusalem, and the Mount of Olives will be split in two from east to west, forming a great valley, with half of the Mount moving north and half moving south."

Yesterday she took a taxi to the tombs and waited until the final tour of the day, when she nonchalantly blended in with Italian tourists streaming out of two big buses. The large group descended a flight of roughly hewn stone steps. They were greeted inside the pitch-black catacomb by a swarthy, middle-aged man holding a lighted candle. "Welcome, my friends," he said. "My name is Jamil; I'm the caretaker of this sacred site."

For fifteen minutes, as Jamil led the crowd through the labyrinthine cemetery, she was careful to trail behind. At just the right moment she ducked into one of the many deep, dark burial nooks carved into the stone walls—"There are fifty in all," Jamil explained—and remained there for the rest of the tour.

"Do we have everybody?" she heard Jamil say at the end. A few moments later, while she held her breath in anxious anticipation, the crowd noise faded away and was punctuated by the loud clanging sound of the metal entrance gate.

Now, as Jamil welcomed the first tour group of the morning, her insides roiled.

"Careful on the steps, please. Everyone must have a lighted candle before we can proceed. Matches are in the small box by the candles."

She listened sharply to Jamil's practiced spiel—waiting for just the right moment.

"Now you are coming into the Tombs of the Prophets..."

Her ears throbbed; her manic heart hammered against her rib cage. *Wait.*

There was the sound of shuffling feet as Jamil led the tourists to the far side of the catacomb.

"On the wall you can see the chiseled marks..."

Now!

Quickly, she lit the candle she'd taken upon entering last evening and crept to the mouth of her small cavern. Poking her head out, she looked around to make certain the coast was clear, then casually walked out. A few anxious moments later, espying the tomb's main entrance at the top of the stone steps, she felt a surge of optimism. The opening was aglow with the bright sunlight of a new day; a day closer to the momentous event she was here to witness.

Thank you, Jesus!

Blowing out the candle, she quickly ascended the stairs and hurried away.

CHAPTER 42

DAMAGE CONTROL

S tanding outside Calder's lab, Allie stared wide-eyed at the explosion of activity. MPs, military reservists, agents from the Secret Service, FBI, and Homeland Security—all were converging on the scene in droves.

"Whoa!" she said to Aragon, who was still shadowing her. "I've seen a whole lot of things as a reporter, but nothing like this."

"Same here. Our orders are to lock down the area and make sure Dr. Sinclair and the lab stay safe. His vehicle, too—when it gets here."

"And when's that?"

He shook his head and shrugged. "Not sure. All I know is Agent Cannatella is with the vehicle now and there's some kind of hold up."

She stared in the direction of the bay, her insides churning. San Diego's power was out. The only illumination was from overhead—stars peeping through the swirling aurora—making the skyline look other-worldly.

A flush-faced Eva suddenly appeared and without explanation led Allie to a quiet spot inside the lab next to a bank of battery-operated playback machines.

"What's going on?" Allie said.

"I've just heard from our IT guys. They've been trying to get through to us for the past hour."

"Go ahead."

"The Quantum chip they've been putting through the paces?"

"Yeah."

"It's bugged."

"What do you mean, bugged? It's got a hidden microphone?"

"No! It's got some kind of virus or something built into it. It went off like a firecracker right at nine o'clock. Our guys say it was pro-grammed to do that."

Allie shook her head. "But I don't get it. What does it mean?" Then she said, "Oh, no, wait. You're not thinking Kilroy has anything to do with it, are you?!"

"Who else?! The Quantum I is his baby—he made sure everybody knew it. Here, take a look at this." She fed a DVD into one of the play-back machines. "This was just taken by our chopper over downtown San Diego."

The aerial video showed people harshly lit by the copter's roving spotlight. They were fighting next to an ATM machine that was spitting out money like a Las Vegas slot machine. Moments later the shoving devolved into fist fighting and gunfire.

"ATMs all over the world are going crazy," Eva said. "Our guys say it's the virus. It's attacking banks, police departments, corporations, power grids, even our own network. Stu says the main studio is still operating on generator power, but with the virus attacking master control and transmission towers—"

"*Dios, chica.*" Allie's eyes remained glued to the video. "This is awful. It's out-and-out anarchy."

"The governor's called in the National Guard, but they're totally outnumbered. Stu says we should keep reporting as long as possible, even though he's guessing nobody's watching."

★

SUNDAY, APRIL 30 (10:52 P.M. PACIFIC DAYLIGHT TIME)

ESTIMATED TIME TO IMPACT: 27 HOURS 56 MINUTES

Allie and Calder were feverishly working on the supersonic booster when Eva stormed up to them.

"Guys! They're saying *Hero*'s coming, she's coming!"

Together, they sprinted to the beach, halted at water's edge, and scanned the night sky.

"Over there!" Allie said, pointing at a moving asterism just above the northern horizon. "You see the little red and green lights?"

Gradually, the small lights resolved themselves into a twin-rotor military transport helicopter that looked like a giant grasshopper.

She stared at it hard.

A Chinook.

Eva, standing next to her, leaned in. "You sure you won't change your mind?"

Allie gritted her teeth.

Eva and Stu were pressuring her to document the story of *Hero*'s disappearance, but so far she'd steadfastly refused—reminding them of her promise to the president. Now that live broadcasting was no longer feasible, however, Allie wondered if it would be ethical to record events for later use.

It was a close call.

"Okay, *chica*, go ahead. But strictly on the QT, understood?"

"Absolutely," Eva said, dashing away. "Trust me."

The massive chopper steadily approached until it was near enough for Allie to make out the lifeless payload hanging on steel cables from its vast belly.

Allie's hand flew to her mouth; *Hero's* exterior was badly charred.

Oh, lord, it's over.

What now??

At last, the Chinook gained a position directly above the pier, where it hovered for a moment, and then slowly began descending. The turbulence caused by its rotors sent many in the vicinity fleeing for cover. She and Calder, buffeted by the powerful downwash, stood their ground, clinging to one another. The tips of her long hair, tossing about violently, whipped against her face and stung.

The Chinook gently lowered the embattled-looking craft onto the water, and then released her from the cabling. Calder, fully clothed, stormed the surf. Others followed him and together they lashed *Hero* to the pier.

Calder heaved himself onto the wooden platform and, soaking wet, fell to his knees. He stared at *Hero*, then began stroking her scorched hull.

Allie wanted to race to his side but didn't, realizing with some jealousy that he needed to be alone. Everyone else stayed away as well.

The unburdened Chinook rose and quickly departed. Allie could feel it: a mood of desolation overtook the beach. Groaning sounds from diesel generators powering high-wattage work lamps around the pier filled the painted night air.

It's like a wake.

She and everyone on the beach watched Calder in anxious, reverential silence as he inspected the blackened vehicle from stem to stern. She held her breath when he opened the bubble-shaped windshield and climbed inside.

Minutes later he poked his head above the cockpit opening and, with a small wave of the hand, beckoned in her direction.

She looked about to see who exactly he was calling for. Seeing no one immediately around her, she pointed to herself and he nodded.

When she gained the pier and was close enough to see his face, she was certain he'd been crying. "Calder, I'm so sorry."

But as she approached more closely, his lips slowly curled into the smallest hint of a smile.

"I told you she was indestructible," he said.

★

SUNDAY, APRIL 30 (11:14 P.M. PACIFIC DAYLIGHT TIME)

ESTIMATED TIME TO IMPACT: 27 HOURS 34 MINUTES

Calder supervised a fast-moving detail of military volunteers who quickly transferred *Hero* back into the lab and onto the lift. As soon as they were out of the way, he went right to work.

Most of *Hero*'s hardware had survived the conflagration, which didn't surprise him. She was built to withstand the atom-bomb-like stresses caused by the Q-thruster's propulsion system. But her software was totally corrupted. Getting it debugged in time would be one of the biggest challenges of all.

He had just started the repairs when Allie showed up with her camera crew. "Calder, you don't mind, do you?"

He checked his impulse to lash out, recalling their amazing kiss earlier that evening. "Go ahead," he muttered, shaking his head. "Just don't get in the way, please."

★

SUNDAY, APRIL 30 (11:31 P.M. PACIFIC DAYLIGHT TIME)

ESTIMATED TIME TO IMPACT: 27 HOURS 17 MINUTES

"Hey, Lois Lane!"

She turned and saw Mike Cannatella marching into the lab—as always, the personification of cool, calm, and in charge. "Keep shooting without me," she said to Eva.

She rushed to Mike and they embraced. His cologne had a strong, sweet fragrance, which she found reassuring somehow.

"Can we talk?" he said, looking to his right and left.

"Sure."

"Somewhere private."

She led him to a corner of the lab, next to the reverb chamber.

"It's about *Hero*," he said quickly. "What we found inside of her."

"Yeah?" She was feeling warm suddenly. "On the record or off?"

"Eventually, on. But right now, off."

"Go ahead."

"We found *Hero* pretty quickly. Compared to everything else on the water, her thermal signature stuck out like Rudolph's red nose. It's too bad we didn't get to her before.... " He looked away.

"Before what?" she said. "All I was told is she accidentally ran into an off-shore oil rig up north."

"Allie, it wasn't an accident. *Hero* was stolen. By Jared Kilroy."

It took a moment for her mind to comprehend. "Kilroy?"

He nodded. "We found him dead inside the cockpit. But not cremated, the ship protected him from that—suffocated. The fire sucked up all the oxygen. You could see on his face how terrified he was at the end. Creepy."

She opened her mouth to speak.

"And that's not all," he went on. "Earlier today we arrested someone—a black bloc anarchist—who says a rich, anonymous mastermind ordered him to arrange the attacks on the protesters last night. When we recovered Kilroy's cell phone from inside *Hero*, it matched the phone number we got from the anarchist."

Her eyes widened. "But it makes no sense!" She began pacing, winding a strand of her hair into the shape of a Twizzler. "Kilroy was into computers, not protests. In fact, Eva—"

"That's the even worse news." Mike looked around distrustfully. "Allie, he's responsible for a major computer virus that just went off a few hours ago."

She stopped. "That's what *I* was going to tell you. Our IT guys discovered the Quantum chip was rigged—like a time bomb."

Mike stared at her. "You know already?"

"Yeah, I just found out from Eva."

"I just found out myself too. For weeks our lab guys have been checking out the chip because the bureau was thinking it could boost the speed and accuracy of our fingerprint ID system, big time. A little over two hours ago, right at midnight eastern time, they noticed the chip suddenly changing behavior—all on its own. It wasn't plugged into a computer or the Internet or anything, just wired to a closed-circuit diagnostics set-up.

"They said it was like watching a monster storming out of a cave. The virus prowled around the circuitry looking for something, anything, to attach itself to. When it couldn't find a way out of the chip, it turned on itself."

She made a face. "Ugh."

"But there's more. As they were watching the virus, something about it seemed familiar. That's when they made the connection—realized the behavior of the virus was the mirror image of the antiviral program on those CDs Anonymous handed out."

"*Dios!* So Kilroy was—"

"Yes. Kilroy was the masked man. We're pretty confident that when we compare voice prints, we'll get a match."

She looked sightlessly at Mike, her mind going a mile a minute. "Eva just showed me video of San Diego. The virus is making ATM machines—"

Wait!

Calder!

"Oh, my gosh!"

Mike looked confused. "What?"

She locked eyes on him. "Mike! Can you get me a copy of that CD? The one with the antivirus?"

"Of course, but why?"

"I'll explain later." She started away and without looking back shouted, "Please, just get it here. Right away!"

CHAPTER 43

ON STAGE

Having been up all night, everyone in the lab, she included, was moving and moping about like zombies, waiting for Calder to finish. Expressing hope he'd finish soon.

Allie massaged her temples and squeezed her burning eyes shut. She'd been able to provide the fix for *Hero*'s infected Quantum chip—the antivirus program on the CD—but not much else. Throughout the ordeal, neither *Hero*'s complex inner workings nor Calder's loner temperament allowed anyone even to get close to the vehicle.

"All set."

The quiet words from behind made her eyes fly open. Whipping around, she saw Calder staring at her, his sky-blue eyes tired but alert.

"Really?" she said in a hoarse whisper. She cleared her throat. "All set?"

He nodded and then turned to leave.

"I really want to go with you," she called after him. *"Please?"*

He stopped and looked over his shoulder, his expression hard as *Hero*'s hull. "For the last time, *no*," he growled. Then he stomped away.

The news of Calder and *Hero*'s readiness spread rapidly throughout the facility, its effect on everyone as bracing as a cup of strong coffee.

Eva ran up to Allie, her salt-and-pepper hair a tangled mess. "I just gave Stu the heads up. Pitsy's firing up the lights. Let's go!"

They rushed away together, Allie's hands instinctively pampering her hair. She laughed at herself.

Vanity, vanity, all is vanity.

Once outside, she paused to drink in the cool sea air. The golden light of the rising sun—its flaming orb now encircled by a broad, diaphanous, orange-red annulus—co-mingled strangely with the garish primary colors of the worsening aurora. It gave her the impression of living inside a giant prism.

Hearing a loud, grating sound, she turned and saw the hangar's tall doors gradually parting. A moment later a large, heavy tow truck bearing *Hero* emerged from inside the lab and rolled slowly through the widening maw.

Hero's ceramic-alloy hull was no longer a glossy, fire-engine red. Instead, it was scarred and mottled, like the heat shield of a spaceship after careening through the atmosphere.

"Allie!" Eva shouted.

"Coming!"

They were going through the motions of normal TV reporting, even though it was unlikely many people were able to watch. Overnight the

Quantum virus had felled power plants the world over, and then turned them back on again, only to dupe their faltering computerized governing systems into thinking they needed to crank up the output. The result were scores of overloaded, blown transformers. The only electricity available now was from generators.

Virtually all electronic devices connected to the Web—computers, TVs, smartphones, you name it—were laid low by the virus. Nevertheless, Allie believed that even if by some miracle only one viewer was able to watch her live broadcasts, it was worth the effort.

Eva dashed up to her. "How much do you love me?"

"Why? What's going on?"

"It's your buddy, the prez. He's just ordered your broadcasts to be carried over the EAS."

"The Emergency Alert System? Seriously? But that's only—"

"Yeah, I know. You've just been designated the nation's one and only pool reporter, Babycakes."

Pool reporter. It meant she was now representing the world's entire press corps!

Eva added, "You're sure you don't want to ask Calder again? Just once more?"

Allie shook her head emphatically. "No! He wants to go solo. Let it be."

"I just thought that if he knew about the EAS, he would—"

Allie stomped her foot. "*Chica! A punto!* Let it go. No!"

★

Calder, inside the lab's locker room, was hurriedly suiting up when a well-dressed young man rushed up with a smartphone in hand.

"Dr. Sinclair, sir! The president wishes to speak with you. He's on a secure line but doesn't know how long it'll hold up."

Calder took the phone, trying to recall how one properly addressed the president of the United States.

"Hello?"

"Dr. Sinclair, I know you've got your hands full right now and I don't wish to hold you up. But you have an important mission ahead of you."

"Yes, sir, I know."

"Have you been given everything you need? Are you all set?"

"Yes, sir. People have been very helpful. I appreciate it, thank you."

"When you get back, I'd like you and your family to visit Martha and me at the White House. In the meantime you'll have our prayers. I only hope you can get to the holes before it's too late. So much is at stake, not just for our country, but the world."

"Yes, sir."

Calder felt honored to be talking to the president, grateful for the man's thoughtfulness and humanity, sensitive to the awful burden he carried. But he just wanted to get going.

"Well, then, Dr. Sinclair, I'll let you go now."

"Yes, sir. Thank you, sir. I'll do everything I can."

"Thank you, Dr. Sinclair. Remember, we'll see you at the White House when you return. God bless you."

Calder hung up and rushed to finish dressing, going over the final plan in his mind. Because of the time crunch, he'd been forced to come up with a strategy for fixing all the holes in one fell swoop. It was a long shot, for sure, but the only one they had left.

Grabbing his helmet, he rushed off.

At the door he paused.

Am I just being stubborn?

Allie had proven herself flight worthy throughout the rescue mission.

No, too dangerous.

He and *Hero* would be hurtling into the heart of the CME storm at supersonic speeds, using a booster never before test-flown.

A suicide mission.

He dared not risk inflicting his jinxed fate on her.

But then maybe, just maybe, it'd work the other way around.

She does seem to have an in with her God.

★

Allie kicked off her live broadcast by introducing Dallan. The signal from the SWPC was fuzzy and unstable. On the giant screen behind him, he explained, was live video of the onrushing CME.

DO: "These images are from the latest generation Advanced Composition Explorer satellite."

They showed a vast, roiling, incandescent orange cloud of radiation bristling with flashes of bright blue and green light and shot through with thin, crooked, yellowish filaments that resembled the skeletal fingers of some grasping beast.

AA: "Pretty scary looking."

DO: Yes…it is. The main cloud is now about twenty-five million miles across and two million degrees Celsius on the surface—about three-and-a-half million degrees Fahrenheit.

AA: And where is it, exactly?"

DO: "It's less than twenty-four million miles away and still averaging about 1.3 million miles per hour. At that rate we expect contact in fewer than nineteen hours."

AA: "In the past few days we've talked a lot about the CME's impact and what we can do to protect ourselves. My question this morning is: Has there ever been a CME this powerful before? If so, why haven't we heard about it?"

DO: "Great question, Allie. The largest CME ever recorded was the so-called Carrington Event in 1859. It was gigantic. In modern terms it had the destructive power of twenty Katrina-sized hurricanes. But it didn't create a lot of damage because the world wasn't electrified and computerized the way it is today. The worst that happened back then was telegraph lines went down.

"According to the National Academy of Sciences, today that same Carrington Event could easily cause trillions of dollars in damage and take years to clean up."

AA: "Yeow. And how does the CME we're facing compare to that Carrington Event?"

Dallan hesitated for a moment.

DO: "It's about ten times more powerful, which is mind-boggling, I know. Even *I* can't wrap my head around it, and I do this for a living."

AA: "But Dr. O'Malley, wait a minute. In the face of—"

DO: "Oh, and Allie, don't forget: those damage estimates I just gave you assume a normal, intact magnetic field. The holes will make things even worse. It's scary, but those are the hard facts. We're dealing with a mind-boggling phenomenon here, not just some hurricane or flood."

AA: "That's just what I was about to say. In the face of that kind of destructive power, people watching might be saying, 'What in the world can I possibly do about it?' So can we go over those survival tips once again?"

On the screen appeared a checklist titled, "How to Survive the CME."

DO: "First, whatever you do, stay indoors. That goes for your pets too. Don't try to evacuate, it's too late for that. What you want are as many layers of solid protection between you and the sky as possible. If you have a basement, then by all means stock it with supplies and plan to hole up until the CME has blown over. Just to be extra cautious, I'd say plan for about two days.

"Second, unplug all electrical appliances. Power might be down right now, but when the CME hits it'll cause electrical surges in the wiring that'll fry anything plugged into the grid.

"Third, stay away from plumbing. Surges will go through metal pipes as well.

"Fourth, wet down your house if possible. In case of an electrical fire, it'll be less likely to burn down.

"And finally, if you have any electrical equipment containing important information that could be erased by surges—a hard drive, for example—put them into cardboard boxes and wrap the outside of the boxes with aluminum foil. It sounds crazy but it works. And people with pacemakers should do something similar. I'd recommend wrapping yourself in one of those aluminized Mylar space blankets."

AA: "Homemade Faraday Cages—I like that, very clever. Good advice."

DO: "Allie, one last thing. These precautions, which I urge everyone to take, are still no guarantee against the CME. People would need to hide in bomb shelters at least three feet underground in order to be truly safe. And for people living under a magnetic hole, the danger of being hit by an unfiltered CME is very real. Expect explosive fires and radiation poisoning to be everywhere throughout a hole site. But again, staying indoors the way I explained is about all any of us can do at this point. There's no other way to protect ourselves from this thing that's about to rain down on us."

Allie, mindful it was getting close to launch time, thanked Dallan and asked him to stand by for further updates.

DO: "You bet. Thank you, Allie. Stay safe."

Allie tossed to Bill Marks, a reporter standing by at the Staples Center in downtown Los Angeles.

"Thanks, Allie. Rioting and looting here are now completely out of control…"

She took the brief opportunity to gulp down some water and communicate with Eva via the IFB. In mid-swallow she heard her name being called. She turned and saw Calder coming toward her, somber-faced and suited up.

"Excuse me, Allie," he said upon reaching her. "But if you're coming with me, you'd better get dressed, *pronto*."

She wasn't amused and said so.

"I'm serious," he said, holding up a flight suit. "You win."

She stepped out of the camera lights. "Calder, I don't want this to be a test of wills with a winner and a loser. Unless you really want me to go, I won't."

He looked her in the eyes. "Okay, I really want you to come with me."

She searched his face for signs of irony and found none. "What changed your mind?"

"Not what, *who*. You." He thrust the flight suit at her. Then gently taking her by the forearms, he murmured, "I want us to be together—no matter what happens."

"Allie!"

The familiar, bossy voice was shouting into her ear through the IFB, but it seemed to be coming from a long, long way away.

Allie, still staring into Calder's eyes, leaned in and pressed her lips to his.

"Where are you?!" the voice shouted. "Allie, Allie, you're on!"

CHAPTER 44

SHOWTIME

MONDAY, MAY 1 (9:15 A.M. PACIFIC DAYLIGHT TIME)

NAVAL BASE POINT LOMA; SAN DIEGO, CALIFORNIA

ESTIMATED TIME TO IMPACT: 17 HOURS 33 MINUTES

As Calder neared the pier, he was taken aback by the large number of Navy people around *Hero* shouting orders as if they were in charge. Under different circumstances he would've stormed down there and chased them all away. For that matter, he would've asked the president on the phone a few minutes ago why in his speech yesterday he'd connected Calder with the Navy.

He let it slide. There was too much to be completed before launch. Like the final stages of evacuating the vacuum chamber and freezing it to nearly absolute zero. There was also the complication of freezing the supersonic booster as well.

Allie, all suited up, rushed up to him. "Okay, put me to work."

He smiled weakly. "Just go ahead and get aboard. Make sure all your cameras are in place and tested." He lifted a forefinger. "And no interviews this time until we've pulled away. We're cutting things really close."

Nearly a half hour later, with every task in the pre-launch sequence completed, he inspected the vehicle one last time. He finished by lifting the vehicle's rear cover and scrutinizing the collision avoidance system. It was the part of *Hero* he was most concerned about; it had never been tested at supersonic speeds.

"All set, everyone," he said at last, in a voice loud enough for everyone standing nearby to hear.

Allie stood up in her seat. "Calder, just a minute. Can we pray?"

He vacillated, but took note of the nodding heads all around him. "Sure." Then in a low voice added, "Make it quick, please."

She thanked her God for the gifts of life, love, and light...beseeched him for mercy...and asked for his will to be done, through Calder.

At the end of the prayer, everyone—but not he—said a loud amen.

"Thanks," he said in low voice, despite himself.

In the distance he heard the beating of helicopter blades.

The media circus begins.

Quickly donning his Kevlar helmet, he stepped into the cockpit and studiously worked through the preflight checklist. When he reached the point of booting up the computer, he held his breath and pushed the green button.

C'mon, baby—do your thing.

His heart sank when the nav screen faltered and began fluttering. A moment later, the display settled down and he heaved a huge sigh of relief.

Immediately, he thrust a fist high into the air and the crowd erupted with loud, raucous cheering. Then he pulled the domed windshield shut.

★

Allie watched the ensigns untying the ropes. When that was done, she heard the telltale whine of *Hero*'s ignition system. She said to her viewers, assuming there were any, "With all systems go, it sounds like the engine has ignited. For the next few minutes I'm going to keep my commentary to a minimum so Dr. Sinclair can concentrate. I'll let the natural sights and sounds speak for themselves."

She pictured the laser and electron beams revving up and colliding—the subzero quantum vacuum shivering in response—sneezing up a spray of innumerable electron-positron pairs. Pictured them being channeled by a magnetic lens into the combustion chamber, like an incendiary river. Imagined them coming together inside the chamber, annihilating one another in brilliant explosions of gamma radiation. According to Calder, *Hero* generated a thrust equivalent to six hundred thousand pounds of TNT *per ounce* of matter-antimatter fuel—enough energy to power the average American home for 60,000 years.

The sudden forward momentum pressed Allie against the seat. She fought to catch her breath, could sense *Hero*'s souped-up propulsion system champing at the bit, like a strapping racehorse eager for the sting of the jockey's crop.

"Joshua One, this is Point Loma. Please confirm your parrot is on. Over."

A subtle but noticeable change in the audio level of her IFB gave Allie the distinct impression she'd lost the connection to the production truck.

"Eva, can you hear me?"

Nothing.

She'd worried about this. The Emergency Alert System had access to the finest, most storm-hardened communications pathways known to science, but it was far from foolproof.

"Hello? Hello? This is Allie. Can you hear me?"

Nothing.

Then scratchiness.

"Ye—we ca—ar you."

"You're breaking up," Allie said. "Try again."

After a few more minutes of futility, she opted to give it a rest.

"Problems?" Calder asked.

She saw he'd already steered *Hero* well clear of the bay and was now headed toward open ocean. "What else? Anyway, once you give me the all-clear I'll ask you some questions as though we were live, okay? They can broadcast it later. We do it all the time—it's called live-to-tape."

"Let's do it now, but fast. I'm about to give the ol' girl her rein."

For the viewers' sake, as always, she'd pretend not to know the answers to her questions.

AA: "Dr. Sinclair, we've just left Naval Base Point Loma. Tell me, what's your plan for fixing the magnetic holes?"

CS: "Sure. There are six holes all together, but I don't have time to fix each one separately."

AA: "So what are you going to do?"

CS: "I'll try to make this simple, but help me out, okay? For starters, there's something called the Riemannian centroid. It's a fancy way of saying that if you have lots of points on the surface of a sphere, like the Earth, there's one unique location that's equally distant from them all. I'm oversimplifying things but that's the gist.

"When I did the calculation, I discovered the Riemannian centroid of the six magnetic holes is located in the Middle East. Specifically, Amman, Jordan."

AA: "But you're talking about an inland city. *Hero*'s a ship. How can you possibly get to the centroid?"

CS: "Well, the short answer is that I can't. But I'm going to get as close as possible."

AA: "What's the plan when you get there?"

CS: "We believe the magnetic holes can be disrupted—snapped back to normal—by hitting them with quantum waves of just the right frequency."

Last night Calder and she agreed not to tell people *Hero* almost certainly created the magnetic holes in the first place. They felt it would only add to their fears. There would be plenty of time afterward to come clean. Assuming the mission was a success.

AA: "Okay. But how exactly do you do that?"

CS: "Basically, I've come up with a makeshift frequency modulator. It lets me change the frequency of quantum waves naturally radiating from *Hero*'s vacuum chamber. Think of it as a jamming device, like what the military uses to block enemy radio signals. I've calculated a very particular jamming frequency that should disrupt and destroy the magnetic holes. And people should know you helped me with this, Allie, so thank you."

AA: "You're welcome, but please go on."

CS: "When I get to the centroid, my job will be to turn on the jamming device and hope it does the trick—that it jams whatever mechanism is causing the magnetic holes. If it works, then the magnetic field should snap back to normal right away, instantaneously."

AA: "Amazing. And by the way, before I continue, I want to make sure viewers understand something. Dr. Sinclair can't make the CME itself go away. All he's trying to do, which is plenty, is close the doors on it, right?"

CS: "Yes—although I wish I could make the CME disappear."

AA: "How long will it take you to get to Amman? It's pretty far."

CS: "Yeah. It's about fourteen thousand nautical miles by way of the Pacific and Atlantic, around Cape Horn. At five hundred knots it would take us more than a day to get there. But we're going to be traveling faster than the speed of sound. And Allie—I'm sorry, but the interview's over. We've gotta get going."

"Allie! Can you hear me? Over." It was Eva's voice, clear as day.
"Eva, not now, I'll call you back. Over and out."
"But I—"
Allie threw the kill switch. "Sorry, Cald—"
Without warning, Allie was squashed against the chair so brutally she nearly passed out.
"Awright, here we go!" Calder cried out, "Beam me up, Scotty!"

★

Calder activated the supersonic booster and felt a slight jolt. An instant later *Hero* accelerated precipitously, as if suddenly unshackled, throwing him back in his seat.

He beamed. It was just as the Haisch theory predicted! *Hero*'s supersonic booster was manipulating the quantum fields—whittling down her inertia, lessening her resistance to motion—causing her speed to surge.

Calder's body was now pressed so hard against the seat he was virtually paralyzed. With all his might, he forced his left hand to keep nudging the throttle forward.

With her mounting speed, he could feel *Hero* straining to hold together.

Please, baby, please.

The anxious seconds ticked away and all continued to go well. No glitches. No alarms.

Still pinned in his seat by the brutal, unremitting G-forces, his gaze flickered drunkenly over the dashboard and landed on the digital speed log. But its cycling numerals were an indistinct blur.

He dragged his gaze over to the navigation panel; the grid lines were whizzing across the screen indecipherably. With great effort he turned his head to the right and left, looking outside for any clues as to *Hero*'s speed. But the passing scenery—what little he could see of it—was no less of a blur.

A few moments later *Hero* stopped accelerating. He stared at the speed log until its indistinct numerals settled down. He blinked at the final reading: 1,446 knots. Mach 1.9! Nearly *two times* the speed of sound—way past his expectations.

Before he was able to tell Allie the great news, he became aware of a strange, disorienting sensation. His limbs moved more freely than normal—even though he felt as heavy (his bum was sunk deeply into his seat) as ever.

He puzzled over the paradoxical sensation—and then it dawned on him. He was experiencing a side effect you'd expect from the Haisch theory. Usually, *inertia*, our resistance to movement, was inextricably tied to *weight*, our feeling of heaviness. It was as though inertia and weight were Siamese Twins. But now they'd become detached. His inertia had plummeted significantly—explaining his newfound freedom of movement—but his weight was still the same.

Holy cow!

The discovery would surely win him the Nobel Prize.

But then pessimism, his familiar nemesis, whispered into his ear.

Wait to see what happens.

Wait to see if you even survive.

CHAPTER 45

WEIGHTY MATTERS

Their pit stop at Cape Horn was as brief as its Chilean Navy station was small. The only year-round residents were a military family who maintained the station's lighthouse, chapel, and memorial sculpture. The monument—a thick metal plate whose center was cut out in the shape of a flying albatross—honored the countless sailors who over the centuries lost their lives trying to round the Horn.

The family helped secure *Hero* to the station's narrow floating pier, remarkable for its bright, tropical-blue color. Then they all rushed up the wooden staircase built into the cove's scrub-covered hillside to a modest, weather-beaten dwelling at the top. There, he and Allie hit the restroom and then wolfed down some *cazuela*, an earthy stew of rice, potato, corn, and meat.

As they hurried back down again, Calder eyed the dark, fast-moving thunderheads shrouding the lowering sun. Powerful winds out of the west were whipping up a heavy chop, tossing *Hero* fiercely about.

When they reached the pier's pitching surface, he shouted to Allie over the wind's blustery voice, "Hold on!"

For many seconds, struggling to keep his balance, he waited for a lull in the choppiness that would make it safe to board *Hero*.

Then it happened.

"Now!" he yelled. "Now!" He bounded for *Hero*, unlocked the windshield, and lifted it.

Reacting quickly, Allie made for a handhold near the cockpit, grabbed it, and pulled herself aboard.

Jumping in right afterward, Calder shut the windshield and immediately began running through the preflight checklist.

By the time he finished, *Hero* was pitching every which way, like a maddened rodeo bull.

"Allie, if you feel yourself getting seasick, I have—"

"Don't worry about me, I'm fine. Just get us out of here. I don't like the looks of those clouds."

He was even more concerned about the icebergs in these waters. *Hero*'s collision avoidance system had worked perfectly so far; but floating mountains of ice were a hazard she'd never faced.

Just as he went to ignite the engine, the dark, pregnant clouds ruptured with fury. Powerful gusts hurled thick, horizontal strands of drenching rain hard against the windshield. The sea all around—where the Pacific and Atlantic oceans collided—rose up and became a white-capped maelstrom.

Hero's engine came to life.

"Fasten your seatbelt, Allie, it's going to be a bumpy night."

"Ha, ha, very funny." Her voice was tight.

Carefully, he steered *Hero* away from the rocky cove and pointed her east. The plan was to head up the coast of South America, steadily angling toward the Straits of Gibraltar, and then directly into the Mediterranean.

Inching the throttle forward, he was comforted by the vacuum-powered engine's ferocious roar.

"Yahoo!" Allie cried out. "Let 'er ri—ayyyy!"

Hero sprang forward like a cheetah charging an impala.

Calder—his hand still advancing the throttle—struggled to keep breathing; his torso was being crushed against the seat. He glanced at the speed log.

627 knots.

A few moments later they hit the speed of sound—and, still, *Hero* kept accelerating. Soon her speed leveled off at 1,074 knots—Mach 1.4. Not as fast as before.

He pressed on the throttle to make certain it was fully open. It was. *Why in the...?*

With no time to figure out why the supersonic booster was under-performing, he forced himself to be happy with going forty percent faster than the speed of sound.

As *Hero* zoomed ahead on autopilot, Calder concentrated on inter-preting the various palpable sensations arising from her deft maneuver-ing through the deadly waters. There were slight pressures on his body—now right, now left—accompanied by periods of weightlessness. And jolts, one after the other, resulting from *Hero*'s skipping over claw-ing waves.

He flinched whenever the dark shape of an iceberg whizzed by in the gathering dusk. There was no choice but to trust their safety to *Hero*'s finely tuned electromechanical instincts and abilities.

Trust.

He thought of Allie.

Faith.

But he admonished himself to stay focused on their perilous situation.

Minutes later, with the last of the icebergs well behind them, he sat back and breathed easy. They were now safely on the leeward side of South America, in the wide open waters of the Atlantic. He kissed the pads of his fingers then laid them on the console. *Hero*'s collision avoidance system had survived its first supersonic trial by fire.

A moment later Allie began filing a report.

He shook his head.

Tireless.

He glanced at the speed log. *Hero* was holding steady at Mach 1.4. At this rate they were on track to reach the centroid in just under eight hours—still plenty of time.

★

TUESDAY, MAY 2 (8:40 A.M. CHINA STANDARD TIME)

SHANGHAI JIAO TONG UNIVERSITY; SHANGHAI, CHINA

ESTIMATED TIME TO IMPACT: 9 HOURS 8 MINUTES

Zhaohui Tang blinked when all the large wall screens went blank, surprised only by how long her hack-proof computer network had managed to hold up against the virus. She called out to her grad students, who quickly gathered around her.

The office lights fluttered nervously, danced to the inconstant current coming from the emergency generator. She knew the students were tired and hungry. The mood was unmistakably sullen.

"Listen, everybody," she said, trying to sound calm. "I'm very grateful that you have all chosen to stay with me for so long. Practically everyone else in the university has left; I'm now giving you permission to leave as well. There's nothing more we can do here."

"What about you, professor?"

"I'm leaving too. But I am not quitting. I'm already thinking of ways to defeat the virus. We must *all* work together to neutralize it. But first we must protect ourselves."

"But how do we get home now?" one student whined. "The streets are jammed and looters are everywhere. We're safer here!"

She looked at them sternly. "Soon the fuel for the generator will run out, plus there is no food here. No, it is better for you to go home and find shelter in your basements. The CME will be hitting tonight."

"Is there no way to get more fuel or food so we can stay here?" said Zhang Wei, her most prized student.

"Believe me, Zhang, I've tried everything. Pulled every string, called in every favor. It's hard now even to get anyone on the phone. Shanghai's like a ghost town."

The students relented and quickly began telling each other what they were going to do—stay or leave. She remained silent, looking blankly at the talking heads all around her. A minute later she felt a queasiness stir within her.

The room began to quiver.

"Duck, everybody!" she shouted.

"Earthquake!" someone yelled.

Zhaohui jumped up from her chair. Feeling lightheaded, she froze and swayed on her feet. A chorus of plaintive, panicky cries arose from the students.

She staggered toward the nearest door frame, but she stumbled and fell. Her hands flew out just in time to keep her nose from crashing into the tile floor.

Several moments later the room stopped quaking. But when she tried to lift herself, inexplicably, her muscles did not obey. Every move she tried making ended up being exaggerated. Every intention led to an overreaction.

Lying on the cold tile, feeling as uncoordinated as an infant, she looked around in confusion. Everyone in the room was either sprawled on the floor or tripping over their own two feet, dropping heavily, like so many bowling pins.

★

TUESDAY, MAY 2 (2:40 A.M. CENTRAL EUROPEAN SUMMER TIME)

POOR CLARES' SACRED HEART CONVENT; SEVILLE, SPAIN

ESTIMATED TIME TO IMPACT: 9 HOURS 8 MINUTES

Mother Yolanda, ensconced in her small, stone-walled cell, was at the radio twisting the tuning knob this way and that, chortling with glee. The world was at her fingertips—the babble of rapidly changing channels like music to her ears.

Abruptly, she became conscious of an indistinct voice shrieking above the noisy electronic rapids. She concentrated on it. Tried to understand what it was saying.

When the task became too difficult, her eyes flew open. It took her a moment to realize she had been dreaming.

But not entirely.

Her radio was actually on, hissing and babbling quietly. She must have forgotten to turn it off last evening after unsuccessfully trying to broadcast her thanks to the world.

She lifted her head from the pillow and stared in the direction of the staticky din, which sounded unusually chaotic. The young sisters would probably blame it on the mischievous sun. But knowing the enemy, she doubted it.

Lying back down, she picked up on the loud chugging sounds of the portable generators outside and prayed the racket was not disturbing the children's sleep. The sisters told her the electrical blackout too was caused by the sun—but none of these disruptions were a coincidence, of that she was sure.

For many minutes she tried unsuccessfully to fall back asleep. At last, sitting up, she reached out in the darkness for the bedside lamp.

It was not there.

Odd.

She tried over and over again but her groping hand found nothing but air. She stopped, closed her eyes, and gave herself a moment to wake up more fully. Then she tried again, but the problem persisted.

Is it my hands?

My mind?

She rebuked the enemy and prayed for help. When she tried again, at last her hand met the lamp and switched it on.

Thank you, Father.

Sliding out of bed, she felt strangely out of control. Her legs, arms—they were not working quite right.

Am I dying?

She heard a scream from somewhere and tumbled onto the stone floor. Her frail body shivered, unable to rise.

The babbling from the radio grew more boisterous and quickly filled the small cell. It no longer sounded like music to her ears, but like pleas from anguished souls on the other side of the grave.

Lying helpless and frightened on the hard, chilly ground, Mother Yolanda crossed herself and prayed.

★

TUESDAY, MAY 2 (10:10 A.M. AUSTRALIAN CENTRAL STANDARD TIME)

CHARLES DARWIN UNIVERSITY; CASUARINA, AUSTRALIA

ESTIMATED TIME TO IMPACT: 9 HOURS 8 MINUTES

Sara arrived at Lulu's tank wheeling a large tub of squid.

"Breakfast!" she sang out.

Sara leaned into the tank and stroked Lulu's nano-rough skin. Sara's academic advisor had explained that a pilot whale's skin secreted a unique anti-microbial gel, which he hoped to replicate in order to create a line of mildew-resistant paint.

"Hungry, girl?" she laughed. "Of course you are." The meds being used to keep the baby whale calm were also stimulating a voracious appetite.

She took a fistful of squid and held it out to Lulu, but her hand overshot the mark. Sara thought nothing of it and simply adjusted her aim. But when it kept happening she felt the hairs on the back of her neck bristle.

Lulu crashed against the side of the tank. Soon the entire warehouse-sized rescue center was alive with the unmistakable sounds of distress—and not just the animals this time. People everywhere were collapsing, as if they were drunk.

"Sara!"

She turned to the voice. It was Dirk. He was lurching toward her from one holding tank to another.

"Dirk! What's happening?"

She took a step forward but tripped over Lulu's feed tub, face-planting into its slimy contents.

★

TUESDAY, MAY 2 (3:40 A.M. ISRAEL DAYLIGHT TIME)

MOUNT OF OLIVES; JERUSALEM, ISRAEL

ESTIMATED TIME TO IMPACT: 9 HOURS 8 MINUTES

Lorena, huddled under a vast dome of stars and a night sky roiling with swirling currents of red dye, was unable to sleep. Drowsily, she lifted her head and gazed across the Kidron Valley at the warm lights of Old Jerusalem.

Hidden by tall landscaping behind the Mount of Olives Hotel, she felt extremely tempted to take a room and sleep in a warm, comfortable bed. But her name and photograph were all over the local news. She couldn't risk being caught, not now.

Lorena had spent the day touring many of the sacred sites blanketing the Mount of Olives—starting with the Garden of Gethsemane. She strolled its cobbled walkways through a small grove of gnarled, ancient olive trees—amongst which Jews of Jesus' day used to sleep *al fresco*.

She loved the garden's magnificent Church of All Nations, with its breathtaking Corinthian columns and mosaic pediment depicting Jesus as mediator between man and God the Father. Inside, she meditated over the enshrined patch of bedrock on which Jesus had reportedly kneeled, prayed, and sweated blood the night before his crucifixion.

After grabbing a shawarma from a street vendor—not as good as Myra's—she visited the Church of the Assumption, the Church of Mary Magdalene, the Benedictine monastery, the Carmelite monastery, and finally the Pater Noster Church.

Now she wished desperately for sleep, but her swelling spiritual excitement kept her wide awake.

She heard screams.

Drunkards.

Even here!

The screaming didn't stop. Nor did it, on careful hearing, sound like revelry. Wearily, she stood up to investigate; but her legs wouldn't support her. With dogged effort she crawled on hands and knees to the edge of the bushes, and then, craning her neck, peeked out at what was happening.

People everywhere were collapsing like pillars of salt!

Instantly, she raised her eyes to the rubicund heavens and gave thanks.

The end—it's finally happening!

★

MONDAY, MAY 1 (6:40 P.M. MOUNTAIN DAYLIGHT TIME)

SPACE WEATHER PREDICTION CENTER; BOULDER, COLORADO

ESTIMATED TIME TO IMPACT: 9 HOURS 8 MINUTES

Dallan, his head resting on crossed arms atop the desk, was awakened by a computer alarm designed to signal changes in the CME. He heard a chorus of shouts outside his closed door.

That bad?

He sat up and began typing on the keyboard.

What the—?!

His fingers were refusing to obey him; they kept hitting the wrong keys. At last, with enormous effort—the shouts outside growing louder—he managed to type a simple command. Matrices of numbers flashed on the screen.

No!

The CME was speeding up.

He reached for the intercom, but his hand missed the call button. Something or someone crashed against the outside of his office door. Agog, he leapt out of his chair and—*whoa!*—his feet left the ground.

A moment later he crashed to the floor like a collapsing stick figure.

CHAPTER 46

POWER OF FAITH

TUESDAY, MAY 2 (TIME ZONE UNCERTAIN)

LOCATION UNCERTAIN

ESTIMATED TIME TO IMPACT: UNCERTAIN

Calder, out of ideas and fighting a rising sense of helplessness, looked out the windshield at the suffocating duskiness and saw nothing to give him any clue as to their exact whereabouts. All he knew for certain was *Hero* was barreling forward—presumably eastward—at some unknown, breakneck speed.

He conjectured they were somewhere in the South Atlantic but couldn't know for sure until daybreak. Even then, given they were probably in open ocean, there was no guarantee of seeing any landmarks.

The crisis began hours earlier, when it became clear the nav system was taking *Hero* farther east than originally planned. At first he chose not to interfere, guessing the computer was optimizing their bearings on the fly and, for that reason, was delaying their turn northward. But when *Hero* continued heading in the direction of the Cape of Good Hope, he knew there was a serious problem.

Over and over he pressed the manual override button. But *Hero* kept streaking toward the southern tip of Africa. He tried other things as well: engaging the emergency brakes, pulling back on the throttle, switching off the ignition, even—and he held his breath when doing this—cycling the computer on and off. All to no avail. Inexplicably, nearly every one of *Hero*'s systems, even the radio, was frozen.

Desperate now, he flirted with the idea of ejecting. But what would that accomplish? The mission, all of his cleverness and hard work, would end in utter failure. He and Allie would land in the ocean—in all probability, in the middle of absolute nowhere—far from any rescue operation and totally at the mercy of the CME.

He rubbed his forehead.

I won't let it end this way.

The curse will not win!

Miraculously, mercifully, *Hero*'s collision avoidance system was still doing its job. Calder could tell from the unremitting parade of evasive moves.

"Any luck?" Allie shouted.

Even the intercom was dead.

"No!"

Calder kept staring at the control panel for signs of life. Its stalled display incorrectly showed them dead in the water just southwest of Cape Town.

"*Aaiy!*" Allie yelled. "What was that?"

Instantly, their speed plummeted—as though some gigantic hand had seized *Hero* by the tail. Calder's body snapped forward; the six-point harness pressed against his lungs and nearly suffocated him. He gasped for air and battled to maintain consciousness, while hastily scanning the dashboard for any explanation of what was happening.

A red warning light appeared on the dashboard, indicating a failure of the supersonic booster.

Damn it, nooo!

"Allie! Allie!" he shouted between gasps, his vision darkening. "Get ready to eject!"

No response.

Hero was shuddering severely now, in the grips of an insanely powerful force threatening to break her apart. On the precipice of passing out, he shouted more loudly, "ALLIE! SPEAK TO ME! ARE YOU ALL RIGHT?!"

Still nothing.

A frisson of fear, like a whiff of smelling salts, crystallized his panicky thoughts.

We're going to die.

"Damn you!" Calder snarled at fate. "Damn you to hell!" Then he shouted, "Allie! Allie!"

He called to her again and again.

But there was no answer.

★

She was aboard a helicopter, the same one she used the last time she visited her mom at the nursing home. It was gently touching down on the roof of the adjoining hospital.

She jumped out and looked around.

How did I get to Los Angeles so fast?

She dashed into the church.

"Hey, everybody, it's me, Allie. I'm home!

But no one was inside the main sanctuary.

¿Dónde están?

She couldn't wait to tell them about Phil—they were finally getting married! She wanted Carlos to officiate.

She quickly searched the church offices—nobody!

"Carlos! *Apa!* Where are you guys?"

She bounded down to the basement, two steps at a time. At the bottom, she took hold of the doorknob—but it was locked!

"Open up, guys!" she said, banging on the steel-clad door. "It's me, Allie. I've come home. I quit the network so I could be with you. C'mon, open up!"

For what seemed like many minutes she kept rapping the door with her knuckles until they bled. Then the stairwell filled with a maroon light.

Ay, Dios, no!

She pounded harder, weeping uncontrollably.

Oh, please, God, no, don't let me be too late!

"*Mamá, Apá,* I'm sorry, I'm so sorry. *Por favor, perdónenme.*"

Finally, the door gave way and she tumbled into the dark room, landing face down on its familiar worn, wooden floor. Before she could pick herself up she was blinded by a flash of brilliant white light and deafened by a chorus of desperate, deathly pleadings. She shut her eyes tightly, covered her ears with both hands, and screamed. But the light and sound and smell of death defeated her puny defenses.

She scrambled to her feet. But when she opened her eyes to see where she was going, she froze at the ghastly scene.

Littered everywhere—prostrate on the floor, slouched at tables piled high with food, lying motionless on canvas cots—were the scorched bodies of her family. Her mom and dad, huddled in the far corner in one another's embrace; her aunts, uncles, cousins, her *familia*—all of them dead.

I should've been here!

I should've been here with you!

Please forgive me!

She saw herself being overtaken by maroon light, drowning in a loudening choir of unearthly voices.

"*Ay, Dios mio, no, nooooooo!*" she shrieked. "*Perdonenme! Perdonenme! Perdonenme!*"

★

TUESDAY, MAY 2 (TIME ZONE UNCERTAIN)

At last *Hero* came to a screaming, trembling halt. Hastily, Calder unharnessed himself and threw open the windshield. Raising himself on shaky legs, he twisted round to check on Allie. It was dawn, so he could see well enough that she was slumped in her seat, eyes shut.

Oh, god, no!

The horizon resembled a dusky stage lit by colorful footlights: red, orange, yellow, and baby blue. The sky high overhead glowed faintly red, as if it were on fire—an inkling, he knew, of things to come.

He called to Allie, but she didn't respond. He looked around for help, but of course there was none. In the far distance he could see land.

Where in the world…?

He lifted his right foot, placed it onto the seat cushion, but quickly withdrew it. *Hero* swayed dangerously in the water.

A few moments later, having decided on a better course of action, he gingerly placed his hands on the rim of the cockpit. Then, holding his breath—hypersensitive to *Hero*'s every tetchy reaction—he pushed himself up and flopped onto the broad bulkhead that separated the pilot and passenger cabins. From this prone position he could reach Allie.

The pitching vehicle threatened to toss him overboard, into the swelling sea. He felt every bit like a cowboy riding an unbroken mustang.

Cautiously, he extended his arm and began unharnessing Allie's seat belt. "Allie!" he said as he tripped the buckles. "Allie!"

But she didn't stir.

Gently, reluctantly, he slapped her face.

Still nothing.

He cocked his right hand and swung it hard against her cheek.

Her head lolled and her eyes flew open.

Those emerald eyes.

Even without their usual luster, they were stunning.

"Oh, thank god." he said.

"God?" she mumbled. "You believe in God now?"

He snickered. "Are you all right?"

Her eyes closed again; her head fell back against the seat.

"Allie!" he said. "Allie!"

He cocked his arm again.

Her eyes flew open. "Don't you dare! I'm fine. Just give me a minute." She shut her eyes again.

A short while later—still reclining with her eyes closed—she smiled, inhaling deeply through her nose. "*Ahh*, the fresh air feels gr..." Bolting upright, she looked around confusedly. "Wait, where am I? Where's my family? What's happened?"

He reached out to calm her, to warn her against making any sudden moves. "Let's not sink her, okay? We've got enough trouble on our hands."

After he was done explaining things, the devastated look on her face summed up their dodgy situation well.

"So what do we do now?" she said.

★

TUESDAY, MAY 2 (TIME ZONE UNCERTAIN)

Kneeling on her seat, facing sternward, she fought to keep the GoPro in her hands steady against *Hero*'s constant pitching movements. She was recording Calder, who was astride *Hero*'s backside troubleshooting the supersonic booster. He believed its gradual breakdown—starting back at Cape Horn—was the cause of all the problems.

She looked askance at the rising sun and felt fear. Its scrim-like orange halo now spanned half the sky—an indication the CME cloud was nearly upon them.

Overlaying the pale orange color was the bright ruddiness of the aurorae, much livelier than the pale tinting she'd seen in San Diego when they departed. Its reflection in the water made the sea look bloody.

"Calder!" she said, her stomach tightening like a closing fist. "How much longer?"

★

TUESDAY, MAY 2 (6:43 A.M. EASTERN AFRICA TIME)

ARABIAN SEA; OPPOSITE MOGADISHU, SOMALIA

ESTIMATED TIME TO IMPACT: 6 HOURS 5 MINUTES

With electrical power restored and both of them back inside, Calder eagerly surveyed the restored nav screen. But his heart dropped. According to the screen's telemetry, they were stranded in the Arabian Sea, off the coast of Somalia!

Without any idea of what to do next, he decided at least to make sure *Hero*'s engine would start.

"Okay, prayer warrior," he said, "now's the time to dial up the Big Guy."

"You got it. Praying…"

He pressed the green button and *Hero*'s engine sprang to life.

He'd heard Allie describe the sound as a whine, but to his ears it sounded more like an ode to joy.

"Strapped in?" he said.

"Roger."

He gave *Hero* her head, but from the absence of any jack-rabbit-like leap forward, he knew instantly his jury-rigging efforts had not entirely succeeded. For some reason, the repaired booster unit was not kicking in.

So much for prayer.

Glumly, he watched the increasing numbers on the speed log: 97...
201...310...425...475...499...502 knots. That was it—all he'd be
able to squeeze from *Hero*'s unenhanced Q-thruster.

"How fast are we going?" Allie said.

He swallowed hard. "Not fast enough."

"Oh." Then a moment later, in a clearly dejected voice, she said,
"Sorry, Calder. You tried. That's all anyone can do."

Calder wondered where to point *Hero*.

Does it matter anymore?

TUESDAY, MAY 2 (6:47 A.M. EASTERN AFRICA TIME)

ESTIMATED TIME TO IMPACT: 6 HOURS 1 MINUTE

Allie alternated between praying for inspiration—for help of any
kind—and recollecting the people she loved most.

She tried picturing her family tucked away safely in the basement of
Carlos's church. But the dream she'd had (or whatever it was) kept intrud-
ing. Was it a premonition? Would the same horrific end come to her and
Calder out here in the Arabian Sea—unprotected from the killer CME
steadily, stubbornly, irresistibly streaking toward them?

She thought of Lolo, presumably still in Jerusalem somewhere.

Oh, Sis, Sis ...

Will I ever see you again?

Then she thought of her lost love.

Phil, please forgive me...I was so incredibly stupid.

She caught herself. These morbid thoughts were getting her nowhere.

"Calder?"

"Yeah?"

"Penny for your thoughts?"

"*Psh!* Right now? They wouldn't be worth a wooden nickel."

She had no immediate comeback but knew they both needed to snap out of their funks, and quick. The clock was ticking.

"You can't give up, Calder. Not now. You're too close, too clever for that."

"Clever!" He made the word sound like a curse. "Ha!"

"Calder, have you ever heard the story of how Kurt Gödel died?"

"What?"

"Kurt Gödel."

Allie, like most others who knew about him, considered Gödel the most profound logician of the twentieth century. According to his famous Incompleteness Theorem, there were absolute truisms that could never be *proved* true using logic alone.

"What about him?"

"He was paranoid, you know. Constantly worried people were out to hurt him. The only ones he trusted were his wife Adele and Albert Einstein. Gödel worked with Einstein at the Institute for Advanced Studies in Princeton. Every day the two walked to their offices together, talking, laughing—they even stopped for ice cream now and then.

"After Adele and Einstein died, Gödel went off the deep end. He refused to eat and eventually starved to death. That's how afraid he was of being poisoned by someone."

"That makes no sense," Calder said. "He let himself die because he thought people were out to kill him?"

"Yeah, I know. But to him it was perfectly logical. Right to the end." Silence.

"Why are you telling me this?" Calder said finally. There was an unmistakable edge to his voice.

"Calder, it shows the power of faith. If you believe we're through here, then we *are* through. And the world, too. Get it?"

CHAPTER 47

SEEING RED

TUESDAY, MAY 2 (7:23 A.M. EASTERN AFRICA TIME)

ARABIAN SEA; BEARING NORTHWARD

ESTIMATED TIME TO IMPACT: 5 HOURS 25 MINUTES

"That's it!" Calder exclaimed. "I've got it!"

His booming voice reached her ears without the aid of the intercom.

"What?! What is it, Calder?"

"Allie, hold on."

A moment later she heard him on the radio.

"Point Loma, this is Joshua One. Can you hear me? Over."

There was no response. Even after *Hero*'s rebooting, the radio still did not work.

For the next ten minutes Calder tried and failed to connect with San Diego. Nevertheless, he did not give up.

"Point Loma, this is Joshua One. Can you hear me? Over."

Still, there was nothing.

"Point Loma, this is Joshua One. Can you hear me? Over."

Nothing.

A moment later there was crackling on the line.

"Joshua One, this is Point Loma. Roger, we copy, and thank goodness. We've been worried sick about you two. We noticed you're way off—"

Calder cut in. "Scotty, please listen, we're changing our itinerary. I'll explain later. We need to go through the Suez Canal. I repeat, the Suez Canal."

Allie understood immediately.

Yes! Atta boy!

"Please secure permission and clearance ASAP. Our ETA there is four hours from now. I repeat, four hours, understood? Over."

There was no immediate reply, just crackling. She held her breath.

At last Scotty said, "Joshua One, we copy. Also, be informed there's been a change in the CME's ETA. The SWPC is now saying T minus four hours, forty-seven minutes to impact."

What??

"One other thing," Scotty continued. "Ms. Freiberg wishes to speak with Ms. Armendariz right away on their com link. Do you copy? Over."

"Copy that, I'll tell her. Over and out."

She congratulated Calder on the plan.

"Thanks, but did you hear about the CME—its new ETA? We've just lost thirty-eight minutes. I'm not sure we're going to make it now. It all depends on how fast we can get through the canal. Let's hope—"

"Calder, we're gonna make it."

Please, Lord Jesus.

He remained silent.

She switched on her radio link. "Hello? Hello? This is Allie Armendariz from Joshua One for Eva Freiberg. Can you hear me? Over."

A wave of static gave way like a dissipating fog to Eva's unmistakable voice. "*Oh, my god! We all thought you guys were dead. Over.*"

"We're fine, Eva, we're fine. Just a little glitch. Over."

"You call being out of radio contact for six hours a 'little glitch'? The transponder thing showed you guys leaving Chile, then stopping. And something else. The weirdest thing happened right after that. People all over the world started to—"

"Eva! Eva! Hold on. First you need to know there's been a change of plans."

★

TUESDAY, MAY 2 (7:43 A.M. CENTRAL EUROPEAN SUMMER TIME)

POOR CLARES' SACRED HEART CONVENT; SEVILLE, SPAIN

ESTIMATED TIME TO IMPACT: 3 HOURS 45 MINUTES

She and the sisters were in the orphanage playground rounding up the kids. It was bedlam. Most of the boys and girls were insisting on staying outside to watch the flamboyant spectacle unfolding high overhead.

"Quickly, children! Quickly!" Sister Theresa cried out.

It wasn't really like herding cats, Mother Yolanda thought. It was harder.

Marte, a dark-haired boy, refused to get off the swing. "Please, Reverend Mother, it's so beautiful!"

The entire sky was now a pale orange, brightly streaked with red. It was, she had to admit, quite a show.

"Yes, Reverend Mother," echoed another boy. "Why can't we stay here and watch? It's like fireworks on a feast day."

"Better!" an older girl chirped.

A symphony of voices arose in agreement.

Mother Yolanda was in a fix. She did not want to scare the children by telling them the truth—the enemy was on the prowl, causing the sun to do a bad thing. But she also could not allow them to stay outdoors.

Early this morning the parish priest himself ordered everyone to take shelter inside the church. It was made of stone and had withstood, he said, every manner of disaster for more than a century.

And there was no plumbing. That was important, he explained, because reporters on TV were saying people needed to stay clear of metal, of anything that could conduct electricity.

He stopped short of ordering that the church's stoup be emptied. Even though, he claimed, he knew enough science to understand water was an excellent conductor of electricity.

"Yes, yes, I know," Mother Yolanda now said to the mutinous children. "But you see, I wasn't supposed to tell you we are planning a very special party inside the church. So if you don't come with me"—she made a sad face—"it won't be much of a party, now will it?"

It worked. The children cheered and sprinted toward the massive stone building. Except for one teenage girl, who look scared.

"Are we going to die, Reverend Mother?"

Mother Yolanda was taken aback by the simplicity of the question. *What shall I tell her?*

The truth?

"We all will die one day, my child. But only God knows when and how." She took the girl gently by the hand, saying, "Now come. I need your help with the decorations. You are such an artist, you know, when it comes to those things."

TUESDAY, MAY 2 (9:18 A.M. EASTERN AFRICA TIME)

GULF OF ADEN; OPPOSITE DJIBOUTI CITY, DJIBOUTI

ESTIMATED TIME TO IMPACT: 3 HOURS 10 MINUTES

Hero whizzed past Djibouti, speeding northward toward the Suez Canal. Calder watched the sky nervously. Its glowering complexion reminded him of raw meat.

"Is that the Red Sea coming up?" Allie said.

He glanced at the nav screen. "Yeah."

It felt as though *Hero* were crawling. He wanted to get out and push her, kick her in the behind.

"Should be at the canal in about two-and-a-half hours," he said. A few moments later he added, "You don't really believe Moses parted this thing, do you?"

He winced.

Am I trying to pick a fight? Now?

"Of course not."

"Really?"

"I believe *God* did." She laughed. "Gotcha!"

"Allie, c'mon, really. Just look at it, how big and deep it is. Parting it would defy the laws of physics."

Why am I pursuing this?

What am I after?

He knew the answer: he was beginning to wonder if God really did exist. It wasn't a question he'd taken seriously since being a boy.

Ridiculous, leave it alone.

He doesn't exist.

"Yeah," Allie said, "well lots of people are saying that about you too, you know, despite the evidence—that you're a fraud for claiming an invention that defies the laws of physics."

Despite his annoyance, he grinned.

Touché.

"All right, smarty pants," he said, "you've got—"

"Joshua One, this is Point Loma. Do you copy?"

"Point Loma, this is Joshua One. We copy, Scotty. Over."

"Be informed the Egyptian government is granting you permission to transit the Ditch. A few ships are still in the pipeline but they're clearing them out. Stand by. We'll update you ASAP. Over."

★

TUESDAY, MAY 2 (3:43 P.M. CHINA STANDARD TIME)

SHANGHAI, CHINA

ESTIMATED TIME TO IMPACT: 1 HOUR 45 MINUTES

Zhaohui Tang, riding a bicycle—one of the few viable means of transportation remaining—was nearing her parents' house. For the past half hour she'd successfully navigated the back streets, avoiding Shanghai's main boulevards, which were jammed with traffic.

She had no idea if her mother and father were even home—bad communications made it impossible to find out. But where else could she go? The only reasonable alternative—her own place, where she surely would be alone—was not an option.

She kept an eye on the sky. Its color was changing by the minute. Its orange-roseate hue brightened everything, creating the colorful impression of the sun rising. Or setting.

In truth the sun was still high enough to be seen above the neighborhood trees. But its shimmering yellow-white face was now obscured by a pall of orange light and a swirling sea of red waves that seemed to be descending rapidly.

The CME??

"But it's not due yet," she muttered to herself, peddling harder.

CHAPTER 48

THE DITCH

Calder was a million miles away, worrying about Sara's safety, when the arrival bell sounded and *Hero* began slowing down. He came to and glanced at the control panel.

"We're here," he called out. "We should be seeing the canal."

Allie cheered. "Thank you, Lord!"

He looked up at the orange sky and fluttering red curtains; they'd grown more intense during the past hour.

"Calder, look at the sky."

"I know, I know. I only hope to god we're not already too late."

"You're doing everything possible, *hombre*, stay positive."

Something caught his eye.

"Allie, look halfway up from the horizon on the right. You see the green?"

Silence.

"Yeah, I do," she said finally.

He wondered if Allie knew what the appearance of a green sky signaled. It meant overly eager particles outracing the CME's main cloud were already sliding down the magnetic field lines, like cars riding the rails of a roller coaster, striking oxygen molecules in the atmosphere's mid-section. Those atomic collisions invariably gave off green light.

He said, "You know what it means, don't you?"

"Yes, Calder, yes."

"Then you know that—"

"Yes, Calder, I know. Let's just keep going."

★

As *Hero* approached the entrance of the Suez Canal, Calder tried repeatedly without any luck to make radio contact.

"Suez Authority, this is Joshua One. Can you read me? Over."

Allie fretted about Calder's frame of mind. He was an incredibly strong person; but she intuited that the stress, the sleeplessness, the lack of faith in himself and in life—in God—were all conspiring to break him.

Lord, please buttress him.

Her thoughts switched to what was immediately expected of her—a report documenting their passage through the canal. Eva told her a local TV crew would be doing the filming.

"Allie, ca—you—ear me?"

Speak of the devil.

"Not great, but go ahead."

"The—ew is waiti—for—ou at the—trance. Look for them."

She scanned the shoreline. "Yeah, I see them. Eva, we need to—"

"Allie, please," Calder said. "Can you hold off with the chatter? I can't hear myself think."

★

He was vexed by the canal authority's radio silence.

Answer, dammit, answer.

"Suez Authority, this is Joshua One. Can you read me? Over."

The radio was swamped with static.

We're running out of time!

"Suez Authority, this is Joshua One. Can you read me? Over."

The mission is finished unless I—

"Calder, look!" Allie shouted. "Out the windshield to the right, on the bank."

He turned and saw a short man dressed in a military uniform waving with both arms.

What the—?

"I think he wants you to pull over there," she said.

"You gotta be kidding me!"

Calder steered *Hero* toward the waving officer. By the time he gained the shore and lifted the canopy, he was ready to kill someone.

"Ahoy!" said the little officer. He was muscular and dark-skinned. "Dr. Sinclair, I presume?"

Control yourself.

"Yes. Are you in charge? We're in a hurry. There's no time to lose."

"Yes, yes, we know. The radio is not working. We're just about ready for you. Only one ship remains in the way. Our tugs are pushing it to the side now. It shouldn't be much longer."

★

"Allie, wh—going on?" Eva said.

The radio reception was a bit better but still barely intelligible. Allie quickly brought her producer up to speed.

"Allie, listen. Mike t—s me the pres—ent and others have been st—fed into a sub—arine for their pr—ection, for g—s sake. Everyone's pan—king because they don't th—you're gonna make it."

Allie felt faint. "Where are *you* right now?"

"Inside C—r's lab. It's packed w—people."

"And Stu?"

"In New Y—k, at the stud—, where else? The—ld diehard."

"You gotta be.... Tell him to get down to the basement. It's crazy for him to be at the studio."

"So are you go—g to film the rep—t or what? It's bet—than ju—ting around waiting."

Allie agreed to do a hurried interview of the military man from inside *Hero*. The Egyptian TV crew chose a spot on the shore with the canal entrance framed behind him.

> **AA:** "There's less than a half hour before the CME hits and we've made it as far as the Suez Canal. With me now is Navy Captain Farouk El Akba. He's been put in charge of making sure the canal is clear before we head into it. Sir, can you tell us how much longer it will be?"
>
> **FE:** "Yes, good morning. I think it will be only a few minutes more."

He was interrupted by someone calling him. He spoke in Arabic but she could tell from his large, animated gestures that he wasn't happy. When he was done, she resumed her questioning.

> **AA:** "Bad news?"
>
> **FE:** "No, no, everything is fine. Please, continue."
>
> **AA:** "Tell us about the canal. What do we face here?"
>
> **FE:** "We affectionately call it the Ditch because it is long, narrow, and shallow. Roughly 120 miles long and 197 feet wide at its narrowest point."
>
> **AA:** "So there's room for only one ship to pass through at a time. Is that the problem?"

FE: "Well, I wouldn't call it a problem. But, yes, there is only one shipping lane. Still, there are several widened places along the way where a ship can pull over and allow another ship to pass. We call them passing bays."

In the background Allie could hear the constant, harried-sounding chatter on the captain's walkie-talkie.

AA: "And so that's what you're doing right now, making sure all the ships inside the canal are pushed off to the side?"

FE: "Yes, exactly. And there is only one ship left in the lane, but that is almost done."

AA: "How long does it usually take for a ship to make it through the canal?"

FE: Well, first of all, let me say there are no locks in the Suez Canal. It's all at sea level so that helps speed things along. But the really big ships—let us say 200,000 tons fully loaded—they're naturally pretty slow. It usually takes them about fifteen hours to get through. At any rate, we do not normally allow ships to go too fast because their wakes speed up the erosion of the canal's dikes."

AA: "But in our case—"

FE: "Of course, of course, in your case Dr. Sinclair has been given special permission to go as fast as he wishes. Of course."

Once again he was interrupted by a voice on the walkie-talkie. The voice sounded flustered. When the conversation was finished, she could see clearly, even though her monitor was tiny, that the captain was sporting a giant, Cheshire-cat-like smile.

CHAPTER 49

ALL CLEAR

"Be safe!" yelled the captain. He was standing on the shoreline waving good-bye. "Go with Allah!"

Calder lowered and locked the windshield. A few moments later the Q-thruster started up without difficulty—but a light indicated trouble with the navigation system.

Son of a...No!

Calder hesitated. Most likely the high-speed atomic particles at the CME's leading edge were already interfering with the GPS satellites, on which *Hero*'s nav system relied. *Hero* had backups—dead reckoning and stellar navigation programs—but they were useless in this situation.

He made up his mind.

"Allie, hang on! I'm taking over the steering. It could get a little crazy."

★

Allie braced herself for takeoff but couldn't remove her eyes from the sky. It was now looking like the ruffled dresses worn by Mexican hat dancers—red on top, bright green below.

If things continued worsening, she knew, the aurora would morph from red and green with yellow highlights to pinkish-purple, the most dangerous color of all. When that happened—*if* that happened—it would mean the CME's charged particles had completely broken through Earth's defenses and made it all the way to the lower atmosphere, where collisions with the nitrogen molecules always produced a purplish light. The barrage of atomic particles would then bombard the earth's surface with the force of innumerable nuclear bombs— something that had never happened before, not even in the Carrington event.

Her thoughts flew to Lolo—her family—the church basement. *Will it hold?*

"I trust you, sweet Jesus," she whispered, choking back tears. "I—I surrender them to you."

★

Calder, right hand wrapped firmly around the joystick, used his left to push the throttle forward. *Hero* leapt into the Suez Canal, knocking him back against the seat.

People waving and saluting him along the shore, the vast desert terrain on both sides of the Ditch—punctuated by palm trees and clusters of small buildings—large ships of every description sidelined out of harm's way in the passing bays: it all whizzed past him faster and faster as *Hero* gained speed.

Moments later the throttle reached its limit; *Hero*'s speed leveled off. He glanced at the speed log: 446 knots. At that rate—his mind rapidly crunched the numbers—it would take fourteen minutes to get through the Ditch and another thirteen minutes to reach the centroid.

He stared straight ahead, staving off any thoughts of defeat.

Better late than never.

★

TUESDAY, MAY 2 (6:43 P.M. CENTRAL AUSTRALIAN STANDARD TIME)

CHARLES DARWIN UNIVERSITY; CASUARINA, AUSTRALIA

ESTIMATED TIME TO IMPACT: 0 HOURS 15 MINUTES

Sara stroked Lulu's face, grateful her chubby little black-and-white charge was calm again.

"Don't worry, girl, I'm not leaving you."

Her faculty advisor and friends, including Dirk, had pleaded with her to evacuate, to flee with them to the basements of the university's tallest, most massive buildings. But she refused, and in the end Dirk opted to stay behind as well.

"Is your dad just as stubborn?" He was standing next to her, leaning against Lulu's tank. His tense face and pale lips telegraphed anxiety.

"Yup." She bent into the tank and kissed Lulu on the forehead. "How do you think he's managed to survive all these years? The critics, the setbacks. Any normal person would've given up a long time ago. But not my dad. And not me either."

Dirk looked away and then back again. "He's quite a guy, your dad. Thank you for letting me meet him." He reached out and patted Lulu on the flanks. "But I feel sorry for you."

She reared her head. "For *me*? Why? Why do you say that?"

"Because you're never going to find a man who measures up to your dad's standards."

Sara, uncertain of what to say, turned her gaze outdoors. The sun was setting, but the sky wasn't darkening on account of the brightening aurorae. The red and green colors looked garish, dangerous.

She shivered, thinking of her dad being out there somewhere, unprotected.

Dad, I love you.

Her attention was shanghaied by a sudden, preternatural silence. She stood stock-still and listened. It reminded her of what it was like just before a tornado, when even birds stopped singing.

The eerie stillness was broken by a loud popping sound to her left. Turning toward it, she saw sparks shooting out from a nearby high-voltage transformer. It looked like a Roman candle on the Fourth of July.

"Sara!" Dirk said, his widened eyes filled with alarm. "Are you sure you won't change your mind?"

She rounded on him. "What did I just tell you?!"

★

TUESDAY, MAY 2 (12:18 P.M. ISRAEL DAYLIGHT TIME)

CHAPEL OF THE ASCENSION; JERUSALEM, ISRAEL

ESTIMATED TIME TO IMPACT: 0 HOURS 10 MINUTES

Lorena stood her ground, while everyone around her jockeyed for position.

"Stop shoving, please!" she cried out. "Give me some room to breathe."

After regaining the use of her legs in the wee hours of the morning, she'd made straight for the Chapel of the Ascension, located next to the Mount of Olives Hotel. She wanted a front-row seat to the greatest comeback story in human history.

Belatedly, everyone was catching on to what was happening and trying to muscle in on her space. People were flocking in from the hotel, from downtown Jerusalem, from everywhere in order to catch a glimpse of the returning Messiah. She marveled at the diversity of their faces and skin tones.

They spoke in languages she didn't understand. But from the snippets of English she was able to pick out from the babble, it was clear everyone was gushing about the Second Coming, about how lucky they were to be here, the very spot where Jesus rose to heaven and promised to return.

She also gathered the Temple Mount was being overrun. By Jews, as well as by Muslims, who were crowding into the Mount's Al-Aqsa mosque and Dome of the Rock, where Mohammed was said to have ascended to heaven.

To each his own.

She elbowed a man next to her who had terrible body odor.

"Please, give me room!"

Someone a short distance from the chapel began shouting. It was a woman's voice, in a language Lorena couldn't identify.

Could this be it?

Another shout, father away, made her muscles tighten. Perhaps Jesus decided to change venues!

"What?" she shouted. "What's happening?"

No one answered.

"I said, what's happening? Someone please answer me!"

She heard a sizzling sound. It took her a moment to realize the air around her was crackling with electricity, the way a woolen sweater did when pulled from a dryer.

"Come on, already, sweet Jesus!" she moaned ecstatically. "Come to us, come to us, *now*!"

CHAPTER 50

FINAL RECKONING

Now that he was doing the driving, 446 knots seemed mighty fast. For the past thirteen minutes, he'd kept his eyes glued forward, knowing one slip of the hand, a single distraction, could spell the end of the mission. But now, entering the final stretch, Calder allowed himself a quick peek at the sky.

The orangish air was roiling with swirls, jets, and curtains of red, yellow, and green.

No violet.

Quickly resuming his forward gaze, he caught sight of something that electrified him: a tugboat on the visual horizon appeared to be in the shipping lane.

Before he could react, the tug whizzed past, accompanied by a heavy thud and the unmistakable sensation of a sidelong collision.

"What was that?" Allie said.

He held his breath, expecting the worst. As a precaution—even though he'd planned to do it only when he arrived at the centroid—he quickly switched on the jamming device and turned up the volume full blast.

Hero kept charging forward and soon he successfully steered her out of the canal. He pressed on the throttle, but it was already wide open.

We can still do this!

Abruptly, he was slammed back in his seat.

What the—?

The sudden, high G force smothered his face like a monster-sized hand. He willed his darkening gaze to focus on the speed log, but its numerals were a blur. He could hear Allie's unintelligible cries coming from behind him, but his mouth was unable to form any words. His scrambled thoughts labored to connect the dots.

Then he knew.

Whatever his earlier repairs to the supersonic booster hadn't achieved, the apparent glancing collision with the tugboat provoked. He strained with all his might to reach out and pull back on the throttle.

Nothing!

Hero had reverted to her catatonic state and was careening across the Mediterranean, toward Amman, in an accelerating, supersonic tailspin.

Frantically, he went through the motions of trying to bring her under control, but of course nothing worked.

He looked up at the sky.

Oh, god, no!

The CME had arrived.

★

TUESDAY, MAY 2 (12:23 P.M. ISRAEL DAYLIGHT TIME)

MEDITERRANEAN SEA

IMPACT

Allie's skin crawled at the sight of purple in the aurora's ruffled hemline, which now danced ominously just above the water. It meant the CME was smashing through Earth's weakened defenses sooner than Dallan predicted.

But he wasn't entirely wrong. From the looks of it, this CME was indeed destined for the history books.

Pinned to her seat like a biological specimen, she struggled to keep from blacking out. She wanted to ask Calder what was happening with *Hero,* but despite her best efforts she couldn't get her mouth to work.

Calder would be happy to know that.

Oh, dear Jesus, why did you bring us out here?

Her harried mind involuntarily formed a sickening picture of the destruction crashing down on their heads. On Calder and on her. On her family in the church basement. On her baby sis out there somewhere. On Eva and on Stu.

On the world.

Surely not to fail.

Then it came to her—a possibility that rattled her soul like a thunderclap.

Yes, precisely to fail.

★

TUESDAY, MAY 2 (6:53 P.M. CENTRAL AUSTRALIAN STANDARD TIME)

CHARLES DARWIN UNIVERSITY; CASUARINA, AUSTRALIA

IMPACT

Sara was questioning her decision to stay with Lulu. But it was too late. The sky was now so bright—the dazzling, threatening flames were dancing all around, hissing and crackling—she and Dirk needed to don sunglasses for protection.

"What are we going to do?!" Dirk yelled. He and Sara were sitting on the cement floor, backs against Lulu's tank, facing away from the outside. "We can't just stay here. We're sitting ducks!"

Their problem was the holding tanks area of the rescue center was protected by what amounted to an oversized pop-up tent: a vast, corrugated tin roof held up by heavy-gauge Lally columns. It had no walls, only an open view of the university campus to the west and east, and of the ocean to the north.

"But Lulu's a sitting duck too!" Sara protested.

As if on cue, Lulu began thrashing around inside the tank. Springing up for a quick peek at what was happening, Sara shied at the sight of plummeting drapes of red, yellow, green, and purple light all around her. There were loud bangs everywhere. Sparks, then flames, burst forth throughout the sprawling campus. A split second later the university's tallest structures—the library clock tower most of all—glowed with a dazzling, violet-blue halo.

"Dirk! Dirk! Oh, my god, c'mon!"

Without thinking, she dove into Lulu's tank and surfaced immediately, her face and hair dripping with sea water. She looked around for Dirk but didn't see him.

"Dirk!"

She spotted him on the beach, running like the wind toward the sea.

What? What's he—?

"Dirk, nooo! Come back!"

She saw him stumble and fall. Felt a familiar queasiness taking hold of her body, as it had that morning. But she didn't collapse again, which confused her. She flexed her arms and legs and quickly it came to her: the water's buoyancy was keeping her upright.

From her right came the sound of explosions. Whipping around, she saw massive showers of golden sparks shooting out from among the flames now engulfing the university.

A shadow swept across the region, plunging the rescue center into a spooky twilight. Angling her gaze upward, Sara saw the cause. The ballooning cloud of black smoke from the campus-wide conflagration was rising high enough to obscure the sun.

The sudden duskiness did nothing to mask the blinding, rambling, red-green-violet aurora pulsing overhead. The scene reminded her of wild, 1960s-syle frat party videos on YouTube.

An off-shore wind kicked up and blew sand in her direction. The airborne grains looked like pale blue glitter. She tried blinking the luminous grit out of her eyes, but it only worsened the pain. She splashed water on them instead, all the while watching Dirk repeatedly fail in his efforts to stand up.

"Dirk, hold on! I'm coming!"

She was shouting as loudly as possible but the wind kidnapped her voice and spirited it away to the east.

As she went to hoist herself out of the tank, the tin roof, the steel posts—the entire infrastructure—began to glow blue. And to sizzle, like meat on a grill. A moment later the very water she was in began to glow.

"Oooowww!"

The electric sting Sara felt impelled her to leap out of the tank. She landed hard on the cold, wet floor, her ears filled with Lulu's frantic clicking and squeaking.

She's being electrocuted!

The surrounding aurorae blinked faster and faster. The pitch of their unearthly screeches rose higher and higher, resonating with Lulu's cries.

Sara heard a scream coming from the beach. Propping herself up on an elbow, peering hard into the malevolent, pulsing light swirling above the beach like a giant whirlpool, she saw Dirk desperately crawling across the sand toward the thrashing sea. It, too, was glowing blue.

Her chest—like an enslaved performer—heaved in synch with the convulsing light. Futilely, she strained to reclaim her feet.

She heard a giant splash, turned, and saw Lulu crashing to the floor next to her, missing Sara by inches. A deathly shriek drew her eyes toward the beach again.

"Dirk! Look out!"

But it was too late. Having finally managed to stand up on wobbly legs, he was instantly immersed in a churning, multicolored cloud descending like a fog from overhead. He glowed blue for a few moments and then disappeared in an explosion of sparks.

She screamed and kept screaming.

Finally spent—with her face buried in both hands, Lulu belly-flopping and squealing hysterically beside her—she collapsed.

"Oh, Daddy, Daddy! Help me! Please help me!"

★

TUESDAY, MAY 2 (11:23 A.M. CENTRAL EUROPEAN SUMMER TIME)

POOR CLARES' SACRED HEART CONVENT; SEVILLE, SPAIN

IMPACT

Mother Yolanda beamed at what the sisters had created on short notice: a rousing fiesta inside the church. They even festooned its hard, cold interior walls with colorful paper decorations made by the children.

The hymn the orphans were now singing—"Jesus Loves the Little Children"—was intended to distract them from the magnetic storm raging outside, to help drown out the terrifying sounds it was making.

Praise God!

She cast an anxious glance at the church's large, stained-glass window, which was lit up exceedingly brightly. She would have described the effect as heavenly were it not for the horrifying reason behind it.

When the hymn was over, she put on a happy face. "Wonderful, children, just wonderful! I can easily imagine the Holy Host applauding your beautiful voices this very minute."

Her attention was stolen by a commotion erupting by the main entrance. She heard Sister Theresa crying out, "No, Marte. Wait!" Saw the tail end of a small boy—the dark-haired rascal who had resisted coming inside that morning—racing out the heavy wooden doors.

Theresa began to give chase.

"Wait, Sister!" Yolanda called out. "I'll go. He'll listen to me. You stay. Make sure none of the others gets out."

Once outside, she shielded her eyes from the blinding, colorful, noisy sky. Moments later, near the playground, her legs buckled, sending her tumbling to the ground. She flashed to the previous night, when the same thing happened.

Lifting her head and looking around, she spotted Marte sitting on a swing. He was staring up with innocent, open-mouthed wonderment at the restless swirls of red, yellow, green, and purple light dipping and dodging immediately above his head.

"Marte!"

He looked over at her and instantly his enthralled little face dissolved into a riot of confusion and fear. With the unmistakable look of boyish bravado, he jumped off the swing. But on landing his legs gave way and he crashed to the ground.

"*Ay, Dios, no!*" she cried out. "Marte!"

He lay crying on the ground. "*¡Mamá! ¡Mamá!*"

Feeling herself buoyed by the Holy Spirit, she struggled to her feet and stumbling and staggering made straight for the boy.

"*¡Mijito! ¡Aqui vengo!*"

Her progress was slow and precarious.

"*¡Aqui vengo, mijito, no llores!*"

Wishing not to risk falling again, she lowered herself to the ground and began crawling, clawing at the dry soil with all her might.

"*¡Aqui vengo, mijito! ¡Aqui vengo!*"

Her body began juddering violently, but still she crawled. Fighting to maintain a peaceful equilibrium, she instinctively recited the familiar words of *San Juan*: "*Nadie tiene amor más grande que el dar la vida por sus amigos.*" (Greater love has no one than this: to lay down one's life for one's friends.)

The demonic attack came closer, falling from the sky like flaming sheets of colored paper. The sizzling and humming sounds were deafening, the furnace-like heat, suffocating.

She tried picking up the pace of her hands and feet, but hesitated when she saw the boy's hair stand on end and glow blue.

"*¡Mamá! ¡Mamá!*" His little hands frantically batted the air above and around him.

A second later the playground equipment began glowing blue.

She felt her own hair shifting around on her head, heard snapping sounds she associated with hot, dry days, when she would reach for a doorknob and be bitten by electrical sparks.

The devil's work!

Doubting she could reach the boy before they were both destroyed by the dense fog of lavender fire engulfing them, she turned to the One she trusted completely.

"Our Father, which art in heaven," she whispered desperately, "hallowed be Thy name…"

Marte's screams grew louder. "*¡Ay! ¡Ay! ¡Mamá! ¡Ayúdame! ¡Ayúndame!*"

"…Thy kingdom come, Thy will be done in earth as it is in heaven."

She felt herself lifting off the dirt. She surrendered to the Savior, to the moment. The sky's voice was now an ear-splitting whine, its waving, spiking, folding sheets of multicolored light a flickering, nightmarish miasma.

Higher and higher she felt herself being lifted. Soon she was suspended in a raucous, stuttering, plum-colored incubus. Louder and louder the satanic sky shrieked. Faster and faster it flickered. Brighter and brighter it blazed.

"Reverend Mother!"

The voice came from directly beneath her feet.

"Where are you?!"

She looked down and recognized herself crumpled on the ground, no more than a few arm lengths from little Marte's quivering, shapeless form.

"Reverend Mother!"

She fought to recognize the familiar voice. Then it came to her and she smiled, with a peace that defied understanding.

"Over here, my child!" she heard herself shouting.

The wildly flickering lights stretched out their flaming fingers and seized her. But with a mighty effort made in the name of Jesus she managed to escape their grasp.

"Over here, my child," she cried out again, though not as loudly as she wanted. "Over here!"

"*¡Ay! ¡Gracias, San Cristóbal!*"

At last she felt her mind shutting down, taking with it the last impression her eyes beheld. It was the vision of a nimble-footed Sister Theresa—her habit wet and fuming like a pot of boiling water, veiled head crowned with a vivid sapphire halo—bending down to her with outstretched arms.

CHAPTER 51

SECOND COMING

When the acceleration ceased, Calder was able to move his arms and mouth freely again. But *Hero* was still hurtling uncontrollably across the Mediterranean Sea at supersonic speed.

Yet again, he tried to bring her under control; but nothing worked. He was close to tearing through the console and ripping out wires to get her to stop, but that would only spell suicide.

He glanced at the chronometer and then at the nav screen, but their information was outdated, freeze-framed. He had no idea how far away they were from the centroid or how much time they had before running out of sea. But it couldn't possibly be much longer, not at this speed.

"ALLIE. I'M SORRY, I'M SO SORRY!"

With the intercom down again, they were back to shouting.

"CALDER, IT'S NOT YOUR FAULT!"

He smirked, while tightening his helmet's chin strap.

Yeah, right.

"GET READY TO EJECT!" he yelled.

Wrapping his fingers around the lever that controlled the ejection seat, he thanked his lucky stars he'd designed it to function manually.

At least I did one thing right.

He'd miss *Hero*. Besides being his greatest creation—conceived, developed, and made in the image of a boyhood dream—she had become his closest friend. Someone, something, he understood completely. Or so he'd thought. Despite everything, he would always believe she was the future of transportation technology.

"READY…NOW!" he shouted.

With a single, decisive movement he yanked on the lever and immediately the canopy blew off and his seat rocketed up and out of *Hero*'s cockpit. The sudden rush of warm air slapped his exposed face like a giant fly swatter.

This is how a bullet must feel!

Anxiously, he looked around for Allie, hoping she'd obeyed his command, hoping her ejection seat hadn't malfunctioned. But it wasn't easy to see anything with so much bright light and air hitting his eyes.

He had the impression of flying through a pool filled with living, squirming watercolors. And the cacophonous sounds riding on the rushing wind, bombarding his ears, were unlike anything he'd ever heard—snapping, crackling, screaming.

Abruptly, he felt himself braking—as if he'd hit a wall of water. He glanced behind him. It wasn't his parachute—it hadn't deployed yet.

Then it struck him.

My inertia.

Hero.

The sudden change in his inertial mass—its instantaneous return to normalcy—could mean only one thing: *Hero* was no more.

But she's indestructible …

He was violently yanked backward yet again. This time, he saw, it was his parachute opening. The restraining harness squeezed his chest over hard. He fought not to black out.

Barely conscious, he was aware of noisy streaks of bright red, green, and magenta light hissing past him, of an all-pervasive, sizzling, violet-blue glow. He wondered vaguely if it was all just a hallucination. But he didn't think so.

Maybe I'm dead.

Calder's faltering senses apprehended in the far distance, silhouetted in the aurora's light of many colors, something that looked like a massive stone fortress atop a mountain.

God?

God lives in a castle?

The idea sounded ludicrous. But before he could argue the point with himself he hearkened to a vast whooshing sound. It was accompanied by a brilliant flash of white light and the feeling of being sucked upward. A split second later the sky turned dark and became still.

It was the last thing he saw and heard before losing consciousness.

★

TUESDAY, MAY 2 (12:24 P.M. ISRAEL DAYLIGHT TIME)

CHAPEL OF THE ASCENSION; JERUSALEM, ISRAEL

TIME SINCE IMPACT: 0 HOURS 01 MINUTE

Lorena—gazing expectantly skyward within the courtyard of the ancient, fortress-like Chapel of the Ascension—continued to stand her ground against the pushing, elbowing masses. The chaotically colored sky was mesmerizing, more beautiful, more awful than she ever imagined from reading the Bible's description of the Second Coming: "For just like the lightning, when it flashes out of one part of the sky, shines to the other part of the sky, so will the Son of Man be in His day."

"Wheee!" a nearby child exclaimed.

She hugged herself, knowing that at any moment they actually would be welcoming the Savior back to Earth.

Then she saw it: a spot of white light coming at them out of the painted skies over Jerusalem, surrounded by ragged fingers of lightning. She fixed her eyes on the fast-moving object, ignoring the raucous, flamboyant, turbulent sky threatening to smother them. She tuned out the excited commotion rising from the mass of spectators atop the Mount of Olives.

"This is it, people!" she said. "This is it!"

The nearby child began to cry.

"*Shhh*, baby, *shhh!*" She pointed at the fast-approaching white object. "Look! It's Jesus! *Jesus Christ!*"

But the child cried even more loudly. She continued shushing him reassuringly but did not, dared not, take her eyes off the white light.

Fix your eyes on Jesus!

Closer and closer the white light came.

Directly toward her!

"Yes, Jesus, yes!" she cried out.

All at once there was a blinding white flash, and the surrounding air was filled with a loud whooshing sound. She felt her body being sucked upward as if by some cosmic vacuum cleaner.

This is it—the Rapture!

She raised her arms heavenward and wailed loudly, "Yes, sweet Savior, yes!"

People screamed and started fleeing in all directions. The child bawled uncontrollably. But Lorena stood her ground, keening ecstatically.

Abruptly, the whooshing and sucking ceased.

The gaudy colors in the sky, the madness on the ground, and the white light as well—it all went away, just like that. In the twinkling of an eye, a sublime and uncanny peacefulness settled on the mountaintop, on the surrounding region, on the entire world, it seemed to her. Eerily, the daytime sky grew black; stars appeared.

She jumped up and down, shouting in the direction from which the prominent white spot had been coming just a moment earlier.

"Come, Lord Jesus, come!"

Then she saw *him*!—materializing out of the preternaturally darkened sky.

Yes! At last!

"Oh, Lord, welcome, welcome! How long we have waited for you!"

Hands stretched before her, tears coursing down her flushed cheeks, she stared adoringly at the slowly descending figure.

It was *Jesus*—she was sure of it—floating gracefully to Earth.

And just as she had pictured him!—shimmering sapphire glory and all.

CHAPTER 52

SECOND CHANCES

For the past three days Calder, bedridden, refused to see any visitors or be interviewed by any reporters. Instead, he stayed fixated on the nonstop TV coverage of the devastation around the world.

Rescue workers were still digging through the rubble, but it was clear the CME's radiation blast killed—mostly incinerated—thousands of people and injured tens of thousands more; still more thousands were missing. Total damage was being estimated at hundreds of billions to trillions of dollars. All of it the result not just of the CME nuking property and equipment for barely more than a minute, but also the rampaging computer virus, which mercifully the FBI was steadily bringing under control.

Allie hobbled in on crutches. "Hey, lazy bones, time to rise and shine."

He stayed glued to the TV and said nothing. But out of the corner of his eye he saw her look to Sara, who was sitting bedside.

"How's the patient behaving this morning?"

Sara smiled and gave a curt flutter of the hand signifying, so-so.

Because his injuries, like Allie's, were not life threatening—mainly some broken ribs and a heavily bruised ego—he knew he'd need to snap out of his funk sooner rather than later. He would have to leave the hospital and face the debate publicly raging about him.

Some people were lauding him for fixing the magnetic field and thereby sparing the earth even worse damage from the CME. Privately, he hypothesized the fix was actually a lucky accident. Pieces of *Hero* had been found in a vast debris field between Beirut and Haifa, suggesting to him she'd blown up from the inside. The explosion, he theorized, had set off a chain reaction in the quantum vacuum that had culminated in a 'big swallow,' which straightway sucked up the CME's charged particles and even the sunlight in Earth's vicinity. He pictured it being the exact opposite of the 'big bang,' which once upon a time reportedly spewed out an entire *universe*.

Nevertheless, he'd be quite happy if people kept crediting him for slaying the CME.

Others were condemning him and *Hero* for creating the magnetic holes in the first place. Bradstreet was among those to raise and prosecute the issue in the media. Allie was forced to concede publicly that Bradstreet might very well be right—and that, in fact, she and Calder had entertained the same hypothesis while brainstorming Project Joshua.

On Wednesday, a U.S. consular came to the hospital and served Calder with subpoenas from Senate and House committees investigating the magnetic-hole-CME cataclysm; they demanded he appear before them immediately upon his return to the States. And if that weren't bad enough, early this morning the National Academy of Sciences announced it was partnering with the United Nations to scrutinize the science and ethics of his research.

The vilest of all were Greenies claiming his method of extracting energy from the quantum vacuum constituted the worst environmental catastrophe in human history. Some of them were even speculating his early work with the vacuum might have exacerbated the CME that killed Nell!

Evil SOBs.

Allie switched off the TV and turned to face him. "Calder—Calder."

He knew what was coming and wanted to hide under the sheets.

"Allie—Allie," he replied sardonically.

Allie turned to Sara. "Do you mind?"

Without hesitating, his daughter—his own flesh and blood—left him alone to face another pep talk from his beloved.

Or would it be another scolding?

"Okay, we need to talk," Allie said, drawing near to the bed.

She looked beautiful, as always, despite the bruises and bandages. That was one good thing coming out of the disaster: *Hero*'s impregnable hull had protected her and him from the CME. The injuries she'd received—the minor burns to her face, the sprained wrist, and the broken leg—came *after* the ejection, the result of her landing in a tree and falling out of it.

"Look, Allie, I know what you're going to say. You've been saying it to me all week."

She pointed an accusing crutch at him. "Yeah, well then when are you going to get your bum out of this bed and start living again?"

"When I'm good and ready."

She snorted. "You need to confront your fears, Calder, or they'll cripple you for life. Like I've told you, there are plenty of people waiting to welcome you like a hero. The president, for one. Ticker tape parade and all."

He rolled over in bed, turning his back to her. "I don't want a parade, for god sakes; it's obscene to even think it. People died because of me. I even killed my own daughter's best friend! Forget it, Allie, *no!*"

"Oh, here we go again. Calder, for the umpteenth time, you didn't kill those people—the CME did. Their own decisions did. With all due respect, had Dirk stayed with Sara he'd still be alive. I told you once before, you can't take all the blame and you can't take all the credit. The world doesn't revolve around you—you still don't get that."

No, he thought, it was *she* who still didn't get it. It *was* all about him—and his blasted black cloud.

Curse me!

He turned around and glowered at Allie. "Say whatever you want, it was *Hero*—my *Hero*—that created the holes. Without the holes, the CME wouldn't have been so damaging."

Her eyes widened. "Calder, listen to me! There's more to heaven and earth than *Hero*, than the broken world we've created for ourselves and that is now out of control. Sure, *Hero* didn't work out like you expected. But she's not all bad. And she's not all your fault."

"But I invented her!"

She leaned in on her crutches. "And who invented *you*, Calder? *Escúchame, hombre.* Beyond *Hero*, beyond even the scientific imagination, is an invisible reality every bit as real as the virtual energy fields inside the quantum vacuum. I believe that. Yes, we have free will—just like when you manually steered *Hero* through the Suez. But in the end, Calder, we operate within a bigger reality. Things happen that are beyond our control, for reasons only known to God. Do you understand?"

Yeah, yeah, blah, blah, blah—religious gibberish.

He hoisted himself up on an elbow. "Oh, so you're saying God wanted this to happen?"

She rolled her eyes. "No! I'm saying we aren't entirely masters of our own destiny. There are forces we unleash through our ignorance, through our hubris—even through our good intentions—that influence the ultimate outcomes of our choices, of our behavior; forces only God fully understands."

He settled back onto his pillow. "Look, Allie, spare me the sermon, okay? All I know is the world is one screwed up place and I just made it worse. End of story."

She shook her head and threw up her hands. "Okay, *hombre,* you win. Go ahead and lie here hiding out and sulking all you want. But I gotta go. Carlos is flying in to visit me; we're having lunch in Lolo's room."

"Great. Say hi to them for me," he muttered, turning his face away from her.

"Sure."

He noticed obliquely she was staring at him.

"Another thing—I'm flying out tomorrow with Carlos. Heading back to Los Angeles to see my family—thank God they all survived. After that, I'm on sick leave for a few weeks and Sara has invited me to visit her in Australia. I've accepted."

What?

He watched dumbly as she turned on her heel and hopscotched on crutches to the door. "You're welcome to join us," she said just before exiting, "if you want."

★

Without looking back, Allie opened the door and shambled into the hallway. Sara was chatting with the security guards assigned to protect Calder from reporters and hotheads gunning for him. On seeing her, Sara broke away and approached her.

"So? What did he say?"

"The most stubborn man I ever met." Allie, leaning on her crutches, put an arm around the teenager and smiled weakly. "Most brilliant one too."

"So are you going through with it? Should we?"

She nodded. "It's our best chance of getting him to face reality."

"Allie!"

She turned. Dallan was striding toward them.

"Morning, Brother." she said when he reached them. "You look rested. Holding up okay?"

"Yeah, we just finished breakfast and now I'm out for my morning exercise. Lolo's getting a rub down."

Shortly following the aborted CME, police found her sister on the Mount of Olives and brought her to the hospital. Dallan flew to Jerusalem immediately upon hearing the news.

During the past three days, he'd not left Lolo's bedside. It really did appear to Allie the change of heart he experienced in the Arctic was genuine. Anyway, she was willing to give him the benefit of the doubt—for Lolo's sake, if for no other reason.

"How's she feeling?" Allie said. "Have they taken her off the sedatives?"

He screwed his lips and shook his head. "No. She still believes she saw Jesus. No one's told her it was actually Dr. Sinclair parachuting in. Video of it is all over the Internet, but we're keeping her from seeing it. At least until the doctors feel she's stable enough."

"Yeah, she was telling me all about it yesterday, although she still can't talk very well because of the medication. Poor thing. She's gonna be disappointed when she finds out."

"Anyway, I've got some big news."

Allie stiffened. "Yeah?"

"I'm officially putting off the divorce—at least until Lolo is lucid enough for us to discuss things. I'm hoping we can make it work. I've done a lot of growing up this past week."

She stared at him. He looked like a different man somehow—above all, happy.

"Dallan, that's wonderful!" She leaned in and pecked him on the cheek. "Love isn't something you just throw away when things go wrong. It's worth fighting for. I'm going to be praying for the two of you."

He smiled. "Thanks, Allie, that means a lot." He added, "I hear Carlos is coming. How's the family doing?"

Not only had her family made it through the ordeal, her mom was now more lucid than before, as though the magnetic storm actually helped her condition. The doctors said it was a case of spontaneous remission, rare but not unheard of; her dad was calling it a miracle. Allie didn't disagree.

The family's church took a hit when the fuse box overloaded. It sparked a fire on the kitchen side of the building, burning a hole in the roof. But the structure overall escaped damage completely.

"Fine, fine," she said. "Except Carlos is complaining he's gained five pounds from all the food leftover because of the shortened CME. 'Shame to let all those tamales and tacos go to waste,' he said—you know him."

Dallan laughed. "Yeah, and I know those tamales too; how good they are. I don't blame him."

"The *hermanos* are all set to pitch in on the repairs, so it shouldn't be long before the church is back to normal. I told Carlos it'll be a great way for him to work off the extra pounds."

Dallan laughed again, then turned to Sara. "How's your dad doing?"

She frowned. "Depends on what part of him you're asking about. Physically he's healing fine, but—anyway, if you get a chance, stop by and say hi. He can definitely use some cheering up."

FRIDAY, MAY 5 (10:06 A.M. CENTRAL EUROPEAN SUMMER TIME)

POOR CLARES' SACRED HEART CONVENT; SEVILLE, SPAIN

Mother Yolanda opened her eyes and saw the stone-faced sisters and children massed around her bed, crammed shoulder to shoulder inside her small cell. She smiled feebly. "Well..." She stopped to cough. "Either I am in heaven. Or the next best thing."

Everyone cheered.

"Welcome back!" Sister Theresa said, her eyes red and puffy.

"What have I missed? Where have I been?"

"You've been with us here the whole time, but unconscious. The doctor, all of us, we have not left your side for a moment. We've taken turns keeping you company."

They all chimed in at once to explain everything that had transpired—how, for protection, Sister Theresa wet herself down before rushing out to rescue Mother; how the magnetic storm was a very scary thing for the kids, who nevertheless were brave and didn't cry; how God spared the church buildings; and on and on.

The rapid-fire accounts were abruptly interrupted by a strong, clear voice issuing from the antique shortwave radio. All heads turned in unison to look at it.

"*Mateo 19:14*, this is Rising Son. Are you there?"

Mother Yolanda pointed anxiously at the radio. "Please, someone help me up."

Everyone made a move to help and got in each other's way. They paused and laughed about it.

"Allow me," Sister Theresa said, extending a helping hand.

A small voice from the very back cried out, "Me, too, please!"

The crowd parted to make way for Marte, whose little body was heavily bandaged. Later she would learn the boy escaped death by managing to crawl inside the playground's little wooden fortress.

"*Mateo 19:14*, this is Rising Son. Please answer."

The children helped her across the room and finally eased her into the chair in front of her beloved radio.

She took hold of the microphone. "Yes, Rising Son, this is *Mateo 19:14*. How are you, my dear sister? How's the convent? Did you make it through the storm all right?"

"Yes," came the cheery reply. "People all over Japan are already busy returning things to normal. It will be some time before everything is fixed, but even the whales are no longer stranding themselves, thanks be to God. And how are you, Mother Abbess? The community has been praying for your recovery ever since receiving news about your distress."

"The Lord is faithful, Sister. I am so old now there is not much left to damage that time hasn't already taken care of." She chuckled.

"And the orphanage? Did it survive all right? Will you need any help to rebuild?"

"It was a miracle, Sister! The kids were just telling me. Right when the storm was about to really attack, it disappeared. The church was spared. And a good thing, too, because now we're able to take in children orphaned by the storm."

The small cell was filled with Mary Pius's hearty laughter. "The enemy should know better than to tangle with you, Yolanda."

Mother Yolanda smiled. Then, feeling enormously grateful for her situation, she looked around the room, taking in the faces of the women and boys and girls who were her *familia*.

At last she spoke into the microphone again. "Yes, Sister. You would think by now he had learned his lesson. When he messes with the Poor Clares and our work, he messes with God."

CHAPTER 53

HOPE

Calder, Sara, and Allie were nearing the massive research ship when Eva, Pitsy, and the crew came into view. They were standing next to the gangplank. Allie leap-frogged toward them as fast as the crutches could take her.

She'd seen Eva briefly while in Los Angeles but this was their first assignment together since Project Joshua—although calling it an assignment was a stretch. Technically, she was on sick leave. But when Stu discovered she was going to Australia to watch a baby whale—a survivor of the CME—be returned to the wild, he insisted on turning it into an inspiring human interest story, symbolic of the world struggling to return to normal. He never missed a beat.

Eva sprang toward her with open arms. "Girlfriend!"

Her producer looked like her old self. She survived the CME unscathed because Calder's lab proved to be as impregnable as *Hero*'s hull.

"*Chica!*" Allie cried out, leaning forward on her crutches and extending her arms.

They hugged long and hard before disengaging.

"How's ol' Stuey?" Allie said.

"Like always—tough as shoe leather. He sends his love, thanks you for doing this."

Eva told her he'd taken her advice and high-tailed it into the basement just before impact.

"He's already counting the money the network's going to make off your special. He wants to talk to you about giving you your own show."

Normally, Allie would be ecstatic. But at that moment her unexpected good fortune felt too much like the exploitation of a worldwide tragedy.

"Great, let's go."

The two started up the gangplank, Pitsy and the crew following right behind with the equipment.

"I did get some bad news from Shanghai, though," Eva said. "Zhaohui Tang was killed. Shanghai was close to the Nagasaki hole, you know."

Allie stopped. "Oh, no, how? What happened?"

"Apparently, she was in her mom's kitchen. The mom went to get a glass of water but Tang told her to stop and pushed her away. Right then, a bolt of electricity came shooting out of the spout."

Allie winced. "*Ay, no!*"

"Yeah, Tang took the hit. Was killed instantly."

Sara ran up to them. "Allie, c'mon, this way!"

Sara led her to the ship's portside and introduced Lulu, who was cradled in a canvas sling held up by steel cables controlled by an electric hoist. The animal appeared calm. A deckhand was keeping her skin moist with ladlesful of seawater.

"Hey, Lulu," Allie cooed, stroking the whale's shiny black flanks. "I feel like I know you, your mama's talked so much about you."

Calder strode up and laid a gentle hand on Lulu. "Your big day, huh, little girl? Back to the ocean."

The ship's horn gave Allie a start. A moment later the engines roared to life and the ship pulled away from the dock.

She turned to Calder. "Calder, I'll be right back."

She set off and quickly found Eva testing the equipment with Pitsy and the crew.

"*Oye, chica.* I need a moment alone with Calder. Do you mind if—?"

Eva held up her hand. "Go. I've got it covered."

She hopscotched back to Calder and they both went to the other side of the ship, settling onto a wooden bench along the railing.

"I'm really glad you decided to come along," she said, fighting a case of nerves.

"Me too."

He made a move to take her hand but she drew it away.

"Calder, there's something I need to tell you. I've been thinking and praying a lot about it since the CME."

"Allie, if it's—"

"The problem is we're worlds apart when it comes to certain things, and not just God. It's also my work. I know you don't enjoy being around the media—although, like it or not, you're going to have to put up with it for a while."

She waited for Calder to say something. But he was looking out to sea and gave no indication of wishing to speak.

"I love you, Calder. I really do."

He turned to look at her, his face a somber mask.

"But," she added, "we're what the Bible calls unevenly yoked."

He frowned. "What does that mean?"

"It means we see things differently and our behaviors reflect it, especially in times of crisis."

"What are you saying, exactly?"

"It's eating you alive that your work hasn't panned out the way you expected. Believe me, I wish it would've turned out differently too. The idea of a clean, limitless energy source is awesome. But the biggest difference between you and me is I allow for the possibility that something good can result even from the terrible way things turned out, crazy as it sounds."

Calder noticeably stiffened. "Good? *Good?* Don't even go there!"

She feared this would happen—Calder's fierce defensiveness in matters even remotely smacking of a spiritual perspective.

"Calder, in God's economy our failing to accomplish whatever we set out to do, no matter how high-minded or well-intentioned, doesn't necessarily spell failure in the grand scheme of things. There's a storyline playing out in the universe, an appointment with destiny, that can be really scary—even cataclysmic—but is ultimately more majestic, more beautiful, more meaningful than anything any of us can possibly imagine." She paused. "But I don't want to argue with you anymore, Calder. You're entitled to your beliefs. I respect them, even though I can't go along with them."

Calder stood up. She had the impression he was formulating a response, but he remained silent. She waited, while he paced.

"Okay, you win," he said at last, stopping and looking down at her. "Tell me what's good about my research being a threat to world safety. Tell me what's good about why I'll probably never be able to show my face in public again. And neither will Sara, all because her old man screwed up royally."

He plopped down on the bench, leaned forward with elbows on knees, and rubbed his hands roughly across his face.

She waited a few moments and then said, "You've heard of the null result, right?"

He turned and scowled at her. "What?"

"The null result."

"Yes, of course."

"Then you know it refers to a certain kind of experimental result that's way different from the one everyone was expecting. The null result seems catastrophic at first, but ends up leading to something worthwhile, even spectacular—more spectacular than anyone ever imagined. Like the Michelson-Morley experiment. Right?"

Allie cited the nineteenth-century experiment because it yielded a null result that trashed long-held axioms in classical physics—a seemingly major calamity. In the end, the unanticipated result led to a new, breathtaking worldview that included Einstein's special theory of relativity.

"The unexpected way things turned out with *Hero* is a null result," she said, "and I get that it looks like the end of the world to you right now. But Calder, maybe, just maybe what happened can do some good— like further open our eyes to the unintended consequences of science and technology, to the dangers we're naively creating for ourselves in the name of so-called progress. That would be a valuable thing for mankind, wouldn't it? And I know you don't want to hear this, but it might even cause our cynical, secular society to stop and at least wonder if perhaps the Bible might be correct about who we are and what will happen to us in the end, both scary and joyful."

He threw up his hands and spat out the words. "Oh, please, don't start with that low-brow mumbo jumbo again. It's the last thing I want to hear right now."

Allie fought to keep her temper. "*That* in a nutshell is the problem with us, Calder. What I take seriously as a well-educated scientist you consider mumbo jumbo. Believe me, I'm not out to convert you anymore. I admit I was at the start, when you first told me you didn't believe in God. But now I'm simply explaining my worldview to you. And you keep putting it down."

Calder leapt to his feet and began pacing the deck again.

She continued, "Is it really that impossible for your genius brain to allow for the possibility—even a very, very remote one—that what I'm suggesting is true?"

"What exactly *are* you suggesting, Allie?" he growled. "Because that's where I'm lost."

And that's where you're right, brother.

She took a deep breath. "What I'm saying is *Hero* is just one more example of our brilliant, inventive ignorance. Proof we are manipulating laws and forces still mysterious to us, no matter what we claim. That's why things go wrong all the time. *Very* wrong."

"Yeah, tell me about it," Calder hissed, running his hand through his hair. "The story of my life."

"It's not luck, Calder, and it's not God. It's us doing it to ourselves. Your well-intentioned research has cracked open a whole new Pandora's box—one infinitely more dangerous than even nuclear weapons. The quantum vacuum is the ground state of the entire physical universe, you know that. And you've discovered a way to toy with it—to toy with what amounts to the foundation of everything we call reality: mass, energy, space, time.

"It's riskier than a child playing with a stick of dynamite. Your discovery now gives us a way to destroy the entire physical world—in the blink of an eye. Your discovery now makes possible—*science* makes credible—the Apocalypse prophesied in the Bible."

Calder stopped pacing and with both hands leaned against the railing, staring out at the water and saying nothing.

She turned in her seat. "Are you hearing me, Calder? We didn't set out to destroy ourselves; the fact we can now do it is a cruel and completely unexpected consequence of our best, most well-intentioned efforts to improve the world, to create a scientific utopia. But the Bible predicted it all along—that's the point. For the first time in human history, what you call religious mumbo jumbo is a scientific reality. We literally have the ability to destroy the entire world. The null prophecy is coming true."

He pushed off the railing and rounded on her. "Good god, Allie, stop and listen to yourself. You're mad! It's ridiculous!"

Allie looked past Calder at the sea and waited before responding. She chose her words carefully and spoke in a quiet voice. "Calder, I know it sounds crazy—and the thought of us destroying ourselves is grim and scary, for sure." She looked at him. "But only if you believe it's how the story ends. I don't. To me, the Apocalypse is like the mother of all phase transitions, you know? A period of chaos that leads to a new, infinitely more hopeful chapter in human history." She stood up, ready to leave. "I believe that, *hombre*, even if you don't."

★

The research ship rumbled to a swaying stop. Instantly, Sara's academic advisor and several other marine biologists scrambled to prepare things for Lulu's release.

The advisor explained to Allie that instruments and observations showed a pod of pilot whales in the vicinity. The scientists were hoping it'd become Lulu's new family but had no way of knowing if its members would accept her.

Sara and Calder were standing next to Lulu, both stroking her gently. Reluctant to intrude on their space—especially given her awkward estrangement from Calder now—Allie kept her distance, opting instead to stay near the bow.

Sara began weeping and buried herself in Calder's large embrace.

Seeing it, Allie began twisting her hair. "Oh, sweetie," she said under her breath, "it's the hardest thing in life to say good-bye to someone you truly love."

"Okay, it's time!" one of the biologists called out loudly.

Sara disengaged from Calder. Then leaning into Lulu, she kissed her on the cheek. A moment later the winch came to life and began lifting the chubby little creature up and over the side.

Sara returned to Calder's arms.

Allie watched with an anxious heart as Lulu was lowered into the water and released from the sling. An underwater microphone amplified the splashing sounds and broadcast them over the ship's loudspeakers.

A few moments hence they heard Lulu's amplified voice calling out plaintively. According to the biologists, she was saying, "Is anyone around? Can anyone hear me?"

The uncertain seconds that followed were agonizing for Allie and, she knew, for everyone else. She overheard Sara saying, "Please, God, please, please, please."

Then everyone heard it clearly. A chorus of clicks and whistles from the pod that, according to Sara's advisor, meant: "Here we are! Come join us! Welcome to your new family!"

"Oh, Daddy!" Sara bawled, burying herself once again in his embrace.

Allie stared at the water and a moment later saw whales big and small, Lulu included, breaching the surface all around the ship, leaping into the air like happy children.

"Sara, look!" Allie shouted, forgetting herself.

Sara tore away from Calder's embrace and, wiping away tears, stared wide-eyed at the exciting celebration. She jumped up and down like a giddy schoolgirl.

"Sara!" Allie shouted. "It's Lulu saying 'Thank you! Thank you for saving me! Thank you for giving me a second chance!'"

CHAPTER 54

THE STUDY OF LIGHTNING

Allie felt her left hand being patted, just as the end credits of her special began rolling on the sanctuary's giant, rented screen. She turned and beamed at her dad, who was sitting next to her in the front row, patting his hand in return.

The *hermanos* and *hermanas* cheered loudly—something she'd never heard them do in church. Turning to her right, she leaned over and gave her mom, who was applauding energetically, a soft kiss on the temple.

"*Muy bien, mija, muy bien,*" her mother said. "I'm proud of you."

Allie inhaled deeply and then slowly exhaled. She felt as good as her mother looked—as if they'd both been granted a fresh start in life. Or as Carlos put it, a new season.

Her mind flashed back to the research ship in Australia, to her telling Calder she wanted things between them to cool down for a while, maybe for good. She would never forget the look of pain and confusion on his face, or her own feelings of crushing sadness at the thought of not seeing him or Sara much anymore.

Ever?

But she also realized that despite its seeming failure, her relationship with Calder wasn't a total loss. For one thing, she was feeling hopeful again about her personal life—for the first time since her devastating breakup with Phil.

Maybe lightning can strike twice.

Her spiritual life was invigorated as well. Calder's arrogant, aggressive, joyless atheism made her value more than ever the company of these humble, hospitable, genuinely happy Christians. And best of all, his constant testing and trashing of her fledgling faith made it grow stronger—the way a steady wind naturally strengthened the fibrous cells of a newly planted sapling.

When the credits were done rolling and a commercial started playing, the feed stopped and the sanctuary lights came on. Carlos got up, mounted the dais, and stood in front of the screen.

"Wow, Allie, that was something. I think you've given me enough material for a month's worth of sermons—more than that."

Chuckles bubbled up from the standing-room-only congregation.

"I'm sure everyone here thanks you for all the work you put into making the special. Let's hope you get great ratings." He paused and grinned. "You should, because everyone I know told all their *tias y tios y primos y primas* to watch tonight!"

The room resounded with laughter.

"Anyway, I hope and pray you do more of these kinds of shows to help people wake up to what's happening in the world—that science is a double-edged sword and the Bible is anything but obsolete."

A short while later everyone was out on the brightly lit parking lot eating and socializing. The church kitchen was not yet fully repaired, so the *tertulia* was being catered by a locally-run taco truck. Still, many of the *hermanos* and *hermanas* were pitching in to help serve the large, hungry crowd.

The warm evening was topped by a clear, starry sky. The kids were either running around—ignoring pleas from moms to stop and have something to eat—or lined up at the *raspa* machine, where her dad was serving up snow cones spilling over with fresh fruit syrups.

Allie emerged from the bathroom and ran her gaze over the celebration with feelings of enormous pleasure and nostalgia.

Some things never change.

The only thing missing—that would've made the night perfect—was Lolo. She was still recuperating in the Jerusalem hospital.

Allie wended her way to Carlos, gladly accepting congratulations from people along the way. When she reached him, she said, "Hey, can I steal you away for a few minutes?"

"Sure, Sis, lead the way."

She guided him to the far edge of the parking lot, by the old sycamore.

"*Hijo!*" he said when they arrived, waving the remaining half of his street taco *al Pastor* at the crowd. "I've never seen so many people here. What a blessing. Thanks again. The show was amazing."

"Thanks, Carlos." She hesitated. "You know, this night makes me realize how much I really miss all this." She gestured toward the lively scene.

"Yeah, it's hard to beat, isn't it?" he said, still eating.

She took in a lungful of the balmy, spring air. "This place is so full of love. I'd really like to spend more time here..."

Carlos brightened. "That would be awesome, Sis, really awesome."

"If only I could figure out how to do it. My job—I love it, but—" She gave out a little growl. "it's so demanding."

He swallowed the last of his taco. "Just come as often as you can, Sis." He pulled a white handkerchief from his back pocket. "Everyone here understands how busy you are." He quickly wiped his mouth and fingers and stuffed the handkerchief back in its place.

She grinned. Carrying around a white handkerchief was a custom Carlos picked up from their father.

Her grin promptly changed to a frown. "But that's the problem, Carlos. Sometimes I wish they weren't so understanding. It just makes me feel more—I don't know—guilty."

"Whoa, whoa! Guilty? Where's that coming from?"

She didn't want to ruin the festive mood; but she needed to get certain things off her chest, which was greatly burdened with revelations from the past two weeks. "Oh, Carlos…"

"Look, Sis, let me take a stab at it. You feel guilty *por que*—why? Because you're super-successful and we're not?"

She reared. "No! God, no! I feel guilty because—"

"Because you're not there for us?"

She wavered, looking down at her feet.

"Okay, yes, *yes*," she said finally, looking up. "I'm always cancelling on you guys or flying off somewhere, like with the CME. I so wanted to be here with you guys. What if—?"

Carlos stepped backward and held up an index finger. "Allie, *mira*, I'm older than you, so listen up. You don't need to earn our love, okay? *Te amamos* because of you, because of who you are, which is a smart, beautiful woman who's doing God's will. Quit and you'd be quitting more than a job or a career, you'd be quitting your calling, your purpose. You'd be quitting on God."

"But Carlos, you don't know the sacrifices I've made."

"*Sí, sí*, I know about Phil. We all—"

"Not just Phil, everything. I've sacrificed family, my personal life, *todo*."

She felt a surge of regret and shame, as she always did when thinking about Phil.

"Allie, *por favor*, doing God's will doesn't mean being happy all the time. Look at Mother Teresa; *mira a Jesús mismo*. Don't you think I don't feel guilty about not being able to give Alicia nice things in life? I've sacrificed *tambien* because of my calling. But let me tell you something." His eyes shimmered. "When I'm at the pulpit or counseling someone, I know I'm doing exactly what I'm supposed to be doing in life, and it makes all the sacrifices more than worth it."

She remained still.

"Allie, when I see you in your element, reporting on a big story or doing a show like tonight—oh, man, Sis, you shine, girl. *Brillas como una estrella*. It's beautiful to see."

She began tearing up.

He took her gently by the arms. "It's okay, Sis, just listen. Ever since we were kids I knew you were different—*todos nosotros sabimos*. We all knew you were going to leave us and go places, and it was sad but also exciting. That's how we feel right now: *triste pero emocionados*. Excited for you and for us. Your success makes us all feel important, you know? Proud to be related to you, *de ser Latinos*. And besides, whenever we watch you on TV, which these days is always"—he chuckled—"we know you're safe, *y es todo que importa*."

She was weeping now, leaning on Carlos's broad shoulder—his arms around her.

"You're where you're supposed to be, Allie, *nunca lo olvides*," He gently patted her back. "The dream you had as a girl? *Fue de Dios*. None of the family doubts it and you shouldn't either."

For the next minute Allie cried and cried some more. When she was done she straightened up and, wiping her eyes, said, "*Gracias*, Bro, you always did know how to speak the truth." Then she smiled ironically. "Anyone tell you, you'd make a good pastor?"

They hugged again in loving silence.

"There you are!

Allie's teary eyes swiveled in the direction of the voice.

"Beto!"

He was holding a taco stuffed with the works.

Of course.

He stopped short and hesitated. "I'm sorry—I'm not breaking anything up, am I?"

"No, no," she lied, pulling away from Carlos and swiping at her eyes. "What's up?"

"I just wanted to say how much I really liked your TV special. Man, it was something really—well, special." He chortled. "I also wanted to catch you up on that new dealership I talked to you about a couple weeks ago. I'm still hoping you'll go in with me."

His sweet smile and handsome face, his indefatigable pushiness, that ridiculously overloaded taco—it all suddenly struck her as utterly charming—and irresistibly hilarious.

She began to laugh.

"What?" he said, looking confused. "What's so funny?"

His innocent reaction made her laugh even harder.

"What?" He wiped at his face, clearly thinking that maybe there was something on it that was busting her up.

She couldn't control herself, but waved a dismissive hand and barely managed to say between laughs, "No, nothing, Beto, nothing. You're fine."

Beto and Carlos glanced at each other and they began to laugh as well.

She watched them—pictured herself with them—and her heart took flight. After two weeks of unrelenting stress and misery—oh, how good it felt to laugh like this again.

At last she gained enough control to speak. Taking in the spirited scene out on the parking lot, she said breathlessly, "*Hombre*, it's great to be home again, that's all I have to say. *¡Se siente bien estar en casa!*"

RECOMMENDED READING

"A Carrington-level, extreme geomagnetic storm is almost inevitable in the future."

Solar Storm Risk to the North American Electric Grid

"The consequences of such an event could be very high...would likely include, for example, disruption of the transportation, communication, banking, and finance systems, and government services; the breakdown of the distribution of potable water owing to pump failure; and the loss of perishable foods and medications because of lack of refrigeration. The resulting loss of services for a significant period of time in even one region of the country could affect the entire nation and have international impacts as well."

National Academy of Sciences

- Bamford, James. "NSA Snooping Was Only the Beginning. Meet the Spy Chief Leading Us into Cyberwar." *Wired*. 2013. https://www.wired.com/2013/06/general-keith-alexander-cyberwar/all/.
- Committee on the Societal and Economic Impacts of Severe Space Weather Events, National Research Council. *Severe Space Weather Events: Understanding Societal and Economic Impacts*. Washington, DC: The National Academies Press, 2008.
- Davis, E. W., et al. "Review of Experimental Concepts for Studying the Quantum Vacuum Field." In *AIP Conference Proceedings*. American Institute of Physics, 2006.
- Haisch, Bernhard, Alfonso Rueda, and Harold Puthoff. "Inertia as a Zero-point-field Lorentz force." *Physical Review A* 49 (2), 1994.
- Institute 511. *Study on Space Cyber Warfare*. Aerospace Electronic Warfare. China Aerospace Science and Industry Corp., 2012.
- Maclay, Jordan G. "Analysis of Zero-Point Electromagnetic Energy and Casimir Forces in Conducting Rectangular Cavities." *Physical Review A* 61 (5), 2000.
- Maclay, Jordan G., et al. "A Gedanken Spacecraft that Operates Using the Quantum Vacuum (Dynamic Casimir Effect)." *Foundations of Physics* 34, 2004.
- Millis, Marc. "NASA Breakthrough Propulsion Physics Program." *Acta Astronautica* 44 (2-4) 2009.
- Millis, Marc, and Eric Davis, eds. *Frontiers of Propulsion Science*. Reston, VA: American Institute of Aeronautics and Astronautics, 2009.
- *Solar Storm Risk to the North American Electric Grid*. Lloyd's; Atmospheric and Environmental Research, Inc., 2013. https://www.lloyds.com/~/media/lloyds/reports/emerging%20risk%20reports/solar%20storm%20risk%20to%20the%20north%20american%20electric%20grid.pdf.
- Tenner, Edward *Why Things Bite Back: Technology and the Revenge of Unintended Consequences*. New York: Vintage Books, 1997.